freewalker

—

DENNIS FOON

ANNICK PRESS

TORONTO + NEW YORK + VANCOUVER

Text © 2004 Dennis Foon

Annick Press Ltd.
All rights reserved. No part of this work covered by the copyrights hereon may
be reproduced or used in any form or by any means—graphic, electronic, or
mechanical—without the prior written permission of the publisher.

We acknowledge the support of the Canada Council for the Arts, the Ontario Arts
Council, and the Government of Canada through the Book Publishing Industry
Development Program (BPIDP) for our publishing activities.

Edited by Pam Robertson and Barbara Pulling
Copy edited by Elizabeth McLean
Cover and interior design by Irvin Cheung/iCheung Design
Cover illustration by Susan Madsen

The text was typeset in Centaur and Disturbance

Cataloging in Publication
  Foon, Dennis
  Freewalker / Dennis Foon.

(The Longlight legacy trilogy ; 2)
ISBN 1-55037-885-6 (bound).—ISBN 1-55037-884-8 (pbk.)

  I. Title. II. Series: Foon, Dennis Longlight legacy trilogy ; 2.

PS8561.O62F74 2004 C813'.54 C2004-902279-2

Printed and bound in Canada

Published in the U.S.A. by	Distributed in Canada by:	Distributed in the U.S.A. by:
Annick Press (U.S.) Ltd.	Firefly Books Ltd.	Firefly Books (U.S.) Inc.
	66 Leek Crescent	P.O. Box 1338
	Richmond Hill, ON	Ellicott Station
	L4B 1H1	Buffalo, NY 14205

Visit our website at **www.annickpress.com**

This book is dedicated to
Dr. H. Mirakal
a.k.a. Ron Foon

IN THE SHROUDED VALLEY, THE PEOPLE OF LONGLIGHT
EVADED DESTRUCTION. FOR SEVENTY-FIVE YEARS
THEY QUIETLY THRIVED, ISOLATED FROM THE WORLD,
NURTURING A SMALL FLAME OF HOPE. IT TOOK LESS
THAN ONE HOUR FOR THEM TO BE ANNIHILATED.

—THE BOOK OF LONGLIGHT

Freewalker is the second volume of The Longlight Legacy.

The first volume, *The Dirt Eaters*, tells the story of Roan, one of two survivors of Longlight. Injured while trying to prevent a raider from capturing his younger sister, Stowe, he wakes to find his village destroyed and its inhabitants slaughtered.

Sifting through the wreckage of his former home, Roan is discovered by Saint, a man who leads a band of warrior-Brothers devoted to a god known as the Friend. Under the tutelage of the Brothers, Roan begins training in the art of war, never forgetting his desire to wreak revenge on those who massacred his people. But soon Roan becomes suspicious of Saint's unwavering interest in the use of power to dominate others, and also of Saint's second-in-command, the manipulative Brother Raven. Just before Roan reaches the final stage of his initiation into their sect, he discovers the dark truth they're concealing. Committing his first act of violence against another human being, he flees, striking out into the uninhabitable lands known as the Devastation.

Haunted by visions of his lost sister, Roan treks through

the ravaged landscape, hiding from marauders and fighting off wild dogs. There he meets Lumpy, a young man disfigured by wounds and scars caused by lethal insects called Mor-Ticks. The two decide to travel together, their destination a hospital rumored to have medicines that will help ease Lumpy's pain.

Throughout the journey, Roan visits a separate plane of reality where mysterious beings (the Dirt Eaters) have been advising and assisting him since his stay with the Brothers. These beings cannot warn Roan of the Brothers who lie in wait for him at Lumpy's fabled hospital. Though the two friends manage a narrow escape, they find themselves trapped in a labyrinth deep below the hospital's ruins. But just as they are on the brink of death, they are rescued by the Forgotten, a seemingly ageless people who live hidden below ground in a community called Oasis.

In Oasis, Roan and Lumpy gradually recover from their journey, forging new friendships with Kamyar the Storyteller, Orin the Librarian, and Lelbit—among others. But when Roan's need to find Stowe is stirred up by a series of new visions, he decides to leave Oasis and press on.

Suffering a near-fatal injury crossing hazardous terrain, Roan, feverish and only semi-conscious, is carried by Lumpy to the destination of his visions: Fairview. There, he is tended by a healer named Alandra, who enlists his help in saving fourteen special children from certain death.

When Brack, the Governor of Fairview, uncovers Roan's

true identity, the friends must make a dramatic escape with the children. With Saint and the Brothers in close pursuit, Roan, Lumpy, Lelbit, Alandra, and their precious cargo reach a chasm that should lead them to a safe haven. And it is there that Roan has his final showdown with Saint.

In *Freewalker*, Roan's quest to find his sister leads him to the City, where Stowe is engaged in her own struggle against the Masters. Both discover that their experience of abduction and betrayal is a crucial part of a battle for control of their world —and perhaps for life itself.

contents

keeper of the city

one rose from the ashes, keeper of the Light
nine close the circle holding him high
twenty-one guardians of hearth and home
ten, eyes scouring the horizon
forty-one are masters of the city
 —the war chronicles

Dirt. Dirt that burns the throat, scorches the insides, makes one see without eyes and journey without feet to far places. Dirt that cleanses, lifts, and makes one whole. Breath of life in a golden bowl. Dirt. Cherished by the Masters of the City. How they hoard it. How they try to shield it from those pilfering cowards, the Eaters. But they fail.

Darius is forever swallowing Dirt. It stains his fingertips, glows violet on his narrow lips. He sits so perfectly still. His watery eyes open in reptilian slits. He looks feeble, translucent skin stretched across a beardless face so tight his head's a living skull. His new lungs wheeze as his latest heart pumps blood that's changed twice daily. He is the Eldest.

His eyelids flutter and open wide. Alert, he listens. His

hands grip the sides of the chair as he rises. Now he is not weak, he is all strength and control and cunning. He is the Keeper of the City, Archbishop of the Conurbation, the Great Seer, and he fills the room with a magnificent, terrifying power.

"Now," says Darius, and with a flick of his wrist, the room is brought to maximum illumination.

The doors open and two clerics, heads bowed, drag in a ragged, yellow-haired detainee, blinking blindly in the glare. His skin has the raised orange blotches of interrogation scourge. Nothing unusual in that, yet he's different from the other prisoners who have passed this way before. He has not been enabled. Who is he?

Darius nods to the clerics, who bow obsequiously, awe glazing over their eyes. They owe all to the Eldest One. Privilege, status, health, and most importantly, that tiny bulge behind their ears.

The dazed prisoner is left sitting on the marble floor. Alone with the Keeper. He poses no danger. So what was his crime?

As the crumpled man's eyes adjust to the light, they focus on the portraits that cover the mahogany walls, paintings of Darius, of the Great Pyramid, of a small girl, Icon of the City. His gaze follows the chrome and crystal desk, the porcelain hands, the ancient body until it finally rests on the visage of the Master. A smile spreads across his face. The man's body expands with delight.

"Oh, Keeper! Keeper, seeing you in such good health fills my heart with joy."

"How quaint that you still hope to flatter your Archbishop," murmurs Darius.

"He should have been executed," declares a dark voice.

The prisoner painfully rises as the tall, thin-nosed man enters from the hall. "Ah, Master Kordan, still imagining threats where there are none. You would be wasting an invaluable resource. The Keeper is wiser. He has conceived of a use for me. Have you not, good Master Darius?"

Kordan frowns. A trace of a smile crosses Darius's face. "An opportunity."

The sniveling scarecrow's face lights up.

"Yes, you love opportunities, don't you?" observes the Keeper.

Kordan steps past the threshold, moving deeper into the sanctum, but a cold glance from Darius freezes him. Poor, bitter Kordan. He never should have voiced his opinions, especially when there was a chance they would clash with the Eldest's.

Darius turns to the prisoner. "I've kept you alive because once you served me well. You discovered the location of the settlement I sought and helped deliver one of the two I desired. Not a complete success but still a worthy feat."

"My Keeper, I live only to serve."

"You live to lie and cheat and plunder—but that can also be useful."

The captive smiles, the gleam in his eye signaling his eagerness to have his many talents exploited.

"Saint has become a martyr to his cause," says Darius. "A true saint. I know you can appreciate the irony. Your former brethren, the Brothers, sow rebellion. The donor deliveries have stopped. Produce is withheld."

The prisoner gives Darius a wary look. "What will you have me do?"

"You know of the Lee Clan. The Fandors?"

"Of course."

"They command half the Farlands," says Darius. "Use them to neutralize the Brothers."

"You honor me, Keeper. What can I offer them in exchange for their services?"

"Our resources are at your disposal."

The man lets out a high-pitched cackle, bows, and makes for the door. "Consider it done."

"You'll want these," Darius says, touching the wall. A large panel, hidden in the polished wood, opens and a glass shelf glides out. Neatly arranged on the surface is a brilliantly feathered gown and behind it, a box. It must be one of those stupid costumes, a consolation prize given to those the Dirt rejects. Poor man, never able to fly the Dreamfield, he's now condemned to walk the earth covered in feathers.

"May I?" the man whispers.

"Of course, Raven."

Look at him! Lovingly caressing the robe with his bony fingers. What a pathetic fool. Doesn't he realize the costume marks his humiliation?

"Thank you, all-knowing one," Raven sighs. He delicately dons the robe, and opens the box, revealing a helmet with a long yellow bird's beak.

Seeing it, Stowe screams—but of course they cannot hear her. She'd gouge out their eyes but her hands are not flesh and she can only hover impotently above them.

No other Bird Man has a mask like that. The harbinger of the end of Longlight—it was Raven, and Longlight was surely the settlement he discovered. It must have been Darius who ordered the Brothers to burn her village to the ground. Darius who required that the Brothers kill every last resident, except for two. The two that he wanted: her and Roan. Raven had the Brothers deliver her directly into the Seer's eager hands, but he failed to bring Roan. And that's why he was punished.

Raven, the first visitor to ever come to Longlight. Raven, with his magical cloak of feathers. Before he came, she'd only seen black crow feathers, white chicken feathers. But he had a rainbow of dazzling plumage. She made Roan tell her all the names, made him write them down. Peacock, eagle, swan, cardinal. She would have given anything for those feathers, more than her two favorite bowls, she'd have gladly given a finger or toe. Roan was so somber that day when he told her about the long-dead birds. He didn't want to talk, he kept looking at Daddy, at the councillors. It wasn't until Mama woke her up and she saw the village burning that she began to understand. What a stupid little girl she was, craving feathers.

When she first arrived in the City she was too angry and

afraid to speak, distrusting everyone she met. But Darius gave her Willum, who made her understand that even if she couldn't give up her anger, she might at least set her fear aside. Then Darius coaxed her and soothed her and coddled her and revealed the mystery of the Dirt—and the Dirt made her more than she was, better and stronger and wiser. She began to forget, and all of Darius's words became her own.

When he'd told her the Brothers were insane, a suicide cult, uncontrolled and dangerous, and that it was a lucky chance she'd been saved by the Masters of the City, she'd believed him. All was not lost, he'd insisted. After all, she had the Keeper himself, Great Seer of the City, to care for her. But he'd lied: Darius had been the one who'd planned it all. The attack on Longlight. Its destruction. The death of her parents. Why had she been so ready to accept his lies?

And how many other lies has he told her?

She must listen. Listen with her eyes as well as her ears. Listen and learn.

"I doubt six months in prison has inspired his loyalty," sniffs Kordan.

"Perhaps you'd prefer the task?"

Kordan stares at the floor, no doubt trying to control the glower in his eye. Such a weak man. So transparent.

"I thought not." Darius looks to the door. "Willum."

Stowe's guardian quickly enters. "I am here, Keeper." Willum is always there, always offering sensible suggestions. He does not lie, never denies a possibility, only states facts. Darius values his opinion, which is a testament to Willum's intelligence and cunning. Willum has never wronged her, it's true. He's never wronged anyone that she's aware of—but she hasn't been aware of much, it seems. That will change, now that her eyes have been opened.

"Where is Our Stowe?"

"She rests, Keeper."

Stowe whirls above them, hovering just over their heads. Fools! She is not asleep. At least not this part of her. She has a secret. She can escape her skin. In her ether body, she can fly where she will, flitting around marble columns, sweeping past oblivious citizens or high above spiral towers, glass domes, wire walkways, so high that people look like dots on the ground, and towers become building blocks. Or here, invisible, able to discover what the Masters try to conceal from her. She'll be their dupe no longer.

"The time has arrived, Willum."

"She is too young, Eldest."

Kordan sneers. "You fretted she'd be damaged by her use of Dirt and were proven wrong."

"With all due respect, Master Kordan, my fears were correct. The Dirt has transformed Our Stowe. It has forced her intellect to mature far beyond her years, and exposed her to a depth of knowledge that has shaken the stability of some of our most accomplished Masters. Stowe's powers are just beginning to blossom and as we suspected, her talents will far supersede our own. But to push her too fast too soon bears great risk.

It is easy to forget in the presence of one so articulate and poised, but allow me to remind you that within Our Stowe lies the volatile nature of a ten-year-old."

"Good Willum, of course all of what you say is true. The unfortunate facts remain, however. The governors are uneasy. Their demands increase daily. Should order not be restored, our energies will be diverted. We can wait no longer," says Darius, regret in his voice.

"I understand that our need is great, Keeper. But it is my duty to impress upon you the danger posed by this acceleration in her development."

"Her contribution outweighs her impairments. What do a few fits of temper matter? Look around you. We need to act," says Kordan.

With a wave of his finger, Darius silences Kordan. "Willum, you are to focus her education on the skills she will require to face the challenges ahead. Directing the ventures has fallen to Master Kordan; he shall inform you precisely what those requirements will be." Darius's tone signals that the discussion is over. As the two men bow and leave the room, Stowe has one last look at the Archbishop, her newfound enemy. She then quickly returns to her bed and slips back inside herself, seething. They think they know who I am. Impairments? Fits of temper? They don't know the power that's inside me. But one day they will. And on that day, I will melt the skin from their bones.

newlight

roan was afloat on it with children he'd stolen from under the nose of the jabberwock when saint set out after them with twelve of his men. not a one returned. the boiling lake forgives no trespass: not even their bones remain.

—Lore of the storytellers

"I LIKE PULLING UP WEEDS!" shouts Lona, holding up a gnarly root in each little hand.

"I pull 'em faster!" says Bub, tossing another weed in his basket.

"No, you don't, I'm winning!"

Roan chuckles as he tends the seedlings. Both the crops and the children are thriving in their new home, this place they've named Newlight. Once Lumpy rejoined them, it took three weeks of trekking to find their way here, no small task with fourteen rambunctious children. Guided by Roan's snow cricket, their search ended in this low valley, as beautiful a place as Roan has ever seen, a spot seemingly unscathed by the ravages of the Abominations that poisoned so much of the planet less than a hundred years before. Its meadows have rich topsoil, its forests abundant timber and firewood, and its pristine river-fed lake provides drinking water and fish. Rolling hills protect them from the worst of the elements and the four seasons they've spent here have been nothing short of idyllic. This is Roan's first real home since Longlight was annihilated and he's continually reminded of his birthplace. Sometimes he mistakes the children's laughter for that of his old friends or imagines his father just under that tree, reading one of his books, or his mother carving a new door for the main hall. They would have loved this land. Once, Stowe would have thrived here.

To maintain security, he's had to avoid the Dreamfield, the only sure way Stowe had of finding him. The fear of losing her forever preys on Roan. But the dream that is Newlight is haunted by many ghosts. Saint and his agonized plea as he fell to his death. The unbearable grief of Lelbit's final breath while Lumpy watched, his hope for love obliterated. Stowe. All calling out to him. Always calling out to him.

As Roan carefully culls the weaker seedlings, he worries that he might never be able to enjoy his new life here—so much suffering took place in the struggle to arrive. His hand, mounding soil around the base of a surviving plant, reminds him of all he lost and how easily it was taken from him.

"Can we go chop down trees with Merritt?"

Roan looks up, grateful that Bub has liberated him from these dark thoughts. "After we finish here," he says, marveling at how the boy's grown in the past year. He must be half a head taller.

"O-kay!" Bub scurries back to the weed-pulling contest.

"What did he say?" asks Lona.

"We gotta finish first!" yells Bub, yanking up roots.

Roan can hear Merritt's axe in the nearby wood. He's a good carpenter and an amiable man, but Roan still wishes they didn't need the help of these workers from Oasis. Alandra had argued that even with the mild weather, they needed more than lean-tos for shelter. Buildings were required. For that task they needed craftspeople with proper tools, and people who could bring food and supplies to see them through the winter. People who knew the lay of the land and could ensure a crop come summer.

"You and Lumpy might enjoy surviving on grubs and termites, but children need a bit more than bugs to eat," she said.

Still, Roan was reluctant to reveal the location of Newlight to anyone, even the Forgotten, and why shouldn't he be— hadn't the first visitor to Longlight brought about its ruin? Alandra kept insisting, though. It wasn't that he doubted her dedication to the children's health and well-being, but in their many disagreements she was always quick to dismiss his concerns. Her relentless single-mindedness was making him wonder where her allegiances truly lay.

In the end, a carpenter and four other workers from Oasis had joined them, a skilled group of people whose commitment is undeniable. For here, unprotected by the caves of

Oasis that had maintained their youth, they've already begun to show their true ages, deep wrinkles appearing on their faces. Loren directs the building construction, Bildt oversees the cultivation, Selden the food preparation, and Terre, an accomplished weaver in her own right, commits time to work as an apprentice healer under Alandra. Roan likes them all, more or less. He has to admit the shelters went up quickly, the gardens were planted with success, and the children are happy, relishing their new lives. What more could he ask for?

And yet, these people from Oasis are clearly more than mere craftspeople. Roan can see the wariness in their eyes, the physical discipline they maintain. They must have been sent not only to help, but as guards—of him and the children. It's not an unreasonable precaution, there is always the threat of the Brothers. But the fact that they do not acknowledge this other purpose has only served to increase Roan's suspicions.

"I won! I won!" shouts Lona.

"I got twice as many as you!" protests Bub. "Plus you got lots of broken roots, the weeds'll grow back!"

"Roan!" Lona wails. "Are my roots all broken?"

Roan, with a deeply serious look on his face, strides over to the baskets, inspecting each one intently. He picks up weeds from each basket, sniffs them, pinches them, and finally bites them, eliciting a squeal of laughter from Lona. Then he pronounces his verdict. "Without a doubt, you are both supreme weed yankers and for this reason I am appointing you both to a new position." And laying his hands on their heads, Roan declares, "I hereby dub you Captains of the Weeds. Congratulations."

Proud smiles break out across Lona's and Bub's faces. "For true?" Lona says. "For really true?"

"For really true."

Lona whoops and elbows Bub. "Come on, Captain, let's yank!"

"I still pull better than you!"

Roan watches as they dive back to the ground, hands gripping weeds. But Lona suddenly stops mid-motion. Her head bobs, her eyes roll back, and she collapses.

"What——?" begins Bub, and without another word, he's crumpled down beside her.

"Come on, you two," Roan smiles, thinking it's some kind of game. As he reaches them, however, he sees that their faces are pale and lifeless.

Terrified, he bends over Lona, and puts his ear to her chest. All he can detect is her hollow shell, and a great darkness within her. Steadying his breath and focusing deeper, he hears it. A faint heartbeat. She's not dead. He instantly reaches with his mind to sense Bub. Like Lona, Bub's consciousness feels so indistinct and distant that Roan can't reach it. Hoping against hope that the other children aren't also stricken, he shifts his attention outward—and the voice of Alandra is the first signal he picks up. Six were with her in the main residence, sorting herbs when they collapsed: Sake, Dani, Beck, Anais, Tamm, Korina. She's already attending to them, along with Runk and Theo.

Anxious shouting draws his attention. In the distance, other cries, other voices. Merritt's screaming for help with Gip. Bildt with Geemo. Lumpy's yelling at Jaw and Jam, splashing them with water but they won't wake, won't move.

Terre, the healing apprentice, ashen-faced, appears at the garden's edge. "It's struck them too?"

"Every one is down," says Roan, fighting to stay calm.

"Could you reach them?"

"No. But they're still alive. Barely. Help me take them to Alandra. "

Roan carefully places Lona in Terre's arms and takes Bub in his own. Moving as swiftly as he dares, he picks his way across the familiar path toward the lake, taking care to protect his charge from jutting branches. He sees, coming from the water, from the forest, from the fields, Lumpy, Bildt, and Merritt, catapulted forward by the burden they hold in their arms. Roan's apprehension grows at the sight of each limp child. But nothing could prepare him for the panic that hits him as he follows them into the residence. Loren and Selden frantically prepare beds for the new wave of victims. Lumpy's beside Jaw, tears filling his eyes, begging the unconscious boy to wake up. Terre, swiftly laying Lona safely down, joins Alandra, who's shouting out instructions as she rushes from child to child.

"Put them down on their backs! Heads slightly elevated! Make sure their airways are clear! Terre, bring me the salts!"

Brushing the hair from Bub's forehead, Roan scans the room and as his gaze drifts across the fourteen small beds, he struggles to control his own anxiety. These children are teetering on the edge of death, and he's responsible for their lives.

"I don't know what's happening yet," Alandra says. "Give me one full day with them to formulate a diagnosis." She holds Bub's wrists, taking his pulses, assessing the strength of his organs and blood and energy fields. Her downcast face tells Roan all he needs about the prognosis.

"Will they last a whole day?" Roan asks.

"The sleep is deep but they live. Go," she says. "And take the others. Let Terre and me do our work."

Roan stands and signals everyone but the healers to leave. Lumpy squeezes Jaw's arm, releases it, and rises. Roan silently guides his friend outside.

Merritt and Bildt, their faces fraught with worry, rush at Roan. "Did she say anything to you?"

"Only that she needs time."

"I've never seen anything like this."

Bildt sighs. "You've never seen anything like those children either, Merritt."

"I don't like the look of it," says the burly carpenter.

"Trust Alandra," Bildt says, her voice quavering.

"I think Bildt's right," says Roan. "We've no choice but to wait and let Alandra do her job."

Watching the Oasis people slowly disperse, Roan can't help wishing he trusted them. They may be visibly shaken, but he's certain they know more than they're saying.

"Want to walk?" Roan asks, turning to Lumpy.

Lumpy, head bowed, his face pinched with worry, blinks away tears as they both head to the lakeshore. "Sorry. I don't know why I'm reacting like this. They're still breathing, Alandra's treating them, she'll fix them." His eyes, red as the craters that scar his face, search Roan's. "Won't she?"

Jaw and Jam had become Lumpy's constant companions, their friendship a salve for the wound of losing Lelbit. Lumpy had wandered the Farlands for years never meeting anyone who shared his experience, but then he met Lelbit, who had been scarred by the Mor-Ticks, too. Like Lumpy, she was the only surviving member of a family devastated by the lethal insects. He had admired her courage, and between them there had grown a quiet tenderness. What her death cost him, Roan has no way of knowing—Lumpy never talks about it—but is there a limit to how much loss he can sustain?

"Yeh," Roan says, trying to believe his own words. "She'll figure it out. If anybody can, it's her."

"You don't sound very convinced."

Though Roan has a theory, he's not exactly sure how to put it into words—or that he should, even to Lumpy. Still, he can't find it in himself to lie, and in the end, his silence tells all.

"If you know something..."

"She asked for one day. Let's give it to her." But the words of Kamyar, the storyteller Roan met so many months ago in Oasis, continue to trouble him. *Ask many questions. Accept nothing at face value. Beware the Dirt Eaters.*

They sit in silence, watching the sun's waning rays shimmer on the water. While the light fades, and the two friends fight to keep their hopes alive, Roan's snow cricket jumps onto the dock and begins to sing.

"Okay, okay," Lumpy says to a rustle near his chest, and takes from his pocket a white cricket with faint black spots on its wings. "Go join him, then."

When they first came to this new land, they were all amazed to see that it abounded with the rare insects. It didn't take long for one to adopt Lumpy, an attachment he'd yearned for ever since he lost the snow cricket that saved his life.

Soon the music of crickets surrounds them. "You think it will help?" asks Lumpy.

"Can't hurt."

It is well into moonrise when Lumpy says goodnight. Roan steps off the creaking dock and winds his way through the settlement, pondering the buildings, the walkways, the gardens. They've accomplished so much, far more than he ever expected. And it will all have been for nothing if the children do not survive.

Following the white stone trail to the top of the spotting hill, Roan hikes to the rise that provides a lookout over the water and forest. Now that he's alone, the dark emotions he's been battling threaten to overtake him. His thoughts keep returning to his sister and the night, three years ago, when her hand slipped from his and he fell face down in the snow, never to see her again. His parents had entrusted him with her care. He had failed them—and her. These children trust him completely, they'd placed their lives in his hands. And now he's failing again.

It could be that this place isn't what he thinks it is. There might be a disease or a toxin in this idyllic environment that only the children are susceptible to. It's possible their gifts created the vulnerability that struck them down. Maybe it's an attack of an altogether unexpected nature. But these suppositions are hollow, meaningless. He knows where the germ of the answer lies. Alandra knows it, too, and she'll have to face the truth in one day's time.

Suddenly the hill, the water, the forest, all vanish. And before Roan, branches with orange, peeling bark hang limply in the humid air. Beside the smooth-skinned tree stands a boy, a few years younger than Roan, face brown and open.

"How do you do that?" the boy asks.

"Do what?"

"Call me this way."

"I'm not calling you."

"You don't need my help?"

"I'm in great need of help."

"Maybe I have what you need."

The boy disappears and the vision ends as abruptly as it

began. But standing alone again on top of the spotting hill, the moon high in the sky, the lake below, Roan knows the boy is of this world, somehow reaching out through space and perhaps even time. The experience was certainly unlike any he's ever had with the Dirt Eaters in the Dreamfield. No. This boy seemed innocent and natural. And his voice so full of hope.

OUR STOWE

OUR STOWE, CHILD OF LIGHT
TURN YOUR MERCIFUL EYE UPON US
THAT WE MAY BE BLESSED
WITH YOUR HELP AND PROTECTION
　　　　　—LITURGY OF THE CONURBATION

"I'T'S STUFFY IN HERE." Stowe is scowling.
Their driver winces. The fan is immediately turned up. No one likes it when Stowe scowls.

"Air circulation is not the problem. I want to stretch my legs. I want to be outside." Stowe glowers at the car-camera that is monitoring her every movement. "These dresses I am obliged to wear are heavy, hot, and uncomfortable. They clench and cinch and are stifling and unbearable. Let me out. I would like to walk to the factory."

"I am sorry, Stowe, but you do know that prolonged exposure of your person is not permitted by security."

"But Willum, everyone in the City loves me."

"You are very much loved, but there are outsiders..."

"Rebels? Are things so out of control that rebels, by the

hundreds, stalk the City streets, waiting for a chance to assassinate me?"

Willum glances at the car-camera. "No, no, of course not. But precautions must be taken."

"You know very well I can protect myself. Besides, they could never get through this." She knocks on the front panel of the dress, which cracks with the sound of fila-armor. She glares at the impenetrable material, which was invented, she is sure, to make her life perfectly miserable.

Her eyes catch Willum's for a moment. She does not miss how carefully he picks his next words.

"... Under most circumstances you are able, yes. It is the unforeseen that worries us and there has been an inordinate influx of people from the Farlands."

"Ooooo! And are they dangerous to me as well?"

"No, of course not."

"Then stop the car."

"The crowds, Stowe. You know how people react when they see you."

"But we're on a bridge, Willum, there's hardly anyone around. Stop the car."

"That is not advisable."

"I need air. I am suffocating!"

Stowe watches the driver's eyes nervously dart in the mirror from her to Willum. She can see the enabler behind his ear throbbing. He must obey—but who? Willum lets out a large sigh and nods. Obviously relieved, the cleric brings the electro-engine to a stop. The cars behind and in front of theirs also come to a halt, the doors fly open, and blue-robed clerics scramble out to either side of the bridge, scanning in every direction.

"Only a few minutes," says the ever cooperative Willum.

Stowe's door opens. She bursts from her seat to stand on the bridge. A strong wind buffets her face, flaps her four skirts; even her high stiff collar is bent back by the force. Stowe loves the wind. It should do nicely to obscure any words passed between her and Willum.

Below her, green water. Above, green sky. And on both sides of the inlet, dozens and dozens of airtight domes, all built during the Consolidation, when the rebels massed against the City and the skies rained red. Once used to protect the elite from the toxins that ravaged the environment, the domes now house the laboratories so crucial to keeping the old ones alive. Beyond the domes the new architecture of the Masters is a testament to their triumph over the traitors. Glittering spires, obelisk-shaped towers and, rising above it all, the Great Pyramid, a masterwork of glass, the throbbing heart of the City.

This is the City, the only metropolis to survive the Consolidation, and it adores her. Her image is everywhere, on posters, signs, even giant billboards, like the one that rises at the end of this bridge. She is the City's own true daughter, a mirror into its future. To the citizens, she is perfection, she is mercy, beneficent beauty, possibility, hope. But it is Darius who has made her so, and what is he to her now? A murderer.

A liar. This City is his creation, its citizens his. And he controls it just as he controls her.

The line-up of cars grows ever longer behind her cavalcade. Judging by their colors, many are privately owned, a privilege reserved for citizens who contribute to the glorification of the amalgamated City—designers, engineers, architects, doctors, and the like. But as with everything in this Conurbation, not a horn honks or driver curses. All will wait patiently for however long the delay may be. No one ever complains in the City. And if they do, they don't complain for long.

"Good," says Stowe. "Now we shall talk."

"You are due at the factory."

"Center of our civilization, I know. Willum, I love these visits. I realize the importance of our workers' contribution and acknowledge that it would never do to keep them waiting. But—"

"The guards are very nervous. The wind is so strong."

"But this won't take long," she insists, turning to him. "I've had a bad dream, Willum."

"You've had bad dreams before," he replies, unsympathetically.

Nevertheless, she can hear the kernel of curiosity beneath his dismissal.

"Not like this one." She scrutinizes his face, ready to detect exactly how much he knows and determine how much she should reveal. "In this dream, I see a man wearing a cloak of many feathers."

He seems unfazed, but she has his attention now, yes she does. "And who was this feathered man?"

"The one who brought death to Longlight."

"Stowe, you should always call me when you have nightmares like that."

That tone, worried like a doting parent. Why does it simultaneously gratify and repulse her?

"Were you able to get back to sleep?"

She feeds him the bait, her eyes steady. "In this nightmare, the Bird Man speaks to the Keeper. He had displeased the Eldest in some way. Failed on a mission. But he has been punished."

Willum's gaze remains unblinking. "Clearly your dream capacity has blossomed."

Oh, he treads so carefully. But he suspects. Will he mention his suspicions to anyone?

"Do you know of such a Bird Man as mine?"

"I know what I have been told. Which is not much. I was a journeyman in the barrens of the outer circle when I was called to this position." He pauses, catching the wary gaze of one of the clerics. "Walk. They will follow."

As they proceed along the walkway, below the massive cables that suspend the bridge over the churning water, clerics fan out in all directions, frantically maintaining their security net.

"His name is Raven."

"Such a beautiful name. Not at all suited to the sly wretch on the Keeper's floor."

Was that a grin? Too swift. She'd catch Willum out yet. His game, his truth.

"He was a failed student at the seminary, they said. He lacked the gift."

"But under normal protocol, world-locked seminarians are given the Enabler and made into clerics."

"Darius stopped the implantation. Raven was extraordinarily clever and manipulative, so the Keeper recruited him to join a new movement in the Farlands."

"The Brothers. So one of Saint's first followers was Darius's spy. How clever."

"Too clever and yet not clever enough. Though Raven was successful in delivering you into the protection of the Eldest, he failed to locate your brother, or so he said."

"I ought to be grateful," Stowe says with a sweetness that could rot teeth. "Darius is like a father to me. His generosity knows no limits."

"Then it was discovered that Roan had been with the Brothers all along, quite under Darius's nose."

"Raven was a traitor?"

"So it appeared. Raven was brought in, interrogated, tortured, but his pleas of innocence were never withdrawn."

"You don't believe him?"

"No."

"Then he may know where my brother is."

"He may have once, but no more."

Stowe's fingers tighten on the railing, as she gazes at the

churning water below. "Thank you, good Willum," she says, smiling up at him.

"I am here only to serve you, Stowe."

"I know."

How did he look at her just then? She could have sworn it was elation, but no—no, she must control her emotions, not see in others what she feels in herself. Careless, that was careless. She had allowed herself a moment of triumph. It was so satisfying to know she had been right about Raven, but she must not let Willum see her victories. She cannot let down her guard, not to anyone. Not even him. And she must always look beyond the surface. On the surface are lies the Masters use to deceive her.

"It's Our Stowe! Our Stowe!"

A man and a woman have stopped on the opposite pavement, both waving enthusiastically at Stowe.

"Our Stowe!" they yell, beaming at her. Stowe raises her fine-boned hand in response, her lips curved into a tight smile. How open and vulnerable she must seem, standing before her own gigantic picture, cherubic grin warming the world. The letters on the billboard read: Our Stowe.

Oh, yes, the City loves her. Its citizens bow before her. But they are not hers. She must never forget that it is Darius who owns them.

For now.

the assignation

the children will number fourteen.
they will know our dreams and be led by them.
where they will go, so will we all.
—book of Longlight

THE MAIN HALL IS THE BIGGEST of the log buildings, harboring the kitchen and dining room. In the morning, Roan, Lumpy, and the Oasis people sit glumly at one of the tables; the other two are conspicuously empty. Selden puts the pot of porridge in front of them and they each fill up their bowls. Loren breaks the silence.

"Did you check on them this morning?"

Selden shakes his head. "I brought them their breakfast, but didn't go in. Terre told me to leave it at the door. Looked like a ghost. Far as I can tell, they worked straight through the night."

"What else would you expect," says Bildt. "Alandra and Terre won't stop till every last one of those little folks is running about again."

"Judging from what I see, they weren't the only ones who couldn't sleep last night." No one answers Roan. Their drawn countenances say it all.

"So reading between the lines, Selden," grumbles Merritt, "I gather that there's not been a scrap of progress."

"I admit I listened at the door," says the cook, just a little embarrassed. "The only voices I heard were those of the two women."

"The smartest thing right now," says Lumpy, echoing Roan's comment from the night before, "is to do our jobs and let them do theirs."

Roan observes the faces around him. He can see they all share his frustration. If he could just get to the bottom of what's happened to the children, he could *do* something, stop feeling so helpless.

After his vision on the lookout, he'd retrieved his hook-sword from its hiding place. He sat with it, for what seemed like hours, before removing it from its sheath. It felt comfortable in his hand, easy. Too easy. He knew it was unlikely he'd have to use it, but he felt better somehow, having it close.

Roan breaks out of his reverie to find breakfast finished, and everyone pushing back chairs to go their separate ways. Grateful to have the gardens to himself, Roan sets to work immediately, sweating in the sun, turning over shovelful after shovelful of pungent earth. His hands are blistered, his back is aching, but he won't stop. The work helps calm him.

He pauses only for water, trying to ignore time, and hoping that somehow the nightmare will magically disappear.

"She's ready," calls out Lumpy from across the fence.

Roan puts down his shovel, washes his face in the trough, and they wind their way back to the residence, the sun low in the sky. Lumpy knocks lightly on the door. It opens a crack. Terre motions them in.

All fourteen children lie on their beds, glistening with needles that pierce dozens of points, from around their eyes to their toes. Apart from their chests rising and falling with each breath, they are still. Alandra is bent over one of the smaller girls, Dani, carefully dripping liquid onto her lips. The healer looks up at Roan, her eyes dark from lack of sleep.

"Nothing works. Not the herbs, not the emulsions, not the aromatics."

"Not even the points?" asks Lumpy, nodding at young Jaw.

Alandra looks up at Lumpy, anguished. "Nothing."

"We both know it's not an illness."

She shakes her head. "You're wrong, Roan."

Roan wants to shout at her. How can she deny what's going on, even now, after all this—why can't she even acknowledge the possibility?

"What's Roan wrong about?" asks Lumpy.

"I took them into the Dreamfield—even though he expressed some concerns," Alandra tells him.

Lumpy looks at Roan quizzically. "It was a necessary part of their training, wasn't it?"

"According to the Dirt Eaters. They were the ones pushing for it." Rounding on Alandra, Roan quietly asserts, "I never agreed."

"I assumed you'd accepted it."

"How convenient for you."

"They were ready."

Torn between his friends, Lumpy tries to reason it out. "But it's part of who they are, Roan, isn't it? The kids have incredible potential. A big reason for bringing them here was to help them develop."

"And you see the result."

"No," says Alandra. "We don't know why this happened. Why should it have anything to do with the Dreamfield at all? I exercised every precaution. I only took them to the nearest edges; they were barely exposed."

"Obviously it was more than enough."

"You have no evidence."

"How many times did you tell me that my sister was being damaged by her early exposure to the Dreamfield and the Dirt?"

Alandra, flushed, snaps back at him. "You really think I'd do to the children what the Turned have done to your sister? You think I would be that reckless after all we've been through—after all I've seen?"

Roan has no reply. He wants to trust her, he realizes—that's always been the problem. He's so sure she loves the children that he doesn't fight her decisions, even when he feels he should. But he can't forget that only part of Alandra is in this world. The rest is with the Dirt Eaters—and he's certain they're the ones who encouraged her to test the children. They may even have lied about the risk, and she believed their arguments. She still does.

"I think Alandra's telling the truth, Roan," says Lumpy. "Don't you?"

"He can think whatever he wants," says Alandra.

"I think," says Roan softly, "that you care deeply for the children. I know how hard you're working. I'm sorry."

Alandra coolly accepts the apology.

"But," Roan adds, "I also think you may not know the truth behind what you've been instructed to do."

"And what truth would that be?"

"For that I need to speak to the Dirt Eaters. I want answers."

"But it's too dangerous. The Turned are still searching for you."

"And so I've avoided the Dreamfield all these months. But I think this qualifies as an emergency. I want to hear what the other Dirt Eaters have to say. My eyes on theirs."

The healer considers, then accepts. "There is one place we control that is believed to be impenetrable by the Turned. We will have to remain cloaked, though—and not move beyond, no matter what happens."

"Agreed."

Alandra takes out a small, plain jar, opens the lid, takes a pinch of the violet dirt inside and swallows it.

"Come back with answers. Please. And Roan..." Lumpy

adds pointedly, "the best way to do that is to actually ask some questions."

Roan accepts Lumpy's admonition with a smile. His friend's right, of course—Roan needs to steer his thoughts away from his own frustrations and focus on the children's predicament. Regaining control over his heartbeat and breath, he slowly draws up energy through his feet, his legs, his spine, and out through the top of his head.

YELLOW CLOUDS HIGH OVERHEAD DRIFT ACROSS THE CRIMSON SKY. ROAN, HIS BODY OF DENSE CLAY, STANDS WITH THE GOAT-WOMAN ON A FIELD OF ROUND BOULDERS.

"HOW DO WE SUMMON THEM, ALANDRA?"

THE GOAT-WOMAN MEETS HIS EYES. A TERRIBLE SADNESS STANDS BETWEEN HIM AND ALANDRA.

"IF YOU TRUSTED ME, WE WOULDN'T NEED TO," SHE SAYS, AND RAISES HER ARMS.

THE FAINT GREEN AURA THAT SURROUNDS HER GROWS BRIGHTER. SOON IT'S SO BRIGHT ROAN HAS TO TURN HIS HEAD AWAY.

"YOU TOO," SHE TELLS HIM.

HE STARES AT HIS OWN AURA AND SILENTLY URGES IT TO INTENSIFY. SOON THEY BOTH BLAZE WITH COLOR, THE LIGHT EXTENDING UP INTO THE SKY.

"THEY COME," ALANDRA SAYS.

SUSPENDED ABOVE THEM, A CIRCLE IN THE AIR, BARELY DISCERNIBLE, BEGINS TO SHIMMER. THE RING TURNS AQUEOUS AND TWO SHAFTS OF LIGHT BLAZE THROUGH IT, STRIKING THE GROUND BEHIND ROAN.

"I SEE YOU'RE STILL WAITING FOR YOUR TRUE FORM, ROAN."

THE CLAY MAN SEES A MOUNTAIN LION SITTING ACROSS FROM THEM. BESIDE THE CAT, A RED LIZARD WATCHES WITH UNBLINKING EYES.

ROAN IGNORES THE SLIGHT. "WHAT'S HAPPENING TO THE CHILDREN?"

THE LIZARD FLICKS ITS TONGUE. "WE ARE SEARCHING FOR ANSWERS."

"YOU PRESSED FOR THEM TO GO TO THE DREAMFIELD BEFORE THEY WERE READY."

THE LION GROWLS. "THEIR POWERS, LEFT UNATTENDED, WOULD FESTER AND GROW TO HARM THEM."

"AND YET YOU CLAIM MY SISTER'S POWERS HAVE FESTERED AND HARMED HER SPECIFICALLY BECAUSE THEY ARE VERY WELL ATTENDED. YOU CAN'T HAVE IT BOTH WAYS."

"THE CHILDREN ARE NOT YOUR SISTER."

STIFLING HIS FRUSTRATION, ROAN TRIES ANOTHER APPROACH. "YOU SAY YOU'RE SEARCHING FOR ANSWERS. WHAT HAVE YOU FOUND?"

THE LION CIRCLES ROAN, THEN ABRUPTLY TURNS TO THE GOAT-WOMAN. "ALANDRA?"

"IT IS NOT A WEAKNESS IN THE CHILDREN, THEY REMAIN STRONG. NOR A TOXIN IN NEWLIGHT, FOR THE LAND IS PURE. IT CANNOT BE A VIRUS. I DETECTED NO SIGN OF DISEASE."

"ANY IDEA WHAT IT MIGHT BE?" ROAN PERSISTS.

THE GOAT-WOMAN IGNORES HIS QUESTION, DEFERRING TO THE LION.

"We have suspicions," responds the lion.

The lizard rises from its rock. "You once saved the children from coming into the possession of the Turned. Perhaps now they have used other means to abduct them."

"Do you have any proof of that?" says Roan.

The lion's and the lizard's eyes meet. They shake their heads. "We have none. But we know of no other explanation."

"If you believe that to be a possibility, then why bring the children into the field in the first place? What were you hoping for? What do the Turned want from them?"

"We are searching for answers."

"So you've said."

A small moth flutters in front of the lizard. And with a flick of his reptilian tongue, they are all gone.

Lumpy waits expectantly as Roan opens his eyes.

"If they know anything, they're not saying," Roan mutters.

Alandra slowly lifts her head. "They're investigating. We should have answers soon."

"How long is soon?"

"I don't know, Lumpy."

Lumpy's about to protest but Roan catches his eye, stopping him. "Okay. We wait."

"In the meantime, I must get back to the children," she says, with a pointed look at Roan. "I won't rest until they're whole again."

Lumpy gives her hand a reassuring squeeze. "I know they're safe in your care."

The moment he and Roan step out of the residence into the glaring sun, the tradespeople swarm about them, all talking at once.

"What'd you find out?" asks Loren.

"Are they going to be alright?" Bildt wonders aloud.

"It was awful quiet in there," says Merritt.

"My guess is you went dreamwalking," Loren hypothesizes. "Sure felt to me like Dirt Eater business going on in there."

"Still no answers. No improvement." Scanning the Oasis people, it's clear to Roan that they expected answers. They assumed the Dirt Eaters would suggest solutions to the problem. Well, they were wrong. "Sorry," he mutters, and using his grief as an excuse to get away quickly, he bows his head and strides toward the wood, Lumpy at his side.

"Do they at least know what caused it?"

"They blame the Turned."

"What do you think?"

"I don't know. But I mean to find out."

"So when do we leave?"

"Don't you want to stay close to Jaw and Jam?"

"I'm no use to them here."

"After dark."

"We tell anyone?"

Roan sighs. "All these people come from Oasis. They're

warriors, Lumpy, our guards. I'm sure that they're all under the direction of the Dirt Eaters." Roan looks at Lumpy gravely. "And so is Alandra."

"I don't believe Alandra would do anything to hurt the kids."

"As our friend, it doesn't make sense to me that she would. But she is a Dirt Eater. I don't trust them anymore, and she trusts them too much. I don't want her to know where we're going."

"And just where are we going?"

Roan smiles for the first time since this ordeal began. "I had a dream..."

Lumpy laughs, rolling his eyes skyward. "Of course."

cooperation unlimited

providers of essential services are now all
alpha-enabled and we are pleased to announce
that this triumph of knowledge and expertise
will soon be made available to all. the
conurbation, striving always to enhance the focus,
strength, and wisdom of its congregation.
—proclamation of master querin

THE ROAD STOWE'S SPED DOWN for the last hour is all
new concrete and high guard towers. This highway is
reserved for the Masters and their minions, while other
ancient broken roads are left for the use of travelers and
refugees, but there is nothing to see apart from interminable
flatlands. Gazing out in bored silence, Stowe's stupor finally
ends with the sight of the forest of sleek windmills that signals their imminent arrival at the plant. She steels herself as
she watches the spinning blades harness the infinite energy of
the wind. She loves what the wind can do. From little innocu-
ous breezes to paralyzing hurricanes, she and the wind share
the same kind of force. Invisible, powerful, and often deadly.
Stowe loves the wind.

When the motorcade stops at the guard gate, Stowe suddenly senses herself being surveilled. Her eyes dart in all directions, but all she sees is a Gunther, peering through his thick glasses at a windmill transformer. With their half-addled minds, Gunthers are said to be good for only one thing: maintaining the power grid. They hide away like mice and speak like automatons and are generally unpleasant. Something about them makes her cringe... maybe it's the large eyes behind the thick lenses. The city's dependence on those pariahs is inexplicable and she's wondered more than once why Darius granted them guild status. Though she continues to scan the area, it is of no use—the chill of being profoundly observed has left her. If that stupid drudge hadn't been working there, distracting her, she might have found the culprit.

As the convoy proceeds through the guard gate, the factory's sign, prominently displayed over the entranceway, becomes visible. COOPERATION UNLIMITED. Stowe sniggers to herself. This should prove interesting.

Before she has a toe out of the car, she's surrounded by a dozen clerics and whisked into the entryway of the pharmaceutical factory. There she is greeted by a large, amiable man with small teeth, the factory Manager. She instantly identifies him as Fortin, the groveler. At the council meetings, he insinuates himself into every conversation, usually through some sort of self-deprecation. And well he might. Of the forty-one Masters, Fortin is the only one with the lowly title of Manager. His singular incompetence is the stuff of legends, the legends of fools. Even dour Kordan loves to mock him.

"You bless us with this visit, Our Stowe." Fortin dabs his right eye with a cloth, but not because he's been moved to tears by the sight of Stowe. The veins in his eyes are red and swollen, constantly oozing fluid. Soon his vision will become cloudy, then obscured by dark spots, until his sight fails completely. Whose eyes will they pluck for you, Fortin the Fool?

"The pleasure is entirely mine, Good Fortin."

"You are too kind. May I have the honor of showing you our facility?"

"I would be delighted."

Willum and the clerics change into white coveralls, cotton mittens, and covers for their feet. Stowe, in her billowing scarlet gown, like any good trophy, is left untouched. No sanitization is required for Our Stowe.

She is escorted through two sets of doors into an enormous room where hundreds of people peer through magnifying glasses, as they work with the most delicate of tools, intricately constructing what appear to be....

"Enablers?" asks Stowe.

"Our Stowe perceives the truth as always," replies Fortin.

"And your rate of production?"

He smiles. "One hundred a day."

"How extraordinary."

Stowe glances at Willum, but he seems in deep concentration, absorbing every detail in the factory. What does he see?

"We have an excellent success rate. Only five in every three thousand are faulty."

"So last year..."

"Thirty-five thousand, seven hundred enablers successfully activated, the Keeper be blessed."

"Yes," Stowe says. "People are so wayward. Your enablers help to unite all of our citizens."

"A tremendous focusing tool," Fortin says. "The clerics' efficiency has tripled since they were enabled. The device has incredible potential. We've only just begun to explore its many possible uses. Terribly exciting, don't you think?"

"Yes. Terribly," Stowe agrees, now understanding Willum's keen interest in this site—and in Fortin. This groveler puts on a show: what appears a lowly position—Manager of a factory—is, in fact, one of the most important in the Conurbation, one that's in the process of expanding. How?

The Manager leads her down countless aisles of technicians working with deep concentration and a smile of satisfaction on their faces, all encouraged by the bulges behind their ears. Not a worker in the building is without. In fact, all citizens in service positions for the Conurbation have enablers—except Gunthers: the electricity they work with interferes with the field the devices generate. Darius has been fascinated with the enablers ever since he invented them; constantly laboring to improve their function and increase their application. And judging by what Fortin's said, the Eldest has even more developments in mind.

As the whistle blows, Stowe is guided up a flight of metal stairs to a balcony overlooking the manufacturing area. The workers, gathering below, gaze up at her in adoration.

Fortin booms out to the crowd. "Our Stowe has blessed us with the radiance of her presence. Her light illuminates our glorious future. Our Stowe."

Every worker cheers. Fortin offers his hand, guiding her onto steps of the amplification platform. How gullible she has been. All those blissful faces worship her, yes. Of course they do. Master Fortin enables them to. And she has been seduced by the adulation. How clear that's becoming. The Masters seek to coddle her, to keep her trusting, vulnerable to their coercion. What would happen if they identified her as the enemy? What then? Would all the enabled be summoned to tear her to shreds? No doubt.

"I'm so honored to be here, among such talented, committed people. I know that Darius and the Masters of the City value your work enormously. As I do."

More cheers and applause.

"Being here like this, so near to you, seeing you at your workplace, witnessing your brilliant accomplishments, fills me with great pride and excitement. I feel so close to all of you. Each and every one of you I carry in my heart because we form a family. And I am little sister to you all."

"Stowe! Stowe! Stowe!"

Stowe, poster-girl for the Masters, for the first time since her factory tours began, feels the ovation for what it is: the trigger response of a controlled population. A well of sadness rises to catch in her throat and she instantly dismisses it. Not allowed, you idiot. You cannot go weak. This is how Darius keeps you under his thumb. Needing, needing. No more. No.

Taking Stowe's arm in his, Willum guides her to the exit, but not before she casts her most beguiling look Fortin's way. The Manager's eyes, despite appearances, see all too much. But those eyes are also certain others don't notice. And that's his failing.

"You did very well," Willum assures her.

"I know. I love these visits," she replies.

"So you said, but today you seemed different."

"Only tired. The speeches are always the same. I find the repetition a challenge."

Willum sips the air, as if he's testing the temperature of a hot drink. "Well, Stowe, you're about to face an even greater challenge."

Ah, here it comes. "And what might that be?" Stowe asks.

Willum looks away, his hands balled tightly into fists.

"Come now, Willum, you've piqued my interest."

"A trek."

"I trek every day, looking for my brother."

"Your assignment's been modified."

"You mean I won't be looking for my brother?"

The cleric opens the car door but Willum does not get in. "No. Not any longer. At least not for the moment."

"Then who will?"

His eyes lock on hers. "No one."

"What do you mean, no one?"

"Darius informed me this morning that Roan has been declared dead."

"He is not dead," she states emphatically.

"I'm sorry, Stowe, truly I am."

"Darius is in error."

Willum looks fiercely at Stowe. "Recall that your father is the Eldest. Keeper of the City, Archbishop of the Conurbation, the Great Seer. No matter what happens, consider that before you speak."

"Of course, Willum, I was not thinking." Stowe feels her whole body begin to shake. When did they find out Roan was dead? How could they know?

"Good then. We will begin to prepare for your new assignment."

For more than two years she's searched for Roan. Three hours every day in the amplification booth, eating Dirt, crying out to a brother who never comes. The mythical brother who holds the keys of destruction and salvation in his hands. And now they're giving her a new assignment because they think Roan's dead. But it's not possible. She would have known.

"It is expected that you will do your duty," Willum warns.

"Of course it is. What does it matter to you? Just another Farlands boy, dead! My brother. Dead!"

She lets the anger rise through her body, red hot—she has

an excuse now, and a chance to see what happens when she explodes.

"You know nothing! Nothing! NOTHING!"

She lets her fury surge until it shrieks out the pores of her skin, out the pupils of her eyes, her guts, her lungs, her heart. Their driver falls to his knees, then onto the ground, writhing. The other clerics sink down in agony.

"Don't, Stowe." Willum winces, then covers his ears. It's very subtle, but she notices a glow around him. He's creating a protective aura to shield himself from her!

"Stop it, Stowe, now!" demands Willum.

But she doesn't stop. She doesn't want to stop, the release feels too good, so gratifying. All the fear, the loneliness, the pathetic wheezing apprehension in her chest, gone, gone.

Willum is far stronger than she thought. She imagines Darius's face and her rage builds, pushing against Willum's aura, knocking him backwards.

"Enough!"

Stowe exhales until there is nothing left. Nothing left in her at all. But she felt it, Willum's aura pushing her back. He can push her back.

She looks around her. All the clerics are lying on the ground moaning, contorted from the pain she's inflicted. But the driver, blood oozing from his ears, is silent and still.

"Have I killed him?" asks Stowe, curious.

Willum's aura vanishes. Bending over the body, he gives her a cold look. "He still breathes."

"Ah," she says, a trace of excitement in her voice. This is an ability well worth perfecting! And she'll need to perfect it. If Willum can push her, Kordan would probably crush her. Never mind what Darius could do. She must get stronger. Much stronger.

Feeling her cuspid with her tongue, she realizes it's loose. Another baby tooth is about to come out.

wetlands

DID THE LAKE TRULY SWALLOW HIM?
HOW COULD IT BE?
TO BELIEVE THAT DENIES THE PROPHECY.
A NEW WORLD WAS PROMISED
SO
IT WOULD SEEM THAT OUR ROAN HAS A LONG WAY TO GO.
                                    —LORE OF THE STORYTELLERS

ROAN AND LUMPY WALK THE LAKESHORE under the waxing crescent moon. Their steps are silent on the rocky beach, and they do not need to speak for they know each other's movements all too well. Once again they are journeying together on an unknown, probably dangerous road, but this time it's not their lives that are at stake—it's the lives of fourteen children, and the weight of it is with them every step.

Just as the trees across the lake glow with the first light of day, Lumpy points out the rivulet that Bildt described when she and the tradespeople first arrived.

"She said they followed this stream all the way from Oasis."

Roan kneels down and stares at the water slipping through the small pebbles at the bottom of the brook.

Lumpy peers curiously over Roan's shoulder. "See something?"

Roan shakes his head. "The pebbles, this stream, they're familiar."

"From the dream?"

"Not exactly. I just feel like this is the way we should go. But, if it's the way to Oasis..."

"Are you worried the Dirt Eaters sent you the dream?"

Roan stares at the rippling water, trying to sort through his feelings. "No. It's not them, I'm positive. We're going the right way... for now."

"Why didn't you tell me you changed your mind about trusting the Dirt Eaters?"

Roan grips a handful of pebbles, worrying the smooth stones in his palm. "Because I felt stupid. How could I trust a man I'd barely met more than a group of people who'd been real friends to us."

"You mean that Storyteller... Kamyar? The one who warned you about the Dirt Eaters."

"You remember that?"

"It's not the kind of thing you forget."

"No, it's not," Roan sighs, relieved that Kamyar's warning stayed with Lumpy, too. He wishes he'd talked to Lumpy sooner... he's felt so alone with his suspicions. "Anyway, I couldn't let it go. It got me worried that the Dirt Eaters had hidden plans for me and the children. It was true we needed the help of Bildt and the others from Oasis, but in my gut I knew it was an easy way for the Dirt Eaters to keep us under their control. And now the children are sick. I should have listened to my instincts, done something, said something, sooner."

"Like what?"

"I don't know. Something."

"We couldn't have done it without them."

Though Roan recognizes the truth of Lumpy's words, it doesn't lessen his feelings of responsibility. He presses the stones back into the streambed, as if he could, by correctly placing each one, bring the children back, and undo the damage that's been done.

"So..." Lumpy shuffles uncomfortably, obviously anxious for them to be on their way, "... based on this vision of yours, you're sure this is the right direction?"

"Yes. Definitely... I think."

"Now that's a comfort."

"I mean we're going toward whatever it is that's drawing me."

"Animal or vegetable?"

"A person. I think."

"This possible person you're seeing—its intentions couldn't possibly be bad, could they?"

"It doesn't feel like it."

Lumpy shakes his head. "So let me see if I understand. We're being drawn away from people who are very nice but who we don't trust, to an unknown, possibly deadly entity who, for no reason whatsoever, we do trust."

"You've got it. Do you want to turn back now?"

"Are you kidding? I wouldn't miss this for the world."

And with a last look at Newlight, they start down the stream.

The uneven streambed doesn't allow sure footing, and with heavy packs on their backs the going is slow. But fine weather, the scent of fir trees, and the singing of white crickets eases every step. Roan's thoughts keep returning to the hook-sword on his back. Though he has no desire to use it again, he felt compelled to bring it. He knows it's likely he'll need all the skills the Brothers taught him before the end of this journey—that is, if he still remembers how to use them.

By the end of the third day, they've moved out of the valley and the air's grown colder. The trees have disappeared, the wild crickets are gone, and wide-leafed ferns converge around them. At a small clearing, Lumpy tosses down his pack.

"This is as good a place as any to spend the night."

Weary after the long day's march, Roan throws down his bedroll and gathers some dry branches for a fire. Lumpy points to the mountains in the distance.

"According to Bildt, the doorway to Oasis is due north, on the other side of those peaks. So... we'll be wanting to go a different direction?"

"More or less."

"Good news. The walking's good going east on the foothills."

"We're going west," says Roan.

"Oh no... west is marshland."

"It's where the marker is."

"Yeah, marking where you don't want to go."

"No, the tree I'm looking for is in the marsh."

Lumpy grimaces. "Well, actually, from what I hear, it's more like... swamp. Huge, impassible, dangerous swamp. Bzzz Swamp. No sane reason to cross it."

"Well, that's the way."

Lumpy lets out a huge sigh. "Just when you think you've found paradise, it's back to the Devastation and bugs for breakfast."

"Could be worse."

"Yeah, and I'm sure we'll get there."

At sunrise, Roan wakes to find Lumpy at the ready with bean stick and water sack. "Breakfast in bed. Enjoy being nice and dry while you can, because after this it's damp and miserable for days."

While Roan chews, Lumpy sifts through a small bag.

"Well, that's a relief," he says, pulling out a small, battered tin. He opens the lid and sniffs. "Umm. Still effective." He shoves it under Roan's nose.

Roan's assaulted by a horrible stench and jerks away, gagging. "It's like... rotten eggs!"

Lumpy snaps the lid back on. "Rotten eggs would be useless as bug repellent. This is dragonweed."

"You don't mean we have to... "

Lumpy smiles devilishly as he smears some on Roan's chin. "And it has the added benefit of clearing your sinuses."

When they set out, pushing through the ferns, a sensation of impending danger eats away at Roan. As if on cue, his mind and body begin practicing the techniques that have lain dormant the last year. He gives complete awareness to every movement, making each footfall an exercise in strength, stamina, and concentration. When the brush becomes too thick for passage, Roan uses his hook-sword to clear the way. Not hacking like any trailblazer, he isolates each stem and the sword slices it in the exact spot he visualizes. With speed and precision, the minimal amount of vegetation is sacrificed, and an opportunity to train is maximized.

"Are you doing what I think you're doing?" asks Lumpy.

"I guess," replies Roan, as another swing of his blade executes a perfect clearing.

Lumpy bends down and inspects the cut. "Won't that wreck the sword? It was made to slice people, not plants."

Roan shrugs. "It will need a good cleaning and sharpening every night, but it's a strong blade, it'll survive."

After two days' walk, their dour expectations of the swamp have been wildly inverted. The marsh is anything but a nightmare of mosquitoes and festering water. Biting insects are mercifully few and the trees, though sparse, are festooned with bright flowers in full bloom. Golden butterflies flutter around them, fluorescent dragonflies dart through the ferns, tiny violet waterlilies float free on the water's surface, and there's enough solid high ground for them to walk at a brisk pace. In the waning light, they make camp on a rise near the water. The trees here are completely unfamiliar, with thick, curling branches and leaves that close up when touched.

"Well, that dragonweed was so effective all the biting bugs fled the swamp."

"In this case I'm thrilled to be wrong."

"So when does this odor wear off?"

"Next bath."

Roan groans.

In the evening mist, a warm fire of dry fern crackles. The aroma of cooking catfish, yanked from the water with bare hands alone, has Roan and Lumpy transfixed. Their crickets perch on their shoulders, still, not a feeler moving.

Across the fire from Roan the mysterious boy slowly takes shape.

"YOU'RE COMING."

"YES."

"NOT ALONE?"

"I'M WITH A FRIEND. IS THAT A PROBLEM?"

"IS HE A WALKER TOO?"

"NO. ARE WE VERY FAR?"

"What is far?"

Then the boy is gone. Roan looks up. Lumpy pokes at the fire, completely absorbed in his activity, unaware of Roan's experience.

"I saw the boy."

"A boy? What did he tell you?"

"He doesn't seem to mind that I brought you along."

"Well, that's a relief," says Lumpy. "I'd hate to think I wasn't wanted."

"It's a good sign. We're going in the right direction."

"Well, believe it or not, I'm having a great time and," he grins as he shifts their fish out of the fire, "it's about to get even better."

preparation for the unknown

the archbishop constructs, in celebration of our ascendance, a monumental structure to equal the lost great pyramid of giza. in order to reflect the vitality the eldest brings to us daily, his great pyramid will be of glass and bear his holy light.

—proclamation of master querin

"MORE SPEED THIS TIME. Go!" Willum shouts. Stowe runs full-out toward the half-wall, leaps onto the springboard and vaults up, her hands reaching for the top of the wall. Swinging her legs high, for an instant she hangs upside-down in the air, and feels in that moment as if she could rest there, suspended. Then she flips over, landing on her feet on the other side.

Willum stands by the parallel bars, taking note of every miniscule element of her technique. "Once again."

"That was my seventeenth vault today."

"Make it eighteen. And this time, name the six Constructions of Darius."

Taking her position, Stowe says: "The Ramparts." She runs to the half-wall: "The Whorl!" Vaulting up, she shouts: "The Spiracal!" Twists in the air, yelling: "The Antlia!" And lands perfectly on the other side of the wall. "The Gyre and Ocellus. That makes six," she smiles. But her triumph is soured by Willum's expression. "What was wrong with that?"

"Your heels were released too quickly off the board. Again."

Stowe thumps onto the polished oak floor of the small gymnasium. "I've done enough."

Willum, a rope in his hand, strides over. "Fine. Then you'll work on stamina."

He's tense, his face is drawn. Has news of the incident with the clerics reached Darius? Will she be punished? How? Stowe drags herself up and, grabbing the rope from Willum, starts to skip. Every muscle aching, she thinks perhaps this workout is punishment enough.

"Which of the six Constructions is for purely defensive purposes?"

"The Ramparts," Stowe answers. She wishes Willum would stop being so stern. How else was she supposed to react to the death of her brother? They must be wrong, have to be. She'd know. She'd feel it. Perhaps they're deliberately lying to her because of her new mission. It's clear Willum's not pleased about it either.

"What is the Well of Oblivion?"

Stowe sighs. Will there ever be an end to this lesson? Well, she can amuse herself by reciting in rhythm to her jumps. "Discovered by the Seer in the fifteenth year of the Consolidation, it consumes the memory of any who partake of it. The Eldest used its waters to build the Whorl, thus those captured within the Whorl lose all sense of their identities and their past." What are they going to ask her to do? Something that will put her life in danger, or Willum wouldn't be so edgy. So it'll be important, very important. And obviously to do with the Constructions.

"What is the secondary purpose of the Spiracal?"

"The Spiracal is the method of termination in any death sentence issued to a Walker for crimes against the Conurbation. As the ether body approaches the Spiracal's pulsing maw, it is transformed into energy and instantly absorbed, rejoining the fabric of the Dreamfield. This final judgment is deemed the most humane and functional form of capital punishment in existence." Wet with sweat, she gasps, "Why are you asking me these questions, Willum?"

"It's important to review them for your training."

"How am I supposed to train effectively when I don't know what I'm training for?"

"It is not for me to reveal your task, only to ensure you are ready for it. But it is quite apparent that at least one or two of the Constructions will be used to test you."

As she suspected. "Is Darius angry at me?"

"I believe he is considering a response to the inappropriate behavior you displayed. Kicks!"

Stowe throws down the rope and leaps into the air, her heels aimed at Willum's ribs. A quick downstroke of his arm deflects her.

"Too slow."

She releases a flurry of kicks, at his shins, stomach, neck. He fends off each blow with a flick of a fist, his control deliberately unnerving. Undaunted, she spins, pivoting her foot around so that it catches him on the knee.

"Good," he says, without so much as a flinch.

She strikes again, knocking him down. Jumps up for another blow to his head but is momentarily distracted by someone coming in the door. Willum's hand reaches up, grabs her heel, and flings her to the mat.

"Not fair," she says.

"You must sense, not look. Reassess while remaining focused on your objective. Any distraction will favor your opponent. A mistake like that could end your life," Willum warns.

Kordan looms over her. "With such poor concentration, you are sure to fail your next exercise."

The thought of Dirt and flight in the Dreamfield overshadows her loathing. Let him gloat if it pleases him, soon she'll be soaring. Away from this grueling session, away from sweat. Willum doesn't feel she's really working unless she's covered in it.

"Now?" she asks Kordan in anticipation.

"We still have several hours of practice before us," Willum says calmly.

Kordan is always on the lookout for an opportunity to undermine Willum. This new mission should provide him with many. Kordan ignores Willum's statement, and dripping condescension, says to him, "I can't see any reason to prevent you tagging along, if you so desire."

"I shall consider it," Willum replies, bowing in deference to Kordan.

As Stowe strolls out the door with Master Kordan she can feel Willum's eyes on her. He's right, she does not need to look, she can sense him.

Taciturn as always, Kordan walks briskly through the transparent passage into the next building while she glides effortlessly behind. She has no doubt he knows of her transgression. How could he not when, wherever she goes, nervous clerics immediately give her wide berth or simply rush off the other way? The entire City is probably babbling about the event.

Kordan opens the door of the Travel Room. Inside are four glass chairs, each curved to the shape of a reclining body. Kordan sits on the chair nearest him, the smallest, the one Stowe always uses.

"That's my seat," Stowe says.

"Why, so it is," Kordan replies. But he does not move.

Stowe meets his gaze, her eyes blazing. These games he plays, these attempts to provoke her, what do they accomplish?

"Today your goal is acceleration. Do you remember your past lessons, or will we need to review?"

Stowe smiles serenely. "I have not forgotten."

With the tiniest of smirks, he rises from the seat, casually picks up the bowl and offers her a spoonful of Dirt. She has always associated her pleasure in taking the Dirt with the possibility of finding Roan, but today is different: they will let her search for him no more. But still, the thrill of anticipation rises, as always. Perhaps it is only the excitement of not knowing what she has to accomplish and whether she will be up to the test. And they are wrong about Roan—she's sure of it, she will find him. One day.

Stowe lets her jaw drop open. The soil touches her tongue and she swallows, savoring the stinging heat.

Kordan holds up the spoon. "Enough?"

She shakes her head. He knows all too well one dose hasn't been enough for weeks. Willum enters the room, and takes his place, not realizing that this spoonful is her second. If he knew, he'd be sure to protest.

Stowe swallows. Ah, there it is.

And the warm glow envelops her and slips her into the Dreamfield.

an assembly of tendrils

THE RED RAIN BURNED ALL THAT IT TOUCHED.
BUT ALL THAT IT BURNED DID NOT DIE. AND THAT
WHICH DID NOT DIE WAS UTTERLY AND COMPLETELY
TRANSFORMED.

—THE WAR CHRONICLES

BY THE AFTERNOON OF THE NEXT DAY, Roan and Lumpy are thigh-deep in murky water, sinking in muck.

"Should've known swamp was inevitable," Lumpy moans.

Gone are the butterflies and the floating flowers. Instead, thick, milky white stalks rise high out of the water. Capped with a tangled mass of crimson tendrils, they have an unpleasant resemblance to raw meat.

"Those hairball things look tasty. Think I'd feel better if I ate one?"

Roan grins. Lumpy's appetite knows no bounds. But just as Lumpy reaches to snap one off, a fat dragonfly swoops down and, within seconds of landing on the stalk, is engulfed by the tendrils.

"Maybe not," Lumpy shrugs.

Chuckling, Roan points to a tall shape rising in the distance. A tree with orange, peeling bark. "There. That's where we want to go."

"That's the marker from your dream?"

"Yeh."

"Well," says Lumpy, unimpressed, "at least it's not submerged in this muck."

Reaching the tree, however, proves no easy matter. Every step plunges them deeper into the mire, so that they seem to be retreating from, rather than gaining on, their goal.

"Now this is more like it," Lumpy comments dryly.

Impatient and irritated, Roan attempts a long step forward. Plunging deep into a sinkhole, he tries to regain his footing, but every movement draws him farther into the muddy bottom. Blind in the dark water, he stops struggling and focuses on slowing down his heart rate.

HE'S SOARING IN A TAWNY, SUN-SPATTERED SKY.

IT'S INCONGRUOUS, HIS BULKY BODY OF CLAY SO EFFORTLESSLY AIRBORNE, BUT HE FEELS LIBERATED. HE DIVES AND SOMERSAULTS, HOPING LUMPY MANAGES TO PULL HIS CORPOREAL BODY OUT OF THE MIRE. AS MUCH AS HE LOVES IT HERE, HE DOESN'T WANT TO BE TRAPPED IN THE DREAMFIELD FOREVER, A MISSHAPEN HUNK OF FLYING CLAY. WOULD HE VANISH ALTOGETHER IF HIS BODY DIED?

THESE MORBID THOUGHTS ABRUPTLY HALT WHEN HE COLLIDES INTO A COLUMN OF PITCH-BLACK STONE THAT RISES FROM AN ISLAND FAR BELOW. IT'S PART OF A LIMITLESS ROW OF EBONY PILLARS EXTENDING ACROSS THE SEA AND SKY. ROAN CAUTIOUSLY

PASSES BETWEEN TWO COLUMNS AND A GIANT SPIKE SHOOTS OUT OF ONE, HEADED STRAIGHT FOR HIS CHEST. HE PIVOTS AND IT NARROWLY MISSES HIM. THE PILLARS BLAST DOZENS OF ARM-LONG SPIKES AND IT TAKES ALL ROAN'S FOCUS AND DEXTERITY TO AVOID THEM. HE MAY BE IN HIS DREAM-FORM, BUT HE'S STILL ABLE TO USE ALL HIS MARTIAL SKILLS, DUCKING AND WEAVING, STRIKING AND KICKING. FINALLY HE FINDS AN OPENING AND RETREATS, SPINNING UP INTO A CLOUD.

SAFELY HIDDEN IN THE VAPOR, HE STUDIES WHAT SEEMS TO BE A DEFENSIVE WALL. THIS TYPE OF FORTIFICATION IS DIFFERENT THAN ANYTHING HE'S EVER SEEN IN THE DREAMFIELD. WHAT DOES IT PROTECT?

BEFORE HE CAN PONDER THE QUESTION FURTHER, A SMALL FALCON APPEARS, CIRCLING BELOW. ITS SHAPE IS SUPERSEDED BY A MUCH MORE TROUBLING SIGHT: HUGE BROWN WINGS. RED, BULBOUS SKIN HANGING OVER A LONG BEAK. IS THIS THE SAME VULTURE-LIKE CREATURE THAT PURSUED HIM ONCE BEFORE? HE DIVES DEEPER INTO THE CLOUD AND WATCHES THROUGH ITS CONCEALING MIST.

A BOOMING SOUND ERUPTS FROM THE SEA BELOW. SMOKE PILLOWS UP AND THROUGH IT BURSTS A SHAPE, ROUGHLY FORMED, ITS TERRA-COTTA SKIN RIPPED AND SHREDDED, ITS THICK HANDS DRIPPING BLOOD. THE FACE IS RUDIMENTARY BUT HE RECOGNIZES HER INSTANTLY. IT'S THE EYES THAT GIVE HER AWAY. STOWE.

HIS SISTER. LOST TO HIM FOR SO LONG. HE WANTS TO SCREAM HER NAME, TO FLY AFTER HER, GRAB HER, TAKE HER BACK WITH HIM. BUT HE'S PULLED UP THROUGH THE CLOUDS, HIGHER AND

Roan is coughing, gasping for breath. "I saw her, I saw
Stowe."

"Easy, easy," says Lumpy, gripping him tight under the
arms. "I had to find a place to get some footing, you were
under a long time. What were you doing in the Dreamfield,
anyway?"

"I didn't mean to be there. It just happened."

"Did Stowe see you?"

"I don't think so, but she wasn't alone."

"Well, there *is* some good news."

"Really? What?"

"You're not dead."

"We'll both be if we don't take it nice and slow to that tree."

They pick their way cautiously, avoiding the ubiquitous
bog holes, and what would have taken minutes on solid ground
consumes precious hours. Soaked with mud, sweat, and swamp
water, they're relieved to find themselves on dry land before
nightfall.

Throwing off his pack, Lumpy examines the tiny patch of
earth that sustains the tree. "How am I supposed to build a
fire on this miserable clump of tree root?"

Roan reaches, grabs a branch, pulls himself up, and in a
moment, he's sitting at the top of the tree, scanning the marsh.

"See anything?"

"Yeh. More swamp."

"I wish I could say this place was growing on me."

"Well, it almost grew on me and I don't want to repeat the experience."

Holding onto the tree trunk and ensuring his footing is secure, Roan quickly hacks off two long branches with his hook-sword and tosses them down to Lumpy.

Lumpy sighs, shaking his head mournfully. "Now why didn't I think of that?"

While they busy themselves cleaning the twigs off for kindling, Roan worries over the events of the day. He was careless in the marsh. For the first time he realizes how excited he feels, how free of responsibility. It's an illusion, he knows, and a dangerous one at that. One that almost got him killed—in more ways than one. What were those strange, deadly pillars in the Dreamfield? Had that vulture or Stowe sensed his presence? Would she pursue him, perhaps even find him?

Immersed in thought over his unbelievable stupidity, it takes Roan a moment to notice that Lumpy's neglecting his freshly made fire to stare, unusually still, at something: two bulging eyes peeking out of the water. In a flash, Lumpy lurches forward and snaps his branch against the green shape. "Dinner!" he smiles, gathering in the huge bullfrog.

Roan's heart sinks. In Longlight, they never killed animals for food. Necessity has turned him into an omnivore; he's even grown used to eating fish—but this?

"Look at the size of it," Lumpy says. "Biggest frog I've ever seen. Ever eaten frog's legs?"

"No," says Roan, looking a little pale.

"You're going to love them." Lumpy waves a shorn twig at Roan. "Perfect size. Almost like you knew we'd be roasting frogs tonight," he chortles, grinning wickedly. He cuts off the frog's legs, skewers them and sets them on the fire.

"I'll be eating a bean stick."

"Oh, no, you don't, we've got to conserve our food and eat fresh when we can."

Aware of the truth in Lumpy's words, Roan prepares himself for the worst.

Lumpy smiles. "Don't worry, it's better than termites."

The meal was easier to eat than Roan feared, and his stomach is fuller than it's been since leaving Newlight. Bedrolls spread out, Lumpy tends the fire, adding the largest sticks to keep it burning through the night. Roan hones the blade of the hook-sword, performing the task with the focus of a sand painter. Completely engrossed in the tiniest action, he transforms the mundane task into an intense exercise in seeing. He carefully smooths his stone across the blade, surveying every nick on its edge, and as he works, a picture forms in his mind. A rough, scarred hand, the hand of the sword's maker. Metal red hot, the maker's mallet pounding it down. Then a young man's face, Brother Wolf, but the same age Roan is now.

"Don't you think you should put that down?" asks Lumpy. "Wouldn't want to fall asleep and slice off a finger or three."

Roan snaps out of his trance. "I was meditating."

"It looked like more than just that. Your eyes started fluttering."

"The blade was showing me its past," Roan says.

"Great, another new trick. Why don't you put your hand in the muck and see if it will show us the way out of here?"

"I wish I could. But it doesn't work that way—you're right, though, I'm bone tired. It's been a long day."

"Been a long four days, if you ask me," says Lumpy, who stretches out on his bedroll, closes his eyes, and is asleep.

Roan fastens the sword on his pack but keeps it within easy reach. He lies back, contemplating a sky clouded with stars, and falls easily into a well-earned slumber.

Something heavy shuffles on Roan's lap, waking him. He touches it with his finger—cold, slimy. He opens his eyes. In the light of the first quarter moon, he makes out a bulbous form. It's a giant bullfrog. Startled, he pushes it off. Wide awake now, he sees that every inch of their little island is covered in bullfrogs.

Lumpy jumps up, throwing a frog off his chest, kicking another at his feet.

"I'm sorry, okay? I was hungry. Sorry!"

Slinging his bedroll over his shoulders, Roan gingerly makes his way up the tree, followed by a thoroughly revolted Lumpy. Side by side, bedrolls wrapped like armor around them, they nestle in the topmost branches, observing the quivering mass below.

"It could be possible they resent us making a meal of them,

but more likely they were driven out of the water." Roan isn't sure which thought makes him more uncomfortable.

"And what, do you suppose, could have done that?"

"A predator that eats bullfrogs at night."

"I was afraid you'd say that."

"Maybe we're sharing their safe haven and don't know it."

"What sort of predator, do you think?"

"Some kind of fish?" Roan replies.

"It'd have to be a pretty big fish to eat one of these giant frogs."

"Snake?"

"I don't like snakes. And I really wouldn't like a snake that eats frogs this size."

"It might just be that they're attracted to the dry ground. Or maybe it's mating season."

"I don't see any mating going on." Lumpy looks nervously at the water. There's no sign of movement, apart from the swaying of the tall, red-tendrilled stalks. Then his eyes narrow. "Wait—the plants... they're moving."

Although they only appear to be bending with the breeze, Roan can see that the plants are actually mobile. Very slow, like the sea anemones he once read about, but there's no question they've changed their position.

"Weren't there only a few around here when we came?"

Lumpy shudders. "They brought friends."

Their island is now encircled by the stalks and the pale glow of daybreak reveals that more are on their way.

One of the stalks closest to the shore suddenly bends over, its tendrils grasping a struggling frog. It's over in a blink. The bullfrog is still, then gone. As if on cue, the other plants bend over, each scooping up its supper.

"Tell me it's a crazy idea," says Lumpy, "but could these plants have herded them here?"

"That would be a pretty complex hunting strategy."

"Have you ever heard of a plant doing this kind of thing?"

"Nope," says Roan.

The feeding frenzy goes on. By the time the sun peeks over the horizon, the only surviving bullfrogs are the few that have managed to leap onto a branch out of the tendrils' reach.

"Natural selection in action," Roan comments dryly.

"Yeah. I'd be fascinated if we weren't surrounded by a forest of carnivorous plants."

Though the vegetation now stands straight and motionless, its relentless carnage is so fresh in Roan and Lumpy's minds that they remain glued to their spots, staring and waiting.

"They haven't fed for a while now," says Lumpy.

"They've probably all eaten their fill."

But the two friends stay safely aloft until all the remaining bullfrogs jump off the island and survive their venture back into the water, undisturbed by the plants.

"As good a time as any," says Roan.

Slowly, they slide down the tree. All remains still. Roan lifts up his pack, which, apart from a bit of slime, seems intact. As they carefully step toward the water, Lumpy instantly lurches backwards. A stalk has swallowed his left hand. He frantically attempts to extricate himself, but within moments his arm is sucked in up to his elbow.

Slipping his hook-sword from his pack, Roan slices the bulbous head off the plant with one hand while the other pulls Lumpy up and away. Two more plants strike, but by then the friends are huddled against the tree, just barely out of range.

"Guess we're the second course."

"Are you okay?"

"I'll be a lot better once I have this thing off my hand."

The neck of the severed stalk gives way easily, but Roan finds removing the sticky tendrils a delicate and painstaking task. Once the last one is detached, Roan sniffs it. A sharp, almost sickeningly sweet scent. Before Lumpy can stop him, Roan tastes it.

"What're you doing?"

"Trying to figure out what it is."

"Why—you sure you want to know this thing better?"

"This *thing* isn't like a normal plant."

"I kind of already figured that out."

Roan ignores the slight. "They have an... energy. Almost like..." Roan stops, struggling for an explanation.

"What?"

"Thought."

"But they're... plants."

"You're right," says Roan. But he's not sure he believes it.

He has a close look at Lumpy's hand. "I think it will be alright. How does it feel?"

"Fine. Just numb, that's all."

"That's why the frogs stopped struggling so quickly. The tendrils must inject a paralyzing venom in their prey."

"Lucky I'm bigger than a bullfrog."

"Yeh. But if five or ten of those things got hold of us at once, it could be lethal."

"Good point."

"Best to wait till sunset. If we're lucky, they'll drift off again, looking to herd some more frogs."

"How lucky are you feeling?"

"Can't say I foresaw being besieged by plants. Not one of the books in Saint's library covered that topic."

"I'd laugh if I wasn't so scared. Hey, what did Bildt say about plants? Sensitive to sound, remember?"

"That's right. She talks and sings to them."

"You should play for them, it might have an effect, maybe drive them away, or put them to sleep."

"Worth a try."

Back up in the safety of the tree, Roan hangs his pack from a nearby branch. He locates his recorder and slides it gently from its sleeve.

"It's hard to imagine a Brother making the effort to find something so... unwarlike."

"Brother Asp was different. I couldn't understand how he could be with them, he seemed so kind, but he said it gave him more opportunities to work as a healer. In the end, I think I felt the most betrayed by him. He knew all the time what Saint and the Brothers did to Longlight, he was there for all the Visitations and bloody rituals—and he never tried to stop any of it."

"Maybe he wasn't what he seemed. Alandra lived in Fairview, and as sick as it made her, she went along with the child harvest. She tolerated it because she was waiting for you, right? For you and our kids. Hey, what if Asp was a Dirt Eater, too?"

"Brother Asp?"

"Well," says Lumpy, "if the Dirt Eaters were watching over you at Oasis and Fairview, then Newlight, what would have stopped them from having someone with the Brothers?"

Roan mulls it over, considering Asp's generosity, his concern for people, his keen interest in Longlight. "I've never thought of that before. But when you put it that way, it seems so obvious."

"Thanks. Now will you play the damned recorder so we can see if there's a chance of hypnotizing those plants?"

Balancing the instrument in his fingers, Roan lifts it and blows, the honeyed quavers of a ballad from Longlight drifting lazily in the early morning haze. The world he lost floats on the surface of his eyes and when he finishes he cannot bring himself to look up at Lumpy.

"Keep playing," Lumpy gently urges.

Roan plays all the Longlight tunes he knows, melodies he heard over and over as a child that he rearranged for the children of Newlight. Lona had started it, demanding that he make her some pipes so she could join his playing, and soon Bub and all the others were in on the act. He and Lumpy had spent many evenings carving flutes for them all—except for Jam, who wanted a drum. They'd played together every night after dinner. In a matter of weeks, their little pipe orchestra was harmonizing at a level beyond anything Roan had thought possible. He shouldn't have been surprised. There was nothing ordinary about those children. Nothing ordinary at all.

One look at Lumpy's misty eyes tells him that the music is evoking similar memories in them both.

The voracious plants, however, do not disperse despite hours of Roan's soulful playing. In fact, quite the opposite.

"The good news is the numbness is gone in my hand," says Lumpy. "The bad news is those plants really like your playing. Hey—they're shifting position."

Roan looks up to see a mass of tendrils swooping toward them. "Lift your legs!" he shouts. The plants smash against the tree, and Roan senses a fine powder drift past his face.

"Do you feel that?"

"What?"

"Something... I'm not sure." Keeping all his senses attuned to the plants, Roan tries to shake off the sluggishness folding over him.

"You're sure this isn't a trap, right? No chance at all the

Turned might have stuck the image of the boy in your mind to draw you here."

"No. I've felt some of their tricks before. This is different." Roan holds out the recorder. "Your turn. At least it kept them at bay."

"I'd try, only, well... you've heard me. I don't want to make them angry."

"I need a break, my fingers are aching. Play Jaw's song," says Roan, pushing the instrument into Lumpy's hand.

Lumpy takes a breath and blows, picking out the notes of a tune he and Jaw wrote together. The only one he knows really well, the one he and his little friend played so often. Eyes closed, lost in thoughts of brighter days, he repeats the simple melody again and again.

The attacks soon abate. The stalks weave and nod. Crimson tendrils wave in the wind, creating a hypnotic vista, the echo of a rhythm to sleep by, a rhythm to die by. Whenever Lumpy pauses, the stalks strike, surrounding them in a cloud of powder. In a short time, Lumpy too is played out and the worried look he shares with Roan speaks volumes. They know in a matter of hours they will succumb to exhaustion and the plants will have them.

When dissonant thumps, not unlike the call of a wild bird, echo through the marshlands, the sound seems an eerie prelude to their demise.

"What was that?"

Roan signals Lumpy to be quiet. Breathing very slowly, he

releases all fear, thought, and self-awareness. When his mind is completely clear, he reaches for his hook-sword.

"Roan!" Lumpy whispers, but Roan's feet are already on the ground.

"Grab the packs and follow me."

Tendrils swoop down, but Roan can see a pattern, like a moving tapestry. He anticipates every assault, slicing the carnivorous plants off at the head, slowly clearing the way to the water.

"There!" Lumpy gasps, and Roan stops.

The stalks are parting. A sleek, low boat is coming toward them. A box is fastened to the bow, thick smoke billowing out of it. The stalks edge away from the smoke. It's oddly comforting to know that the sword is not the only way to manage this threat. The paddler draws in, close enough for Roan to see his face.

"Get in," the boy says.

perfect body and mind

oh, to be a doctor in the city
you'd be rich, well fed and witty
but to keep the masters pretty
is a job some would deem... gritty
and that's the ending to my ditty
—Lore of the storytellers

A MASS OF WIRES extends from every part of Stowe. Each wire connects to a machine where technicians hover anxiously over dials. Dr. Arcanthas has been testing her for hours, scanning, monitoring, probing.

"I want to see Darius." The imperiousness in Stowe's voice causes the doctor's tiny eyebrows to lift.

"Pardon me?"

Stowe shoots him a rabid glare. "I want to speak with Darius."

His face tics nervously, his cheek lifting. "I relayed a message, as you requested, one hour ago, Our Stowe, and every hour before that."

"Do it again," she snarls.

Dr. Arcanthas freezes, as do the three technicians. They cannot leave their posts, but it is clear they wish they could be anywhere else but here, close to her. They are all terrified of what she could do to them, cowed by the dreaded wrath of Our Stowe.

Good. She smiles. "Until he comes, we wait."

Bowing until he's backed out the door, Dr. Arcanthas leaves the technicians standing rigid at their posts. Stowe promptly forgets them to ponder her situation. After her session with Kordan in the Dreamfield, she had felt elated. Having successfully accomplished his every test, she felt sure Darius would see her. But he rebuffed her request. Then, this morning, she awoke to be told the Eldest had ordered tests. She went instantly to talk to him, hoping that if she could see him, she could make him understand. But his door was shut to her. For almost three years, she's had access to him whenever she desired, night or day. Now, because of one small incident of "inappropriate" behavior, it's as if she exists simply as an object to experiment on. Is that her punishment? How long will it go on? It's difficult to stifle the urge to leave her body and get some answers. But if Willum mentioned her "dream" to Darius, then her new ability might be suspected. One of these machines might be set up to detect that kind of astral movement and she must not play into their hands.

For the past few nights she's had real dreams, dreams about Roan. In these dreams, his eyes are crystals, and when she looks into them, she sees a great iron gate spanning an abyss.

Its bars have eyes that slide open to stare at her. And lips that seem to say something, relay some message, but she can't quite grasp it. She wakes burning with frustration and doubt.

She shouldn't have mentioned Raven to Willum. She revealed too much. And what she did to the clerics... stupid. But Willum used an aura to protect himself... she's never seen that except in the Dreamfield. Stowe realizes with a start that she has no real idea of the extent of the Masters' powers. If her lowly tutor can do that, they all must be able to. And yet, Darius is having her wired and probed—he must want to know whether her power is starting to surpass theirs, like Willum said.

The doctor returns, but it is Willum who follows, not Darius. His impassive face is a sure sign he's annoyed.

Willum hesitates for a moment, his glare ensuring her silence, then addresses the doctor. "The report, please. Turn the viewer so Our Stowe can see, and explain with precision."

The doctor nods furiously at a technician who rushes over, pushing the screen close to Stowe's bed. Numbers fly across the illuminated surface.

"These represent readings of all of your systems: respiratory, circulatory, nervous, digestive, endocrine, excretory, immunological, lymphatic, muscular, skeletal, your tissues and organs."

"And?" she asks.

The doctor's mouth moves but no words come out; he can't seem to find them.

"If you please, Dr. Arcanthas," urges Willum.

"You're a perfect human specimen. Better than perfect.

Every one of your systems is functioning at an extraordinary level. I understand now, from a physiological point of view, why Our Stowe is so honored. You are the best of us all."

"Then she is fit enough to continue the next phase of her training," says Willum. "If you would be kind enough to disengage her, we might commence."

Once inside the confines of the Travel Room, Stowe relaxes considerably. Darius had only wanted to ensure that her body was strong enough for what lay ahead. A practical but also fatherly concern. Could it be that he's not so terribly mad at her after all?

Willum is about to push her, she can tell, but a part of her enjoys his challenges. She's always surprised at how much she is actually able to accomplish. Still, it's difficult not to drop her guard around him. She doesn't find him threatening, although she cannot put her finger on exactly why. That in itself should disturb her. How much of what she reveals to him does he pass on to Darius?

Willum reaches into his pocket and takes out a velvet bag. "Today we will work on changing your composition in the Dreamfield."

Stowe smiles at the concept. "Sounds intriguing."

"You are aware that the form you have is temporary, a kind of interim body. But it can be manipulated to serve you in different ways. For instance, as a form of protection."

"Like armor?"

"Exactly. You choose a substance, and with proper concentration it can be called upon to replace your clay form."

"How do I do it?"

Willum hands the velvet bag to her. Stowe tips the contents into her hand. A diamond the size of her thumb tip glistens in her palm.

"Contemplate it. Take in every facet. Feel the weight. Find its internal resonance. You need to imprint the diamond essence on your consciousness."

Stowe rolls the gem between her palms. Squeezing it between thumb and forefinger, she sits down in her glass travel chair, and raises it to her eye. She submerges herself in the light reflecting off each facet. Her breathing becomes shallow, her vision fixated, her entire being engaged with the stone. She's unaware of the passage of time, of where she is. All is one with the diamond.

A tone, barely discernible at first, purrs against her fingers, then the hum increases in intensity. She lets it in, allows the pulse to spread through her organs, her bones, her marrow, until her entire body is filled with its ephemeral vibration. When every cell is touched, the essence of the crystal is available to her. She opens her eyes and hands the diamond back to Willum.

"I won't need this anymore."

Willum nods approvingly. "When you enter the Dreamfield you have simply to recall the resonance for it to manifest. The process can be painful, but if you do not falter, you will be successful. There is no other way to accomplish the tasks set before you."

The door opens and a grating voice contaminates the air behind her. "It's time we began. You've been at this for the best part of the afternoon. We'll see now if the time's been wasted." Kordan lifts the silver lid from his bowl of Dirt. "Is Willum joining us today?" He sneers as he offers Willum the container. "Worried over how well you've done?"

Willum disregards the remark and, taking a tiny pinch, settles serenely into his chair. Kordan takes the same amount for himself, then turning so that his back shields her from Willum's view, he slips a heaping spoonful to Stowe, who eagerly gulps, then holds her mouth open for another. Kordan, grinning, obliges.

Waves splash against the shore of the sandswept island. No more than a league away, the vaulting beams of the Ramparts rise from the sea. The first of the six Constructions, it is an impenetrable barrier demarcating their eastern boundary from the Eaters.

A falcon perched on Stowe's terra-cotta shoulder whispers, "Begin the process now."

Stowe finds the tone and nurtures it like a tiny flame, letting it rise and build inside her, directing the vibration. A terrible pain stabs into the soles of her feet as diamond erupts over their surface. She cries out, and the transformation stops.

THE VULTURE LOOMS OVER HER. "THERE, YOU SEE! IT IS BEYOND HER ABILITY," SNEERS KORDAN.

WILLUM, THE FALCON, GENTLY ENCOURAGES HER. "JUST A LITTLE AT A TIME. MAKE THE PAIN SERVE YOU. FORCE IT TO DRIVE THE CHANGE."

SHE RETRIEVES THE TONE AND RECALIBRATES HER ANKLES, HER CALVES, HER KNEES TO ITS RESONANCE. BENDING HER LEFT LEG SLIGHTLY, AN EXPLOSION OF PAIN SENDS HER REELING TO THE SAND.

"RIDICULOUS!" MUTTERS THE VULTURE, BLACK EYES MOCKING.

BUT THE FALCON'S CLAWS, STEADY ON STOWE'S SHOULDER, REMIND HER TO SWALLOW THE PAIN, USE IT AS FUEL.

SHE COAXES ANOTHER SERIES OF ERUPTIONS, CRYSTALS FORMING THROUGH HER THIGHS. WHEN THEY REACH HER HIPS, WILLUM ORDERS HER TO STOP.

"GOOD, THAT IS ENOUGH FOR TODAY."

STOWE SIGHS, THE AGONY ABATING, AND FOCUSES ON THE TASK AHEAD.

"WE'LL SEE IF SHE'S ABLE TO MAINTAIN THE DENSITY IN HER LEGS WHEN SHE RISES," THE VULTURE SAYS DISPARAGINGLY, THEN SWOOPS AHEAD, LEADING THE WAY TO THE RAMPARTS.

"REMEMBER YOUR PROTECTION IS ONLY PARTIAL. EMPLOY YOUR ARMS IN YOUR DEFENSE AND YOU MAY LOSE THEM," WILLUM WARNS, THEN DIVES TOWARD THE ISLAND.

ACCELERATING RAPIDLY, SHE CALLS UP ALL SHE KNOWS ABOUT THE RAMPARTS. IT WAS ON THIS BORDER THAT THE EATERS ONCE ATTEMPTED TO EXTEND THEIR TERRITORY. THE COLUMNS THEM-

SELVES ARE ALL THAT REMAINS OF A PREVIOUS STRUCTURE THAT PRE-DATED THE DISCOVERY OF DIRT. DARIUS SECRETLY REFURBISHED THEM, CREATING AN IMPENETRABLE BARRIER THAT PUSHED THE EATERS BACK AND HAS CONTINUED TO PREVENT FURTHER INCURSIONS.

STOWE FLIPS OVER SO THAT HER DIAMOND LEGS ARE WHAT PASS BETWEEN THE COLUMNS. SPIKES BURST OUT, BUT WITH A FLURRY OF KICKS THE PROJECTILES SHATTER. THE MORE SHE DESTROYS, THE FASTER THEY COME UNTIL SHE IS A BLUR OF MOVEMENT, SHARDS OF METAL AFLAME ALL AROUND HER.

CONSUMED WITH THIS ORGY OF DESTRUCTION, SHE ALMOST MISSES THE SCREECH OF THE VULTURE. SHE BACK-FLIPS AWAY FROM THE GIANT PILLARS, REJOINING HER TEACHERS.

"WELL DONE," SAYS WILLUM. THERE IS NO MISTAKING THE SWELL OF PRIDE IN HIS VOICE.

"IT WILL BE A GREATER CHALLENGE WITH FULL ARMOR. WE'LL SEE HOW YOU MANAGE TOMORROW," SNAPS KORDAN.

Stowe rises from the glass chair and looks at her two instructors. "What is the mission I am training for?"

Willum is silent. Kordan grins, relishing the hint of pleading in her voice. "As you've been told, only Darius has the authority to discuss this with you. And Darius will do so when he pleases."

Kordan's tempting her to strike out, but she will not lose her discipline again, certainly not on account of him. No, all will come if she is patient.

How she hates patience.

mabatan

the friend commanded the prophet to leave
the world and prepare a way for the one.
and saint spoke the friend's word to brother
wolf so that he might continue to preserve and
enforce it in the prophet's stead.

—orin's history of the friend

At Roan's signal, Lumpy tosses in the packs, then delicately steps into the craft, careful not to capsize it. Once he's seated, Lumpy turns to the boy. "I may look it, but don't worry, I don't have Mor-Ticks."

The boy looks at him curiously.

"I mean, I did, but not anymore."

The boy shrugs, unconcerned.

Lumpy smiles. "I'm Lumpy, by the way. And that's Roan."

Roan puts one foot in the bow and pushes them off the shore with the other. Hook-sword in hand, he sits warily, unwilling to put all his trust in the musky smoke.

"I am Mabatan. We travel until the sun sets." Seeming to respond to an unspoken command, the boy turns the boat around, adroitly maneuvering through the narrow passageway between the plants. As the boy paddles, Roan admires the workmanship of the craft. Its skin is made of thin tree bark strips lashed to a wooden frame, so it's light in the water, perfect for a shallow swamp. He moves his fingers along the craft's smoothed edges, and takes a long look at the boy. The child of the visions, certainly, but much younger in appearance than Roan imagined. No more than eleven or twelve years old, he guesses. The boy's dark hair is long and tied back, his tawny pants and shirt woven from rough fiber. His paddling is stronger and smoother than it should be for a child of his age. This is someone who fends for himself, Roan thinks, who probably spends all of his time alone.

Emerging from the plant-infested waters, they're welcomed by the glow of late morning sunlight. Roan lifts his head, enjoying the warmth on his face, and finally feels free to speak.

"How did you find us?"

"I followed the Skree."

"Is that what you call those plants?" asks Lumpy.

"They are not plants. They are Skree."

"How long have Skree been in this swamp?"

"They were here before my father," the boy replies. "But they were smaller then. They had only begun to wake."

Roan stares at him. "Sentient beings?"

The boy nods.

Hanging his head, Roan murmurs, "I killed dozens of them."

"How were you supposed to know?" says Lumpy.

"You did not kill any Skree. What was cut will grow back."

"That's a relief," Lumpy sighs, with half-concealed sarcasm.

"You should know that your friend had won their respect."

"By hacking their heads off?"

"By cleansing his mind. An attack on the Skree is impossible otherwise. Thoughts are what draw the Skree."

Lumpy mutters, "Those must've been pretty deep-thinking frogs."

"They are not drawn to frogs. They harvest frogs. But they like eating larger game better. Especially strong-smelling ones like you. The reek of dragonweed alone would have been enough to track you."

Lumpy laughs. "Do you have an extra paddle?"

"You must rest. You have not slept. You have much more traveling to do."

"Not before we wash up, I hope," says Lumpy. "Wouldn't want to tempt any other creatures looking for an overripe lunch." Then he opens his pack, takes out some bean sticks, passes one to Roan and offers one to Mabatan.

The boy sniffs it. "Good," he says, and starts chewing. He reaches down and lifts the lid of a basket. Inside are dozens of small, charred globes. "Eat."

Lumpy takes one and examines it. "Is it a larva?" he asks hopefully. Roan's never shared Lumpy's appetite for eating bugs and fervently hopes this food does not have legs that wriggle.

"No, an egg," replies Mabatan.

Lumpy hands it to Roan, who happily pops the whole egg, shell and all, into his mouth. A couple of quick chews and he swallows. "Better than grubs," he says, and with that pronouncement, Lumpy grabs a few and gulps them down. Stomachs soon full, their lack of sleep quickly catches up with them, and it isn't long before the glare of the noonday sun reflecting off the water lulls them to sleep.

A scraping on the keel wakes them. Roan's eyes open as Lumpy groggily sits up. To their surprise, the western horizon already glows with the pale green haze that anticipates darkness.

Lumpy gives Mabatan a suspicious look. "Did you put something in those eggs?"

"Just eggs. The Skree made you tired. They always do. It's in their dust."

"I sensed it," says Roan, getting out of the craft and carefully stepping over the mossy rocks. "But I didn't realize what it was."

"You were not meant to."

Lumpy grins at Roan. "Wow, he doesn't just know what they are, he knows what they're thinking."

Mabatan smiles. "He?"

"Lumpy's talking about you," says Roan.

Mabatan laughs, a sound like the tinkling of bells.

Both Roan and Lumpy take another, closer look. "You're a girl," says Lumpy, astonished by their mistake.

"I am a girl." With an amused smile, she pulls the boat onto the shore.

Seeming to not quite believe her, Lumpy leans in closer, then turning to Roan wide-eyed, he exclaims, "Look!"

There, perched contentedly on Mabatan's shoulders, are both of their crickets.

"Remarkable," Roan says, his voice filled with awe. There's rarely been a time when Roan's cricket has gone near another person, and he's certain Lumpy's shares that shyness.

"They tell me they are fond of you both," Mabatan says. "That is good." Her face grows suddenly somber. "I have seen the little ones."

"Little crickets?" asks Lumpy.

"The children," she replies.

"In Newlight?" asks Roan, barely able to contain himself.

"Only their bodies remain there."

"What do you mean?" demands Lumpy.

"Please explain," Roan urges.

"I can do more than that, Roan. I will take you to them."

"Are they with the Turned? In the Dreamfield?"

"They are not where those who eat Dirt can go."

It's much more than Roan had hoped for. But his excitement is tempered by just the slightest of doubts. Can he truly believe what she is telling him?

As if reading his mind, Lumpy stares at the crickets on Mabatan's shoulders. "The crickets wouldn't go near her if she couldn't be trusted."

"I am just a guide. Nothing more."

"That's good enough for me," smiles Roan.

"I'd go in a second, too, if I could," says Lumpy mournfully.

"Whether you could or not, we would need you to stay here," she says, patting her chest, "to look after our shells."

"I'm not going anywhere."

"Good. Thank you, Lumpy." Mabatan grins widely as she says his name, but when she turns to Roan her tone is more pressing. "We must make haste."

Mabatan leads them to a grove of huge, ancient red cedar and sits beneath the giants on the mossy ground.

Lumpy looks up, admiringly. "Must be five hundred years old."

"Older," says Mabatan.

Roan and Lumpy stand quietly for a moment, appreciating the grandeur of the trees, breathing in their sweet fragrance.

"This area, there's something about it," says Roan.

"You can feel it. Good. This is an earth place," says Mabatan. "Very special." She reaches into the leather pouch dangling from her neck. Between her thumb and forefinger, she draws out a silver needle. Roan leans over for a closer look. Miniscule symbols are etched into the head. "Do those mean something?"

"It's the old language. It says, the earth remembers."

"What does the earth remember?"

"Everything."

"What's the needle for?" asks Lumpy.

"It sings the path. Are you ready?"

"Yes—where is your Dirt?"

Mabatan's eyes darken and she spits with a contempt that startles both Roan and Lumpy. "I eat no Dirt. I follow the call."

Roan has never met anyone else who can travel without Dirt. He watches Mabatan, fascinated as she pushes her needle's sharp tip into the exposed edge of a thick tree root. Kneeling before the tree, she touches her forehead to its bark—almost as though she's asking a favor of it. Then, drawing herself up, she strums the needle's exposed end. A very quiet but clear tone slips into the silence. The tiny sound is penetrating; it echoes through Roan's head, peals through his bones, and his whole body begins resonating, ringing, vibrating. It's a feeling completely unlike anything he's ever experienced.

The reverberation suddenly thrusts forward out of his chest, generating a blistering heat that collapses him into a blinding flash of light.

THE GROUND IS CHARRED AS FAR AS THE HORIZON. DUST, GRAVEL, GIANT STONES, ALL BLACK. ROAN'S EYES BLINK AT THE DARK EXPANSE AND HE ATTEMPTS TO TURN HIS HEAD FOR A LOOK IN THE OTHER DIRECTION, BUT HE CANNOT. HE CANNOT MOVE AT ALL. IT SEEMS HE'S CAUGHT IN ONE OF THE STONES. A SINEWY RABBIT WITH AZURE FUR JUMPS BEFORE HIM, NOSE QUIVERING.

"HOW DO I GET OUT?"

"DIDN'T YOUR FATHER TEACH YOU?"

"NO."

"YOUR MOTHER?"

"Neither of them told me about these things before they died."

"But you know you are never changing and always changing, don't you?"

"The Dirt Eaters told me I was gestating until I found my dream-form."

"You don't know what to do?"

"No, I don't."

"I will wait."

While the rabbit busies itself chewing a tuft of grass, Roan closes his eyes and concentrates, trying to find his form within the solid rock, straining to burst through it. He feels the effort, can sense himself pushing, but it's useless. He tries to open his eyes but can't. They aren't there anymore.

Blind and caught in a stone. Perfect. Why is it that every step forward puts him ten steps back?

Roan tries looking at the problem the way Lumpy would: first, he would make a joke, second, he would explore, and then he'd examine the information at hand. Finally, he'd come up with a plan.

Right. Well. First of all, this is no joke. Second, Roan can't explore. Information? The girl—Mabatan, she's not one of the Turned, not a Dirt Eater, she hasn't trapped him, he knows it, he can feel it. Plan: His job is to get untrapped.

He focuses all his thoughts on the surface of the rock,

PROBING IT, PRESSING IT, PULLING IT, NUDGING IT, USING ALL OF HIS MENTAL STRENGTH. PAIN RENDS HIM, AS IF HE'D BEEN RIPPING AT HIS OWN SKIN.

HIS OWN SKIN. COULD IT BE THAT HE'S NOT TRAPPED IN THE ROCK—BUT THAT HE *IS* THE ROCK? NEVER CHANGING, ALWAYS CHANGING. ROAN CONCENTRATES AGAIN, FEELING THE ANCIENT SOLIDITY OF THIS FORM. THE COOLNESS. THE JAGGED EDGES. THE DENSITY. HIS ENTIRE BEING HAS BECOME STONE. STILL AND SLOW, THE WAY HE'S BEEN FEELING. WHAT ELSE CAN HE FEEL, COULD HE BECOME? ROAN PICTURES HIS HUMAN BODY, HIS HANDS, HIS FEET, HIS HEAD. AND IN THAT MOMENT, THE STONE TURNS TO FLESH AND RECONSTITUTES ITSELF. ROAN STRETCHES OUT HIS ARMS, FEELS HIS FINGERS. HE'S NO LONGER THE ROCK, BUT IN HIS OWN SHAPE. NOT THE CLAY MAN. HIMSELF.

THE RABBIT LOOKS UP FROM THE GRASS. "YOU HAVE ARRIVED."

"IS THIS MY DREAM-FORM—MY OWN BODY?"

"THIS IS NOT YOUR BODY. IT'S WHAT YOUR MIND MADE YOU."

"WHY DON'T YOU TAKE YOUR HUMAN SHAPE?"

"I CANNOT. I AM NOT LIKE YOU. NO ONE IS LIKE YOU. YOU ARE ABLE."

"ABLE TO DO WHAT?"

"WHAT YOU HAVE DONE. IT IS ONE OF YOUR GIFTS. COME."

THE RABBIT LEAPS. IT JUMPS SO FAR, SO FAST, ROAN ALMOST LOSES SIGHT OF IT. HE RUNS, BUT FALLS TOO FAR BEHIND. HE THINKS OF THE RABBIT, OF ITS SUPPLE FORM, ITS POWERFUL LEGS, ITS INCREDIBLE ABILITY TO LEAP IN THIS ENVIRONMENT. AND ROAN JUMPS, MATCHING ITS BOUNDS. HE'S SOON CAUGHT UP WITH

Mabatan, who waits by a huge fracture in the ground, nearly as wide as the human Mabatan is tall.

"What's down there?"

"Emptiness."

Roan walks, following the jagged rupture. In the distance, he sees a storm pummeling what appear to be iron statues stretched across the gap. He moves forward, fighting wind and lashing rain. He can make out the hands of the metal statues gripping one side of the fissure. Their feet are buried in the other side. The first statue's head pivots slowly on its neck. Its lips curl sweetly upward. It's Lona.

"We knew you'd come."

"Are all of you here?"

"Every single one," says another iron child.

Roan sees his face. "Bub!"

"Hi, Roan!" yells Jaw, and his voice is followed down the long line by Gip and Runk and Jam and Dani and the other seven children of iron.

"I have to get you out." Roan reaches to pull Lona up but she screams.

"No!"

All the heads of the iron children turn slowly to Roan. "We have to stay, Roan," says Bub.

"If we let go, it'll just get bigger," Gip tells him.

"So we can't let go," adds Runk.

"Got here just in time," Sake pitches in.

"Who brought you here?"

"Nobody," Lona replies.

Dani nods. "We just came."

"We knew what to do," Bub says.

"Wasn't hard to figure it," says Jaw.

"The crack was getting bigger and bigger," Gip pipes in.

"And bigger and bigger and bigger!" shouts little Dani.

"Why didn't you tell me?"

"Happened too fast," Jaw says.

"We couldn't wait," Bub adds.

Lona's eyes shine in her face of iron. "Now you know where we are, so don't be mad, Roan."

Roan's face softens. "I'm not mad. I'm not mad at you at all." But turning back to Mabatan, his gentleness turns to fury. "Who did this?"

The rabbit twitches its ears. "Those who eat Dirt fight to control this place. Their battle has made the Rift. If it is not stopped, the Rift will grow. The children will break and be lost. This place, you call it the field of dreams, it will be forsaken and we will change. This vast emptiness that lies beneath the children will overtake us."

Roan considers her words, the first anyone has spoken that help make sense of the situation. What choice does he have but to trust her?

"What can we do?"

"End the conflict."

"How?"

"I do not know. This is the struggle we face." A shudder runs down the length of the rabbit's long body; its pink eyes dart away from Roan's. "There is a place that calls for you."

Roan turns back to the children.

"Go, Roan, go!" shouts Bub.

"Roan, go, go!" the others cry, one voice echoing after the other.

"We know you won't forget us," Lona says.

"We're strong!" hollers Bub.

"Stronger than you think!" yells Jaw.

Is this the fate Roan saved them for? They seem to know this is where they belong. Not for the first time, Roan wonders who these extraordinary children really are. And though it feels wrong to leave them here, it's obvious there is nothing he can do for them—not here, not yet.

"Promise you will call for me if you need help!" he shouts.

"We promise!" they all cry at once.

Reluctant to leave, Roan waits for the rabbit to leap away, then follows her to the edge of a vast expanse of water. Mabatan jumps, sailing onto an ice floe. Roan does the same. As they bound from floe to floe, the air becomes stifling. The water around them steams. In the midst of this roiling, foaming sea, they alight on a jagged rock.

Mabatan points out the nexus of a whirlpool. "This is the way in."

"You first."

"It does not call for me."

"Does it matter?"

"It will hold only those to whom it calls. I would not survive the passage."

"But I can?"

"Yes. It would hold you, whether you were called or not. You are a Freewalker, Roan, you travel where you will."

"Is that part of my gift?"

"Some of it."

"You seem to know an awful lot about me."

"I have spoken to the children, I have felt you. You know more about yourself than you want to know."

Scanning the raging water, roan experiences a strong apprehension that there is something beneath the whirlpool, something that is desperate and that wants him.

"Trust what has been given to you," Mabatan urges.

He stares into the maelstrom, the water swirling down into an infinite descent. The eye of the vortex draws Roan in, tugging on him, coaxing him to surrender.

Casting all doubt aside, Roan yields to the inexorable pull and jumps. Caught in the current, he's swept in endless circles, tossed and dragged and spun as he's drawn deeper into the eddy. His limbs ache, the current threatening to rip them from their sockets. But just as he presses his arms to his sides, he topples into a void.

As he spirals downward, he hears singing, a choir of

MEN'S AND WOMEN'S VOICES. HE RECOGNIZES THEM IMMEDIATELY. THE VOICES OF LONGLIGHT.

ON THE DAY OF REMEMBERING, AT THE FIRE HOLE, THE ENTIRE VILLAGE WOULD COME TOGETHER. HIS FATHER WOULD SPEAK OF THE VISION OF THE FIRST ONES, AND THEN THEY WOULD ALL SING. MOURNFUL SONGS, SONGS FOR A WORLD LOST, SONGS FOR THE INNOCENT DEAD.

BUT THIS SONG IS DIFFERENT. THIS SONG HAS NO WORDS. ROAN SEES THE EXPLOSIONS, THE FIRE, THE SKULL-MASKED INVADERS. REMEMBERS SLIDING WITH STOWE THROUGH THE ICY WHIP-GRASS. AND THEN, THE GLIMMER OF A MEMORY HOVERS AT THE EDGE OF HIS CONSCIOUSNESS——AN EERIE RUMBLING SOUND, LIKE HUNDREDS OF VOICES HUMMING IN UNISON. THE PEOPLE OF LONGLIGHT LIFTING THEIR VOICES, WHILE THEIR VILLAGE BURNED.

THE MEMORY OF HIS PEOPLE'S HELPLESSNESS IN THE FACE OF THAT RUTHLESS VIOLENCE IS A BRAND SEARED ON HIS HEART. HE HEARS HIS MOTHER'S SOPRANO LIFTING ABOVE THE OTHERS. "MOTHER," HE WHISPERS. "FATHER." BUT AS HE DROPS, THEIR VOICES GROW FAINTER, AND EVERY CELL IN HIS BODY GRIEVES FOR THE LOSS.

ROCKED BY WAVE AFTER WAVE OF ANGUISH, ROAN IS SUDDENLY CONFRONTED BY THE REEK OF BURNT FLESH. HE FIRST ENCOUNTERED THIS STENCH THE MORNING HE RETURNED TO LONGLIGHT, AFTER THE BUTCHERY. BONES FLOATING ON THE SURFACE OF THE FIRE HOLE, HIS FATHER'S SHOE CLUTCHED IN HIS HAND, THE AIR TAINTED WITH DEATH, INFINITE DEATH. IT GAGS HIM AND HE CHOKES ON IT.

Reaching out, he claws at a warm, soft wall, his fingers digging in. Thousands of wailing screams assail him and in the rising light he sees the wall is made of raw bleeding meat. Strands of flesh hang from his fingernails, his hands swim in blood.

Horrified, he jerks away, and tumbles through a thick gray mist. Below, he scans an endless flatland. The sun, halved by the horizon, casts a dim amber glow across a landscape that seems to shift and writhe. Roan topples into that living surface. Ankle-deep in undulating slime, he's deafened by a symphony of sucking. Leeches! Endlessly sucking at whatever is in their reach, a whatever Roan has no desire to investigate. He frantically scrapes the bloodsuckers off as they begin to inch up his legs.

With one wild swipe, he brushes against something solid in the quivering mass, and exposes the shape of an ear. Startled, he carefully pulls the leeches off, exposing a nose, a mouth, an eye. Until he finds himself staring into the face of Saint.

His dead mentor's eyes open slowly and look upwards. They widen in satisfaction when they see Roan. The mouth opens, but before it can utter a sound, leeches topple into it by the hundreds, stifling it. Saint's eyes scream out their desperation. His hand shoots out and grips Roan's arm, drawing him down. Leeches slide up Roan's hands, his arms, covering his body, then his face.

Roan convulses with a pure primal fear that instantly

TRANSFORMS HIM INTO FLAME. HE BURNS INSIDE AND OUT, THE WHITE FIRE THREATENING TO CONSUME ITSELF AND EXTINGUISH HIM AS SURELY AS THE ARM THAT SOUGHT TO HOLD HIM CLOSE. TOO CLOSE.

the god of the city

eldest who knows all my needs
the secrets of my heart
guide me into paradise
your wisdom to impart
that i might join with the wonders
you have created there
eldest who knows all my needs
accept my humble prayer

—Liturgy of the conurbation

"Fingertips, fingertips!"

Not fingertips again. "Where's Willum?"

"This level of training comes under my tutelage." Kordan claps his hands in annoyance. "Now. Make your energy push through each tip."

Stowe hates the whine in Kordan's voice, his acrid smell, his constant demands. But most of all, she hates Kordan's finger exercises.

Imagining her fingertips puncturing his eyes does the trick. Heat begins surging through her hands.

Kordan nods with approval. "That's the kind of focus you require."

Stowe can barely stifle her laugh. So imagining his dismemberment will get her through his relentless training sessions!

"Now, heels!"

Stowe sighs. "Where are we going to fly, Master Kordan?"

"Heels!"

She gathers the energy around her and, channeling it in through her head, pushes it down into her body. Then she directs it out toward Kordan, just to see if she can make blood come out of his thin nose.

"Focus! Your heels!"

Did he feel her attack at all? True, it was just the tiniest burst, but she'd hoped it might have at least brushed the punctilious fool.

"Are you awake?" Kordan snaps.

Stowe immediately pushes the energy into her feet.

"You were letting your mind drift!"

"Apologies, Master Kordan, it's just... we've been practicing all morning and..."

Kordan frowns. "You will continue."

"Yes, Master Kordan." Worm that he is, he's right. Why does she feel so listless when what she needs is to focus, to become stronger?

"Abdomen!"

Stowe, biting her tongue until blood trickles in her mouth,

gathers in her frustration, and funnels it into her abdominal muscles.

"Lungs!"

Off come his arms.

"Navel!"

Off come his legs.

"Eyes!"

Off comes his head.

And thus Stowe survives the drills that continue into the early afternoon.

Finally satisfied, Kordan rewards her with a smug little smile. "*Now* we are ready to fly."

But Stowe doesn't care. For as Kordan's hands press on the wall, a drawer emerges. Her heart bangs against her chest, her body courses with adrenaline, her fingers tremble.

He lifts the silver vessel. She resists the urge to rush over, grab the bowl, and swallow it all. Dirt is power, Dirt is strength. Dirt will take her away from here, where she is barely more than a child and a slave to the whims of the Masters.

She bows her head. She must not appear too eager. She opens her mouth and Kordan spills in the contents of the spoon. As she gulps the Dirt down, there is a faint glimmering at the edges of her consciousness, but she knows she cannot reach it, she need not even make the effort. "More, please."

"As you wish," says Kordan, with an ingratiating smirk. Taking his time, he leisurely dips the spoon into the bowl and raises a heaping spoonful. And with excruciating slowness, he brings it to her mouth. He so enjoys making her squirm. After she swallows, he takes a pinch for himself. The drawer slides shut, the wall closes, and they settle into their chairs.

Stowe shudders as Dirt sizzles through her veins and surges under her skin. She shimmers, then bursts into the Dreamfield like an exploding star.

STOWE, HER SKIN TERRA-COTTA, STANDS UPON A MOUNTAIN RIDGE UNDER THE PULSATING GREEN SKY. THE VULTURE, SALLOW FEATHERS AND BULBOUS RED FACE, HOVERS BESIDE HER.

"BEGIN THE TRANSFORMATION."

STOWE FOLDS ENERGY INTO HER FEET, BUT CRIES OUT IN PAIN AS THE CLAY FLESH CRYSTALLIZES, TURNING TO BRILLIANT DIAMOND.

"TOO FAST!"

RECALLING WILLUM'S INSTRUCTION, SHE SLOWS THE FLOW, PERMITTING THE CRYSTAL TO ONLY GRADUALLY INCH UP HER LEGS, OVER HER PELVIS, AROUND HER TORSO. THE METAMORPHOSIS FIRES A MILLION TINY KNIVES INTO HER NERVE ENDINGS. THE CRYSTALLIZATION OF HER FACE IS AGONY. AS HER EYES TURN TO DIAMONDS, HER VISION KALEIDOSCOPES. SHE REFOCUSES, INTEGRATING THE INFORMATION FROM ALL THE FACETS TO FORM ONE COHERENT IMAGE. SHE HAS BECOME ENTIRELY DIAMOND NOW EXCEPT FOR HER RIGHT HAND, AND THOUGH SHE WILLS IT WITH ALL HER MIGHT, THE CRYSTAL WON'T MOVE DOWN HER WRIST.

THIS HAND HOLDS THE MEMORY OF HER BROTHER'S TOUCH— HOW HIS GRIP TIGHTENED AROUND HERS BEFORE SHE WAS TORN AWAY THAT TERRIBLE NIGHT. WHEN SHE CLOSES HER EYES, SHE CAN STILL FEEL THE WARMTH OF ROAN'S FINGERS.

"Finish it," says the vulture. "Every part of you must undergo the change."

She pushes with her mind, but she cannot make the crystal move into her hand.

"I see. You still nurse this weakness. Sentiment is dangerous."

Stowe bristles. She'd lash out at her teacher, but that is what he wants. Instead she eradicates the last semblance of her vulnerability. Erasing the sensation of her brother's touch from her mind, she spreads the diamond rapidly over her hand, and instead of pride at her successful transformation, she is left with a plaintive, searing ache.

"Good. Maintain that density as you rise."

But she cannot move.

"Raise yourself!" demands Kordan.

The weight of Stowe's limbs is too great. Kordan's contempt distracts her and siphons off her energy. Her efforts become brittle and every time she tries to lift off, the challenge increases. Then Willum's instructions drift into her crystalline consciousness: pain is a fuel, swallow it, make it serve you.

Following his teaching, she eats her pain, and as she rolls it back into her control she slowly levitates, rising to the same height as the vulture.

"Now let's see if you can soar."

The last visit, she'd transformed only half her body.

Now, carrying this greater density, it's difficult to pick up speed.

"Why so cautious, Our Stowe?"

If pain is fuel, then hatred is its igniter, thinks Stowe as she blasts into the mist. Soaring high above Kordan, she can almost imagine being free of him, of any responsibility to the Masters or the City. But not today. Today she will suffer his taunts and obey his every command. With another thought, she plummets, then comes to a dead stop inches from the vulture, her crystal fingers curved into a sharp point at his breast.

"You waste your efforts," says Kordan. "Do not make the same mistake when you pass through the Whorl."

"What if I become trapped in it?"

"You will only fail if you falter."

All that he says is aimed at the core of her pride. He has always treated her like this, forever preying on her weaknesses, seeking to keep her in his thrall, daring her to crave the mystery of his power. So obvious. Not like Willum, whose hold on her and on his position is a puzzle. Willum appears open, vulnerable, but he feigns this transparency. He keeps his secrets and, if the ease with which he repelled her attack on the clerics is any indication, they are secrets worthy of her attention.

Stowe contemplates the towering waterspout that obstructs the horizon: the Whorl. Set in the middle of what the Masters call Blind Man's Desert, it dominates

A LANDSCAPE THAT IS SAID TO HAVE ONCE THROBBED WITH ACTIVITY, ACTIVITY THE MASTERS HAD TROUBLE POLICING. DARIUS'S CONSTRUCTION IS INSPIRED IN ITS SIMPLICITY. THE WHORL'S WATERS WERE DRAWN FROM THE WELL OF OBLIVION, AND ITS ENERGY FROM ANY ENTITY FOOLISH ENOUGH TO APPROACH IT. SOME CLAIM THAT AT THE VERY MOMENT IT WAS SET IN MOTION, ALL THE BIRDS IN THE CITY FELL FROM THE SKIES, THEIR SPIRITS FOREVER CAUGHT IN THE WHIRLING CASCADE. CHILDREN WOKE SCREAMING FROM NIGHTMARES THEY COULD NOT REMEMBER.

STOWE HAD ALWAYS BELIEVED IT WAS DRIVEL, A TALE TOLD TO TERRIFY THE UNINITIATED, KEEP THEM IN AWE OF THE DIRT AND ITS POWER. BUT FACE TO FACE WITH THE WHORL AND THE LIFELESS LANDSCAPE IN WHICH IT PULSES, SHE HAS NO DOUBT THAT THE STORIES OF ITS LETHALNESS ARE IN FACT UNDERSTATED. A GREATER CHALLENGE THEN, BUT SHE IS STRONG. STRONG ENOUGH.

SHE BULLETS STRAIGHT TOWARD THE WHORL. CLOSER AND CLOSER, UNTIL SHE CRASHES INTO IT. THROUGH HER HEAD FLASHES THE FORCE OF AN INESTIMABLE NUMBER OF BEINGS, THEIR MEMORIES INTERTWINING. THEY ENVELOP HER WITH THEIR PLEADING, URGING HER TO JOIN THEM. SHE COULD LEAVE ALL HER PAIN BEHIND WITH THEM, THEY COO, NO NEED TO LOOK BACK, OR TO CARRY SUCH DEVASTATING ANGUISH. SHE COULD GIVE IT ALL TO THEM. THEY WOULD CARRY IT FOR HER. THEIR CALL IS A DIVINE MUSIC THAT WINDS AND WRAPS LIKE VELVET OVER HER LIMBS, HER HEART, HER MIND.

YEARNING, SHE REACHES OUT, BUT HER MOMENTUM THRUSTS

HER FORWARD AND THROUGH THE OTHER SIDE OF THE WHORL TO WHERE KORDAN WAITS. HER CRYSTALLINE SKIN IS SHREDDED, HER HEAD HALF-HANGING TO THE SIDE, BUT SHE IS STILL THERE, ALL THAT SHE IS AND THAT SHE KNOWS, ALL THAT SHE REMEMBERS INTACT. LOOKING INTO THE VULTURE'S EYES, IT SEEMS FORTUNATE THAT IN HER CRYSTALLINE FORM SHE CANNOT CRY.

She unsteadily picks herself up from the floor, ignoring Kordan's gaze.

"You successfully completed your task." His normal whine is tinged with resentment, and Stowe takes some small satisfaction in the fact that her accomplishments irritate him.

Her skin feels like it's blistering, but a quick glimpse assures Stowe that the sensation is simply a side effect of her ordeal. The throbbing ache, however, is no illusion. It takes all her strength to remain vertical, and maintain her pride before this preening, disdainful ogre. She smiles at him.

"I thank you from the bottom of my heart, Master Kordan. Your instruction is invaluable. You make me better than I am."

Kordan, peacocking, bows his head with false modesty. "I am here only to serve Our Stowe."

Ah, flattery. Such an effective tool.

A quiet knock on the door and Willum whispers into the room, "I trust your venture was successful."

"All is satisfactory."

"The Keeper would like to see Our Stowe."

Now. Finally. The verdict.

"Why wasn't I notified?" snaps Kordan.

"You'll have to ask him that yourself," says Willum, turning to leave.

"Wait," Kordan hisses before pompously directing his scowl at Stowe. "Tomorrow you will be challenged. Make sure you are up to it."

Stowe gives him her most ingratiating smile. "Thank you again, my teacher."

As she and Willum step into the hallway, he offers her his handkerchief. "How much have you been taking?"

She ignores his offering and licks the corners of her mouth. "Enough."

"And that is?"

"Two spoons."

"That's enough for ten Walkers."

"The Dirt makes me stronger."

"Stowe, do not be deceived by the semblance of a thing."

"Nothing can be done, Willum. It is in the interests of the Conurbation."

"Nevertheless, I will speak to Darius."

His troubled expression seems quaint, but Stowe's not blind to the consequences of his disquiet. He must not ration her Dirt. It's unthinkable; Kordan will not let him.

"There is nothing to fear in Dirt, good Willum."

"I do not fear it, Stowe, but I am concerned with its abuse."

She will divert him, bury the issue among all the other matters Willum must attend to. "Why has Darius waited so long to call on me?"

Willum's silence is his answer. Darius's withdrawal from her has been part of her punishment. He may be old and mainly made of replacement parts, but few have survived his wrath. How angry at her can he be?

"What will he do to me?"

Willum stops midstep. "He does not share his judgments with me. You must prepare yourself for whatever may come." Rounding the corner, Willum leaves Stowe to take her final steps to the ornate oak door, portal to the Archbishop of the Conurbation, alone.

Stowe stares at the brass doorknob wrapped in the claws of an animal. But what kind of animal? Not an eagle or a wolf. Something smaller, sharper, more devious. One day she must bring a book with pictures and identify the beast that Darius honors. When she first arrived in the City, she was brought here trembling, but Darius was kind and gentle. He delighted her with intricate wind-up toys and sweet cakes. Plush toy animals from the time before the Wars, a monkey, a lion, and a donkey. He would read her stories, and taught her to build houses of cards.

But that time passed once she voyaged to the Dreamfield. Once she became Our Stowe. Now her visits are always official, matters of state, and Darius expects her to take her role seriously. A major breach of protocol has been committed so he has kept his distance. Well, she will accept whatever punishment he inflicts without argument, as it is imperative she regain his confidence. All of his questions must be answered as truthfully as possible. She needs his trust to destroy him.

She takes in air through her nostrils, calming herself, ready for whatever she is facing. Stowe touches one of the claws on the doorknob and the door opens. She steps in, leaving the safety of Willum behind. She listens as the door slides shut.

Darius is imposingly erect in his chair. His eyes snap on Stowe, his skull-like face grim and unyielding.

"Do you know why I've called you here?"

"I was rude to your clerics after our visit to the factory."

His thin lips curl upward. "You left one man deaf, another comatose, another paralyzed on one side of his body. Is this what you call rude?"

She exudes shock and dismay, and quickly bows her head, hoping to indicate shame. In fact, she feels a quiver of excitement. She had the power to do all that?

"You realize, of course, that there must be ramifications."

"Eldest, though I am distressed at my lack of control, I honestly did not know I was capable of such a thing. What is to be done with me?"

"Your victims have been... adjusted. Since your outburst, or should I say, test, took place in a reasonably secure area, there were not as many casualties as there might have been."

"I was not aware I was being tested, Eldest."

"Clever girl. You make me very proud. I believe it was you who was doing the testing, was it not?"

Holding his gaze as steadily as she can, Stowe wonders how much Darius knows, how much she should admit to. Damn

Willum, what did he tell? The effort of not averting her eyes is causing them to tear up. She must not let that happen.

"Willum tells me you were distraught to hear that Roan has been declared dead."

"He is not dead," Stowe whimpers. There, let him think it's grief. Something she can play.

"Perhaps you are right, perhaps he is still alive somewhere, disabled or in hiding. What is important for you and I is the realization that he is no longer a necessary part of our plans."

Our plans? Here it comes. How easy it must have been these last few years, to mold and shape her.

"Imagine. If he came into our fold, you would be halved, dominated by your older brother, sharing everything when you've worked so hard. Why shouldn't it all be for you? You are becoming something even greater than I hoped for. You are my adopted daughter, and you must rule one day."

Yes, Our Stowe. Our Stowe should have it all. And what, oh adopted father of mine, shall be the nature of my gilded cage?

"But Father, you shall rule forever. I have no such desire."

"This flesh is an unbearable burden. I have waited long to slough it off and take my place forever in the Dreamfield. It is for you that I have waited, Stowe."

He is lying, of course. But why? Is the sacrifice he will ask of her so great he feels he must offer his place to secure it?

"What is it, Darius, that I must do?"

His leathery fingers lightly touch Stowe's curls. She bends her head into his hand, feigning ecstasy.

He's like the monster in the picture book her mother used to read her. Luring her in with candy because he wants to devour her.

She keeps that thought firmly in the back of her mind as he lifts her head and gazes fondly at her face.

"*Must* is an inappropriate word. There is a mission before you. An experiment that could turn the tide forever in our favor. But you are under no imperative. You should think on it, evaluate the risk, and then decide. If you refuse, it shall not change my plans for you."

She realizes with an icy chill that he intends to destroy her. How she knows, she's not sure, but she's certain of it. He will kill her whatever she does. A tremor passes through her. Fear? Yes, but also relief. He will develop her powers until they are ripe for his use. That will give her time to find a way to turn the tables and destroy *him*. He's taught her perhaps too well, this false father of hers.

"What is the task?"

"The immediate task is to pierce the Wall."

"The Eaters' barricade?"

"Yes."

"I thought it was impenetrable."

"It is of a most ingenious design, but I don't think they had you in mind when they built it, my love."

"You really think I can get through?"

"I am sure of it. We must undermine the Eaters' plans to dominate the Dreamfield. For ten years we've searched for a way through their wall—and you are it, my daughter. I would like you to take careful note of its structure. And observe the Eaters' response. Also... we need to assess the feasibility of bringing one back."

"What—an Eater?"

His lips spread across his face, stretching his skin to its limits. "A wonderful thought, isn't it? So much we could learn. How quickly we might hasten their demise."

The Keeper's eyes flutter and he sinks deeper into his chair.

"Keeper? Father?"

"Do not underestimate the difficulty and the jeopardy. This is a dangerous task."

He holds out his hand. Stowe kisses it.

"What power you have, my little one. Something our clerics have grown to appreciate. We must put it to better uses."

Stowe sets Darius's hand down just as he begins to gently snore. She looks at him, a black well of hatred collecting behind her eyes. He had made her believe he loved her, cared for her, when all he wanted was to use her. Well, I hunger for your touch no more, monster. You tried to become my father so that one hand could squeeze the life from my heart, while the other tore the sight from my eyes. You are responsible for all the death, all the lies. You destroyed my world. You and your City. I will find out what you want to steal from me. I will rise up, and nothing, no one, will ever control me again.

the fevers of hell

most of those who wander are thought to be lost
in the devastation. we have no knowledge of their
origins, beliefs, or numbers. all we know is that
where they have passed, the white cricket thrives.
——the war chronicles

HEAT RADIATES FROM HIS BODY, the taint of his ordeal
with Saint torching his insides, but Roan is certain he's
alive, alive and back in the world. He knows it because he
senses the coolness of the air, the rich scent of cedar, his back
upon the mossy ground. He can hear voices, can see faces
through the fog, but they rise and fall, in and out of view.

"It's been a whole day and night and the fever hasn't quit."
Lumpy.

"It's not unusual after visiting the place of torment. He must
have resisted it. Fled when he should have embraced. Glimpsed
instead of becoming. That is the reason for his sickness."

"We should move him. Get help."

"He has everything he needs. He is strong and my medicine is good."

"Then he'll get better?"

"His fever will end, but he cannot fully recover until he returns to the place that called him."

Roan feels himself writhe on the ground; he tries to call out Lumpy's name but there's a stick in his mouth.

"The cloths," says Mabatan.

Cold, wet cloths are spread across his chest and legs, quelling the fire under his skin. Roan opens his eyes a little more, trying to focus.

Lumpy's face is very close. "Roan? It's me."

Roan tries to say, "I know it's you," but all that emerges is a strangled sound from his throat.

"Take out the stick," says Mabatan.

"You were convulsing before," Lumpy explains, removing the obstruction. "This kept you from biting your tongue."

"Lumpy. I saw the children," Roan stammers. "Mabatan took me. There's a rift. In the Dreamfield. They hold it together."

Roan closes his eyes and moans, his body wracked with pain. Mabatan touches his forehead. "He is too hot."

She crushes a piece of bark with a stone. Putting some of the powder into a cup, she adds a little water and puts it to Roan's lips. "Drink. This will help you."

As Roan sips the liquid, a calmness settles over him. His body sinks into the moss. Lying there, half awake, he hears Mabatan whistle softly and senses his cricket responding to the call.

Lumpy's cricket jumps down beside Roan's, and when they

begin to sing, three more white crickets emerge from Mabatan's pocket to join them. Within moments, crickets descend from the tree, from under rocks and fallen branches. Dozens of them surround Roan, singing.

Roan sighs heavily, feeling himself enveloped in a cloak of mist.

"They have taken him to the place between. He is awake to the sounds of the earth but his spirit is resting safely. When he rises, he will be stronger."

Relieved, Lumpy sits beside Roan, careful not to disturb the crickets.

"Mabatan, what do you know about the crickets? I mean, apart from the fact that they are creatures of the earth."

"But that is the center of their being. That is exactly what they are. More fully that than any other creature in the world. You must know this, for they chose you."

"Well, since the first one I had got crushed, I don't know how wise a choice it made." Lumpy lets out a self-deprecating laugh.

Mabatan, however, remains quite earnest. "The crickets, all of them, they chose you."

"You can't be serious. How would you know something like that?"

"They told me."

"They talk to you?"

"Talk, no. Tell me things, yes."

"Like that I was chosen."

"Yes. That you were chosen."

Lumpy's hand goes to the craters that landscape his face. Craters formed by the Mor-Ticks that attacked him and his family. All dead except for Lumpy. He was saved by a white cricket, when it killed the parasites that were consuming him. Almost breathless, he forces out the words. "I never understood why I lived and my family died. Why there was only one cricket, and why it picked me to save."

"It is because you will save many."

"Me?"

"Yes."

"Listen, you've made a mistake. I'm not the hero. That job belongs to Roan."

"I do not know that saving many and being a hero are always one. I wish I could say more, but that is all I understand."

In the fading light, as the clouds shift across the gibbous moon, Roan rests peacefully under the soothing scent of the cedar tree that towers over him. He has thought more than once that his friendship with Lumpy was fated. If what Mabatan says is true, then maybe Roan has more than just a friend watching his back. With all that he guesses lies ahead, it's a comforting possibility. He wants to open his eyes now, but he knows he must wait. Listen. Though he is unsure why.

"Do you have a family?" Lumpy asks the girl.

"I did once."

"You seem young to be on your own."

"I am not on my own."

Lumpy, bemused, restates himself. "I don't mean now, I mean before you met us."

"I have never been alone."

"You have the crickets."

"The crickets come and go as they wish. Even still, I have much company. What I touch, what I smell, what I see, what I taste, what I hear, all of this is with me. As long as I use my senses to open my spirit, I have the world... I have the world for now."

Mabatan is silent a long time, but Lumpy knows better than to interrupt.

"The world will be lost to us if we fail to close the rift, our spirits taken. I have been told this. The gift we have been given will be withdrawn."

"You mean the earth will die?"

"No. The earth has millions of summers still before it. But she will shrug us off her shoulders and we will be returned to dust."

Mabatan and Lumpy become as still as the air Roan breathes, and the night is filled with the song of crickets.

The sun rises, casting its bloody palette across the cloud-filled sky. Roan wakes to see Lumpy and Mabatan hunched over a small cooking fire.

"Good morning," says Mabatan. "We've made a soup. It will comfort you."

"Feeling better?" asks Lumpy.

"Way better," Roan replies automatically. But when he tries to stand, he stumbles, falling back on one knee. Lumpy grabs his arm and eases him down onto the thick moss.

"Take it easy," Lumpy cautions, as Mabatan offers Roan a clay cup of broth. "She found a place where tawny mushrooms grow. Best sick food around."

The soup's rich fragrance makes Roan's mouth water. He starts to gulp it down.

"Sip slow," says Mabatan. "You've been two days without food."

Despite the warning, the soup is quickly gone and Lumpy refills the bowl. Handing it back to Roan, he hesitates before asking a question.

"You were calling out Saint's name."

Roan shudders. "I saw him."

Lumpy's face crumples in horror. "He's still alive?"

"No. He's in a place. A terrible place." Roan turns to Mabatan. "What was it?"

"When the body dies, the mind makes a place for itself. Some know peace and return to oneness. Others do not."

A strange, excited look crosses Lumpy's face. "And you can visit someone else there, when they're dead?"

"Some can. Not many. Most can only go to the common place. But Roan walks freely."

Lumpy looks imploringly at Roan.

"It's not like you think, Lumpy. Not like ghosts or spirits. It's not the person, it's a jumbled-up idea of themselves, surrounded by whatever torment they invent. The Lelbit you knew is not there. I don't think you'd want her to be."

Lumpy's face is tight, eyes red. Realizing the pain that Lumpy's feeling, Roan whispers, "I'm sorry," as Lumpy, downcast, turns away.

Roan looks inquiringly at Mabatan. "I don't understand what Saint wanted, why he called."

"If you had stayed, you would know. But instead you escaped and now the thing has yet to be done."

"What waits to be done?"

"You are called. You must be reborn inside the mind of the dead."

The expression on her face is so somber, so devoid of humor, Roan can't help but take her words seriously, despite how absurd they sound.

"What do you mean?"

"Were you with him when he died?"

Roan nods.

"He was trying to kill you?"

"He was about to. Lelbit got him instead."

"It is possible that he is caught in the moment of his death, seeking forever to complete the action that brought him to his fate."

"I didn't kill him."

"But you believe you are responsible for his death."

"So I should go back and let him *kill* me? Why?"

"Then you could enter his mind, discover what he is trying

to offer. If you fear this, if you run in terror, the knowledge he wishes to share will be lost."

"I don't know if I can go back."

Mabatan shrugs and breaks up the smoldering sticks from the cooking fire. Roan turns to Lumpy for support, but what he encounters is not solace but grim determination.

"How long will they survive, Roan? The rift—Mabatan said it will tear them apart."

Roan glares at Lumpy. "You weren't there. You didn't see what I saw, hear what I heard..." But the hurt look in Lumpy's eyes stops him. They've faced so much together and never backed away. And now, when the need is so great, what is Roan doing but turning away, afraid that if he goes he'll never come back.

"I can't imagine what you went through, but I saw what it did to you. You couldn't go now, even if you wanted to. Not yet. No one's asking that."

Lumpy's pragmatism immediately lifts Roan's spirits. Right now, he'd rather face anything than return to that horror. But maybe with a little time, he'll feel differently. Or better yet, find another way. "How long before I can try again?"

"You must gather more strength," the girl replies.

"I'm going to the City."

A laugh explodes out of Lumpy. "You actually think the City's less risky?"

"It's not about risk. Mabatan says there are things in the Dreamfield that only I can do. But that's not completely true. There is someone else who can match me. My sister."

Mabatan closes her eyes. After a moment, she nods her head, as if having consulted with someone in her mind. Her eyes snap open. "She will not help you make peace with Saint. But she may help close the rift."

Lumpy shakes his head, distressed. "You said yourself she's damaged. She's one of the Turned."

"In all this time, I've only seen her in the Dreamfield. There is blood between us. We love each other. If we actually set our eyes on each other, touch each other, maybe I could win her back."

Lumpy sighs. "You're serious." Turning to Mabatan, he shakes his head in mock disbelief. "He's serious. I recognize the symptoms." But the frown on Lumpy's face becomes increasingly genuine. "I wish you weren't. If you get caught in the City... and how do you expect to get in? They'll be looking for you. I'm your backup and I can't go anywhere near those gates. I'm covered in Mor-Tick scars, in case you forgot."

Mabatan places a hand on each of them. "I know someone who can take you."

the hole in the wall

DEMONS SEEK TO RUPTURE THE HARMONY OF THE CITY. THE MASTERS BATTLE THEM DAILY IN PARADISE. IN ORDER TO ACCOMMODATE THE OVERWHELMING REQUESTS TO JOIN US IN OUR STRUGGLE, ACOLYTE INITIATION HAS BEEN DECLARED ONGOING.

—PROCLAMATION OF MASTER QUERIN

STOWE STARES AT WILLUM sitting sullen in his blue lacquered chair. She will wait him out. Whatever it is that's eating away at him, she suspects it will be aimed at her and that she will resent it.

After an interminable amount of time, and with a great exhalation, he finally says what's on his mind. "You have become addicted to the Dirt."

"What it allows me to do is beyond the imagination."

"The price you have paid is past reckoning."

"Master Darius has made certain requests. You have always advised me to follow his directions, not fight them," says Stowe. "Are you now saying that he's trying to harm me?"

"I am suggesting that you take a substantial amount more Dirt than you need."

"A great deal is required for what I'm attempting."

"That may be what you have been led to believe, but it is not necessarily so."

"Willum, must we go round and round? These are things beyond our power to change."

For a brief moment, she is overcome with a longing to blurt it all out, tell Willum what she fears, what she intends. Almost as if he were a friend. But she's not stupid enough to believe in that possibility. Willum, like all the others, wants something from her. What, she cannot guess. He slumps in his chair and gulps his water. She can see he's resigned himself. Kordan he will fight, but when Darius commands, Willum obeys. He is no fool. Come at him the right way and he might even help.

Stowe shifts her chair closer to Willum. "Tell me what you know of the Eaters."

"A great deal. You must be more specific."

"I've only heard the official histories. The stories of the Five who discovered the Dirt. How Darius broke from the other four in order to protect it. How their lust for power caused the civil war. And how Darius won that war, leading the City to victory."

"We have discussed the fact, have we not, that history is written by the victors."

Leaning closer to Willum, Stowe whispers, "There is more?"

Willum smiles as he pulls back. "There is always more. History says that seventy-five years ago, Darius's air machines eradicated all but four of the renegade armies. These four scattered. One was discovered and eliminated. No trace of the second remains. The descendants of the third were recently crushed by Darius, leaving only two survivors."

Stowe grows cold as the realization sinks in. She and Roan are those two survivors. They come from Longlight, where the descendants of one renegade army sought to conceal themselves. A strange emotion surges through her. Her face pinches, her eyes sting. Is this grief? She swipes it away like foreign matter. The irritant purged, she locks eyes with Willum.

"Longlight is gone, and if any Eaters lived there, they are now dead. So that leaves the fourth group of renegades. Are they all Eaters?"

"No, not all. But... they are rumored to be powerful in other ways."

"Are they as dangerous as I've been told?"

Willum's fingertips squeeze his temples, he breathes, then looks in her eyes.

"Darius ensures that only the most rudimentary technology is allowed outside the City gates. Thus, as far as we are aware, they have no weapons other than those they might make themselves. This would limit the effectiveness of any army they might have. But, as you are well aware, the body and the mind are quite lethal tools when one knows how to employ them. And then, there is their belief system."

"Which is?"

"They believe the Dreamfield empowers the human spirit. Rule the Dreamfield and you control the essence of life itself. That is the theory. The many defenses the Keeper has created have up till now prevented any confrontation. However, Darius believes their construction of the Wall is the first move in a new attempt at a takeover."

"Are they capable of threatening our defenses?"

"It would not be politic to say such a thing, even if I knew it with any certainty. Naturally, there is conjecture."

Ah, yes, here is the Willum she needs. Those eyes that see beyond the apparent, the ears that evaluate speculation.

Suddenly Willum is alert; she senses it, too. Kordan. The man loves to make his presence known.

Willum whispers, "Do not underestimate them, Stowe. These are not village idiots."

"The conjecture?"

"The death of only one of the original Five has ever been confirmed. Roan of the Parting, he was called. Your great-grandfather."

Stowe is startled by the news. "My great-grandfather was one of the Five?"

"He discovered the Dirt. It was your great-grandfather who led the rebellion. He believed the use of Dirt should be terminated, the substance destroyed. And the others..."

The door opens and Kordan steps in. He is smiling, a rare event, and when he looks at Willum his smile broadens. "I will be taking her now."

Ignoring Kordan's smirk, Willum addresses Stowe. "Well, then, good luck. Remember, what can be used to attack may also be employed as a defense."

She sees the day she attacked the clerics reflected in his eyes. He shielded himself. Can she?

"I will see you later at the Masters' banquet."

"Oh," says Kordan, the acid dripping off his lips, "I didn't realize you were invited."

"As Our Stowe's Primary, it is my duty to be on hand."

"Ah, yes," Kordan says. "How could I have forgotten." And grandly sweeping his robes, he pivots back out the door with Stowe.

Amused, she catches Willum's eye. "Thank you. I will be careful."

The Destination Room is the most advanced of all the travel rooms to be found in the Great Pyramid. Designed for maximum amplification, it is used only for the most important excursions. It is made of clear glass triangles, and sits atop the pyramid's apex. Even the curved beds, perfectly molded to suit the reclining body, are made of glass. This extraordinary environment became a second home to Stowe these past two years, when daily she would set out to search for her brother. Call to him. On occasion bring him visions and dreams. Kordan always at her back, pushing, pushing. Those isolated moments, when she felt the touch of Roan's consciousness, so much like her own, have the same clarity and resonance now as when she first experienced them. He would always escape her, though, always run away. Kordan had said the Eaters interfered, set up barriers between her and Roan. Did Roan sense another presence with her as well? Would he have made contact if they'd both been alone? She was sure she'd heard him call out to her. But that had been so long ago. She has not felt him for... No! He is not dead. He can't be... though he has stopped searching for her.

"It is a fine day, Our Stowe. Today we come to the fruition of all our hard work."

"Will others be witnessing?"

"No, it was determined the added complication of an audience was inadvisable at this juncture."

"Lest I fail and ruin the celebration," Stowe says, her eyes keenly fastened on the silver bowl.

"You are very talented, perhaps the most talented of all of us. But in the challenge you face, talent is of little import."

It was important last week, last month, last year, Stowe thinks. But no matter, the Dirt is in his hand and if she listens quietly she will get it all the sooner.

"Density. Impermeability. Sustaining mass will be key to dominating your opponents."

"Opponents?"

"Traitors are everywhere. You must learn to defend yourself as well in the Dreamfield as you have learned to here in the real world. There are many threats to the Masters now. Irritants that must be set aside forever."

"I am to fight an Eater?"

"Yes. Perhaps more than one."

"The one who kept me from finding my brother?"

"I do not command the Eaters, Our Stowe. I cannot say who will meet our challenge. But I am sure they will be there. The Eaters would all dearly love to see you dead."

Does Kordan also want her dead? Does he know of Darius's plans for her future? She could hear the contempt in his voice when he said her name. It was greater than when he spoke of the Eaters.

Kordan takes a pinch of dirt and places it on his tongue. Smiling, he offers a heaping spoonful to Stowe, who cannot help but devour it hungrily. After a moment Kordan presents another. Willum's warnings echo at the back of Stowe's mind, but he doesn't know how hard it is, how much easier the Dirt makes it for her. And this is important, too important. Maybe next time she'll heed him and take less. But this time, Stowe accepts the extra dose and, lying back on the smooth curved bed, lets her mind focus on the inward journey.

On a beach with sand the color of burnt umber, vulture beside her, Our Terra-cotta Stowe surveys the watery landscape.

"What's our approach?"

The vulture steps into the sea and disappears. With a downward sweep of her hand, Stowe glides effortlessly into the water, despite her form of clay.

League after league of vast coral beds, pulsating fields of anemones, schools of tiny glowing fish and their lumbering solitary predators all zoom past her. Moving at fabulous speeds, she barely glimpses the sights as they whisk by, the struggle between her resolve and her anxiety consuming all her attention.

"Here." The voice of Kordan intrudes upon her thoughts. How free he feels to invade her in this way. She is partially to blame, she knows. At first it seemed a most appealing magic, an entertaining game, but she was mistaken. Now she recognizes it for what it is, this barging into her mind. An assault. When the time comes, she will make him suffer for it.

Lifting her clay head so that her eyes skim the surface of the water, she gasps. How could they call this a *wall?* Were they so petty, so afraid, that they could not admire the accomplishments of their enemies? The surging cascade of energy drapes like a luminescent, liquid fabric. Its length and height are impossible to determine, for it sprawls across the horizon in all directions. This Wall is so large that, far to the west, the Spiracal, Darius's most dangerous Construction, appears tiny and inconsequential. Sinking, she observes that the Wall extends to the

OCEAN FLOOR AND PROBABLY BEYOND. SHE CAN SEE WHY IT IS CONSIDERED A THREAT TO THE SECURITY OF THE CONURBATION. DIPPING AND FLARING AS SPARKS OF LIGHT SHOOT ACROSS IT, THIS BARRIER APPEARS TO BE ALIVE AND IT IS MOST CERTAINLY DANGEROUS. VERY DANGEROUS.

AS IF SENSING HER DOUBTS, KORDAN JOLTS HER BACK TO THE TASK AT HAND. "ONCE YOU HAVE PENETRATED THE WALL, DO NOT TARRY. BLAST BACK THROUGH IMMEDIATELY, AND RETURN TO ME."

"WHAT IF I'M PURSUED?"

"ANY STUPID ENOUGH TO FOLLOW, I'LL CATCH AND BRING HOME AS A SPECIAL TREAT FOR THE ELDEST. AFTER, OF COURSE, I'VE PERFORMED MY FIRST DUTY, WHICH IS TO PROTECT YOU."

AND TO MAKE SURE I DON'T THINK TOO DEEPLY ABOUT WHAT I'M DOING, REALIZES STOWE. BUT THE UNDERTAKING IS IMPOSSIBLE TO AVOID, HER PATH AND THE MASTER'S STILL INEXTRICABLY INTERTWINED. EMBRACING THE PAIN, SHE TRANSMUTATES UNTIL THE WHOLE OF HER BODY, EVEN HER PRECIOUS HAND, HAS CRYSTALLIZED INTO DIAMOND. READY, SHE FOCUSES HER INTENT ON THE NEAREST POINT OF THE UNDULATING CURTAIN. SHE LEAPS, NEVER TAKING HER EYES OFF THAT POINT, STEADILY ACCELERATING AS SHE ROCKETS TOWARD HER GOAL, BRIMMING WITH ANTICIPATION.

SHE SEES THE FLICKERING RAYS OF LIGHT FORM A LIVING TAPESTRY, BUT WITHIN SECONDS SHE'S TOO CLOSE TO DISCERN ITS MESSAGE. IF ITS SURFACE IS IMPOSSIBLE TO DECIPHER, THE NATURE OF ITS DEPTH IS EQUALLY ELUSIVE. SINCE ITS OPACITY PREVENTS HER FROM SEEING THROUGH IT, THERE IS NO WAY OF KNOWING IF ANYONE WAITS IN AMBUSH. BUT ON THIS SIDE OF THE WALL, THERE

ARE NO DEFENDERS, NO ONE TO SLOW HER APPROACH. THAT, AT LEAST, IS AS EXPECTED.

WHEN SHE'S CLOSE ENOUGH TO HEAR THE INTERTWINED WHISTLING AND HUMMING OF THE BARRIER, SHE REALIZES WITH A SHOCK THAT SHE'S ALREADY IN. THIS WALL IS DEEP—SO DEEP THE OTHER SIDE IS BEYOND THE REACH OF HER VISION. THE LIGHT IS FANTASTIC, VIBRANT COLOR JUMPING, DANCING, FLARING, BOUNCING OFF HER CRYSTALLINE FORM.

SHE CHECKS HERSELF FOR ANY FLAWS. THERE ARE NONE. HER IMPERMEABLE ANATOMY PROVIDED SAFE PASSAGE THROUGH THE WHORL, AND THE THREAT IN THIS WALL OF VISCOUS ENERGY SEEMS MINIMAL BY COMPARISON.

CONFIDENT, STOWE STAYS ON COURSE. SHE WATCHES, INTRIGUED, AS A SHAFT OF LIGHT GLANCES ALONG THE EDGES OF HER PRISMATIC SKIN UNTIL IT COURSES THROUGH HER, BLENDS WITH HER—THEN, SPLITTING INTO AN INFINITE ARRAY OF COLORS, IT INFUSES HER WITH RAPTURE. AND THOUGH SOME SMALL PART OF HER KNOWS SHE SHOULD DEFEND HERSELF, SO CERTAIN IS SHE THAT THE EFFECT OF THE DIRT IS BEING AMPLIFIED SHE BELIEVES HERSELF INVULNERABLE, UNTOUCHABLE, UNSTOPPABLE.

AS THE FAR SIDE OF THE WALL BEGINS TO COME INTO VIEW, SHE REMEMBERS WILLUM'S WORDS. WHAT CAN BE USED TO ATTACK MAY ALSO BE EMPLOYED TO DEFEND. AS IF A NOTE OF TRUTH HAS BEEN PLAYED ON HER SURFACE, SHE REALIZES HER MISTAKE. THE ENERGY PULSING THROUGH HER IS OPENING HER, ILLUMINATING HER, OUTLINING A MAP OF HER INTERIOR. FOOL GIRL! FOOL TO TRUST KORDAN. SHE CHOSE THE WRONG DEFENSE; SHE SHOULD

HAVE SHIELDED HERSELF, CREATED A PROTECTIVE AURA. TURN AROUND, TURN AROUND! TOO LATE. SHE WAILS AS SHE EXPLODES OUT OF THE TRANSLUCENCE AND INTO ENEMY TERRITORY.

FOR ONE BRIEF MOMENT, SHE FEELS SHE'S BEEN GRANTED A REPRIEVE. NOTHING BUT OCEAN AND A PERFECT SKY. THIS IS THE ESTEEMED LOCALE OF THE EATERS? SHE COLLIDES WITH A CLOUD, PUFFY WHITE, COOL AND COMFORTING. BUT HER RELIEF IS SHORT-LIVED: SHE CANNOT MOVE.

MOBILIZING ALL HER RESERVES, SHE EXTRACTS HERSELF FROM THE CLOUD ONLY TO SEE THE OCEAN FOAM AND RELEASE FOUR FIGURES FROM ITS DEPTHS. MOUNTAIN LION, LIZARD, JACKAL, AND BEAR. HER ONLY HOPE A RUSE, STOWE PRETENDS TO CONTINUE STRUGGLING WITH THE CLOUD. AS SOON AS THE LION IS UPON HER, SHE KICKS OUT, HER DIAMOND FOOT CONNECTING WITH A FORCE THAT SPINS IT WILDLY INTO THE WAVES. THE JACKAL'S AT HER HIP, ITS TEETH SOMEHOW PIERCING HER. STOWE PRIES ITS MOUTH OPEN, SHAKES IT HARD UNTIL SHE HEARS BONES CRACK. SHE TOSSES THE JACKAL INTO THE SEA, BUT AS SHE WRAPS HER LEGS AROUND THE BEAR, SHE'S JERKED AWAY FROM THE CLOUD.

THE LIZARD INSTANTLY ATTACHES ITSELF TO STOWE, SINKING ITS TEETH INTO HER SIDE. CATAPULTED VIOLENTLY BACK INTO THE BARRIER BY THE SEARING PAIN, SHE FEELS HERSELF REPLEN-ISHED BY THE SURGING CURRENT. HER KNEES SQUEEZE ALL BREATH FROM THE BEAR. SHE LETS IT DROP AND GRABS THE LIZARD BY THE TAIL, YANKING HARD. THE TAIL SNAPS OFF. THE LIZARD CLAWS BENEATH HER RIBS, BURROWING DEEP. SHE REACHES INSIDE HER-SELF, FOLLOWING THE CURVE OF THE REPTILE, AND CLOSES HER

HAND AROUND ITS SOFTEST PART. BONES CRUNCH AND THE LIZARD'S VISCERA SPILL THROUGH HER FINGERS INTO HER CORE. STOWE FEELS A MINISCULE JOLT IN HER ABDOMEN AS ITS LIFE FORCE DISSIPATES.

DISGUSTED, SHE HURLS THE DEAD THING WITH ALL HER STRENGTH OUT OF THE WALL, FAR INTO EATER TERRITORY. SHE IMMEDIATELY REGRETS THE ACTION. SHE SHOULD NOT HAVE KILLED IT. SHE COULD HAVE TRAPPED IT, BROUGHT IT BACK, A GIFT FOR DARIUS. SO MUCH FOR CALM UNDER FIRE.

SUSPENDED IN A WEB OF LIGHT, SHE CENTERS HER ATTENTION ON HER WOUNDS, ERASING THE VISUAL EVIDENCE OF COMBAT FROM HER CRYSTALLINE FRAME. THE PAIN, THOUGH, IS DEEP AND NOT SO EASILY QUELLED. HOPING THEY WILL EFFECT A CURE, STOWE HAS ONE LAST WHIRL IN THE INVIGORATING PULSATIONS, THEN LAUNCHES HERSELF BACK TO WHERE KORDAN WAITS. SHE SOARS GLORIOUS, TRIUMPHANT, TEEMING WITH NEWFOUND POWER.

trail of the misbegotten

as long as their territories remained exclusive,
the clerics and the brothers kept an uneasy
alliance. but before saint walked into the
devastation, he foresaw that worship of the friend
would come to clash with worship of the masters.
—orin's history of the friend

Mabatan stands beside the middle of her boat, puts her hands on the gunnels and effortlessly lifts it over her head. Setting the middle thwart down on her shoulders, she begins walking down a rough trail, only her torso and legs visible. Roan and Lumpy follow, the grove and the sweet smell of cedar soon a fond memory.

Surrounded by a tall sea of briar, Roan is unpleasantly reminded of the Nethervines that once almost killed him.

"What happens if you touch one of these thorns?" he asks Mabatan.

"If you touch a thorn, you will get cut," comes the muffled reply from beneath her craft.

"That's it? No poison?" Approaching the plant, Lumpy

sniffs, "I guess the stink's enough of a defense."

"It is the smell of a difficult labor," counters Mabatan, offering no further explanation.

Picking up her pace, she moves adroitly, easily navigating the twisting trail despite the boat on her shoulders.

Something about the briar seems familiar to Roan. Examining it more closely, he realizes why. "These are cleansing plants I found out about in a book of my father's. I told Brother Asp about it and he organized a planting to reclaim contaminated farmland. In less than a year, the land was producing again."

"The Abominations tainted this soil much more deeply than that. My grandmother planted these briars when she was young." Mabatan's voice is tinged with a wistful sadness. "It will take ten more summers for this land to be whole again. Then, their job done, the plants will die."

"Not much of a reward for the service rendered," complains Lumpy.

"The reward is the work itself," says Mabatan.

The air is thick with the moldering heat of the noonday sun when they come to a narrow lake. Mabatan flips the boat off her shoulders and carefully sets it in the algae-blighted water.

Lumpy gags. "Talk about going from bad to worse. Are we really going to paddle in that?"

The lake's stench is so powerful, Roan's struggling not to retch.

"Be thankful for the smell—it means these waters are seldom

traveled." Mabatan takes out a steel flask and sprinkles some of its liquid onto strips of cloth. Handing them to Lumpy and Roan, she continues, "It is an infusion of coltsfoot, sage, and knapweed. Hold it over your mouth and nose when you breathe. It will filter the toxins. And if the water touches you, quickly use the cloth to wipe it off." Walking to an overgrown log, she moves a rock and reaches in. Withdrawing two paddles, she hands them to Lumpy and Roan. "This time you can paddle. If you know how," she smiles.

"We can manage," says Lumpy, as they step into the boat. "We've been in waters like this before."

Roan shifts uncomfortably. "In Fairview, the lake was used as a graveyard."

"Then you will not be surprised by what you see," Mabatan replies.

They draw their paddles through thick blooms of orange algae, careful not to splash. The oppressive atmosphere matches the bleak landscape. Though they make their approach to a bend in the narrow lake with anticipation, their hope of relief is instantly stifled.

"It smells even worse here, if that's possible," says Lumpy.

"And it's probably more dangerous," Roan adds, indicating the shore. Here the lake is barely a stone's throw across, and rust-colored rushes flourish to a height that could easily hide an ambush. Roan scans the area, absorbing every sound, but all he hears are the whir of dragonflies, leaves falling in the water, and mice scampering through the weeds. Their journey continues in a similarly uneventful manner until, arms aching, they see the disappearing sun mark the end of the day.

Noticing a crest of rocks obstructing their passage down the lake, Roan silently signals the others to raise their paddles. He points at suspicious shapes sprawled across the obstruction and extends his attention beyond the shore. But he senses no threat and as Mabatan slowly guides the boat closer, the forms become easily identifiable: the decaying bodies of two human beings.

Roan steps out of the boat and stares at a man and a woman, near in age to his own parents. Their sodden clothing is simple, their hands and feet dissolved by the toxic waters. He surveys the gray puffy skin, the gaping mouths, the slashed throats. He reaches out, gently lowering the lids on the sightless eyes, and begins the prayer of passing:

That the love you bestowed—

"Raiders?" Lumpy whispers beneath Roan's prayer.

Mabatan looks closely at the wounds on the victims' necks. "No," she says, "Raiders battle. They do not slash the throats of farmers with razor knives. This is the work of the City. The way of the ones with eyes that are not their own."

Lumpy shudders. "Clerics? But they never used to come into the Farlands."

"All is changing," Mabatan says. "I have seen them many times in the last two seasons." Suddenly she stops, sniffs the air. "We must leave here. They are close."

"Roan," urges Lumpy.

Ignoring them, Roan completes the blessing.

"Quickly!" Mabatan insists.

As the whine of an engine rises over the still water, Roan rolls the first body into the lake.

Lumpy grabs Roan's arm. "No time!"

Mabatan pulls her boat up onto the shore. The engine grows louder. They tear at the rushes, throwing them over the craft until it's indistinguishable from its surroundings.

Suddenly the motor cuts out. Lying low in the brown foliage, six eyes silently watch as a flat-bottomed boat drifts up to the remaining corpse. Its passengers are three gaunt men in blue robes. One stares through a scope that's mounted on a crossbow, scanning the river. The second, armed with a bladed spear, steps onto the shore, dangerously close to where they're hidden. The tallest one, grim-faced, with owlish eyes, moves from the boat and crouches near the body, closely inspecting the rocks. Did Roan leave some tell-tale sign that could be traced? The cleric shifts to focus on the body. His hand grazes the dead woman's leg, moves up her torn jacket, touches her arm. He stops, scrutinizing the woman's face. His finger rises, touching her eyelid where Roan had touched it moments before. He is so close that Roan can see the hone of the blade at his side, the tension in his neck, the bulge behind his ear.

With a sudden thrust of his arms, the cleric pushes the corpse off the rock. He watches it slowly dissolve in the acid water, then, seemingly satisfied, motions to his companions.

He pulls the boat through the rocky passage, climbs in, and the clerics motor off.

Mabatan emerges from the rushes, her face grim. "I have seldom seen another traveler on these waters. Now clerics in powered boats appear. We must abandon this route and go on foot." Without hesitation, Mabatan ensures her boat is well-hidden and sets off through the lush rust-colored rushes. Staying low, she follows the narrow lake, Lumpy and Roan close behind.

Roan cannot dislodge the ravaged corpses from his mind. So ruthlessly killed, by the soldiers of the City, men called clerics. What if they're looking for him? Could Stowe have seen him in the Dreamfield? Or perhaps that vulture spotted Roan and sent out an alert. Whether or not that's the case, anxiety presses him to exercise supreme caution.

Hands covered in small cuts from the sharp-edged leaves and soaked with sweat, at dusk they seek a brief respite from their arduous trek. Mabatan and Lumpy are about to settle into a small clearing, when they notice Roan shifting anxiously.

"Smell that?" he asks.

Lumpy and Mabatan silently join him as he makes his way through the foliage to the water. Dozens of bodies lie scattered over an embankment.

Dizzied by the sight, Roan starts to count them. One, two, three... eight, nine... thirteen, fourteen... twenty, twenty-five...

He counts every person, hoping to make some kind of sense of what he sees, make the deaths less anonymous, even though he knows there is no sense to be made. Counting does nothing; nothing can give a massacre meaning. Thirty-seven. Thirty-seven people lost their lives here.

Mabatan's face has gone pale. Lumpy's breath catches in his throat. For several minutes, no one speaks. Then Mabatan turns. Beyond the shore, at the crown of a knoll, stands a village. A village without movement, without sound, without light.

"Silenced," whispers Mabatan.

"Why?" asks Lumpy.

"That only the City knows."

"Somebody may still be alive."

Mabatan gives Lumpy a doubtful look. "They do not leave survivors."

"Someone may have had a chance to hide. Maybe children," says Roan, embracing Lumpy's hopefulness.

"The moon is nearly full," Mabatan informs them, exasperated. "We must leave before it rises and travel in the shadows."

Lumpy looks at her, eyes awash with grief. "We can't just leave the bodies."

Looking at Roan and Lumpy's determined faces, Mabatan sighs. "You are both right. We cannot leave without honoring these lives. I was wrong to think only of our safety. I thank you for reminding me of who we are."

The three share a somber look, the task they've agreed to take on weighing heavily on their hearts.

The swollen moon hovers over the village, and the three friends stand bathed in its unearthly glow. Exhausted from the sorrowful labor of consigning the dead to the lake, they join in speaking the prayer of passing:

That the love you bestowed might bear fruit
We stay behind.
That the spirit you shared be borne witness
We stay behind.
That your light burn bright in our hearts
We stay behind.
We stay behind and imagine your flight.

Picking up their packs, they move cautiously up the hill.

"They had no wall to protect them," says Lumpy.

"Maybe they figured they had nothing worth coming this far to take," Roan says, thinking of Longlight.

"They were wrong," Mabatan utters with a dour finality.

Careful to remain invisible and silent, they approach the cluster of buildings, seemingly untouched by any act of violence.

"Fine craftsmen lived here," Roan whispers. "Each stone was squared and fitted. Look, no mortar was used."

Coming to the first house, Lumpy runs his finger along the junction of two stones, admiringly. Roan looks inside to see breakfast dishes in the sink, beds unmade, a pot of beans soaking by the stove.

"It must have happened early morning," observes Mabatan.

"Why, though?" asks Lumpy, taking in a row of child-sized shoes by the door.

Roan shakes his head sadly. "Does there have to be a reason?"

It's not until they've explored every home and come at last to the community building that Lumpy finds his answer.

Unlike the residences, which were left unscathed, the interior of this building was savagely ransacked. Benches, chairs, and tables are strewn everywhere, the tapestries on the walls torn and thrown into the dust. Moonlight spilling through the windows reveals the inky stains of blood sprayed everywhere.

Roan breathes deep, trying to slow his heart. "This is where they were all executed."

"And this must be why," says Lumpy, straddling a hole that floorboards had once clearly covered. A candle and a firestone are secured under one edge. He hits the rock on the sharp bit of metal hanging at its side, and lights the candle with the spark.

A ladder leads them to a large, once hidden room. Even in the flickering candlelight, the room's purpose is apparent. There are cribs for babies, a feeding table, a play area filled with toys for small children. Mabatan runs a hand over the wooden trains, rag dolls, dress-up clothes, and building stones.

"How many kids do you think they had in here?" wonders Lumpy.

"At least six. All ages," she states, without looking up.

Lumpy picks up a counting stick, and moves the beads up and down, an almost absent expression on his face. "So... the clerics came for the children. They took them and killed the adults as a warning. And that's why they left the bodies exposed, as a message to anybody who passes. Give up the few or we take all."

Something on the wall catches Roan's eye. Taking the light from Lumpy, he moves closer. When he makes out what it is he's seeing, he reels, nearly dropping the candle.

It's a picture of a girl. Her clothing is extravagant, regal, her smile angelic, and benevolence seems to radiate from her. Her hand is slightly lifted, as if she's about to gently stroke the head of the viewer. At the bottom of the picture are two words: OUR STOWE.

Roan gapes at it, uncomprehending. He moves closer, taking in her eyes, her mouth. He leans his head on the wall, close to his sister's image. "She's growing up."

Lumpy says nothing until Roan has stepped back again. He tries to sound out the words, something Roan's been teaching him. "Our... St... Sto... Stowe," Lumpy reads. "Our Stowe. Like she belongs to everyone."

Mabatan lays her hand over the image and closes her eyes. "This picture was left by the clerics."

Roan's stomach burns. "It's like saying she's responsible for this."

"Like she is the City." Lumpy adds in grim agreement.

Mabatan shrugs. "She might not know anything about what's happening."

"I wish I could believe that." The sound of motors echoes across the water, silencing their conversation. Roan reaches out to the wall, touches Stowe's picture, and scrambles up the ladder after the others.

Taking no chances, they crawl to the door. Peeking around it, they can make out two boats in the distance, silhouetted in the moonlight. "We run for it?" asks Lumpy.

"Past the buildings, to the other side of the fields," whispers Mabatan, and disappears into the shadows just as an arrow meant for her thuds into the stone beside them and blasts apart.

"He must have night glasses," Roan says, pulling Lumpy behind the doorway. "Saint had some, a gift from the City. They won't need much light to find their target."

Another arrow soars through the doorway, smashing into a pillar behind Lumpy, and sharing a quick look, he and Roan charge off.

The roar of the engines cuts out. The clerics are on land. Doubled over, Roan and Lumpy run through furrows of cornfields too young to provide much cover. With arrows whistling past them and the shouts of their pursuers close behind, they weave across the rows of plants in hopes of throwing their pursuers off course.

Lumpy falls. Hard. "I'm alright, keep going!" he shouts as Roan rushes to him.

"Don't be stupid, your foot's caught in a hole!" Roan grabs Lumpy's leg, heaves, then heaves again.

"And I used to think gophers were cute," Lumpy winces as his mud-covered foot finally dislodges.

"Can you run on it?"

An arrow thuds into the ground between them.

"Absolutely," says Lumpy, and he's off in a flash.

The clerics are already crashing through the corn when Lumpy and Roan spot Mabatan crouched by a large tree stump, signaling them to hurry. As she reaches between the thick tree roots, they hear something click. The ground on the far side of the stump opens, just wide enough for a person to fit through.

"Lie flat, your packs between your legs. The tunnel will be tight and steep."

Lumpy puts his legs in, sets his pack, and slides out of sight. Roan does the same. Weaving and looping through the ground, the tunnel is at times so narrow it scratches his nose.

Suddenly, after a second of free fall, he thuds heavily into a roughly hewn room to find Lumpy already struggling to his feet. The ceiling is barely high enough for them to stand, the walls covered in a series of holes much the same as the one they used to enter. A gas flame flickers, providing an eerie bluish light. A reassuring thump behind them means Mabatan's made it in safely.

"Pretty handy escape hatch. Did you build it?" Lumpy asks her.

"No," she replies, her voice flat. Roan notices that her eyes are darting from hole to hole. Within seconds, figures slide out into the blue light. Waxen skin, smooth earless heads. Their pink eyes narrow and they slowly rise, moving closer, baring their fanged teeth. Blood Drinkers.

the trailblazer

BLESSED BE THE TEN,
PYRAMID OF LIGHT
BLESSED BE THE SEER
HIS GUIDANCE, OUR SALVATION
BLESSED BE OUR STOWE
WHO BREATHES NEW LIFE INTO OUR HEARTS
——LITURGY OF THE CONURBATION

"STOWE... STOWE... CAN YOU HEAR ME?" Stowe's eyes
open blearily to see Darius peering down at her. His
smile tests skin already stretched past its limit so that his lip
curls up, exposing his small incisors. Where is she? How long
has she been unconscious?

"I can hear you, Seer," says Stowe softly. "I almost brought
you back a present." The sadness in her voice is genuine. Best
to tell the truth; who knows what he might have discovered.

Darius is pleased. "A present?"

"One of the Eaters. But the thing irritated me so much, I
killed it. I am sorry."

Darius's milky eyes barely conceal their sparkle; excitement trembles beneath the steady calm of his voice. "You killed it? Are you sure?"

Ah, he didn't think she could do it. Make it seem easy. "I crushed it in my hand. It was dead."

He ponders each sentence, savoring it, turning each over in his mind.

"Have I done something wrong?"

"On the contrary. Killing an ether form with your bare hands, this is good news indeed."

Could it be no one's accomplished this before? Stowe knows the Dreamfield itself can consume lives, and so can the Constructions the Masters have made within it. But to kill in hand-to-hand combat appears to be something new. It must have been the energy from the Wall, the light coursing through her, that amplified her strength. "What about the corporeal body?" she wonders aloud. "Is it dead too?"

Darius laughs. "They are part of the same whole, my Stowe. If one dies, the other passes also or, at least, ceases to function in any meaningful way."

"It was a lizard, the one I killed."

Darius, usually so restrained, gasps with delight. "Ferrell! Finally we are rid of him."

"How old was he? What did he do?" Stowe hungers for details about him, wanting proof he was the enemy she thought he was, to justify, perhaps even magnify, her triumph.

"He would have been a little older than Willum. A tactician," Darius purrs. "One of the designers of their Wall."

"You've met him?"

"My Stowe, I have never set eyes upon him. What I know is based on our intelligence. And this I can say with authority: Ferrell was a great threat, a scheming, word-twisting, treacherous opponent, and his loss to the Eaters will immeasurably weaken their cause. You have made us proud. Now you must tell me of your experience in its entirety. I want to hear every minute detail."

Stowe dutifully describes the Wall, careful to leave out her absorption of the energy. She tells of the cloud that almost trapped her and how her attackers rose like demons from the sea.

As she finishes, she realizes she's been unconsciously stroking her abdomen. It tingles where the lizard clawed into her. Lingering effects from the bite? Or maybe it's not the wound at all, but an aftershock where the light penetrated her form more deeply and intensely.

"Are you alright, my darling?" asks Darius. He's being more doting than usual and she's no longer naive enough to think that these attentions are benign.

"Yes, fine, thank you," she says, hoping to appear stoic. He must not find out what's happened; it's her trump card. No one else is capable of entering the Wall and coming out unscathed. Only *she* has real knowledge of what it offers, and what she knows is precious little. She needs to know more. She needs to go back. "Father, I felt strong, so strong. You have taught me well. But now, I am so tired."

"Yes, of course, rest, my Stowe, rest. Then we will celebrate you, my dearest. You most certainly deserve it." He strokes her hair, blessing her with a look of... pride? Triumph? Her killing of the Eater pleased him. Is this how he plans to use her? She manages a slight look of bliss before she closes her eyes. The power of the Wall must be hers. It will be. Her wellspring. Her treasure trove. Their demise.

The Grand Epulary is reserved for the Masters' celebrations, a stark, imposing room with high vaulted ceilings and massive skylights. Its austere design belies the wealth assembled here. When Stowe enters, the applause is deafening. Every man and woman is standing, no mean feat, for most are ancient, their decrepitude barely kept at bay. She scans their faces. Their transplanted eyes are riveted on her. They are all here, the forty-one Masters of the City. How delightful. All that newly replenished blood pumping through artificial veins— she can see it throb beneath the skin grafts that strain their corpse-like smiles.

She bows and raises her hand magisterially. "Thank you, esteemed ones. Your appreciation fills my heart with joy." Stowe then puts her hand to her heart, pausing for effect. All of them in one room. Does she have the power to burst all their skulls with one scream? Perhaps, but first she must be certain. She will preserve this thought as a future pleasure to savor. It could be amusing, imagining all the varied ways in which she might obliterate them.

"You are my elders." She pitches her voice perfectly: respectful, yes, but with the vibrant power of her youth pulsing beneath each word. "And I thank you for your kindness. Most of all, I must thank the Keeper of the City, Archbishop of the Conurbation, The Great Seer, my godfather, Darius. It is to him we owe all our good fortune."

More applause. They will always applaud, long and loud, for Darius. Especially when his eye is upon them. Bowing her head, she sits demurely between Darius and Kordan. Darius squeezes her hand. "You owe nothing to anyone, my sweet," he whispers under the applause. "You were born to be where you stand today. I only provide the proper environment for your talents to blossom."

Stowe strokes his hand as the first course is set before her, an asparagus and endive salad. Her favorite. Mesmerized by the variance in the greens, her head begins to throb. The plate begins to waver as if she were seeing with two pairs of eyes. She braces herself against the table.

"Is everything all right, Our Stowe?" asks Kordan, an arch coldness in his voice. He's jealous of her triumph. His place by Darius's side hangs by a thread. And that thread is her willingness to have him there.

"The kitchen must not have been aware of my allergies. I cannot eat this," she smiles sweetly at Kordan, the lie like sugar on the tip of her tongue. "Could you return it, honored teacher, and ask that they prepare something else?"

She's pleased to see her demand has made Kordan blanch. Yes. He must accept his new place in her scheme of things.

"Apologies, Our Stowe. Someone will be punished for the oversight," he hisses, and sweeps away.

She can feel Willum's eyes burning into her. He's leaning against a pillar, a drink in one hand. His face seems relaxed but his eyes never leave her, a sure sign of irritation. She wishes she could ignore him. The reason for his displeasure is transparent. Why must she always leap to strike at Kordan, like a spoiled child? And why will the throbbing in her head not stop? It's like a screw twisting into her brain. She squeezes her temples with her fingertips, pushes hard, trying to stop the ache. Her hands go clammy, the back of her neck flares, her legs tremble.

"Here. Drink this," Willum whispers and places a glass of juice in her hand.

The liquid is lusciously sweet and cool. She gulps greedily, her body absorbing it as the desert absorbs rain. What is the flavor? Delicious yet unfamiliar.

"What's this?" she asks as he replaces her empty glass with another. Water. Only water. But no less satisfying.

"All of it," Willum coaxes.

There. Relief. Was that it? She'd been dehydrated. Was that all? Ha!

How worried Willum looks. It pleases her, this look. But soon he turns away. He is reading the crowd, always the teacher. Of course, she should be doing it as well. They are all hungry, these Masters. So hungry for whatever it is they believe she will deliver. Hungry for what Darius has planned. How much do they know? What a surprise they are in for.

"That was lovely," murmurs Stowe. "Thank you, my Primary, for your kind attentions." Then, with her most beguiling smile, she turns back to Darius.

Though the evening was to be a celebration in her honor, it had proved, rather, to be a test of her perseverance. Exhausted from the unrelenting tedium of it, her face aching from hours of false smiles and feigned sentiment, all Stowe wants to do is sleep.

Instead she's lain here for who knows how long, twisting under the covers, memories racing. Gwyneth, her servant, dutifully brought the relaxation tea she always drinks before bed, but for the first time it's had no effect. These memories are a plague.

Mama's hands pulling a sweater over her head. You have to go! Roan will keep you safe. Be brave, little pumpkin!

Stowe clutching her doll, the one with the shawl she dyed herself. Show me your brave smile, says Mama, covering her face in kisses. Kisses and tears. Why is she crying? Stowe doesn't want to let go, but Daddy lifts her through the open window.

Hide in the blue brush! Run, run!

Roan gripping her hand, pulling her away. Mama! Stowe screams.

Huge monster men on horses, throwing fire. Everything burning.

They run, run, run past the wall. They're on the icy whip-grass, the blue brush isn't far.

She feels a hand go around her, lifting her. It's hard, hard and cold. She looks into the monster's face. A red skull! She grips Roan's hand as hard as she can but the man kicks him. Roan! She reaches, reaches for him, almost touch-ing, but the red skull's club smashes him and Roan falls. Her doll drops and she screams and screams and screams.

"Our Stowe, you were shouting."

Stowe, sweating into the sheets, sees the ever calm Gwyneth standing by her bed. The servant's inner peace is gained from the alpha enabler buried in her neck.

"Was I? Every time I shut my eyes I see things, Gwyneth, horrible things. But you wouldn't know about that, would you? You aren't capable of visions, nightmares. You have no need of dreams."

"I remember that they were unpleasant. We thank Our Stowe daily for taking on this unfortunate burden. Would you like another night draft? Perhaps it will ease your sleep."

"No, they're useless tonight. Bring me a glass of wine."

"I have not been instructed to offer you—"

"Gwyneth, I have made a request."

"Yes, Mistress."

"Have you been instructed to obey my requests?"

"Yes, Mistress."

"Then get me a glass of wine. Now."

As the servant scurries away, Stowe leans against her head-board, but the moment she rests her heavy eyes, it begins again.

She kicks and yells and bites. Screams "Mama!" over and over until she hears her. With a hundred other voices. Humming. Like a cat purrs. The red-skulled rider spurs the horse and it gallops away. Stowe's insides bounce, her throat goes sore from screaming, her eyes reach for anything familiar, but rocked and jostled, it's all a blur. Then the horse stops abruptly. She watches the steam rise off its neck and flanks, feels the chill on her feet, the tension in the man's arm.

"Just one?" says a voice.

"The search continues," says Red Skull, shifting Stowe into the arms of blue-robed men.

"Have you ever tasted ice cream, little girl?" says one. His voice sounds kind but his face is leaden. "It is the most delicious thing in the world."

"Our Stowe. Lady."

Stowe looks up to see her faithful servant hovering, her face frowning with concern. But her eyes are devoid of light, of solace of any kind.

"Yes, Gwyneth?"

"You were smiling, Our Stowe. Are you sure you want this?"

"Yes, thank you." She remembers how she used to throw things at the women they sent to care for her. Scream at them. Hurt them if she could. Until she realized that they would each be replaced by another, exactly the same. What had she been hoping for?

Gwyneth quickly pours her a glass. Stowe swallows it all despite the bite of fermented grapes. Anything to stop these infernal memories.

"Another," she calls out. Gwyneth flinches. But Stowe doesn't care. Why shouldn't the blazing mistress of the Dreamfield, the Breaker of the Wall, indulge in this petty drug when she has tasted much stronger? The servant dutifully pours her a second glass. But as Stowe brings it to her lips, the glass slips from her hand, and splatters onto the floor. The lights dim darker and darker until all fades to black.

IN THE LAIR OF THE BLOOD DRINKERS

THEY SLEEP IN THE EARTH LIKE THE WALKING DEAD,
THEIR LANGUAGE CLICKS LIKE THE INSECTS THAT
SHARE THEIR BEDS. GIVE THEM NO QUARTER FOR
THEY ARE NOT HUMAN.

—THE WAR CHRONICLES

ROAN, HIS BACK AGAINST the earthen wall, slowly reaches for his hook-sword. The Blood Drinkers inch toward him, their small silver knives glittering in the blue light. He's been forced to fight them before, knows his blade will take its toll.

One of the ugliest, his arms and chest patterned with swirls of scars, leaps at Roan, fangs bared, tongue flitting over his lips, knife flashing from hand to hand. Roan breaks the hook-sword from its binding, whips it forward. The scarred creature steps back and circles as Roan lifts his weapon, ready to strike. Three drinkers slink alongside the first, blades jutting toward Roan. He swings, knocking the knife out of one hand, kicking another. He whirls, but before he can strike again, a hand grips his wrist like a vice. Mabatan.

Lumpy, confused, gapes at her. "What are you doing?"

Roan, respecting Mabatan's will, lowers his sword. Letting go of him, she steps up to the first Blood Drinker. Soft gurglings rise from deep in her throat. The scarred one stares at her with pink, unblinking eyes, then hisses and clicks his tongue. Mabatan carefully takes off her woven rucksack and reaches in, bringing out a small red bag. She lowers her head and offers it to the Blood Drinker, who bows as he accepts it. Opening it, he carefully shakes several dried yellow flowers into his palm. He sniffs, then signals to a young female with bright red eyes. Head bowed, she cups her hands with great reverence. He lets Mabatan's flowers tumble into them. Two sharp inhalations and the value of the contents is determined. With a quick nod, she slips the fragile petals back into the bag, then leaves through one of the holes.

Roan listens to the hissing and tongue clicks Mabatan exchanges with the scarred one, trying to discern their meaning. Without unlocking her eyes from the Drinker's, Mabatan whispers, "This is Xxisos. He invites us to the Khonta."

"Is that a good thing or a bad thing?" asks Lumpy.

"Good. They had need of the flowers," Mabatan replies.

Lumpy gives Roan a nervous look as the other Blood Drinkers slink back into the holes and disappear. Xxisos nods for them to follow, handing each a dense felted mat.

Mabatan takes hers and lays it at the edge of the hole. Then, lying on top of it, she pushes herself forward, disappearing in the darkness.

"Do you mind if I go next?" asks Lumpy with a cautious look at Xxisos, who is watching them, tapping his fangs with his fingertips. "After all, you're the one with the hook-sword."

Roan smiles uneasily and nods. Lumpy lays out the felt, and with one last look of reassurance from Roan, slides away.

Roan is about to get on his mat when Xxisos makes a terrible hiss and leaps at him. Roan pivots, ready for anything. The Blood Drinker reaches past him, and with a chastizing click of the tongue, flips over the felt, placing the slippery side down. With a nod of thanks, Roan sets off. His first push only takes him a short way down the narrow tunnel, but he soon discovers ridges that can be used as finger grips to thrust himself forward. Since the smooth material glides unimpeded on the polished clay surface, as long as Roan remembers to keep his feet slightly lifted, he travels at a high speed through the twisting tunnel.

With no way to judge how far he's gone but the ache in his arms, Roan's relieved when he sees a faint light ahead. A few more pulls hurtle him into a large dugout room, much like the first but at least twice the size. As his eyes adjust to the light, he sees a group of Blood Drinkers, thirty or forty, seated in a large circle. Lumpy and Mabatan are surrounded by five children, each no more than two or three years old. They are albinos, like the adult Blood Drinkers, and though their teeth have been filed, they still have ears.

As Lumpy motions for Roan to join them, an ancient Blood

Drinker rises. Plainly one of the eldest, his face is deeply creased and raised scars pattern the entire surface of his chest and arms. He hisses and the others hiss in response, percussive and unified, like a perverse parody of song. Listening carefully, Roan can detect small variances in the rise and fall of the tones, small pauses and clicks. It occurs to him that a language like this might carry well in those long tunnels, and be much easier to understand than words.

The speaker, his eyes white and unmoving, lifts a battered plastic bottle that's filled with blood. Roan remembers seeing some Blood Drinkers collect animals' blood in bottles like that. They chased them down on horses and used weighted ropes to capture the frantic beasts. He'll never forget the groans of the terrified animals when ghouls like these sank their fangs in and drank the blood directly from their throats. And now blood, no doubt from a similar hunt, is lifted to the elder's lips. He takes a long drink and passes it to the creature beside him, who also drinks and passes it on.

Roan watches with growing discomfort as the bottle comes closer. When it's finally given to him, Roan smiles politely and tries to discreetly pass it on to Mabatan. But she will not accept it. "Drink," she says. "They honor us."

"I've seen what they do to those animals," Roan whispers.

"This is not animal blood."

Roan stares at her. "It's human?"

She nods.

Roan shudders. "I can't."

"You must. It will be a deep insult not to partake. We will not leave here alive."

Three years ago Roan had never tasted meat, had never raised his hand against another human being. He'd found the body of a man who'd been ravaged by these vampires. And now he is expected to swallow human blood. The blood of who knows what victim.

All eyes are on Roan, mouths gaping, fangs red.

"There is no evil in this." Mabatan's tone is insistent—she is not lying, he would hear it.

"I will if you will," Lumpy urgently whispers.

Xxisos hisses menacingly.

Roan breathes deeply and closes his eyes. Raising the bottle to his lips, he drinks. The blood is warm, salty. He chokes it down, stomach spasming, and his breaths come fast and deep. Dizzy with revulsion, he hands the jug to Mabatan. Barely able to watch, he rocks to quell his sickness as she and Lumpy drink in turn.

When everyone has swallowed from the bottle, the elder continues to speak. He hums, hisses, and clicks, every utterance nuanced and filled with emotion. The Blood Drinkers, engrossed, sway in response. Roan and Lumpy share a queasy glance, completely unnerved by the proceedings.

Pulling them to either side of her, Mabatan draws Roan and Lumpy in close and whispers, "He tells the origin tale of their people, the Hhroxhi." Closing her eyes in concentration, she translates: "Once our ancestors lived in the sun. Their bodies were whole. They chewed their food like any man. They lived in peace with all. But then the Wars began. Our ancestors would not fight, would not take sides. Still they were attacked. Their villages burned. Their people killed. They left their ancestral lands and sought a land far from the people of war. But everywhere they turned there was fighting. Then came the explosion and with it the Brightness."

Roan watches the listeners reenact the trauma. They all writhe, hiss, clack their tongues, and hold their eyes. The elder, trembling with emotion, runs his fingers over the swirling scars on his chest until all grows quiet again. When he resumes the history, Mabatan continues: "Our ancestors lost their hair. Their skin turned white. Many were blinded. This made them easy prey for the men of war, so they burrowed. The earth welcomed them. She sheltered them. Protected their eyes and skin."

The ecstatic audience warbles, their throats vibrating, their hands slapping the floor. Their homage to the planet for having saved them.

"No longer would they be cursed by the disease that plagued the upper world. This so-called 'humanity.'"

They snarl and shriek, their teeth bared. Lumpy looks nervously at Roan. Would they turn on the three humans sitting here? Mabatan steadies them both with a reassuring hand as the elder reaches the climax of the tale.

"Our ancestors rejected the world of men. They removed

themselves. They transformed themselves. They shed their 'humanity.' They became something better. Us. We are Hhroxhi."

"Hhroxhi, Hhroxhi, Hhroxhi... " the crowd chants, and the fever builds. Even Mabatan joins in. How can she? It's a testament to hatred, a cry against humanity.

"Hhroxhi, Hhroxhi, Hhroxhi!"

The red-eyed girl bows and offers the bag of dried flowers to the elder. He takes a few, crushes them in his palm and lets out a low hum. The Blood Drinkers add their voices, making the entire chamber vibrate with sound. As the elder raises his hands, the humming grows louder. The first child is brought to him. Though sightless, he quickly finds the child's ears and rubs them with the crushed flowers.

It happens so quickly, Roan almost misses it. One of those small, shining blades appears in the old one's hand, and with two quick flicks, the child's ears are gone.

"No!" Lumpy cries, jumping to his feet.

Mabatan grabs Lumpy's wrist and yanks him down hard. Luckily, the Hhroxhi are in such a frenzy, no one's noticed Lumpy's transgression.

"We can't let them!" Lumpy whispers furiously. Mabatan forcibly turns his head so he must watch the proceedings. More flower powder is rubbed in the child's wound, immediately staunching the flow of blood. The child smiles, his little fangs glinting in the gas light. Two of the Blood Drinkers, evidently his parents, proudly hug him. The child beams.

Roan and Lumpy watch in dismay as the other children's ears are sliced off. All the severed ears are laid in an oval pattern on the floor. Then, after more blood is drunk, they're all on their feet. In a frenzy, they stomp and shriek, grinding the ears into the dirt with their heels. Roan watches, filled with horror as these vampires, these Hhroxhi, celebrate the transformation of their children from members of the human race into something foreign and terrifying.

Roan's first to arrive at their sleeping chamber, but Lumpy and Mabatan slide in quickly behind. In the gas light, they silently lay out their bedrolls. Roan sits, back against the wall. Unable to keep the resentment from his voice, he confronts Mabatan. "Why are we here?"

"We need their help."

Roan shakes his head skeptically. "Why would they give it?"

"They do not wish us harm."

"Who did they harm to get the blood we were drinking?"

"The blood was their own. Everyone gives a little."

"They don't drink their own blood for their meals, do they?" Lumpy asks.

"No. But they do not kill; they borrow from animals."

"I've seen them kill. I've seen their victims," Roan insists. "I was there when an army of them attacked Fairview."

"Do you know why they attacked?"

Roan doesn't know. The question never even entered his mind. "They just came at us out of the blue and they paid the price. Every single one of them was wiped out once the Raiders showed up."

But Roan knows Raiders weren't the only ones who killed Blood Drinkers that day. He himself slew more than a few. Mabatan's disapproval is all too clear. Roan's indignation mounts at what he feels is an undeserved reproof. He had no choice, had he? Hundreds of raging Blood Drinkers were storming the poorly defended walls of Fairview, inside of which were the children. He had to protect them. How many did he actually wound or kill that day? No one counts in the heat of battle. There were many, though, of that he is sure.

"I like their language," Lumpy says, trying to change the subject. "There's a rhythm to the sounds they make. By the end of the night, I was almost beginning to understand what they were saying."

"They're dangerous," Roan mutters. Monsters. She's seen what they can do.

They sit quietly for a long time, then without a word, they prepare to bed down.

After a fitful sleep, Roan reaches into his pack, takes out some jerky, and chews it in the darkness. Lumpy snores softly as Mabatan shuffles in her blanket, sits up, then stretches. She lights the gas lamp with a spark, reaches into her pack, and hands Roan a charred egg.

"I want to leave here now," says Roan.

"One more day," she replies. "When the Hhroxhi have found those we're looking for, they will tell us. They may not have earlobes, but they hear a great deal."

Lumpy stirs with a great yawn. "They must have tunnels everywhere."

"Mostly only through soil," Mabatan says, "though they use the many caves of the mountains to shelter their horses. And where the tunnels must cross water, they imitate the old natural beaver dams." Putting her finger to her lips, she gestures for silence, as a low, clicking hiss echoes in their tiny room. "Hhroxhi knocking."

Lumpy hisses back and Xxisos's head appears out of the tunnel, giving Lumpy a curious look.

"I said 'come in,' didn't I?" murmurs Lumpy out of the corner of his mouth.

"You told him he smelled good," Mabatan gleefully informs him.

"Is he smiling?"

"No," she says with a teasing grin, then rises to greet Xxisos as he slides into the room.

Roan and Lumpy stand at a respectful distance while Xxisos and Mabatan converse. Glancing back, she announces, "I am to search with him."

"We'll come too," says Roan.

"You have not been invited. We need help to get into the City. Better to seek this help quietly and quickly. You must stay here. You know the wisdom in this."

"Yeh," Roan sighs in reluctant agreement.

"Xxisos invites you to explore their domain. It is a rare offer, Roan. We cannot do this without him. You must keep in mind that nearly all that is told of these people is false. Some say they burn their ear stumps or wait until they are thirteen to drink blood." She eyes Roan. "Some even think they eat people. This is your chance to find out the truth. Mhyzah will be your guide."

With a nod to Mabatan, Xxisos disappears in the tunnel. After one last probing look at Roan, Mabatan quickly follows.

"Great," sighs Roan.

Out of the other tunnel hole, a face appears. It's the red-eyed girl from the night before, the one with the flowers.

"Mhyzah?" asks Lumpy.

Mhyzah hisses, extending her palm in greeting. Eager to try out a reply, Lumpy hisses back. As Mhyzah's eyes flare, then narrow, Lumpy turns nervously to Roan.

"I just said hi... I think."

"Maybe you shouldn't press your luck," says Roan, unable to stifle a grin.

"I want to learn. She seems like the understanding type, doesn't she?" Lumpy asks hopefully.

"Go on, explore. I'll stay here."

"What are you going to do?"

"Nothing."

Lumpy squints at Roan, suspicious.

"I promise. I just need time to think."

"Don't go anywhere I can't go. You know what I mean."

"I promise. No Dreamfield."

"Aren't you the least bit curious about this place? Come on."

"No," Roan insists.

With a shrug, Lumpy slides off with Mhyzah.

As soon as Roan is sure they are gone, he finds himself a comfortable spot against the wall. Since they seem to be under Xxisos's protection, for the moment at least, Roan feels certain he will not be disturbed.

What Roan plans to do is not something he's shared with Lumpy—or anyone, for that matter. He's only left his body a few times. He's been reticent to do it the last year—like traveling in the Dreamfield, it might somehow alert the Turned to his presence. But after all that's happened, it seems irrelevant now. Mabatan may trust these people, but he still has his doubts. The face of the dead man he found in the Devastation still haunts him. A man whose throat was punctured by fangs. If there are secrets the Hhroxhi are keeping, a danger unknown to Mabatan, Roan will find out.

He reaches into his pocket and the white cricket crawls onto his finger. As Roan sets it gently on his knee, it begins to sing and Roan breathes in the rhythm. Nothing happens for the first thirty breaths, but then a spark flashes. Roan does not reach for it with his mind, just lets it float, continuing his breathing. The spark begins to multiply until Roan is enclosed in light. He focuses on a point at the top of his head and inhales the glow. The light fills him, flows down his bones and out again—only this time, he goes along for the ride.

From above, he looks at himself, sitting on the bedroll, the cricket still singing on his knee. How peaceful he looks. How free of anxiety. If only he really felt that way.

Roan soars through the tunnel Lumpy left by. Hhroxhi move quickly through the winding pathways, but within moments Roan sails past them.

He is quick to recognize the intricacy of their architecture. Every tunnel leads to a chamber, and each chamber offers multiple exits that lead to more chambers. An infinite web of channels just beneath the surface of the earth. How extensive are they? Roan wonders. What a tool they would be in the right hands.

Roan is stopped by the sight of a family of four. The boy and girl are his and Stowe's age, their parents not much different than his might be if they were still alive. The mother is gently filing the girl's teeth, the father twining rope with his son. Somehow, this is not what he expected to see. But fondness for their children doesn't necessarily make these creatures any less dangerous.

Roan goes on, slipping through the tunnels, visiting chamber after chamber. Every type of worker is housed here. Weavers, drillmakers, cleaners, cobblers, potters, blacksmiths, miners, toymakers. There's a large hospice where the old and dying are cared for, a hospital where a woman is giving birth. He watches the infant emerge, covered in blood. As the midwife cleans it off, Roan can see the infant is precisely the same as any newborn. And the fanged, earless mother who holds it in her arms, nuzzling and cooing, is as loving and nurturing as any mother he's ever seen.

In this ether form, Roan's lost all sense of time. He wonders where Lumpy might be. He pictures Lumpy's face and is instantly in a room where Lumpy and Mhyzah are sitting cross-legged, objects littered around them. She holds up a bowl, softly clicks her tongue, and coarsely hisses. Lumpy repeats with a similar click and hiss. She smiles and Lumpy smiles back. She passes him the bowl.

Lumpy was alone for so long he cannot resist the company of people. There are so few who do not fear him. Do these Blood Drinkers see him as not quite human as well?

The loss of family and friends is a tragedy he and Lumpy share, but Roan's been betrayed too often since to welcome anyone with open arms. He trusted Saint once. There was a time he trusted Alandra completely. Now he's learned to trust only Lumpy and solitude.

Suddenly feeling claustrophobic, Roan leaves his friend to his language lesson and seeks the open air. He finds himself hovering high over fields of tall red-brown grass. Dust billows on a hard dirt road. At its center are several dozen wild-looking men on galloping horses. Fandor.

And riding point, his cloak of feathers swirling behind, is Raven.

But Raven's a Brother. Why is he with one of their most hated enemies? Much has changed, Mabatan said, and Raven always was treacherous. Even Saint didn't trust him. But to turn against the Brothers? Or maybe they've turned against him? Could it be possible that they disbanded after Saint's death?

Desperate to find out, Roan flies beside them, hoping to catch snippets of conversation. But invisible strings pull on him, the separation between his body and spirit straining. He fights against it, trying to stay close to Raven, but it's no use. He's reached his limit.

Frustrated, Roan envisions himself back in his body, and upon contact, is, as always, startled by the heaviness of his flesh. Opening his eyes, he's welcomed back into the world by a glowering Lumpy.

"What were you doing?" he demands. "You didn't look like you were asleep."

"Traveling."

"You promised not to."

"Not the Dreamfield. I can leave my body, see things. But I can't go very far. At least, not yet."

"Not another new trick," Lumpy moans.

"Not new, but I haven't done it in a while." Roan rises unsteadily, his limbs numb.

"Have you been in that position since I left?"

Roan stamps his feet and waves his arms to get his blood circulating. "I'm not sure how time works when I do it. It just felt like a few minutes."

Lumpy laughs. "No wonder you're stiff, I've been gone all day. See anything interesting on your travels?"

"Raven. With the Fandor. I don't understand what he was doing there. They were battle-ready."

"How far away?"

Roan shakes his head. "Don't know." Then a smile curls on his lips. "And I saw you with Mhyzah."

But instead of the surprise or embarrassment Roan expected, Lumpy looks gloomy.

"Sorry. Did something go wrong?"

"No, we got along really well. She was teaching me their language, it's fascinating. By the end of the day, we were able to communicate a bit."

"So why the long face?"

"Nothing, really."

Roan had thought meeting Mhyzah might have triggered memories of Lelbit, but it's not sorrow Roan hears in Lumpy's voice.

"What is it? I want to know."

Lumpy raises his head and looks at Roan with steady eyes. He breathes deeply, then speaks. "It's about that raid by the Blood Drinkers on Fairview."

"I threw a lot of them off the wall that day. We were fighting for our lives."

"So were they," says Lumpy. "Governor Brack was using Fairview's lake water to flush them out. The men were out on the surface when it happened. Somehow Brack discovered the entry to one of their tunnels, then pumped thousands of gallons of lake water into the hole. Hundreds of Hhroxhi were killed, mostly women and children. When the men returned home and discovered what happened, they went berserk. And did something they never do."

Roan is staggered. Having experienced Brack's cruelty first-hand, he knows the Governor is all too capable of mass murder. Everything Roan thought he knew about that battle is apparently wrong, and though he doesn't doubt the truth of what Lumpy's said, he finds himself going back to that day, trying to align his experience with this new information. "That's why the Blood Drinkers were so unprepared. Just those ladders. And why they seemed oblivious to pain."

"Mhyzah's mother was one of those killed. She couldn't stop her father before he ran off to battle. He was one of the first up the ladders."

"I remember," says Roan, softly.

"Very few of the Blood Drinkers escaped the Raiders. Those they caught after the battle were thrown dead or alive into the lake. But one of the few young warriors who did make it back told Mhyzah that a human who dressed differently than the others had pushed over that first ladder. Mhyzah's father's neck was broken in the fall."

A grave stillness settles behind Roan's eyes. "It was me. I killed Mhyzah's father."

the craving

there are claws on the handles of darius's door
none have dared ask the master
whatever are they for
but this a wise man once whispered in my ear
"you need not waste your fear on them,
they're not what they appear."

—Lore of the storytellers

STOWE STIRS FROM THE THICK COCOON of sleep, the dreams still sticking. All night long, she's had to endure a barrage of every single thing that's happened to her since she was old enough to remember, unmercifully intertwined with screaming, and burning, and terror. Why now? It's as if something has been opened that she is powerless to close.

She does not move, does not lift her heavy lids. What if someone finds out? What if she's been shouting in her sleep? She listens. Someone's beside the bed. Gwyneth? No, not the shallow breaths of Gwyneth's tiny frame—these are steady and measured. Gwyneth has told someone about her night screams. Why? Normally she'd be too afraid, as it would mean having to admit to giving Stowe the wine, and facing the ensuing punishment. Whatever Stowe was doing in her sleep, it was enough to seriously frighten Gwyneth. Who has she told, that's the question.

Stowe opens her eye a crack, just enough to recognize Willum's silhouette. Good. Gwyneth has some sense left in her adjusted brain. With any luck, Willum will understand. Willum will protect her. Lying still, Stowe ponders the yellow canopy above her bed. The slip of light piercing the heavy curtain tells her it's midday.

"Have you been sitting there long?" asks Stowe.

"As you know, time is relative. But for me, no, not very long at all."

Stowe can tell by his dark puffy eyes that he's been there most of the night. "I think there was something wrong with that wine."

"Stowe," Willum whispers, moving closer to the bed, "you were dreaming of when you first came here, what it was like, weren't you?"

Willum's smile is tired but warm, and perhaps it would help to tell him so. She nods. "I remember the red skull man giving me to clerics. And the truck that brought me here. I'd never tasted ice cream before. They let me eat as much as I wanted."

"Not all children are provided for in that way." Willum frowns, as if attempting a solution to some intricate puzzle. Then looking back up at her, eyes brimming with concern, he murmurs, "But they feared for your life. You were very thin, very pale. You wouldn't speak. My aptitude with children was brought to Darius's attention and he had me in to meet you."

"You showed me all those skipping games to try and get me to talk."

"I tried but it didn't work. You'd been broken, torn from everything you knew, but you still had your rage. Your rage told you to keep from the Masters the one thing they desired: your presence. You withdrew completely into yourself, refused to respond to anything. Kordan claimed the Dirt would be a means to connect with you, and I could offer no alternative but giving you time. I knew if enough time passed, you would gradually recover. But," Willum smiles softly, "time is relative. And to the Masters, my choice seemed too great a risk. What if your decline continued, they asked? What if it took your life? Darius admitted the Dirt was a dangerous alternative but thought it necessary."

"Not necessary," she says, "just expedient."

"Yes, the results were immediate. But in the long term, expedience has its pitfalls. You lost your childhood and gained an unhealthy dependence. Stowe, you've been unconscious for two days. For a time, you had no pulse at all."

Stowe stares at him. "That can't be true." It felt as if she'd just closed her eyes.

"Stowe. Have you ever known me to lie?"

Then they know, they all know. There will be questions. Investigations. She won't be able to conceal the power she's absorbed from the barrier. The power she needs so desperately to overcome her adversaries.

"I'm going to help you, Stowe."

"Good Willum, kind Willum, why are you being my friend?"

"I will guide you in overcoming your dependence on the Dirt."

Stowe goes very cold. "Darius approves?" she says incredulously.

"It came to Darius's attention that Kordan's demand for Dirt had tripled in the last four months. And that the greater portion was going to you. Kordan has proved himself an inadequate teacher. Everything is on hold until you become healthy again."

She's caught in an impasse. No Dirt means no more traveling to the Dreamfield. No new opportunities to absorb the energy inside the Wall. But Willum is offering to shield her from questioning, the blame laid squarely on Kordan and the Dirt. Play the part and she might live to finish the game. She wants to scream in frustration, but instead she sighs in weary resignation.

"You've always looked after me, Willum. You know what's best. How long do you think it will take?"

"Only a matter of weeks."

Weeks!

"All right then," Stowe agrees. The more quickly they become satisfied that she's recovered, the more quickly she can return to the Wall.

She finds a wan smile to put on and squeezes Willum's hand with her little fingers. Locating her most sincere tone, she humbly says, "Thank you, Willum. For being by my side. For giving me hope."

Willum's gaze, however, remains inquiring. He is observing her in the probing way she's seen him, on countless occasions, examine others. What is he looking for? What does he want?

If the days pass slowly, the evenings are interminable. Every night, without fail, as she drifts off to sleep, her mind starts to race.

Are you not Our Stowe? Face on every wall, sister to all, the glue of the fragile alliance that is the City? And how do they treat you? No better than a prisoner! What right have they? One small weakness and through no fault of your own. How dare they! You have to get out! Out!

Shut up! Shut up! Useless, relentless, she can't seem to control the direction of her thoughts. How can she get out when she's crouched in a corner whimpering, trying to hide from the red mask, the fire, the stench of burning... burning...

She counts backwards, forwards, breathes deep, tenses and relaxes every individual muscle, but it won't stop. Doubts, fears, ambitions, all echo in an irritating, endless loop.

Stowe is tired, with a fatigue that goes deep into her bones. She knows this ordeal will not end quickly. Perhaps if she leaves her body...? But no. Her instincts tell her not to; she fears that if she left she might not be able to get back. She doesn't have the strength, anyway—or is it the focus? Whatever it is, it's stopping her.

If she could shout loud enough, she might stop her mind racing. But she can't; everyone would wake up, they would see the extremity of her condition. Then where would she be? She must prove that she's recovering, recovering quickly. She bites her hand, letting the pain shut out her thoughts. She paces the corners of her prison endlessly, her mouth clamped to the side of her palm. Focusing on the pain, she swims in it until finally, she's rewarded with a sweet silence. Only then does she feel the throb in her hand, and opening her eyes, she sees that the floor and her clothes are spotted with her blood. But her head is clear. Clear and blessedly silent.

Two hours later, all evidence of her despair is erased. She's wiped the floors clean, removed the traces of her ordeal from her body and clothes, and felt happy doing it. Happy in the blissful simplicity of her actions, for while she was engaged in them, the nightmare had stopped, the terror—

The red skull smashes at Roan's head. Blood on the snow. His hand, his hand slipping away.

Stowe hurls herself on the bed, burying her face in the pillow, and screams and screams and screams.

At the rise of the waning moon, Stowe quietly opens her door a crack and peers up and down the dark hallway. The only sound is the circulation fan that drives purified air through the building. Staying close to the wall, she glides along almost imperceptibly, controlling her breath, the weight of her foot-falls, the way her shadow plays against the wall. She stops at the door to Darius's office. Listens. Nothing.

She stares at the claws on the shining doorknob. The door will not be locked. Security around the perimeter of these quarters is stiflingly efficient, and the penalty for anyone daring to enter the complex without authorization is death. Stowe runs her finger over one of the claws. Was it ones like these that ripped into her dream-form? No, these are not the claws of a reptile. Wrapping her hand around them, she pushes the door open, just a little. All is quiet. No one in the corridors, no one in this room. She slips inside.

There it is, the golden bowl, gleaming in the moonlight. Her relief grows with every step. Just a couple of spoonfuls, that's all she needs to quiet her mind. He'll never know it's missing. She leans over the precious, beautiful bowl and lifts the lid. She stares uncomprehending. The bowl is empty. Not a fingerful of dirt. Not a grain.

It must be in here somewhere.

Stowe jerks open the top drawer of the desk with a thud. NO. Why look here? Darius does not hide Dirt. Why should he?

Shh.

She freezes, realizing how much noise she's made.

Caution, caution, if you're discovered, all your play-acting will be for naught.

Slowly, quietly, she opens drawer after drawer, her fingers

slipping over the contents. Her eyes ache from the sensation of being pushed, moved without her consent. Why does she feel this way? Tense, her entire body sleek with sweat, she reaches beneath the drawers, feeling for a hiding place. Looks behind the portraits, even the dead-eyed picture of herself, but there are no secrets here, no hidden compartments containing a prize. She presses on the mahogany wall panels, each glass shelf rolling out, revealing Darius's ridiculous collection of antique bottles, ticking clocks, ancient coins... But what is she thinking? There is no Dirt. If the bowl is empty, there is no Dirt in this room. None! Stop it. She must stop...

Calm yourself. Do it now. What good are you if they find you like this?

She's shaking uncontrollably. The pain in her side so intense it almost takes her consciousness.

Go to where the pain is, Stowe. Kind Willum, gentle Willum. Remembering his words always helps her. *Embrace it, cradle it like a crying child. Love the pain and it will quiet. Go to where...* Perhaps he likes her a little, after all.

Go to the source. The source. So much to explore.

Shut up! Go away! Breathe into the pain. Love it, love it. There, there.

Go to the source. The source!

The tremors are abating. Her skin cooling. The moisture evaporating into the dry air of this sterile room.

The source. Yes. She knows where that is now.

mhyzah's justice

only those who wander will see the fourteen truly
for what they are.

—book of Longlight

ROAN SITS BY THE FLICKERING GAS LIGHT, unable to move, overcome with guilt and rage. He believed the Blood Drinkers were monsters, had fought and killed them without a second thought. But now he knows their name, their history, their way of life. Hhroxhi. People who attacked the walls of Fairview in desperation because their families were massacred as cruelly as the people of Longlight.

Roan suddenly stands. "Where is she?"

"In a room, about four thrusalls from here."

"Thrusall?"

"Their name for a tunnel between two chambers."

"Take me to her."

Lumpy stares at him in disbelief. "Mhyzah doesn't know, Roan. I didn't say anything."

"I need to speak to her."

"I know that fighting and killing were sins in Longlight.

But you weren't in Longlight. You were defending the children. You didn't know."

Roan points to the tunnel Lumpy and Mhyzah left by earlier. "Is this the way?"

"Just... don't do it because you feel guilty."

"That's not the reason," Roan says, trying to curb his impatience.

"She'll have to demand revenge. Do you really want to put her through that?"

Roan remains resolute, however, so Lumpy leads the way, brow knotted in distress.

Mhyzah is sitting in a small chamber, slowly rubbing the edge of her razor knife against a sharpening stone. She turns at the sight of Lumpy and Roan and smiles.

"Tell her."

"You're sure?"

"Now."

"I don't know how well I can express it. I hardly know their language at all."

"Do it."

Lumpy sighs and, sitting down with Mhyzah, begins a series of hisses and clicks. Her expression grows more and more troubled. Finally, she stands, and with one long look at Roan, disappears through one of the holes.

"I hope you think this is worth it," Lumpy mutters, so obviously confused and worried that Roan feels compelled to at least try to explain.

"I know it's a risk, but since I saw Saint, I feel it more and more—the children, the rift, what we saw in that village—I think I'm supposed to help change what's been happening, and I know that if I walk away from here without doing this, I'll set off on the wrong path. I'll fail."

They sit together in silence and wait. Lumpy's eyes stay glued to the gas flame until finally, bewildered, he shakes his head. "You know what scares me most?"

"No."

"I think I understand."

A whooshing sound announces the first arrival, the ancient Hhroxhi who led the mutilation ritual of the night before. Five others join him, followed by Mhyzah and Xxisos. All look very grim. Mabatan, her expression impenetrable, is the last to enter. With grave solemnity, she addresses Roan.

"These Hhroxhi are the surviving family members of the four you killed. You wounded several more, but according to Xxisos, the Raiders did most of the killing."

Roan stands facing the families who mourn four individuals, dead at his hand.

Xxisos looks directly at Roan and lets out a low grumbling growl, followed by an intense battery of hisses and clicks.

"You killed my people," Mabatan translates. "But I am told you are not one of the men of Fairview, and that you fought to protect the Novakin."

"The Novakin?" asks Lumpy.

"Hhroxhi legends speak of the Fourteen who will mend

the world. I have told them that Roan is the Novakin guardian."

Roan can feel Lumpy's tension ease ever so slightly, but Mabatan's bleak expression soon squelches any secretly harbored hope of forgiveness. "Blood demands blood. That is the Hhroxhi way."

The Blood Drinkers all draw their razor-sharp knives.

"This is insane," whispers Lumpy.

Roan does not budge and faces the Hhroxhi. "I come to make amends."

Lumpy sighs. The old one barks out an instruction.

"Take off your shirt," says Mabatan.

Roan immediately obeys. As Mhyzah steps forward, her blade aloft, Lumpy catches his breath. She ignores him, her eyes planted squarely on Roan, and with a wide swipe she slices Roan across his chest.

There's a thin line of blood from his hip to his shoulder, but Roan does not falter. The other seven Hhroxhi take their knives to him, each crossing a central point. When the last has finished, the front of Roan's body is covered by a bloody star. The Hhroxhi all touch his blood with their fingers and taste it.

Then the old one rubs a sepia powder into Roan's skin.

"What's that for?" asks Lumpy.

"It will help with the healing, but it will also make the scars permanent," Mabatan explains. "If he survives."

Before Lumpy can react, a strange guttural drone fills the chamber. Led by the old Hhroxhi, throats tighten and together the group raises the pitch to an overpowering whine.

When Roan's white cricket hops onto his torso, the Hhroxhi increase the tempo, the cricket vibrates with the rhythm, and Roan finds himself joining in. The star on his chest bursts into flames that spin faster and faster until the room blurs. Only a giant hole remains where Roan's torso should be and, as he tilts his head forward to look, he is swept into it.

A GLARING SUN BRINGS OUT THE BRILLIANT GREEN OF THE CARPET ROAN'S SITTING ON. ITS EXTRAORDINARY PATTERN OF INTRICATELY SPLAYED VEINS HAS FLUID MOVING THROUGH IT. ALARMED, HE RISES AND BACKS AWAY, NEARLY FALLING OFF THE EDGE. THE CARPET IS SUSPENDED IN THE AIR. IN FACT, THERE ARE THOUSANDS OF THEM, ALL AROUND. LEAVES. HE'S ON A LEAF. WITH A START, HE REALIZES HE MUST BE THE SIZE OF A FLEA.

SUDDENLY THE LEAF ROCKS WILDLY, THROWING ROAN TO THE SIDE. HE CROUCHES, HANGING ON TO A VEIN FOR SUPPORT. THE SWAYING STOPS AND ROAN FINDS HE'S NO LONGER ALONE. TOWERING IN FRONT OF HIM IS HIS WHITE CRICKET. IT TILTS ITS GIGANTIC HEAD, ITS MOUTH MOVING CLOSER TO HIM. IT COULD EASILY BITE HIM IN HALF, SWALLOW HIM WHOLE. HE TAKES A CAUTIOUS STEP BACK, BUT THE CRICKET LEANS CLOSER, ITS HUGE EYE DIRECTLY IN ROAN'S LINE OF VISION.

HE GAZES INTO THE MOSAIC OF HEXAGONAL LENSES, SEEING A THOUSAND REFLECTIONS OF HIS OWN FACE. THE LENSES WHIRL, SHIFTING THE PICTURE. THE FACE OF KIRA APPEARS AND IN A BLINK IS EXCHANGED FOR THE FACES OF BUB, LONA, GIP, RUNK, ALL OF THE FOURTEEN NOVAKIN, AND THEN HUNDREDS MORE CHILDREN ROAN DOES NOT RECOGNIZE.

There are more, many more, all at risk. All at risk in different ways. And Kira? A threat? It didn't seem so. Was she was trying to save children? Save these children?

"How do I help, what do I do?" asks Roan, hoping that the cricket might respond.

But it only rubs its massive wings together, producing an ear-shattering buzz. The sound knocks Roan off his feet, and lifted by the vibration, he is released into consciousness.

Roan opens his eyes, locking them with the old one's, who gives a satisfied nod and hiss-clicks to Mabatan.

"He says it is true. You are the defender of the Novakin."

"How can he be so sure?" asks Roan.

"You are not dead."

By the time he rises from a long sleep, the cuts on Roan's chest have already scabbed. The scars will never leave him, but it seems a small price to pay.

"That was some beauty sleep," says Lumpy. "Don't know if it worked, though." He's trying to sound lighthearted, but the concern beneath his jovial tone proves he's feeling otherwise. A quick, relieved glance between Lumpy and Mabatan confirm his suspicion—they've been keeping watch over him all night.

"Were you afraid I wouldn't wake up?"

"It happens," says Mabatan.

"But now that you're up, we can get out of here."

"Xxisos has located the ones I was looking for," says Mabatan. "He will guide us there."

After a quick breakfast of charred eggs and jerky, the three follow Xxisos and Mhyzah through dozens of thrusalls and chambers. As they speed along the polished floors, the connecting rooms become less and less frequent and the muscles in Roan's arms burn by the time they arrive at their destination. It is a chamber that has many entrances, though one of them is covered with a stone hatch secured by a metal bar. They share some water with the Hhroxhi, whose taste for liquids apparently extends beyond just blood.

"I have no idea how far we've gone or where we are," Lumpy sighs.

Roan's about to speak when Xxisos hisses, quieting them. He puts his earhole against a smooth wall and listens.

Curious, Roan follows suit and is rewarded with a cacophony of thumps and vibrations. Just above a whisper, he says, "People. A lot of people."

After a few clicks from Xxisos, Mabatan says, "This is the place."

Mhyzah turns to Roan and hisses something. There's no hostility in the sound, maybe even a trace of warmth.

"She thanks you," Lumpy says, eager to translate. "For helping her part with her father."

"Tell her I thank her and her people for the honor they have shown me."

Lumpy translates and Mhyzah, never taking her eyes from Roan's, speaks again.

"She says that now you are marked," Lumpy interprets. "Like the Hhroxhi, you are set apart from humankind. But you already know this."

"Tell her I carry the mark of the Hhroxhi with pride."

Mhyzah faces Lumpy, placing her palms on his chest and they exchange a flurry of clicks and hisses. Roan makes out a word that Mhyzah repeats again and again. Gyoxip. Lumpy seems humbled by it. Mhyzah takes a leather band off her neck. A long, round piece of silver is attached to it. She loops it over Lumpy's head.

"What's Gyoxip?" Roan asks Mabatan.

"One who stands between Hhroxhi and humans. An intermediary. That is what they have asked Lumpy to be."

"And the silver thing?"

"A whistle. When it is blown, they will come," says Mabatan. "Let's go. Xxisos is ready."

Xxisos moves the steel bar and opens the hatch. With a hiss and click of farewell, the three humans leave the Hhroxhi domain.

the quarry

insofar as the sacramental dirt is for the exclusive use of the masters in their ongoing battle with the demons, unauthorized possession of this substance is strictly forbidden and the clerical assembly is hereby empowered to deter illegal use or possession by any means necessary.

—proclamation of master querin

STOWE, PALE, HER EYES DARK, moves past a large window that overlooks the newest part of the City, a medical complex to accommodate the growing demands of the aging Masters and their minions. Five square blocks of domes, all connected by clear tubes abuzz with hundreds of people contently occupied, a little lump of coercion behind their ears.

She despises this place and its smells: sweet pungent florals over the bitter reek of dying flesh. Darius had made her want to be part of this. Now she wants... she wants...

The source.

Yes. And it is only through Darius that she can get there.

"I'm sorry, Our Stowe, my orders are no... no visitors," stammers the cleric guarding the door.

"Since when am I a visitor?" Stowe inquires imperiously.

Before the cleric can squeak out a reply, Darius's voice rings out from within the room. "Let her in!"

Her best cherubic smile in place, Stowe sweeps past and enters the white room. The Eldest is sitting up in bed, sipping tea, she's sure it's verbena, his favorite. But how ridiculous he looks: a multitude of wires snaking into every pulse and errant nerve of his body, sacks hanging above his head dripping blood and other disgusting fluids into whatever it is he's had newly replaced. His glance, however, is no less probing than usual.

"Stowe! How are you feeling?"

"Much better, thank you."

Darius pats the bed, indicating that she should sit, the attached medical paraphernalia all quivering with the motion.

"But I'm the one who should be concerned, dear Seer. Such a difficult operation. You must be very uncomfortable."

"Comfort? I have only vague recollections of what that was. I'll be up on my feet in a few days, that is the important thing. The transplants have taken perfectly. Our science steadily improves, and as it does, it answers our needs with greater expedience."

Expedience, yes, that's always the answer, isn't it? Stowe wonders how much he's had replaced this time. Heart? Liver? Lungs? He looks pale and decrepit. Is there any of the original Darius left? Is it possible that he's become someone else entirely? Some... conglomerate thing?

He strokes her hair.

The bones. Some of the bones are surely his.

"I've been terribly worried about you."

His touch is weak, it would be easy to snuff him out.

No, no, what is she thinking? She's not ready yet. Do it now, and where would she be left? No Dirt. No power. No escape.

"You are so kind to me, Father. In fact, everyone has been so generous and caring. And I am grateful, deeply grateful. Though I have to admit, all this rest and system cleansing is making me a little stir-crazy."

The ancient one laughs, his implanted teeth bared, but when he finishes laughing, it is abrupt. Too abrupt.

"Your energy, child, astounds me. There's not a Master among us who could have survived that journey. Never mind one who's been weakened by a bowlful of Dirt each week."

He is brooding over Kordan. What will he do to the poor vulture? Then again, what does she care? She'll never have to deal with that vile, preening oaf again. It seems Willum is not so soft after all. He has orchestrated Kordan's fall with brutal effectiveness.

The Master's tone shifts to mild condescension. "... And after only a week of rest, you're ready to go again."

She won't take it personally. When one is as powerful as Darius, it is difficult not to condescend—she has only ten years to his hundred and twenty. Let him go on thinking that her mind is feeble compared to his.

"Stowe, much rides on your strength and ability. We must

not take unnecessary risks. I cannot allow you to return to the Field too soon."

"Oh, Master, no, of course not. I do not want to go to the Dreamfield, I just want to go outside."

Darius laughs again. "That's all?" He caresses her cheek with the back of his hand, tubes grazing her neck and shoulder.

Careful, careful.

"I miss the outdoors. The open air. I've been invited so many times to the Quarry, don't you think it's time they had a visit from Our Stowe?"

"But you have always turned down their requests. Why the change of heart?"

"Dirt is magical to me, it touches my spirit, as you do, Father. The thought of seeing it pulled from the ground by mere workers repelled me. But now that I've been without it, I've felt another side of its power and I've grown curious to learn more."

"You want to pick at the scab. I understand." Darius nods. "Well, quarrying is lonely and dangerous work. A visit from you would be very affirming. And who knows, perhaps the country air would be good for you as well. When would you like to go?"

Stowe smiles. Her most childlike smile. At least what she imagines a child's smile to be. Innocent, enthusiastic, and devoid of all suspicion, malice, and fear.

The drive to the Quarry is lovely but sedate. Stowe, in a near perfect mood, is happy to contemplate the endless flatlands, all overhung with gray looming skies. Today, her cumbersome, heavy dress feels comfortable and warm, the air of the car well ventilated and fresh. It's a wonderful day. Clearly this plan is perfect, for it has settled her mind. She has no reason to argue with herself, because both sides of her are in total agreement. She is ready and Dirt is the answer.

Willum looks sullenly out his window. He hasn't spoken to her since he was informed of this outing.

"Don't pout, Willum."

"Forgive me, Our Stowe, for being so deep in thought. I am here only to share in the glow of your presence."

Stowe smiles in the face of his sarcasm. "Willum, there is no need to be so formal."

"No?"

"I need to tempt myself so that I can resist. There's no challenge otherwise."

"Your wisdom in this matter is unassailable, My Lady."

Stowe glowers. If he wishes to act like a servant, why should she care? Why does it unnerve her so? He's probably just angry, worried about her, but never mind. She has other concerns. She will think about how to deal with him later, but for now she can simper as obsequiously as he.

"I am honored, my Primary, by your trust."

The vehicles stop at a security point, where heavily armed clerics carefully examine everyone's identification. One more sign of the Masters' growing fear of the Eaters. For years, the Eaters have found ways to smuggle Dirt out of this facility, the only place in the world where it is mined and stored. Darius would like to starve them out of the Dreamfield—the way she's being starved right now.

She wishes her eyes would stop aching. Dr. Arcanthas has prescribed drops, but they do nothing. Nothing!

The guards wave them on to the second of the five gates. Each inspection promises to be as long and tedious as the last, but Stowe is sanguine. With every security check, they draw closer to the source. She can sense it. There's Dirt in the air.

At last the vehicles arrive in front of a small concrete bunker. The reinforced steel doors are thrown open and Master Fileth, the new Overseer of the Quarry, emerges.

"Our Stowe," he says, with a reverential bow. "We are honored by this visit. So happy to see you have recovered from your illness. You've been in the thoughts of us all."

Darius has high hopes for Master Fileth, the latest in a long line of Overseers of the Quarry. His predecessors have all failed to stem the leakage of Dirt, but Fileth has already implemented exceptional security measures and this has raised the Eldest's expectations. How sad it will be for poor Fileth if he fails. Judging from his appearance and demeanor, though, Fileth has every intention of making his appointment a success. He's exceedingly self-assured, a small, elegant man who looks to have retained his original external parts. Stowe wonders if torture hurts more when your body's still completely your own.

"Thank you, Master Fileth. I have waited too long to visit the quarry and its workers."

"You give us nothing but pleasure."

You must see every inch of the complex.

"I want to see every inch of the complex."

"Then you shall."

The entourage walks behind the building and through another high fence, this one electrified, its wiring being repaired by two of those brain-addled Gunthers, with their hideous eyeglasses scrunched up their noses. Darius says there's only a few dozen of these wretches, that they perform a valuable function and should be tolerated. But to Stowe's eyes they're everywhere, and loathsome like insects—she would like to stamp them all out.

At the next gate, Stowe watches as workers pass through security on their way out of the facility. Everything they carry is being investigated, and one by one each is escorted into a hut, to be strip-searched, no doubt. Will the guards dare be so brazen with Our Stowe?

With every step, Stowe's sensitivity to the Dirt increases. Her body trembles with anticipation. Though she can feel Willum's eyes on her, she is unconcerned. What could he possibly see that he doesn't already know?

But nothing could have prepared her for the sight of the quarry. It is a massive deep hole as large as the entire village of Longlight. At its edges caves have been dug out, great stone arches supporting the ground above. The workers all wear goggles and masks, identical to the ones that Felith is passing out now.

"You will need these. Inhaling Dirt makes one an excellent candidate for early lung replacement."

Stowe examines the equipment, then looks up into Willum's watchful eyes.

"Better eaten than breathed," she says to her guardian. And with a mischievous grin, she dons the goggle and mask, then fairly bounces after Felith down the steps into the excavation.

"As far as we can tell, the meteor struck somewhere in the center of this area. As it blasted apart, it irradiated the earth's crust up to a depth of approximately three stories, over the entire impact perimeter. Gleaning the Dirt from the soil was not difficult, though purification proved a challenge. But about three years ago, that supply was exhausted, and we were forced to start excavating from the stone."

Exhausted three years ago. It wasn't long after that they invaded Longlight and took her and Roan. Could there be a connection? Could they have—

Keep your eyes focused on your surroundings. Observe carefully. Every nook. Each crevice.

What was it? She lost the thought. Something about her brother. No matter, it will come back to her.

Felith guides them through the first sandstone arch into a shallow cave, where workers painstakingly scrape with flat metal sticks at the purple veins in the rock. Bits of stone corrupt the crystalline powder collecting on the oilcloth that's spread at their feet. Every few minutes the material is carefully swept up and placed in a large metal jar.

"These jars are transported hourly to Processing. Shall we continue?"

Stowe doesn't reply. Instead, she edges closer to the workers. "How did the Dirt come to be mixed with stone?" she asks, the urge to stick her hand in one of the containers and gorge almost overwhelming.

"The simple truth is that we do not know. There are many theories. Some believe the heat at impact melted parts of the stone, weakening it, permitting the surrounding soil to penetrate. Others think that in the explosion, fragments of the meteor fused with the softer rock in the ground. There has been a great deal of investigation attempting to determine relative potency. But as our supply of Dirt is finite, caution has slowed the process somewhat."

Explore. There must be a stockpile. Open every door.

Indicating that they should proceed, Stowe presents her arm to Fileth.

"I am honored, Our Stowe," he says, awe in his voice as he proudly extends his wrist.

Not so honored if he knew she only offered because she can barely stand, her head spinning from the proximity of the Dirt. It must permeate her whole body, because her every cell is screaming, demanding that she join with the Dirt in the rocks. Lick it, rub it on her face, squeeze it in her fists, roll in it.

Breathe. Breathe. Control.

She allows Fileth to guide her back to the small concrete building. More guards. Steel doors. Inside, additional security people and yet another set of metal doors. Felith and one of the guards each place a key in separate locks, together they turn them, and the doors slide open. An elevator. The members of her entourage paste themselves against its walls to make room for her voluminous skirts as they descend several levels. When they step out into a huge, brightly lit room, their relief is visible.

Here, the floor, walls, and ceiling are a pristine white, as are the fully hooded suits worn by the dozens of workers who stand over conveyor belts, sifting through the violet compound.

"This is the epicenter," says Felith. "All the Dirt that exists in the world is refined in this room."

"How much do you process each day?" asks Stowe, now grateful for the mask, as she struggles to control the twitch in her cheek.

"There was a time when this facility produced a pound a day. But since we have resorted to drilling the rock, we are lucky to garner a pound in a week."

Stowe stares at him, appalled. "That's *all?*" she whispers. That's how much she's been eating for the last six months.

No wonder Willum was able to expose Kordan so easily. An even greater wonder Kordan took the risk at all.

"When production was higher, the wisdom of past Masters demanded the Dirt be stockpiled. There are well over a thousand pounds in safe storage."

A thousand pounds!

"Though the amount appears generous, at our current rate

of consumption, it will be depleted in the next five years."

"But surely what the workers draw from the stone will continue to serve, used more prudently."

"I regret to inform Our Stowe, the trickle we're mining now will be exhausted in the next decade."

The stockpile, you must see it!

She permits herself a questioning glance in Willum's direction. But he has forgotten her. As is his normal practice, he is scanning the room, recording everything. Later he will call the information up in perfect detail, perhaps for a report. Is that what these demands are she hears in her head? Have his lessons become so much a part of her they command her from within?

As they pass door after door, Stowe feels compelled to ask that every one be opened, every room looked at. No, this can't be Willum and his teachings. She's searching, but what is she looking for? There's no Dirt in these rooms. Why is she wasting the time?

The stockpile. Locate it.

"I couldn't have seen everything, could I?"

Felith smiles. "All that's left is the safe storage facility. But it is a bit of a journey."

Stowe fights hard to keep her voice steady. "I should like to see it."

Another elevator shaft, even more cramped and festooned with security devices, plunges them deeper into the earth. Upon arrival, they are greeted by two guards who, after confirming their identities, escort the visitors to a small foyer with walls of thick steel.

"One moment," says Felith, pressing a black square on one of the walls. A flat stick, the size of a thumbnail, emerges. Taking a pin from a second packet, Felith pricks his finger, squeezes it, and places a drop of blood on the stick. After a moment, with a clicking sound, the wall slides apart. Moving through a long corridor, they find themselves in an open area surrounded by a transparent material, somewhat like glass but not nearly as fragile, Stowe is certain. For behind it, on all sides, is the violet glow of Dirt. More Dirt than she could ever imagine. Enough to bury herself standing, a hundred times over. She touches the wall, trying to feel for the Dirt's resonance. Even through this barrier, perhaps it can impart its magic. But the wall is so thick, the Dirt might as well be a million miles away. Stowe's head starts to throb; her legs shake and sway.

Who's laughing? She looks at the people surrounding her. All masked. She can hear them breathe, the trickle of their sweat, their heartbeats. But she cannot tell who's laughing. The laughter's so loud she cannot concentrate, she cannot focus, she cannot fly.

Stowe buckles, but before she falls, a firm hand grips her arm, propping her up.

"Very impressive, Overseer Felith," says Willum. "Now I think a bit of fresh air would do us all some good."

The ascent in the elevator gives Stowe time to clear her

head, but her heart is sinking. So close, so very close.

There are other places to look. We will investigate them all.

To look. To look for what?

Dirt, of course. You must have Dirt.

Yes. Dirt.

To return to the Wall.

Yes.

Three sets of steel doors open and close and Stowe is outside, blinking in the sunlight, dazed by thunderous applause. All the workers have assembled there to see her. They cheer and shout "Our Stowe!" Every single one of them beaming.

Willum, still squeezing her arm, hisses, "Smile and wave!"

Master Felith hands her the ampliphone.

"Focus yourself," whispers Willum. "Do it. Now."

Trembling, Stowe struggles to twist her lips into something resembling a smile and raises a hand. A hush descends over her audience.

"You dig and scrape and sift. Labor unceasingly. What you pull from the rock is beauty. It is the life's blood of our City. Without it, our Masters are nothing. Without you, all would be nothing."

Stowe's voice quavers. "Our thanks to each and every one of you. We are forever in your debt."

"Our Stowe! Our Stowe!" the workers chant.

Willum supports her as she is paraded through the crowd.

They shake her hand, touch her, praise her. Can they see the desperate pleading in her eyes? The unspeakable need for Dirt? Any Dirt. Just a little Dirt.

But they're all enabled, and the eyes she looks into are blank, the smiles hollow. They move in close to her, sniff her scent. But they are deaf and blind to her torment.

The drive back to the City is an ordeal. The car is stifling, the fabric of her dress unbearably itchy, and the landscape a wasteland. Willum remains silent, removed. It's just as well, as she cannot meet his eyes.

He uses you. He abuses you. Fills your head with lies. It isn't Dirt that harms you.

She needs some Dirt, just a little. Not a whole bowl, just a spoonful. Willum does not mean to hurt her. Of course not. Ridiculous. Willum is her teacher. He's teaching her right now, with his silence, leaving her to stew in her boundless inadequacy. *The best lessons learned are those we discover ourselves.* How often has she heard him say that? And he is right. She must gain more control. Her lack of poise at the mine was appalling.

The power of the Wall can give you the strength you need.

I discovered the power of the Wall, yes, but I need Dirt to get back there.

Dirt is where the Walkers are.

Yes... Yes.

"Willum."

"My lady?"

"I'd like you to arrange a visit to the Department of Importation."

"It is a great honor, Our Stowe, to have you here at our facility," says Master Watuba. Her head is disproportionately large, seated uncertainly between her narrow shoulders, making her unnervingly frog-like. Watuba oversees the importing of the Masters' most cherished product from the Outlands: children whose young bodies will be harvested in order to prolong the lives of the Masters.

Open every door. Look in every room.

"I am a simple servant of the City," Stowe says. "Ready to meet the new recruits and give them my blessing."

"What lucky few to have such favor bestowed on them." Watuba, exquisitely mannered, bows. "This way."

Like most, this surgical facility is spotless and reeks of antiseptic. Stowe senses she's being observed, by eyes peeking through spyholes, faces pressed against one-way glass, as she is paraded along the endless array of doors. Doors, doors, and more doors. She knows she tries Master Watuba's patience as she asks to view what lies behind each and every one. Then she sees a door she remembers. Kordan brought her here soon after her arrival in the City, to meet one of the Nine. This door is black, its handle embossed with the Egyptian hieroglyph for sky. She'd loved running her fingers along its sharp grooves. Within, there is sure to be some ancient one floating in the Dreamfield, waiting for the candidate who will provide his new liver or kidneys or eyes. His rotting, corpse-like hand dipping into the precious treasure she seeks.

"Oh!" she shouts and suddenly stops. Willum and Watuba turn. "I'm sorry, but I must have snapped a button." She blushes. "Please, excuse me for a moment."

Before Watuba can stop her, Stowe steps up to the black door, slides it open, slips through, and snaps it shut. Inside, however, there is not one person, but eight. Sitting in soft leather chairs are children, several years younger than Stowe, younger even than she was when she first ate Dirt. They all look up at her and smile. But Stowe does not smile back, she is too busy stifling a scream.

"What a surprise," whines Kordan, stepping out of the shadows. "Children, look, it's Our Stowe. How nice of you to come, my Lady. The children are about to partake for the first time and your words would be an inspiration."

Stowe does not move. She is rigid. Face pallid, she stares at the children.

They are cultivating your replacements!

"Stowe?" inquires Kordan, eyes flashing behind a ruinous smile.

Kill them. Kill them all.

A thin, high sound emerges from her mouth, a sound that makes the children recoil and slashes Kordan like a surgical blade. The children scream until they collapse. Kordan buckles, falling to the floor.

She hears the door open. Shut.

Willum lifts her, slams her against the wall. "Stowe, get hold of yourself!"

She looks intently at Willum, sees herself reflected in his eyes. Herself calm. Powerful. Silent. Resourceful.

"You can put me down."

Gently lowering her to the floor, Willum rushes to the bodies, touching every one. Their eyes flutter for a moment. "You could have killed these children. And Kordan. Go. Go now! Tell Watuba I have business with Kordan and will follow."

Kill them now. You must kill...

Stowe can feel her mouth opening, another scream welling up. Willum looks up, startled. "NO!" he shouts, but it's not just his voice that touches her; it's his mind. He's pushing her with his mind. How could he do that to her? Not Willum. He moves closer to her, gazing deep in her eyes. A wave of tranquility washes over her. Somehow she feels lighter.

"I am trying to help, Stowe. You must leave this instant! They must not remember what happened. I will take care of it."

Swift, the movement of her feet. Cool, the smile on her face. One last glance. Willum's fingers press on Kordan's temples. His memory is being adjusted. She had no idea Willum had such power.

She slips out the door. The frog-woman stands before her. "Ah, Master Watuba. My apologies. Shall we continue?"

The clerics warily watch the road while Stowe and Willum stand on a viaduct overlooking a sea of broken concrete, the last vestiges of the City before the Wars. Though her behavior on the rest of the tour was impeccable, it in no way expunged her lack of judgment from Willum's mind. No doubt he's stopped here to express his disappointment in her, yet he says nothing. Between the sound of rain pelting on the umbrella and his silence, Stowe thinks she will go mad.

"How old were those children?" she ventures.

"Five, maybe six years old."

"I assumed Kordan was ruined. I was wrong."

"He was removed from responsibility for your care but was given alternative duties. It's as if they're still looking for..." Lost in thought, his voice trails off.

"Children with my powers? You didn't know?"

Deeply worried, he shakes his head. It must have taken quite an effort to keep that scheme from Willum's sharp eyes.

"Do you think they are like me?"

"No one is like you, Stowe, apart from your brother."

"But they must have special gifts, or why else would the Masters bother?"

Willum, however, is in no mood to answer any further questions. "You must remain silent about what you have seen today. And go nowhere near those children again."

"They made me so angry, Willum. I..." She wants to tell him that it wasn't like when she attacked the clerics. That was deliberate, she was in control, she was testing her power. This was different. This time she had no control at all, as if... something exploded inside, driving her, pushing her to attack. But...

when Willum looked into her eyes, that something was silenced. Willum made the voice stop.

"Promise me."

"I promise."

Not that her promises mean any more than the million promises that have been made to her. All broken, shards of glass at her feet.

"Remember your strength, Stowe. That is what will get you through this."

Stowe takes his hand as they stride back to the car. She keeps step with him and does not tremble. Her look into Willum's face as he helps her into the vehicle is as penetrating as she dares. Who is he? She realizes she has no idea. But he is certainly much, much more than he seems.

the storytellers

HAVE a Letter that needs writing
or a parcel to convey?
a mug of beer or glass of wine,
we'll do whate'er we may
and for a slice of bread with cheese
we'll tell a tale that's sure to please
—Lore of the storytellers

FOLLOWING A RUSH OF FRESH AIR and a shaft of sunlight, Roan pulls himself out of the ground only to land in a thick patch of briar.

Mabatan motions him out of the way and slides the bracken-laden cover back over the hole. With a shudder, it locks in place and the entry point vanishes, doubly camouflaged by its inhospitable location.

Roan can barely see through the tangle of twisting vines but, just as he starts to push through to get a clearer view, the trill of bugles and thundering drums sends him diving to the ground, Lumpy in tow. They soon realize, however, that there is no threat as Mabatan has remained stock-still, a look of fond anticipation gracing her elfin features.

"They are here," she murmurs reverently.

Motioning Roan and Lumpy to stay on the ground, she crawls ahead, leading the way. The maze-like route winds beneath the prickly brush, and out into a small glade of hemlock trees. From here, Roan can see the walls of what must be a large town, its stone and mortar bedecked with brightly colored banners. A crowd of gaily dressed people are laughing and clapping as they enter through the formidable gates.

"Come," says Mabatan, getting to her feet.

But Lumpy shakes his head. "I'm staying here."

Roan knows his friend has good reason to avoid this place. One look at his face and the festive villagers would turn into a rabid mob. Lumpy learned that lesson the hard way when he first tried to get help after surviving the Mor-Ticks. He'd been beaten and stoned everywhere he went and he has no desire to repeat the experience.

Mabatan, though, is unconcerned, and reaches into her pack. Unfolding a canvas cloth, she gently lifts up a strange mask, woven of reeds, painted green and red. "I made this for you yesterday," she says as she hands it to Lumpy.

"Thanks. This'll really help me blend into the crowd."

"It's a festival. Many are wearing masks. Here's yours." Mabatan gives Roan a mask of brown grass and dons a similar one herself.

Thus disguised, they slip out of the trees on the far side of the village, then wind around on the road, slipping in among the other new arrivals. Moving through the gates, the three friends choose the least crowded path they can find while still following the flow of brightly costumed people.

It's a sprawling town with many buildings of stone and brick. But evidence of decay is everywhere: windows boarded up instead of repaired, the paint on shutters and doors left to peel, and what once must have been paved areas are now uneven paths of broken stone. This town had been prosperous, but those times are long past. Unlike the citizens of Fairview, these people had obviously fallen out of favor with the City.

The three friends drift among the stalls in the open marketplace at the town's center. True to Mabatan's word, many of the townsfolk and visitors are in gaily painted masks. A burst of laughter draws their attention to a platform in the middle of a makeshift stage, where a deeply wrinkled man with long white hair is limping and moaning.

"Ohh... ohhh..." the old man groans, swaying extravagantly.

A cleric in a tattered blue robe and huge red wig, eyes wide and crossed, rushes in and tosses himself at the ancient one's feet. With a look of desperate terror and an obvious apprehension of being kicked that sets the crowd to giggling, he whines obsequiously: "Master, Master, what ails thee, Sire?"

"My heart is dying," the old man replies, rubbing it. "Oh!

And my poor bladder. I haven't had a proper piss in months! But my intestines, my intestines are the worst!" He bends over and lets out a thunderous fart, causing the cleric to roll right off the stage and into the crowd. The audience collapses with laughter.

Roan can't take his eyes off the old actor. There's something familiar about him. He knows him, but from where?

Climbing back onto the stage, and making a production of trying to conceal that he is holding his nose, the faux cleric resumes. "And what would you have me do, Oh Rectum of the City, Archangel of Flatulence, Our Great Stinker?"

"Get me new parts!"

"But Oh Smelliest One, Commander of the Cheese, the people in the Farlands have no more parts to spare."

"No more, you say?" he thunders.

"Not I say, Oh Malodorous One, they! They say!" the cleric screams, pointing at the crowd.

"Then, my servant, it shall be your honor to give!"

"But my parts, Oh Master of the Swamp Gases, my parts are not up to standard!" cries the cleric, backing away.

The old man suddenly reaches out and grabs an apple-sized lump on the back of the cleric's neck. The cleric immediately relaxes and smiles.

"I am yours, Oh Great Fluttering Sphincter."

Two official-looking clowns wheel in a draped table, upon which the donor cleric lies. From beneath it, the old man pulls forth a huge, oversized saw. He careens wildly from one side of the stage to the other, dragged by the weight of the saw, until the clowns steady him. With their assistance, he runs the saw back and forth over the cleric's torso. Leering at the audience, he cackles.

"Now, I will live forever! Nothing can stop me!"

"Go stuff yourself, Darius!" shouts a heckler.

The old man points at the heckler. "You're next! When I need a new anus, I'm coming for yours!" Everyone guffaws, and then the audience grows quiet as the old man reaches his arm deep into the cleric's body. Up to his elbow, he feels around and smiles. "My new heart!" And he pulls out an old tire. Tossing it into the crowd, he reaches in again and again, with growing desperation, pulling out a cabbage, an old sock, a bag of garbage. "A heart, a heart, my City for a heart!" the old man plaintively yowls.

Everyone is jeering and shouting, booing the crazy villain, when suddenly the old man stops. Listens. The crowd goes silent, thinking it's another comedic turn. But then everyone hears it. The unmistakable pounding of horse hooves. Many horses galloping in from the distance.

"Raiders!" someone shouts, and there's instant pandemonium. Men push the gates closed, people run screaming or calling out for their children. The merchants close their stalls and the actors collect their costumes and props and disappear into the confusion. Lumpy turns to Roan. Only his eyes are visible through the mask, but Roan can see the panic. Where will they go?

The question is answered by the old actor. Charging up to

them, he shouts, "Follow me!" and leads the way down a winding street.

Before turning the corner, Roan looks back. The gates
burst open and the riders gallop through, cutting down any
in their way. He recognizes them at once. Fandor. The same
ones he viewed from his astral body. And safely ensconced
in the rear is a figure Roan has hoped never to see again, the
pernicious Raven.

"Over here," the old actor says, waving them down a lane
and toward a weathered house. A villager opens the door and
they flock in. As soon as they're inside and the door's barred,
the villager rushes them through the cooking area and into a
pantry. He opens a cabinet wide and urgently directs them
down into a hiding place.

"Hurry. Quickly now. Quickly!"

Lumpy and Mabatan are the first down, followed by Roan.
A woman and three small children are already huddled in the
corner of the hidden cellar. The woman looks suspiciously at
Roan as he steps onto the floor of hard-packed earth. The
rage and terror he can read in her face and body as she shields
her children make him turn away in shame. He should be outside, defending these people, not hiding with them. He looks
up just as the cabinet is closed and manages to catch a glimpse
of the ancient actor as he descends the ladder. He's agile, Roan
realizes, far too limber to be as old as the man he played. And
against the light, the powder in the actor's hair creates a halo
of dust around him.

"So, Roan of Longlight, we meet again," grins Kamyar the Storyteller as they are cast into darkness.

Roan's surprise barely registers before there's pounding on the upstairs door. Frozen in position, they can only listen while the door is smashed open.

"Bring me your children!" orders a Fandor voice.

"I have no children."

"Stinking liar."

There's the sound of a blow, then a smash as the man who concealed them falls to the floor.

Footsteps. Crashing. A thud and the villager's groan.

Roan reaches for his hook-sword and moves toward the ladder. But a hand stops him.

"Wait," whispers Kamyar. "Do you hear that?"

Fighting. In the streets.

The voice of the Fandor upstairs sounds strained. "Get out there! Now!"

After the group of Fandor clamber out of the house, the cabinet is opened and the bruised face of the villager appears. "The Brothers have come. This may be a good time to make your exit!"

"Brothers?" asks Roan, turning to Kamyar.

"They've offered protection to any and all who break with the City, and who are we to argue?"

"Hurry!"

Roan, Lumpy, and Mabatan quickly follow Kamyar up the ladder, leaving the man's family safe below.

Showing them all to the back door, the man asks Kamyar if he remembers the way.

"How could I forget?" smiles the Storyteller. "Thank you again, old friend, for the courage of your hospitality."

After giving the man an embrace worthy of his honor, Kamyar signals for the others to follow. He leads them down a winding path between houses, avoiding the battle that rages all around them. From behind fences and around corners, Roan catches glimpses of the Brothers, and he recognizes every one. Even his old teacher, Brother Wolf, is here, his hook-sword, the pair to Roan's, slicing through a Fandor. Roan reckons he could expect the same fate if Wolf saw him now. It is difficult not to face him, not to face them all, these Brothers who annihilated Longlight.

Hesitating for a moment, Roan realizes he is flanked by Mabatan and Lumpy. He knows they aren't just there to keep him safe, but are ensuring his direction doesn't alter. There'll be no detours to exercise revenge.

When they reach the town perimeter, Kamyar has them wait while he goes to the outer wall, and discreetly holds back a curtain of vines. One by one, the friends covertly pass through the small gap concealed there. Kamyar is the last to scrape through, and heaving a sigh of relief, he leads them away from the village, leaving the battle behind.

Roan's many questions for Kamyar have to wait, for the rest of the day is spent in a furtive trek through a scraggly forest. It's a narrow trail that avoids the settlements along the main road, but the stunted trees provide little cover, so they need to remain quiet and stay low to elude detection.

By nightfall, they arrive at a glade where the other three members of the acting troupe are waiting. The pony that pulls their small wagon is grazing contentedly, and several rabbits are smoking on the fire.

A small woman, her hair a mass of tight black curls, grins widely at Kamyar. "Glad to see you're in one piece. Mejan bet me five to one you'd finally taken an arrow."

"Mejan!" Kamyar admonishes, waving a long finger.

"Bound to happen sometime, the way you carry on," growls Mejan, a tall, broad-shouldered woman with spiked, sandy hair.

"She cares deeply for me, she does," jokes Kamyar.

"Only when she wins the bet," says the small woman, in a tone that Roan immediately recognizes as the faux cleric's in Kamyar's play.

"Meet Talia," says Kamyar. He waits as she bows ceremoniously to each of them, then introduces Dobbs, an amiable giant who seems built of round corners. Roan and Lumpy share a smile at the sight of the troupe, for they're all sitting around the fire knitting, and the clack of their long shining needles seems a comic accompaniment to their banter.

"Come, come, sit! Are there tubers roasting in the ash for our vegetarian friends?" inquires Kamyar.

Jabbing a stick into the fire, Mejan spears a couple of steaming sweet potatoes.

"I'd be happy with a vegetable, of course," says Lumpy, "but that rabbit looks pretty tasty to me."

"We have never formally met," says Kamyar, extending a hand.

"Lumpy."

"Yes, I know."

"And you're Kamyar. But I thought you were a Storyteller, not an actor."

"Anything can carry a story, young Lump. Whether it's a song, a tale, a poem, or a play. Our objective remains the same: to plant the seeds of doubt and righteous indignation in the people."

Lumpy grins. "You didn't have to plant anything in that town."

"It's true, we are well received there. They've felt the heavy hand of the City for too long. But it's not always so easy."

As they all take a place by the fire, Roan asks, "When did the Brothers start fighting the City?"

"They claim it was the wish of their leader. Before he was slain, he'd received a new directive from the Friend, I am told."

"Just like that?" Roan asks doubtfully.

"Apparently. What matters is, the Brothers stopped both their raids and their deliveries to the Masters. But recently, Darius released Raven to lead the Fandor in an attempt to enforce the laws of the City and gather the food and children the Brothers now deny them."

"The Brothers may defend the towns, but only because it serves their struggle for control," says Roan. "Fighting the Fandor ensures the City starves. If the Brothers were ever to win the City, they'd start bleeding the villages dry again. They're not heroes, they're killers."

Mabatan shrugs. "You thought the same of the Hhroxhi."

"I didn't know the Hhroxhi and misunderstood their actions. The Brothers I got closer to than I ever wanted. They're marauders and mass murderers and they justify it with their religion."

"Well, I don't think we'll be getting to the bottom of it tonight," Kamyar pronounces, ending the argument. "Mabatan tells me you want help getting into the City, Roan."

"If it's possible."

"It's serendipity, in fact. An old friend's urgently requested a meeting so that's exactly where we're headed. Of course, you'll have to earn your keep."

"What do you have in mind?"

"I could use a couple of extra actors in my next opus, *A Clerical Error*. An incompetent cleric seems to be the death of all who come in contact with him. Interested?"

Roan blanches. "I've never done anything like acting before."

"You just need to be able to keel over and look dead in a funny way. You've survived hoards of Raiders, a sojourn with the nefarious Brothers, the Nethervine, and a trek into the Devastation. Surely some crossed eyes and a lolling tongue are not too much to ask."

"What's Mabatan going to do?"

"I have a talent. I will play the drum," she replies.

"I can play the recorder," Roan says eagerly.

"Ah, well," says the Storyteller with an exaggerated sigh, "perhaps I can make do with one less actor. Are you any good?"

"I can vouch for him," says Lumpy. "Roan recently performed for a crowd of man-eating plants. Had them mesmerized."

Kamyar laughs. "Excellent preparation for the audiences we'll be facing." He leans in on Lumpy. "My friend, you'll never guess what I have in store for you."

"You won't be putting a Mor-Tick victim on the stage," Lumpy says with a grimace.

The Storyteller grins wildly, slapping him on the back. "Yes, I am! It's brilliant! See, in the play, the muddled cleric is sent to capture a child for the City. But instead, the fool will bring back someone already dying from Mor-Ticks! It'll save a fortune in make-up."

"That's not much of a joke," grumbles Lumpy.

"Oh, but I'm deadly serious, young Lump. You're leading man material if I ever saw it."

the inquiring mind

the masters fight demons each day,
it would seem.
what?
was that just something i heard in a dream?
no! no! how ridiculous! of course it is true!
have i seen a demon? well... maybe... have you?
—Lore of the storytellers

THE VISIONS ARE UNRELENTING. The flash of fire, her mother's wet face against hers. She can even see them with her eyes open.

Only one way to stop it.

No, I promised Willum.

Why do you think he's not like the others? Can't you see he's manipulating you? He's only using you to climb to the top.

No, he's loyal to me. He's good. It's Darius and the Masters who've been using me.

What else could Willum want but to be a Master? You said yourself you don't know who he is.

"No!"

Her shout jolts her back into consciousness. Walking to her basin, she splashes water over her face. Why is she assailed by these doubts? Willum is the only one who's ever helped her. It's as if—

She senses a presence outside her room. Who is it? How long have they been there? Stowe puts on her dressing robe and slippers and grimly opens the door. Clerics.

"Yes?"

"We are here to serve, Our Stowe. The Archbishop awaits you."

"Is he ill?"

"He has requested your presence."

"I will prepare."

Gwyneth is summoned but Stowe, her mind whirling with questions, almost overlooks the servant when she arrives, she stands so meekly by the door.

"The mint gown," Stowe snaps. Gwyneth obediently enters the room and goes into the huge closet. They must have had strong words with her if she's afraid to even speak.

Gwyneth emerges with the pale green dress, and after getting Stowe into it, helps her fasten the dozens of tiny pearl buttons. This is the dress she wore when she was first presented to the public as Our Stowe. Before that day—how long ago was it? Eight months?—she was simply the ward of the Archbishop. Darius oversaw the design of the dress himself, and Stowe recalls how he looked at her when the last fitting was completed: as if she were his creation.

"Will that be all, My Lady?" asks Gwyneth, backing out the door. With a wave of her hand, Stowe dismisses her, then quickly joins the clerics.

Footsteps ringing down the hollow corridor, she tries to anticipate the possible reasons for this summons, but her thoughts are a muddle of ridiculous fears.

What if the transplants didn't hold? A man of his age, the Eldest, can't expect to be rebuilt forever, as much as he might will it. There might be some kind of infection. Could Darius be dying? You don't want him to die on his own, unassisted; you'd be robbed of your revenge.

Stowe stops at the glass hallway that leads to the medical complex. "Am I not to be taken to Darius?"

"He is no longer in Renewal," replies the cleric and motions Stowe to follow.

He has been transferred.

Already?

He is still strong. Why would she think, even for a moment, that he would succumb? It is clear to her now where they are headed.

The clerics stop outside the Eldest's office, the claws on the shining brass doorknob forbidding.

"Stowe, come in!"

His voice is so vibrant, so sure, that she shudders. In his office. Whole. How could she have come so unprepared to face him? Stowe lets her breath flow to empower each cell, then draws it to her core, feeling the wholeness of her being.

As she steps into the room, she silently thanks Willum and his insistence on having meditation exercises in her regimen. She'd never guessed the well of power woven into his every word. Darius rises from his chair, all toothy smiles.

"What's wrong, my dear? You're pale as a ghost."

"I thought... I thought..."

She allows a small portion of her frustration in the shape of a single tear to trickle down her cheek. Darius takes her arm and gently seats her, chuckling. "They told you nothing? Did you think the worst had happened?"

Stowe allows her lip to quiver. "I don't know what I would do without you."

"I know how concerned you were about me, but you needn't have worried. I told you the procedure had become much more efficient."

His eyes are watery, his entire body plump with pumped-in fluid, his skin smooth and bronzed. It's astonishing. "You seem reborn, Master, your vitality renewed. It is marvelous. I am incredibly relieved."

She *is* relieved, but why? Only then does she realize that the voice in her head is silent. Quiet, yes, blessedly quiet, but perhaps too much like a crouching cat, preparing to strike. Oh, what does it matter?

"Come, Stowe, and look at the night lights with me."

She joins Darius at the window, where the celestial firmament glitters. It is said that once the City's brilliance obscured the stars, but the Gunthers have been unable to accomplish the old wonders. They claim the power grid is unstable. Incompetent fools, all of them. Now the City lights are so feeble they cannot even diminish the meanest star in the constellations.

"Look to the east. Scorpio is rising. This is the same moon phase, the same arrangement of stars, as the night the meteor fell. The sky lit up as if it were day. The impact was so powerful it caused an earthquake that destroyed the City and much of the existing coastline. People were terrified."

"But you weren't."

"I was frightened enough. But I did not believe it the end of the world as some did. That could not be, not while I lived upon it. Oh, I was full of myself. I had some great part to play, I was sure of it. And when your great-grandfather came to me with the Dirt he had found, I knew I was glimpsing the future. It was amazing. A whole new world to discover. I didn't hesitate, I took it, and the expansion of awareness I experienced confirmed my path. The voyages we went on, the places we saw."

"What kind of person was my great-grandfather?"

"Ah. If there was one word I could use to describe him, it would be integrity. He was fairly bursting with it. Roan was my best friend, I trusted him completely. No one knew me so well. We rebuilt the foundations of the City together, maintained it through the world wars and the environmental shifts that destroyed so much of civilization. We were the saviors of our people. But we started to change, and the qualities I had so valued in him as a friend became, well... counter-productive at the least. And more than a bit of a burden."

"Was it the Dirt that changed you?"

"In a way. It unleashed remarkable powers in us. Heightened senses, foresight, energy. And in Roan, something more. To this day, I've never seen a person so adept. But he began obsessing about the nature of the Dreamfield and all the possible abuses of its power. He found the responsibility too much to bear. In the end it destroyed him. He became paranoiac; he actually began thinking our work together was a threat to the very fabric of the universe. I laughed at first—couldn't he see what a grandiose notion this was? But he wouldn't let go of the idea, and it gnawed at him, became a mania. Logic, reason, nothing could dissuade him."

"And he led the rebellion against the City."

"You can't imagine the pain I felt at his betrayal. All his doubts were transformed into a bitter hatred, a personal vendetta that nearly destroyed everything we'd worked so hard to accomplish. It was a terrible blow."

"But you defeated him, utterly."

"Yes, I did. So it all turned out, didn't it? Except now that I'm thinking on it, it comes to me that you share his bloodline, Stowe. And I can't help but wonder how much of him is in you."

There's a hard edge to his voice that makes Stowe shiver. "I would hope that I would never prove myself so unworthy of your trust, Eldest."

"I too have the same hope."

In the silence that follows, the repercussions should she fail him are all too easy for Stowe to imagine. "In preparation for your future as leader, I will share one of my many trials with you. A few years ago, it came to my attention that a new breed of human had begun to make itself known. Children with uncanny powers of perception."

"Like myself?"

"Possibly. I never discovered the extent of their capability because they were stolen by your brother to give to the Eaters. This would have proven disastrous had they not all perished."

"My brother died with them?"

"I cannot say. I do know that they are no longer a force in this world. So now, I search for others. Every new recruit is tested. Recently I went to see one such group and noticed that one of them had a faint trickle of blood coming out of his ear."

Stowe, trying not to tremble, fixes on his reflection in the glass. It has an eerie quality, Darius's face, littered with stars. It is the negative space that fascinates her, as if all the dark matter in the universe were contained in his visage.

"Did you have a doctor examine them?"

"I needed no doctor to tell me what I discovered. They had been tampered with. Even Director Kordan had his short-term memory erased. Or so it would seem."

"You suspect him?"

"I consider all possibilities. Director Watuba tells me that other than the victims, there were only two people who'd been in the room. Yourself and Willum."

"That can't be true!" Stowe exclaims, trying desperately not to falter.

"Are you saying Watuba is lying?"

"But Willum...?"

"Willum said he observed nothing unusual. Of course, his powers are so weak, he could never detect such a subtle attack."

Willum. Who is this Willum who deceives even the great Master? And if it's not him, that leaves only you.

"You suspect me, Father?" Stowe gasps.

"Master Kordan is certain it could have been no one else. You were in the room. The attack was much like your previous aggression against my clerics. But to enter their minds and remove their memory of the event, why, that is very advanced. Very impressive. I think you brought more back from the Eaters' Wall than you shared with me."

Why didn't he erase those little mental footprints? He deliberately left clues. This Willum is looking to betray you.

No! No! Shut up. Can't you see I have a crisis here? Shut up!

"Father, I did not bring back anything, not that I'm aware of. I would have told you. I swear I do not have that kind of power."

Darius's eyes pierce hers. It's fortunate she was telling the truth, for he would most certainly have caught a lie. "Perhaps. Your great-grandfather began to realize that his unconscious desires were being asserted in ways that he could not always control. It was one of the things that terrified him. So there is a possibility that you accomplished a goal of which you were unaware."

"You think I could do something like that and not realize it?"

"I don't know, darling."

"You think I wanted to hurt the children and didn't know it?"

"Stowe, you have a very special place in my heart. Please, do not doubt it. I will get to the bottom of this aberration. We shall perform a few more tests. And then... I think we'll send you back on another voyage."

Stowe's heart lifts. It is exactly what she's hoped for, to eat Dirt again, and have access to the Wall and the energy it offers. Dirt. Her need for it makes her reel. There is, of course, danger. That dampens the thrill somewhat. Darius's motivations are not what he says they are. She will be subjected to Dr. Arcanthas again and there is no possible way for her to discover the true nature of the tests he will conduct. She'll need all her wits about her if she hopes to survive. She will need Willum's help.

Willum—

Shut up!

"I am forever your obedient daughter, Father."

"You need not humble yourself before me, Stowe. I do not require it."

Oh no, not at all, Stowe thinks sarcastically as she kisses his cheek. It depresses under her lips like a sodden sponge. "Thank you, Father."

"And Stowe—the results on the recruits proved negative.

They were sent to recycling," he says, lightly. "So no real damage done."

"I'm relieved to hear it."

He strokes her hair, holding one of her curls between his fingers. "So lovely," he says. "So very, very lovely."

Hair cannot feel, cannot cringe. Yes, Eldest, stroke it all you want. It senses nothing, reveals nothing.

the value of knitting

knit and purl for peace of mind
cable if you have the time
needles are a cunning tool
to pick a stitch or trick a fool
— Lore of the storytellers

"You are an amazing cook," Lumpy mumbles through a mouthful of porridge. And Dobbs, with a satisfied snort, ladles him another serving.

Lumpy grins in thanks. "I haven't had such a good breakfast since, since..."

"Oasis," Roan finishes for him. "But I don't think we saw you, Dobbs, when we were there."

"Don't expect that you did. Can't bear those caves. I'm more the open-air type. So I just stay long enough to take advantage of the library and then I'm off again."

"Do you use Dirt?" Roan warily asks.

"Nay, nope, no, I like my feet on the ground. No fancy aerial maneuvers for me. Besides, you can't eat in the Dreamfield," says the big man, patting his ample stomach. "Where's the pleasure in that?"

"There's more than enough that needs doing in this world, that's what I think. No need to go flitting around in the next," adds Talia.

"I took Dirt once," admits Mejan. "Got me nothing but a headache. If I could do what Mabatan does, though, I'd try a walk or two. Unfortunately, I haven't got the stamina for the fifteen years or so of training it takes to learn the technique."

"You must be a quick study," says Roan, looking admiringly at Mabatan.

"No, same as everyone, but my father started my practice when I was three."

Lumpy goggles at her. "You're eighteen?"

"I am."

"You don't... look that old," Lumpy stammers.

Mabatan smiles. "I do not feel that young."

Banging his spoon on his empty bowl, Kamyar announces, "Well, now that we've had a good night's sleep, a satisfying meal, have registered our surprise at Mabatan's remarkable appearance, and decided that we all hate Dirt, let's run that new scene before heading off."

"Always the taskmaster," sighs Dobbs.

Lumpy gulps. "You mean... my scene?"

"None other. Did you have a chance to look at your lines?"

"Well, I looked but I'm just learning to read, you know, and your handwriting was impossible to make out."

Kamyar laughs. "Then you'll just have to improvise."

"But there's no stage, where are we supposed to rehearse?" asks Lumpy, hoping for a reprieve.

"The world's our stage, young Lump. That stump will do just fine. Ready, Talia?"

"Always," says Talia.

Head bowed, Lumpy steps up on the stump. He does not move.

"Come now, give it some oomph." Kamyar gestures inquiringly at Talia. "What is his action, Talia dear?"

"He's begging for his life!"

"Come on then, young Lump, beg!" orders Kamyar.

"Please, please, no..." Lumpy mumbles.

With one hand over his face, Kamyar groans, then with an appraising eye on Lumpy, he sighs. Deeply. "You can do much, much better than that. On your knees. That's right. Lift up your head. Good. Now, look that cleric in the eye."

Lumpy does everything as instructed, but Talia crosses her eyes just enough to make him explode with laughter.

"Could you manage not to be so terribly funny, Talia dearest?"

"It's not Talia's fault," Lumpy manages between guffaws.

"It isn't, is it? Then if you wouldn't mind, can we resume the begging, Master Lump? Come now, a bit of zeal, if you please: BEG FOR YOUR LIFE!"

Somewhat humbled by Kamyar's booming command, Lumpy attempts to take the whole thing more seriously and actually manages to speak the line with conviction. "Please, please, no, don't send me to the City."

"Yes. Yes. That's it. With gusto!"

When Lumpy and Talia have completed their scene, Kamyar circles them, muttering. "Not bad, not bad. Needs business, though. Talia, teach Lumpy some business!" Then he lifts an eyebrow at Roan. "Now that you've come to a firm decision about Dirt, how do you feel about those who eat it?"

"Can't be trusted, can they?"

Kamyar shouts out, "Faster!" as Talia chases Lumpy around the stump.

"You know, Roan, not all the Dirt Eaters believe the same things. When the time comes, they won't all end up on the same side."

"Do you know Alandra?"

Kamyar laughs. "She was such a sad, sweet little waif when I first met her. My god, the sacrifices they had her make. Committing her to that demented Fairview, where she had to help with the exportation of their children. It's a wonder she didn't go stark-raving mad."

"She claims it was a struggle," Roan agrees. "But she's Dirt Eater through and through."

"The Forgotten saved her, you know. Raised her as one of their own. They saw her potential, and that was that."

"Yow!" shouts Talia.

Lumpy, sitting on top of her, quickly gets up. "Sorry, sorry, did I hurt you?"

"No," she replies. "That's called acting. That 'yow' was my line."

"Sorry," Lumpy peeps.

"Well, I'm so happy that you've worked that out," Kamyar bellows. "Now could we run the whole thing again—staying in character, if you wouldn't mind, young Lump."

Suitably chastized, Lumpy resumes his place on top of Talia.

"Yow!" she screams, grimacing broadly.

Then, without any warning, Roan throws Kamyar to the ground. An arrow bolts into a tree.

"Clerics!" whispers Mejan.

Mabatan holds up five, then four fingers. Nine clerics. Another arrow blasts by, nearly piercing her hand. As two more arrows fly past, Kamyar motions for everyone to stay low and scatter.

Diving for his pack, Roan can feel the star-scab on his chest split open. Still, he reaches for his hook-sword. He knows he's the only one here with the skill to protect them.

The handle secure in his palm, he listens as heavy footfalls move closer. Peeking from behind his rock, Roan sees a burly cleric, crossbow raised, rapidly bearing down on him. Roan leaps up, knocking the bow away. The trigger releases and the string snaps the arrow into the ground at Roan's feet. Unsheathing his sword, the cleric slashes at Roan. Roan avoids the blow, then parries with a strike at the man's blade. He spins and kicks the cleric hard in the chest, knocking him backward against a tree. The cleric yanks a short, translucent rod from his belt and points it at Roan. As it emits a gentle thrumming sound, Roan feels a slight twinge in his chest. The twinge becomes a numbness that overtakes Roan's whole body: his hand goes limp, he loses his grip on his hook-sword, his knees give way. Falling to the ground paralyzed, Roan hears dying groans all around him. Watching helplessly as the cleric raises his sword, Roan's final thoughts are of how his quest has led his companions to their deaths.

But before the cleric can thrust his weapon into Roan's chest, his eyes widen and his mouth opens in a fish-like gasp. He falls, a knitting needle lodged firmly in his back.

Kamyar pulls out his needle and grins at Roan while he cleans it. "We Storytellers are all compulsive knitters. A wonderful way to abate stress, don't you think?"

One sound rises in the sudden stillness, a perfectly pitched middle C. "Talia," says Kamyar. An A joins it. "Dobbs." Then an E, to make a flawless three-part harmony. "Mejan," Kamyar smiles. "Everyone's accounted for."

Trotting up, Mejan has a close look at the rod, while Lumpy rushes over to Roan. "Are you hurt?"

"Can't... seem... to... move," Roan manages to say with his uncooperative jaw.

"Don't worry, Roan, the effect of the stunner will wear off within the hour," Mejan declares, brandishing the weapon.

Kamyar takes the rod and pockets it. "We consider ourselves lucky that this is the most advanced weapon they're using. The City, quite justifiably, fears any arms they manufacture being turned against them. So for the moment, a modicum of skill and an intrepid nature are an adequate defense. But who knows what will happen once the heat gets turned up."

"Nine clerics pierced clean through," says Lumpy, scanning the scene. "Those the same ones you use to knit?"

"Effective, aren't they?" says Mejan. "They're longer and much heavier than a true knitting needle, but the weight builds up hand strength. A bit sharper on the ends, too, so you can do this with them."

She raises the needle and flings it at a skinny tree twenty feet away. The spike thuds into the trunk with lethal force. "Worth a few nicks in the fingers now and again, wouldn't you say?"

"I'll never turn my back on a knitter again," vows Lumpy solemnly, hand over his heart.

"Praise heaven!" announces Kamyar. "I've created an actor!"

As promised, within the hour Roan's skin begins to tingle, and soon, with a little help, he's able to stand up and start walking.

"Sorry if I upstaged you with my needle," Kamyar apologizes. "I'm sure you could have still killed him using your teeth."

"Maybe. I'd have to really want to, though, wouldn't I?"

"And you didn't? Perhaps that's why he got the upper hand."

"Perhaps."

"One more tale to add to our Saga of the Promised One," mocks Kamyar. "He'd rather die than fight, a true son of Longlight."

"That's not exactly true."

"Ah! What is truth, Roan? You were raised to honor all life—that's a tale well worn. Then you were forced to become a warrior."

"I wasn't exactly forced."

"You loved it, of course you did. You've a talent. A gift, some would say. You enjoy using it."

"That's what Saint said."

"Perhaps he wasn't wrong about everything."

Roan, unsure, casts his eyes down at his feet. "I thought that once."

"And now?"

Carefully lifting his shirt, Roan flinches as it separates from his newly opened wound.

Kamyar whistles. "It may not be pretty, but it's big."

"A gift from the families of some of those I killed, using my 'talent,'" says Roan.

"Speaking of your talent—forgive me, but I need to know: if we meet the clerics again in any numbers, can I be sure you will fight by our side?"

"If it comes to that, of course I will. It's not as if I heave at the sight of blood."

"Well, if you do spew, aim on the enemy."

Laughing, Roan extends his hand to Kamyar. "You have a deal."

It's almost evening when they emerge out of the brush, and step onto a wide, overgrown road that goes as far as the cloud-streaked horizon. Lumpy, who's been walking ahead, calls back, "Look at this!"

It's an ancient sign that's toppled in the dirt, covered in rust and grime. "Highway One," reads Roan. "This was the way into the City."

"Yes," says Kamyar. "Still is."

"Are we safe?" asks Roan. "Seems awfully exposed."

"Under normal conditions, we might avoid it."

"But normally those Blue Robes aren't sniffing around in the woods," says Talia.

"What I'm wondering about, if you please, is why those clerics attacked us at all," Dobbs chimes in. "The Blue Robes usually question you before they kill you."

"They are changed these last weeks," says Mabatan. "Anyone off the roads is considered an enemy."

"There you have it. We go openly into the City," Kamyar pronounces as he takes his first steps on the old expressway. "Ah, the high road. Don't you just love what it feels like?"

Talia steps over to the wagon and, with a pat to the pony, pulls out two long gowns. "Apprentices!" she commands.

Roan and Lumpy reach for the ocher robes.

"You'll notice the hoods, you will need to make use of them."

Roan throws on the robe, concealing his pack and sword. The seven march down the highway, eyes alert. When Mabatan stops to put her ear to the ground, all halt at the ready and wait for her sign before moving on.

"Talia tells me we're only three days from the City."

"Have you a plan, Roan of Longlight?"

"No plan at all."

"A plan is always useful," advises Kamyar. "Especially if you expect to get out of there alive."

Mabatan shoots a side glance at Kamyar. "Roan seeks his sister."

The Storyteller stops in his tracks. "Really? Your sister?"

"Our Stowe," says Lumpy.

"Did you hear that? He wants an audience with Our Stowe!"

The other members of the troupe fidget uncomfortably. Kamyar levels his gaze at Roan. "You're committed to this?"

"Completely."

"And there's nothing I could say to dissuade you?"

"Nothing."

Taking a long, deep breath, Kamyar shakes his whole body like a dog sloughing off water. Then he stops and looks at his associates. "Well, friends, he appears to be standing firm." He turns back to Roan. "What do you know of the City?"

"I saw it once in the Dreamfield."

"And what kind of perspective did you get from there?"

"Not a very clear one. But I do know it's dangerous."

"Ah, that's a start, he knows the City is dangerous."

"Belly of the beast," confirms Dobbs.

"Your sister being the beast itself," mutters Mejan, rounding on Roan.

"She can't be more than a symbol, she's only ten years old."

"Believe what you want," she tosses off. "But our ears hear a lot of what goes on. And rest assured that sister of yours hasn't become the icon of the City because she has a sweet disposition. She's overseen the dismemberment of kidnapped children, some say she's even participated in it."

Roan shudders from a memory he has of Stowe in the Dreamfield, blood dripping from her hands.

"One witness even saw her blast open the heads of her own servants on a public road."

"How could she blast open somebody's head?"

Roan winces at Lumpy's question, but he doesn't doubt any of it. Nevertheless, the child he knew, the sister he loved, must still be present in the so-called monster of today. He will call that child out. And hope like hell she answers. "I have to see her. Face to face."

"She's closely guarded. Never emerges from the Pyramid without a small army around her," Talia warns.

"If she doesn't kill it first," Mejan adds wryly.

"Well," says Kamyar, "we aren't without our contacts in the City. I'm sure they'll be loath to get involved, they always are, but there's no harm in hoping for a miracle."

Mabatan raises a hand to silence them, then lowering her head to the ground, states grimly, "Two riders."

"Clerics?" asks Kamyar.

She shakes her head, rising. "No. The horses are big."

"This is the time, my friends, that we prove our talents as actors. If you would be so kind, Roan, to earn your keep by playing a little tune."

Roan reaches into his pack, pulls out the recorder.

"Hoods up, apprentices. A jig, if you please."

Within moments, two riders appear. Brothers. One of them, Brother Wolf.

Roan and Lumpy bow their heads, faces disappearing deep inside their hoods. Out of sight, like all good apprentices.

"Stop the ruckus, apprentice! Can't you see we have company!" Kamyar smiles at Wolf's impassive face.

"Why, Brothers! For a few coins we'd gladly give you a command performance."

"How long have you been on this road, Storyman?" asks Wolf.

"Only the day. We were performing at the very town where you made such a timely appearance. Blessings upon you for saving us from those fiendish Fandor."

"You'll soon be rid of them, and the traitor who rides alongside," says Wolf, reaching a hand to calm his horse.

"If only that were the end of our troubles. The City already sends out clerics in their stead."

That gets Wolf's attention. "You've seen clerics?"

"Oh yes, in fact, just yesterday eve, back in the woods. How many would you say?" Kamyar asks, turning to Talia.

"Ten, I think. Or was it nine?"

"And we hear there's a ravaged farm village by the east Finger Lake," mutters Dobbs.

"That was the clerics' work, certainly," chimes in Mejan.

"We seek," shouts Wolf over the mounting clamor, "a fugitive from our brotherhood."

"We exist to serve."

"Tall, fair-haired. Uses a sword like this one." He holds up his hook-sword. "He'd be about eighteen years old."

Roan wonders if this is Brother Wolf's solitary quest, or if all the Brothers want to make him pay the price for their prophet's death.

"Are you speaking of Roan of Longlight?" inquires Kamyar.

"What do you know of him?" asks Wolf.

"Only that he perished in the Devastation. At least that's the story we tell."

"We have reason to believe he is alive."

"Well, a young man with a reputation like his shouldn't be hard to spot," says Kamyar, tapping his cheek. "Do you want him dead or alive?"

"We want him alive. No one touches him. He's ours."

"If I may be so bold, Brother, is there a reward?"

"Three horses. And a hundred gold coins."

Kamyar's eyes light up. "Now that is a prize! We may only be a motley band of players, Sir, but we're clever and we don't miss much."

"So I have heard."

"Thank you. If Roan of Longlight is truly alive, we'll be the ones to hear of it, and if at all possible, we'll deliver him to you. A hundred gold coins!"

"Don't underestimate his power, Storyman. He will not be easily subdued."

"We've heard the stories—in fact, we tell them. But where there's a hundred gold coins, well, there's a way! Not to scoff at the three horses, of course."

"Indeed," murmurs Wolf. And at his signal, he and his companion guide their horses past the rest of the company. Setting his eyes on Roan, however, he pauses. "I've seen an instrument like that before."

Roan freezes, not daring to move a muscle.

"No doubt," says Kamyar, "but could it be played like this?" He swats Roan hard on the back. His face still hidden beneath the hood, Roan's fingers fly over the holes to deliver a wild, frenzied variation of an old reel. Talia and Dobbs start dancing, stomping a rhythm to the crazed tune.

A hard-won smile spreads across Wolf's face, and with a shake of his head, he leaves the eccentric band of Storytellers far behind. The apprentice with the recorder keeps playing, but once the Brothers are safely gone he shifts to a haunting tune once heard in the village called Longlight.

the rise of the vulture

for many years, trade was under the guidance
and protection of the friend. but corruption
ruled both master and governor and they were
found unworthy in the friend's eye. the prophet
ensured the alliance was severed and chaos
rose in its wake.

—orin's history of the friend

"Excellent," says Dr. Arcanthas, "your precision is extraordinary!"

While the doctor makes his notations, Stowe observes the mole-rat's final convulsions. It's the eighth rodent she's terminated today and she's had enough. "Dr. Arcanthas, I need rest," she says as pleasantly as she can manage. He's had her in his laboratory since early morning. Surely he has all the information he needs.

"Of course, of course, Our Stowe. Forgive me, I become so engrossed I forget myself. I must say, the potential applications of this ability of yours are staggering. I'm afraid I lost all track of time." He looks like one of his rats as he fidgets in the pristine white room, quickly gathering his precious printouts, fussing over the eight blood-splattered bell jars as if they were about to move on their own.

"Perhaps you might wake me in half an hour?" Stowe gently inclines her head as Arcanthas bustles past the monitors, and settling herself down on the cot, she closes her eyes with a dramatic sigh. She listens for the satisfying click of the door shutting behind the irritating doctor.

There. Now she can stop playing games and find out what Darius is up to.

Though the fear of being stranded outside her body has not left her, the danger of walking into her test unprepared far outweighs any anxieties she might have about traveling. Filling her lungs with air, one breath after another, she patiently controls their flow until the spark arrives. She does not worry it, but continues her measured breathing until the spark turns to flame. As soon as the flame becomes a column of light, she follows it, leaving her body behind. In a moment, she's floating past the good doctor, then along corridors bustling with clerics and technicians and on through the clawed brass door— to find Kordan fawning all over Darius.

"The Brothers continue their disruptions of our commerce, and Raven is helpless to stop them," Darius states.

Kordan's glee at Raven's failure can barely be contained. "I tried to warn you..."

"When will you let go of your petty jealousies?" Darius snaps. "Have you learned nothing?"

Kordan turns pale. "My role is to advise, my only desire to serve."

"We must send the clerics farther afield."

"But many clerics have been killed. The defense of the City—"

"Inform Fortin to step up production on the alpha Enablers. Master Querin has arranged a new campaign that should encourage enlistment..."

"But Keeper, the training, the enhancements, they take months. And then the—"

"Do not waste my time with the details of a program I designed. They will be ready when replacements are required. The elite guard stays in the City. If the people of the Farlands have grown brazen enough to kill our clerics, we must send out more spies."

"I will make the necessary arrangements."

"Be certain that you do. We have little time and much to accomplish. The summation of my architecture depends on Our Stowe and you came perilously close to undermining our achievements."

She chuckles at the quiver that shudders up Kordan's spine.

Don't gloat. You fare no better when you stand before the Archbishop.

He deserves it.

And you don't?

"But I did not call you here to rebuke you. I wish to discuss the next step in Stowe's education."

What? Kordan as her teacher again? Impossible!

"I exist to serve, Keeper. What will you have me do with her?"

"*You* will do nothing with her. Stowe will open the way into the Wall. I want her to fetch me an Eater. I believe I have found a means to have you and Willum follow. Then you will be able to help her grapple with it. I need an Eater, Kordan. Alive."

Alive. What a thought!

"Make the arrangements for an early morning entry."

Kordan bows with a flourish and leaves. The moment the door is closed, Darius sits wearily in his chair and reaches for the oxygen mask behind his desk. He takes several deep inhalations, reviving himself.

So fragile—from where does he draw his strength?

Why does Darius still trust Kordan to be his assistant when he has failed the Keeper so completely? It is true that Kordan is transparent and his flaws make him easy to control. Could it be that Darius can only abide rank servility? This might be a chink in his armor, a weakness, perhaps fatal, and certainly worth remembering.

"Come," the Eldest calls out. Stowe's startled, fearing that somehow he's sensed her presence, heard her thoughts, but then Willum enters and she instantly relaxes.

"You requested me, Keeper?"

"Sit, Willum, sit," says Darius. His tone is uncommonly warm. "I wanted to tell you how much I appreciate the care and attention you've given Our Stowe. Your report on the over-use of Dirt was most appropriate."

"Thank you, Keeper."

"The disturbance over those recruits, however, remains a concern."

"It is certain, then, that she acted against them?" Willum's dismay is so sincere even Stowe believes it.

She studies every nuance, every flicker on Willum's face, but it reveals nothing.

"I am afraid, Willum, that I see no alternative to that analysis."

"She's a sensitive child, Keeper. Perhaps she felt your love for her was threatened by their presence."

"Perhaps. Yes. Love. It does play some part, I imagine, but I cannot allow such extravagant displays of emotion to interfere with the greater plan. There is a new breed of human come into existence and I must continue to search for specimens. They will assist me with my latest creation."

"Has the Eldest conceived a new architecture for the Dreamfield?"

What had he said to Kordan? "The summation of my architecture depends on Our Stowe." So, he needs her but also these children. To do what? What can it be?

Something to ensure his domination of the Dreamfield.

"I have not called you here to discuss myself but to ask your opinion. Is Stowe ready to Walk again?"

How impassive Willum looks. You'd think he hasn't had any thoughts on the matter until now.

"Perhaps not ready, Keeper, but able."

Such a perfectly balanced answer. Worried teacher, yes, but as always the faithful servant.

"Kordan will provide you with details of the task."

"As the Archbishop wills it," says Willum.

Stowe follows him down the corridor, drifting close to see what he might betray. A hint of nervousness, of consternation. But Willum's face is a perfect mask.

Too perfect.

the bespectacled man

"Today's the day," says Lumpy as he pokes his head through the tall grass that's provided both bed and concealment for them. "Crickets have been going crazy. Hopping around, wiggling, singing. I think the City's giving them the heebie-jeebies."

Roan drags himself out of his bedroll. His head feels dense, his limbs heavy, as if he got no sleep at all. He stretches, hoping it will help him shake his grogginess, and from under an arm he raises an eyebrow at Lumpy. "What about you?"

"Oh, me? I've got it all worked out with Kamyar."

As if on cue, Kamyar brays loudly into the morning haze. "Enough beauty sleep, my uglies, it's time to rise out of the weeds and move on. The festivities in the City await us!"

Careful to make her approach heard, Mabatan joins them. "You slept a long time. Food's all gone," she says as she hands a few of her charred eggs to Roan.

But Roan has little appetite—the closer they get to the City, the more Stowe's face, or fragments of her thoughts, flash through his dreams, and whether sleeping or awake, the torment is unbearable. Not his, Stowe's. He's not sure if she's doing something to others or something is being done to her. But the pain, confusion, and fury are unmistakable.

"You sense her. So do the crickets. Her mood is dark."

"We have to get her out of there."

Lumpy grins ruefully. "Yeah, if we survive meeting her."

They secure their packs as they step out to face the road before them. Far in the distance, a waning crescent moon hovers over the towers of the City, ghost-like in the livid dawn.

Ruins of neighborhoods that once extended around the City's core litter the landscape, and the dust rising from them streaks the sky in shades of burgundy and mauve. At the sight, Roan experiences an unsettling déjà vu until he remembers the journey he made here with Alandra just over a year ago— but that was in the Dreamfield.

Alandra. Roan felt that since she'd nursed him back from the edge of death, salved the pain of Lumpy's scars, and risked all to help them rescue the children, she was too good a friend to choose any side but his. At least that's what he'd hoped. Maybe it was too much to ask. He supposes he cannot blame her for her commitment to the Forgotten. Kamyar's right: they saved her life, were her second family.

Looking around, he can tell Kamyar and his troupe are growing increasingly uneasy. Even Mabatan's usual serenity has been superseded by a grim alertness. Everyone is on edge. Including him.

"Mabatan, is it the approach to the City that's worrying everyone?"

"Your sister affects them also, but they cannot tell her feelings from their own."

"It's not as if the walk through these ruins is lifting anybody's spirits either," chimes in Lumpy.

"I know something that might lift the mood," says Roan. But when he takes out his recorder, instead of smiles, he's greeted with a chorus of groans.

Dobbs rises to Roan's defense. "Now, hey, hey, be easy on the boy, come now!"

Mejan's in no mood for compromise. "For the last two days, you've played nothing but dirges."

Talia agrees. "All those doleful notes have been killing me."

"I believe a few died at *your* last performance, Talia," quips Kamyar.

She launches a pebble at him, hitting him squarely on the nose. Nursing his bruised snout, Kamyar ambles up to Roan.

"Take pity on us, would you, and sweeten the bitter tea so we may all swallow it."

Roan can't help but laugh and launches into a snappy reel.

Mejan quicksteps to the beat, shouting happily, "That's more like it!"

Midday finds much of the good humor roused by Roan's music evaporated in the sun's unrelenting heat. Initially grateful that Kamyar halts the caravan, the troupe heaves a collective sigh when he announces, "Time to costume up."

But when Dobbs opens his trunk, the performer in all of them rises to meet the challenge. Circled around a gaudy array of masks, fingers twitch until they reverentially make their selections. A glittery human half-mask is chosen for the pony after an intricately constructed horse mask is donned by Dobbs himself. "Neigh!" he whinnies, then trots after Mejan, who kicks him away. Roan absently takes the first mask he touches. A glowing spectrum of red, orange, and yellow, it sets his face alight with flames.

"These are all half-masks," Lumpy complains. "They'll show too much of my face."

"But these are not for you," says Kamyar. "For you we have a new creation." Opening another box, he pulls out a gorilla head.

Lumpy groans.

"Tsk, tsk, be more appreciative, Lump. You are to have the privilege of resurrecting the spirit of this regrettably extinct species."

"An inspired choice," says Talia, wickedly.

"I was about to say the same, only humility hindered me," Kamyar demures.

Mabatan shudders. "So many animals gone," she says softly.

Ever practical, Lumpy asks, "How do I breathe in this thing?"

"There's plenty of ventilation built in," says Dobbs. "Try it on."

Lumpy does, and immediately starts prancing around. Talia chuckles and hands him a tambourine. "Since you'll be getting all the attention!"

Kamyar, sporting a devil mask complete with horns, inspects the company. "Good. We look every inch the revelers."

"Thrilled to be celebrating year one hundred and ten of the Consolidation," mutters Mejan.

"Come, come, everyone loves the jollification of the Archbishop's Triumph!" shouts Kamyar.

"Exalted for crushing the rebel traitors!" adds Dobbs.

"Adored for his beneficence!" Talia pitches in.

"He raises the City up!" chants Mejan. "He saves the people!

"For their parts!" Kamyar counters.

"Delivers them from evil!" she continues.

"And into the hands of the devil!" Kamyar shouts, waving his pitchfork.

"All hail the Archbishop!" the Storytellers shout, and with great gusto, they make the sound of a huge, resounding fart.

The old highway slopes down. Walls rise on either side, but huge slabs have broken away to create a perimeter of concrete debris.

"This was a tunnel, once," says Mabatan. "But the waters dried long ago—" She freezes, listening. Her eyes catch Roan's. "Clerics coming," they assert in unison.

"Our cue!" Kamyar hands Mabatan a drum and Mejan some cymbals. Talia pulls out a ukulele and Dobbs a trombone. After Kamyar plays an introduction with his penny whistle, the unlikely combination of instruments meld to form a peculiarly harmonious band.

But even the clatter of Mejan's cymbals is soon topped by the roar of a pair of three-wheeled trucks. Each has a few clerics on board, all heavily armed. They screech to a stop before the revelers. Dobbs welcomes their arrival with a booming run of ear-splitting notes.

"What is your business?" the foremost cleric demands.

"We are the Promethean Players," Kamyar modestly replies. "I'm sure you've heard of our ensemble. We are the Archbishop's favorites."

The head cleric gives the others a questioning look. They all shake their heads. He strokes the lump on his neck, thinking. "We have no such information."

"Well, for the last five years running we've been the mainstay of Consolidation Weekend. You must come and see us this year, all of you. It's an experience not to be missed."

"We've been assigned to the Farlands," a young cleric sighs from the back.

But he's quickly brought to attention by the head cleric's scowl. Turning to the troupe, the older cleric warns, "Do not veer from the main road or you'll not live to give your performance."

"Thank you for the wise advice. A fine day to you all."

The clerics roll off. When they are well out of earshot, Talia bursts out laughing. "The Archbishop loves us!"

"Why aim low, my love?" grins Kamyar, and turns to the group. "But they were an easy test. The true gatekeepers await."

The ruined tunnel opens onto a huge steel and concrete bridge that spans the fetid waters surrounding the City. There the Promethean Players stop to gaze awestruck at the metropolis in all its glory. Though Roan has glimpsed it through the lens of the Dreamfield, in reality this island-city of steel and glass is much more impressive, more massive than he ever could have anticipated. Wandering the Farlands with its wasted forests and tiny settlements, he's rarely seen a structure with more than one floor. Here, towers rise forty stories tall and gargantuan domes and pyramids of glass rival them.

"You're sure you want to do this?" mutters Lumpy, the apprehension in his voice apparent even through his mask.

"Yeh," says Roan.

At the end of the bridge, a group of glowering clerics, looking very official and very well-armed, stand before a barricade of reinforced concrete. "State your business."

Kamyar steps forward. "We're here for the..."

"Your papers."

Through the holes of their masks, Roan and Lumpy's eyes meet. Papers?

With a flourish, Kamyar pulls a scroll out of his coat. "I believe this is what you seek."

The cleric unrolls the document and studies it while Kamyar looks steadily at him and elucidates. "As you can see, there are seven in my company. And our visa has been signed by *Master Kordan.*"

"Signed by Master Kordan," the cleric repeats, awestruck. Kamyar plucks the document from his hand.

"We must not be late." Kamyar smiles broadly at the cleric, who waves them on.

"Where did you get that document?" asks Roan.

"Ah, now, Roan. A magician never reveals his secrets."

"It's real?"

"When your subject has that little bulge in his neck, real is relative." Kamyar's eyes shift to Lumpy, who is craning his neck to take in the height of the tower before him. "Be advised, young Lump, if you lean back much further, the mask'll fall off your head."

"Then you'll hear screaming like you've never heard before," adds Dobbs.

Lumpy straightens out. "From far away, it looks so clean, like a crystal. But close-up... it's more like lead."

"I'm glad you're impressed, but we have things to do, people to see," says Kamyar.

Roan stares at a gigantic billboard of Our Stowe, illuminated by a hundred spotlights. Dressed in exquisite clothing, she looks as if she's been constructed, like some weird artificial flower. As he juxtaposes his memory of Stowe, enthusiastic, intelligent, vulnerable, against this image of her as Our Stowe, deity of the City, he shudders. His emotions have been fluctuating wildly, their intensity and unpredictability demanding a significant portion of his energy to control. If he is experiencing the echo of Stowe's mental state, then he fears he must prepare himself for the possibility that she has gone insane.

"... And with a benevolent smile, she watches over all..." intones Kamyar, bowing with a flourish.

"That's not the Stowe I knew," says Roan.

"Well, she's on every block, so you'll have a chance to become better reacquainted. You and Lumpy keep close together. Talia, Mejan, take the rear with Dobbs. Mabatan, you're with me."

Kamyar leads the band of players down a meticulously clean thoroughfare teeming with street cleaners and merchants. Medical personnel roam the boulevard, all identified by large badges sewn into their brightly colored uniforms. Official-looking men and women, dressed in dark suits topped with robes in an array of beiges and browns, clutch their cases as they scurry about their business. What their jobs might be is impossible to discern; perhaps they are bureaucrats. But all passersby lift their eyes and nod respectfully to the blue-robed clerics, guardians of order, and Roan's peculiarly masked companions are no exception.

Despite the rush of bodies in these crowded avenues, there is an eerie order and strange listlessness to it all. There are more people here than Roan has ever seen before, and the notion that anyone would seek such a life is difficult for him to comprehend.

No trace of a tree or bush or blade of grass is in evidence. Roan's careful not to let himself be jostled and pressed by the crowd, and his discomfort is easily read by Kamyar, who veers off the large street and into an alleyway.

"One more minute and I was about to start screaming," groans Dobbs.

"Oh, you thespians are so hard to please," says Kamyar. Then he stops and looks around. Colorful facades have given way to nondescript concrete walls, iron bars and grates, large rectangular recesses, and indecipherable signage. Kamyar frowns. "Our contact's not here."

Talia slips in quietly beside him. "I don't like being out on the streets this long."

Dobbs nods. "I hope nothing's wrong."

"Do you want to split up, search in two directions?" asks Mejan.

"No," Kamyar says firmly. "We stay together. Keep moving." And at that very moment, three clerics round the corner, walking pointedly toward them.

"Our lucky day," mutters Talia.

"Do we fight?" asks Roan.

"Far from it," replies Kamyar, who strides toward the largest of the Blue Robes, waving. "Thank goodness you've found us. We seem to have lost our way."

"You certainly have."

"We're such bumpkins and the streets are so many, perhaps you could direct us to Conurbation Park."

The cleric points due east.

"Many thanks," says Kamyar, and hastily directs the troupe away from the cleric. But it is to no avail, as one of the guards extends an arm to stop them.

"You there with the monkey head." He moves in close to Lumpy, who stands rigid and silent. "That looks real."

Dobbs steps over, a proud smile adorning his face. "It's a gorilla actually, mountain gorilla to be precise. I put in every hair individually."

Lumpy remains stock-still while the curious clerics touch the mask.

"Gorillas haven't been seen on the face of the earth for over a hundred years. This mask is my tribute to their memory. I have more masks if you'd like to see them," says Dobbs, trying to draw the clerics over to the wagon. But they don't follow. "I want to try on this one," says the guard, slipping his fingers under the edge of Lumpy's mask.

The self-assured look that usually graces Kamyar's face is wilting as he tries to insert himself between Lumpy and impending disaster. "We really must be getting back to work. We have papers."

"Oh, I'm sure you do. You will get back to work, don't worry." Nose to nose with Kamyar, the largest cleric shoves him gently but firmly away. "When we tell you to." He motions to his cohorts. "Take off the mask."

Lumpy doesn't move, though Roan can almost hear the sweat trickle down his back. It's looking more and more as if Roan's willingness to battle will be tested sooner than he or Kamyar suspected.

"Wait. Wait, please," begs Dobbs. "It's custom-fitted, very difficult to take on and off. He needs expert assistance, and there's my tools..."

While Dobbs rummages in his tool kit, making a great show of the special devices he uses to create the masks, a balding worker wearing thick glasses shuffles down the alley, pushing a small cart in front of him. The disheveled little man stops and gawps at the rising confrontation he's blundered into.

"Do it. Now!" the cleric orders Lumpy.

Roan, dreading what's about to happen, reaches under his cloak, hand curling around the grip of his hook-sword.

Dobbs bumbles back, but the eager cleric puts both his hands on the gorilla head and pulls. Everything slows as Lumpy's cratered face is revealed.

"Mor-Ticks!" come the clerics' drawn-out cries. They fall back and raise their stun sticks.

Roan leaps in front of Lumpy, his sword raised. The clerics stiffen. Eyes rolling up, all three crumple to the ground.

The rumpled little man ambles closer. He hovers over the clerics, all the while tapping at his thick glasses and clucking his tongue. "Pity about these stun sticks. Very unreliable. Always shorting out. And at such a high setting. There's certain to be significant memory loss."

He wanders back to his cart and starts to push it again. He slides his glasses up his nose and squints at the players. "Are you coming or not?"

the snare

S TOWE EATS HER BREAKFAST CHEERILY. The smile she has
for Gwyneth is so bright the poor woman drops the tea
service. Still, nothing could spoil Stowe's mood today. Dirt!
The Wall! She dresses in her most comfortable smock, and
eagerly awaits her escort to the Travel Room. But to Stowe's
surprise, it is Willum who comes knocking at her door. One
look from him sends Gwyneth scurrying away, and he is eye
to eye with Stowe before she can even blink.

"Our journey into the Field is to be monitored."

"Why?"

"For your safety, of course," he mumbles, barely concealing his sarcasm. "Darius is bringing Scrutineers."

The dreaded Scrutineers. The original nine Masters who
stand next to Darius. Their power nearly matches his. They
are ruthless and brutal, and their distrust of each other is what
Darius uses to control them. Though one of them, Querin,
masterminded Stowe's deification, he and the others have

always been suspicious of Darius's intentions concerning her. They've survived by second-guessing the Seer's every move and it is obvious they fear that Darius will use her against them. The question is, has Darius called in the Nine to interrogate the Eater he hopes Stowe will capture—or to observe and pass judgment on *her?*

"Kordan and I are to aid you in the capture of an Eater. Darius believes that connecting our nervous systems will enhance the power of our ethereal forms, allowing Kordan and I to follow you into the Wall."

"Will it work?"

"The Keeper's knowledge in this matter far supersedes my own. Regardless, the journey will be perilous. The Eaters will be waiting. I only pray we are able to serve you as we must."

Without another word, Willum glides into the hallway. Following, she notices the stoop of his shoulders, the heaviness in his step. He fears for her safety, questions Darius's plan, and has taken no small risk to inform her of these doubts. But there was something more. Their nervous systems are to be connected. Does that mean their minds will intermingle too? Will Kordan have access to her innermost secrets, her plans for revenge, the strange murmuring in her head? Is that the real purpose behind this merging, to expose her? No. She can't allow it.

Think. Scar tissue disrupts the flow of energy in the nervous system. You have a scar, an energy disruption, from the wound you sealed in the Dreamfield.

Could she manipulate that disruption when she transforms? Use it to create a shield?

If you are quick enough.

"Stowe." Willum's quiet assertion startles Stowe out of her reverie. "We're here."

Ignoring his questioning stare, she draws strength from her breath as she allows it to radiate outwards to the soles of her feet, the tips of her fingers, behind her eyes. And when she is ready, she signals Willum to open the door.

The facility has three beds in it, and is filled with monitoring equipment. A handful of doctors are in attendance, led by the ubiquitous Dr. Arcanthas. Kordan's already sitting on one of the beds, awaiting them.

"You're late, so we must begin at once." Kordan snarls, not bothering to conceal his irritation. "On your last incursion, you penetrated the Wall alone and entered Eater territory, but you destroyed your captive. Today you go there again, but this time we go with you."

Ignoring the reprimand, Stowe replies, "What am I to do?"

Kordan waves disdainfully at Willum, who bows in acknowledgment before turning to Stowe.

"The resonance of the diamond can be used in many ways. You used it as armor, but it can also be formed into a net. It implements with the speed of thought."

"The Eaters will be on guard, so it should be no problem to draw one out," snaps Kordan. "The net should succeed as a stopgap until we are able to aid you in subduing it."

Dr. Arcanthas, with great deference, shows Stowe the bed she'll be using. She and her fellow travelers are barely seated before electrodes are strategically attached to points ranging from their heads to their toes.

Darius chooses this moment to make his entrance. He fusses over the machinery like a doting parent. "Good, all the preparations have been executed precisely to my specifications." His eyes, black and shiny as an insect's, settle on Kordan.

"As you well know, I have great hopes for this expedition." He waits for Kordan to bow before moving on to address his greater audience. "Our medical staff shall be monitoring you constantly to ensure your connection is not broken. You are not to take any unnecessary risks." Placing one finger under Stowe's chin, he lifts it until her eyes meet his. "Make me proud, daughter."

Darius brings out his own precious bowl and, lifting the lid, presents the Dirt within to Willum and Kordan. They bow reverentially as each man permits himself a pinch. Stepping over to Stowe, Darius carefully scoops the violet powder with a golden spoon, but Stowe shakes her head. Lifting one tiny hand, she pinches as much Dirt as she dares between her thumb and index finger. Her other hand, as if holding hair back from her face, conceals the twitch in her cheek.

"I shall do my very best," she promises, avoiding Darius's eyes. She rolls her tongue over the Dirt, coaxing each individual crystal from her damp fingers. It will be enough. It must.

Darius leans in so close that his cheek brushes against hers.

He whispers in her ear. "Be careful, my Stowe. I won't rest easy until I see you again." His voice extends a tendril that winds round the light spiraling up her spine. "Your Eater must be interrogated in the Dreamfield. The Scrutineers and I will be waiting."

Stowe fears she will not reach the glimmer, it seems so far away. But before her anxiety can take hold, an ethereal hum pulses through her. She moves faster than light along its thread and the tendril that binds her to Darius is soon snapped.

Stowe is on her way.

A BILLOWING CLOUD OF MOON JELLY FLOATS PAST VULTURE AND FALCON, AS OUR TERRA-COTTA STOWE PERCHES ON A BED OF BRIL-LIANT YELLOW CORAL. TAKING THE LEAD, KORDAN UNFOLDS HIS MASSIVE WINGS AND HEADS TO THE SURFACE.

HEAD BOBBING ALONG THE WAVES, STOWE FEASTS HER EYES UPON THE SIGHT SHE'S CRAVED: THE UNDULATING CURTAIN OF THE WALL. SHE IMMEDIATELY BEGINS TRANSFORMING.

"IT MIGHT BE PRUDENT TO CAMOUFLAGE YOURSELF." WILLUM SOARS PAST HER AND DIPS ROUND KORDAN. "DON'T YOU AGREE, MASTER KORDAN?"

"EXCELLENT IDEA, IF YOU CAN BE SWIFT ABOUT IT," KORDAN CONCEDES GRUDGINGLY.

THIS PROVIDES EXACTLY THE OPPORTUNITY STOWE NEEDS TO CREATE A SHIELD. CASTING HER EYES UPON THE WATER, SHE FOCUSES ON ITS COLOR. THEN, WHILE KORDAN IMPATIENTLY WAITS, SHE TAKES ON AN IDENTICAL AQUAMARINE, BEGINNING WITH HER spine. Around this, she layers the scar tissue from her wound like an invisible scabbard, then continues outward. Soon she's impossible to distinguish from her surroundings.

"Ready?" says Kordan. "We must move quickly."

Desperate to distance herself from the Vulture, Stowe skims the waves and propels herself toward a low point in the curtain.

Mesmerized by the extraordinary architecture of the Wall, she could almost forget who she is and the danger she faces, almost not wonder why she risks so much for so little or what would happen to her if she were captured by the Eaters—or if Kordan saw into her mind. How she would love to forget it all. An intense thrumming reminds her that she's about to pierce the barrier. Will her shield deny her companions entry?

If they are unable to follow, it will arouse Darius's suspicions.

Sensing the flow of the energy, she shifts her facets to deflect it, creating a pathway for Kordan and Willum. In doing so, her form is revealed, rendering the camouflage useless. But what does she care? The shimmering haze inside the Wall is even more dazzling than she remembers it. This is the power she's waited for.

"Where are you?" hisses Kordan. He's flailing, flying aimlessly this way and that, dazed by the wall's interior.

Willum, seemingly unimpeded, finds her. "Something is blocking our connection."

Ignoring him, Stowe calls out to Kordan. "Right next to you!"

"Guide me!" he orders, clutching at Stowe. "Take me out of here!" He's completely blind. The fear in his voice is palpable. This is not going according to plan.

With a flash and a shattering crack, five gleaming disks materialize.

"What is it?" Kordan shrieks.

"Don't move," Stowe warns, as each disk snaps open, revealing—"Eaters!"

Bear and mountain lion are now joined by a weasel, a wolverine, and an old woman with the legs and tail of a goat.

"Five of them."

The goat-woman moves forward. "You don't belong in this place."

"I don't understand, old woman. Come closer and explain yourself," says Stowe.

But the goat-woman remains still, eyes latched on Stowe.

"I am a friend of your brother's. I am asking that you withdraw. Failure to do so will be treated as an act of aggression."

"Get her!" screams the vulture. Negotiations closed, the goat-woman vanishes and the other four Eaters are upon them. The lion swipes at Kordan's back. Oozing brackish fluid, the vulture flails, panicked, endangering them

ALL. STOWE, TRYING TO GET SOME DISTANCE FROM KORDAN'S LUNGING TALONS, KICKS AT THE BEAR. WILLUM LAUNCHES HIMSELF AT THE WOLVERINE'S JUGULAR, HIS CLAWS RIPPING OUT ITS THROAT. THEN HE LODGES HIMSELF FIRMLY ON THE LION'S HEAD AND TEARS AT ITS EYES WITH HIS BEAK.

ATTACKING FROM BEHIND, THE WEASEL SINKS ITS TEETH IN STOWE'S ARM, CHEWING INTO HER, DIGGING. REMEMBERING WILLUM'S INSTRUCTION, STOWE UNLEASHES A WEB OF CRYSTAL, SECURING THE WEASEL'S HEAD TO HER ARM WHILE THE FRENZIED ANIMAL SCRATCHES AND SQUIRMS. AS SHE FRANTICALLY KICKS AWAY RELENTLESS ATTACKS BY THE BEAR, STOWE'S ATTEMPTS TO LAYER MORE CRYSTAL ON THE STRUGGLING WEASEL ARE CONSTANTLY THWARTED. BUT FINALLY SHE'S ABLE TO BRACE HER FEET AROUND THE BEAR'S NECK AND, TWISTING WITH ALL HER FORCE, IS REWARDED BY A CRISP SNAP OF BONE.

BEFORE THE EATERS CAN REGROUP, STOWE GRABS KORDAN BY A WING, HOPING TO DRAG HIM AND HER CAPTIVE TO SAFETY. THE MOUNTAIN LION'S ANGUISHED SCREAMS LEAVE LITTLE DOUBT THAT WILLUM WILL SOON FOLLOW.

THE INSTANT STOWE BURSTS OUT OF THE WALL AND BACK INTO THE MASTERS' DOMAIN, KORDAN SHRUGS HER OFF. SPOTTING THE WEASEL THRASHING WILDLY ON STOWE'S ARM, HE HOOKS HIS TALONS DEEP INTO ITS FLESH AND RIPS IT OFF. "YOU'RE MINE, LANIA!"

LURCHING ERRATICALLY TO FREE HERSELF FROM KORDAN, THE WEASEL FORCES THEM CLOSER AND CLOSER TO THE SPIRACAL. STOWE KNOWS THAT IF THEY ARE UNABLE TO SLOW DOWN THEY WILL SOON COME WITHIN ITS LETHAL RANGE. KORDAN WHIPS

Lania violently in the opposite direction, but the weasel snaps at him, biting off a talon. The vulture screeches in pain as he bats at the weasel with his wing. "Do something!" he cries.

But Stowe's approach is hampered by her bulk. She cannot reach past Kordan's pounding wings to dislodge Lania, and as the weasel sinks her teeth into yet another talon, the vulture's ability to maintain his hold is grievously impaired.

Just then, Willum emerges from the Wall and dives toward them. It seems to Stowe—or is she imagining it?—that Willum has linked with Lania, almost as if issuing a silent command. But before he can reach her, she plummets, bursts into flame, and is swallowed by the Spiracal's hungrily churning maw.

An overpowering grief detonates inside Stowe. Blind with despair, she tumbles.

Willum soars beside her. "Are you hurt?"

"I don't know..." her voice trails off. It's too hard to talk; her throat's constricted in anguish. She's aware of Willum beneath her, buoying her up and away, but none of that matters, as she is drowning in a well of sorrow.

The beach is smooth, the rock curved in frozen waves, the crest of each a perfect perch for the flock of nine raptors that awaits them. Led by an enormous red eagle, the Scrutineers' angry screeches guarantee no quarter will

BE GIVEN. THE EAGLE'S EYES LOCK ON THE VULTURE AND, RAISING A TALON, HE RIPS THE SIDE OFF THE VULTURE'S FACE.

KORDAN CRIES OUT.

"STOWE, WILLUM, RETURN TO THE CITY," DARIUS ORDERS.

"MASTER..." WILLUM BEGINS.

"NOW!" HE SNARLS, THEN RETURNS HIS ATTENTION TO KORDAN. "I HAVE BEEN BETRAYED," HE WHISPERS.

"KEEPER, I LIVE ONLY TO SERVE YOU!"

"YOU HAVE FAILED."

Before Stowe opens her eyes, she hears their voices.

"I don't understand why the connection was broken." Darius's voice is unnervingly calm.

"It was strong enough to get us into the Wall, Keeper."

"But not enough to sustain you."

"No."

"Something must have been blocking the flow. Or perhaps, as you said, it was too soon and she was not at peak strength. Although she did capture one, didn't she? Tell me, Willum, what was it?"

"A weasel."

Sadness. Overpowering grief and sadness. Why? She doesn't understand these feelings.

Darius gulps out a laugh. "Lania! I should have guessed! She would have done anything to avoid my grasp."

She chose death!

The very thought sends a convulsion through Stowe.

"There is a lovely symmetry to this death, Willum. Her husband was the lizard dispatched by Our Stowe, not so long ago. Ferrell and Lania were inseparable, together for decades. They alone rivaled my talent for construction. As you know, having experienced their Wall."

"Yes, Archbishop. An extraordinary accomplishment. It must be investigated further. Kordan and I were completely overwhelmed. But for Our Stowe, we both would surely have perished."

"Would that Kordan had, then I might have had my prize. Fool. But my disappointment is somewhat mitigated by the fact that I need suffer rivals no more. Ferrell. Dead. Lania. Dead. I wish I could have seen it."

A flood of rage fills Stowe's head. So sudden, so intense, she cries out.

"Stowe? Stowe!" Willum's face is blurry. His eyes seem to be probing inside her brain. He scowls, staring so deep something shudders, something not herself. He looks up at Darius. "You were right, Eldest, she should not have gone. It was too soon."

"Yes," whispers Darius. "Too soon. And yet, in so many ways, Willum, not soon enough."

the gunthers

VOLUME IV, ARTICLE 7.8, SECTION 3, APPENDIX C,
SPECIAL REQUIREMENTS: AMEND TO INCLUDE THE
SPECIES GRYLLUS NIVEUS, COMMONLY KNOWN AS
SNOW CRICKET.

—GUNTHER LOG

ROAN GASPS AND FALTERS.

Lumpy's immediately by his side. "What is it, what's wrong?"

"Stowe. Something happened. She was excited, then afraid, then grief—this terrible grief—and now nothing. I feel nothing. I can't feel her at all."

"Can you walk?"

Roan nods. They have to move quickly to keep up with the bespectacled man. The streets he leads them down do not resemble the sleek and glossy boulevards they saw when first entering the City. Refuse, stray cats, and toppled garbage cans obstruct their passage. Here, the buildings are made of brick. Most have boarded-up windows and some even appear to pre-date the Consolidation. Shabbily dressed people haunt shattered doorways, staring at them with vacant eyes.

Mejan slips her arm in Roan's and shudders. "The other face of the City. Many of them come here when their villages are destroyed, hoping to peddle a kidney to survive. But they're too old, the Masters don't want used parts. That leaves them with nowhere to go, no skills to sell. By the time they realize the mistake they've made in coming here, it's too late. When their hunger becomes unbearable, if they have children, they sell them, whole or in parts, whatever they think they can make peace with. They have no choice but to take the money. They wander these buildings like lost souls, living on whatever scraps they can find."

Against one derelict building, a woman is bent before a shrine that's been constructed inside two stacked wooden boxes. It's decorated with red ribbons, shiny paper, and burning candles. Roan looks closer to see what she's praying to and turns in shame at the sight. A picture of Our Stowe.

"She's their god. They believe she's going to save them from their misery one day. That's the bill of goods they've been sold by the Master of Inculcation, Querin the Insidious, and the sorry sots fall for it."

"The City does nothing for them?"

"They're not killed as long as they don't stray from this quarter. The City in its magnanimity has termed them 'absent' and tolerates their use of these buildings for shelter. Just one more example of the 'interceding benevolence' of Our Stowe."

These people, the Absent, had homes once, families. Dignity. They lost it all and now they worship the image of his sister. Was this what Saint saw himself fighting against? Saint and Kira had been the children of people like these, turned from their homes and killed—whether by the sword or by the slow rot of despair, did it matter? Roan is on a mission to save children, special children, but don't the children of these people also deserve to be freed?

The bespectacled man opens a ramshackle gate tucked in the recess of a crumbling stucco wall. He pushes his cart through and the group follows. Dobbs leads the pony and Mejan takes up the rear. With a quick look behind, she swings the gate closed. In the center of an asphalt courtyard stands a feature-less white concrete cube. Roan and Lumpy stop, puzzled.

"Don't just stand and stare. Tie up the horse and come inside," the little man says, motioning at a hitching post. He touches a corner of the cube a half dozen times in an intricate pattern. There's a click and a panel flips open, providing just enough space for them to enter.

The room within is as nondescript as the exterior. Two other rumpled, bespectacled workers in green fatigues stand by the opposite wall, gawking at them. One is tall and hunched over, the other's face is covered in freckles and she's wiggling a finger in her ear.

Kamyar grins. "It's good to see you Gunthers again. Gunther Number Six, we are grateful for your timely—"

"Take off your masks," orders the bespectacled man, with no trace of hospitality.

"Even me?" asks Lumpy.

"Even you."

They all obey, though Roan can see Lumpy's more than a little uncomfortable.

"There are only supposed to be four of you," the small man says.

"That's true, but the guests I've brought are somewhat illustrious," says Kamyar. "Allow me to introduce Mabatan."

The Gunthers all peer over their glasses for a better look. "Well. Well, well. So you do exist."

"For now," Mabatan replies. "As you do, Gunther Number Six. And you are?" she inquires of the tall, ungainly Gunther.

"Gunther Number Fourteen, at your service," he says as he shambles forward.

The Gunther with the freckles removes her finger from her ear and nods. "Gunther Number Seventy-Nine."

"There are more of you than I thought," says Mabatan.

"Ninety-six in total," states Gunther Number Fourteen. "Who are the other two that were not invited?"

"You can call me Lumpy. And by the way, I'm not contagious."

"We know," says Gunther Number Six. After conferring excitedly with Numbers Fourteen and Seventy-Nine, Number Six squints at Roan suspiciously. "And him?"

A little smile plays across Kamyar's lips. "Roan of Longlight."

The Gunthers step closer to Roan, their faces tilting all around him. He realizes that rather than looking directly at him, their eyes are flitting between him and the surface of their eyeglasses.

"Are the glasses some kind of scanner?" Roan inquires, fascinated.

"Yes, they are," confirms Gunther Number Six. "And they verify that you are Roan of the Parting's great-grandson. We were under the impression you had left the known world. You are not safe here in the City."

"I've come seeking my sister. I need to see her in person. To speak with her."

The three Gunthers look at each other, seemingly absorbed in silent communication. The troupe also remains uncharacteristically mute as Roan awaits an answer. It is Gunther Number Seventy-Nine who finally speaks. "What you ask may be impossible."

"Because of security?" asks Roan.

"Because she may be dead," replies the Gunther. "Our last observation of her indicated that she's had a neurological crisis, consistent with stroke."

"She was in some kind of pain," Roan says in affirmation.

"You sensed her thoughts?"

"No," Roan admits. "Not thoughts, feelings. Confusion. Distress. Fear."

The Gunthers look grimly at each other. "Your sister's body would not be allowed to be wasted. She could have died a physical death, but parts of her would be kept alive."

Roan's eyes dart from one to the other, panic rising. "What parts?"

"Most certainly her brain. We could try to locate it."

Roan leans against the wall, his hands pressed against his face, fighting despair.

"The Gunthers do not truly know. They like to make guesses. Dark, troubling guesses. They do not know for sure." Mabatan's words would be more comforting if Roan hadn't felt Stowe's suffering, then lost her presence after that last sharp, terrible pain. What if these people are right?

Kamyar scowls at the Gunthers. "Perhaps it would be possible to acquire some accurate information. Hunches and guesswork do not further anyone's objectives."

"Guesses are the building blocks to theory. Theory leads to the discovery of fact."

"Might we move right on to the discovery phase, then? Please."

The Gunthers share a sour look, then agree grudgingly. "Very well. We will not share our hypotheses, only the facts. If we find any."

Standing in the courtyard with the rest of the troupe, Roan scans the sky above the wall, searching. He hasn't seen a bird, or a bug for that matter, since his arrival in the City. Could it be that no life other than human exists here?

Talia hands him a brush. "Here. You're even making me nervous."

"Sorry. Do you have a name for her?" Slipping his hand over the brush, Roan begins to groom the shaggy, dappled pony.

Talia laughs. "Many. When she's acting high and mighty and won't condescend to pull the cart, she's Marie Antoinette. If she's feisty and refuses all reason, we call her Joan of Arc. Elegant and beautiful like she is right now: Queen Nefertiti. Mejan once owned a dog and when she misses it, Nefertiti becomes Fido."

"My name for her's Black Beauty," says Dobbs.

"But she's brown and covered in spots," protests Lumpy.

"Yeah, I can see that, but I've read the book some twenty-two times."

"You must really like it."

"It was the only book in my village. I found it buried in the floor of my grandpa's house. I used it to teach myself to read, best I could."

"You can imagine his reaction when he saw Orin's hoard," says Kamyar. "Couldn't drag him out of the Oasis library for weeks. Truth be told, it's still a little difficult trying to pry him out of those comfy chairs."

Dobbs flashes a toothy grin. Mabatan, who's been gently stroking the pony's muzzle, looks up at them. "Her true name is Shanah."

Talia and Mejan gasp, "You mean it?"

Mabatan shrugs. "Next time the pony acts like Marie Antoinette, call her Shanah. You'll see."

"Shanah," Dobbs murmurs. The pony snorts and nuzzles him. Dumbfounded, Dobbs scratches her behind the ear.

Gunther Number Seventy-Nine appears in the doorway.

"The adjustment for the additional three has been completed. Dinner is served. Fact."

"And blessed be the theory that led to it. I'm starving," Kamyar replies.

"Judging from the surroundings, I'm afraid to feel too hopeful," Lumpy grumbles under his breath as they enter the uninviting cube. There are no tables or chairs, and there is certainly no food, not even the smell of it.

"Sit," says the Gunther. Talia shrugs and plops down on the cement floor. The others follow suit. Gunther Number Seventy-Nine stands by the wall, a genial look on her face, but does nothing.

Lumpy nudges Roan. "Think they're bringing the food in from outside?"

"Guess again," says Kamyar, as a low rumble vibrates through the foundation of the small room.

Roan attunes his senses, trying to determine if they're in danger. But there is no immediate threat, as far as he can tell. He watches as the ceiling recedes further and further. "This must be an elevator!" Roan exclaims, delighted.

"Of a fashion," confirms Gunther Number Seventy-Nine. "This structure was called a 'pay parking facility.' Every family would receive a small coupon to store their gasoline vehicle on one of these floors."

"Why go to the trouble?" asks Lumpy.

"Vehicles without coupons were towed away at the driver's expense and taken to vehicle cemeteries," replies the Gunther.

"Graveyards for machines?" Lumpy sounds skeptical.

"It's logical," replies the Gunther. "People were very emotionally attached to their automobiles."

Suddenly, the troupe's eyes widen with a hunger that has nothing to do with food. The object of their wistful sighs is obvious as Roan takes in the entirely new level revealed below them: a vast library of what must be thousands of books.

"Do you think we might make a brief stop?" Kamyar implores. "It's our favorite room."

"Food is waiting." The Gunther's tone suggests that no amount of begging will dissuade her.

This is by far the greatest collection of books Roan's ever seen, much larger even than the one at Oasis. "How did you acquire a library like this?"

"We do what we must. We need to read," states the Gunther. "Reading feeds our compulsion to make things."

A collective groan of disappointment accompanies the library's rapid disappearance. Roan guesses Gunther Number Seventy-Nine is in for an afternoon of haranguing from the frustrated bookworms.

On the next floor down, Gunthers oversee massive spinning cylinders, shuttle metal boxes to and fro, hover over squares of thick glass that shimmer with symbols and opaque images, and pour clear, steaming fluid from vats into molds.

"What is that material?" Roan asks.

"Something we've developed. Almost weightless, pliable, heat resistant, and if we want it to be, impenetrable."

"Do the Masters know about it?"

"Oh, yes. They use it for security windows." Gunther Number Seventy-Nine points to a chest plate being woven and pressed from transparent filaments. "And armor. But it has many other possible applications."

"And what are those?" Roan points to the illuminated glass squares.

"We're great collectors of antique garbage. You'd be surprised how many of those we find in ancient landfills. Thousands. And they're so very, very useful."

At this, Gunther Number Seventy-Nine becomes preoccupied with her glasses, leaving Roan to contemplate these fascinating and bizarre people. He wonders about the nature of the Gunthers' allegiance to the Masters, and to what extent they share their technological expertise with them.

With a shudder, they arrive at the third level. The group steps off and is greeted by Gunther Number Six, who ushers them through a huge crop of fruits and vegetables that grow under bright lamps.

"Fact: dinner awaits your consumption on table number three."

Kamyar pats his stomach as he greedily assesses the green salad, steamed broccoli and cauliflower, tomatoes, and large bowls of noodles. "What wondrous synchronicity to find the table so full and my belly so empty!"

It's a greater variety of fresh food than Roan's had the privilege to enjoy in a long time. "Number Six, how do you manage to keep this place hidden right here in the heart of the City?"

"We have designed many safeguards that give us warnings, but we rarely use them. Invisibility is our best defense."

"How do you become invisible?"

"We are Gunthers, idiot savants of the City. We stumble through their streets, live in their worst slums, speak only in grunts. They believe our brains are genetically damaged and our eyes weak, so they do not covet our children. We are harmless and feeble-minded. They trust us with the task of maintaining the energy grid because most other workers have the misfortune of dying when they come into contact with it, but we seem to have a thick-headedness that makes us impervious to the dangers. We are reviled, the butt of jokes, taken for granted. This blinds them to us. Thus, we become invisible."

Lumpy looks around at the huge room. "How long have you been doing this?"

"We're the fifth generation. Our ancestors came to the City after the Parting."

"Gunthers were one of the Four?" asks Roan.

"We were," says the Gunther.

Roan's breath catches in his throat. There were four groups at the Parting, each agreeing to leave and start a new society. His great-grandfather Roan led one to found Longlight. The second group created the cavern city of Oasis, where many of the Dirt Eaters live. Haron, an elder of Oasis, told him there were two other groups who had gone into deep cover.

How much deeper could you go than directly under the nose of your enemy?

"Are there Dirt Eaters among you?" asks Roan.

"No. But we have agreed to smuggle out Dirt to Oasis."

"And provide them with information about what's going on here," suggests Lumpy.

"We speak with the Storytellers, but it's doubtful they require what we offer. They have their own means of obtaining information."

"And the fourth group. Do you know where they went?" asks Roan.

The Gunther's usually placid expression grows sad. "We never discovered their location. Darius, however, did. Forty years ago, he released a plague upon them, causing their annihilation. We later confirmed that an epidemic killed thousands in the Farlands."

They share a grim look. Without question, the two surviving groups, Oasis and the Gunthers, would face the same fate if Darius found them.

Gunther Number Fourteen enters from a stairway on the other side of the tomato crop and comes to them. "Information. Our Stowe is alive."

Roan's stomach churns. "Is she alright?"

"According to our sources, she is in perfect physical condition."

"How can I reach her?" Roan asks urgently.

"She is scheduled to attend your performance at the Consolidation Festival."

Kamyar's face is taut. "Sharpen minds and needles, my friends. Where Our Stowe goes, so go the clerics."

"And so go I," whispers Roan.

DIAGNOSIS

RE: INCURSION ON FORESIGHT ACADEMY.

DATE: YEAR 31 OF THE CONSOLIDATION.

SUBJECT: ARCHITECT AUGUST FERRELL.

ALL 74 BLUEPRINTS, DRAWINGS, AND PLANS RECOVERED FAIL TO REVEAL THE LOCATION OF THE HIDDEN COMMUNITY OF THE RENEGADE HARON.

—ECCLESIASTICAL ARCHIVES

DOCTORS HOVER AROUND STOWE. They evaluate information, then consult anxiously over the wires and tubes that link her limbic, circulatory, and endocrine systems to hardware.

She tries to quiet the weeping in her head. It's hard to believe that they cannot hear it. Even if the machines were to find something, she's sure they'd never identify it as a persistent wail echoing in her skull. Only she can hear that. Only she can feel its torment. Perhaps it is not real at all. What if she's imagining it? What if she's going mad? Darius must not, under any circumstances, find out.

"Is this really necessary, Father?"

The Great Seer, standing by the window with Willum, shakes his head. "It's possible, dearest Stowe, that you have suffered a stroke. I'm afraid this is a matter for doctors to decide."

"Was it something that happened on the journey?" probes Stowe.

"The monitors detected nothing, but it appears there may have been a malfunction."

Dr. Arcanthas bows his head to the Eldest. "All her vital signs are better than perfect. If anything, she's stronger than before. There are, of course, fluctuations in her endocrine system, but..."

"But?" snaps Darius with thinly veiled impatience.

"In a girl of her age, fluctuations of this nature are typical. Our Stowe's are perhaps of a more extreme, uh, that is, I should say... extravagant nature. No surprise, as all her graces are thus multiplied."

Darius's eyes sparkle. Maliciously? "You are becoming a woman, Stowe."

An ocean of unspent grief for the loss of her mother overcomes Stowe. One small tear escapes before she manages to forge a dam behind her eyes. With a Herculean effort, Stowe manages to give Darius a small smile.

"There, there, daughter. It will serve only to increase your power. It is good news, good news indeed."

Dr. Arcanthas interjects with a predictable suggestion. "A few more days of tests may reveal more. Perhaps a probe—"

"Enough tests!" growls Stowe, with an edge that forces the doctor a few rabbit hops backwards.

Willum, taking his most conciliatory tone, addresses the Eldest. "If I may be so bold, Keeper. Rest, fresh air, and a temporary withdrawal of Dirt may be the best treatment."

Stowe casts her most evil eye at the doctor and delights to watch him sputter nervously. "I... I definitely can see the wisdom in that."

"Yes," condescends Darius. "I'm sure you can."

"Perhaps... she could attend some of the festivities celebrating the Consolidation. The many pageants and masques might serve to amuse her," suggests Willum.

"Oh, Father, might I go? I've always wanted to see those things." Maybe she could get away from this. All of it. Escape for a while.

The only way to escape Darius is to kill him.

The Eldest ponders Stowe's request. "She'll be swarmed. She's in no condition to make public appearances."

"I'll go in disguise."

"I cannot allow you into the streets of the City without security."

"Willum will accompany me... won't you, Willum?" Stowe begs.

"He alone would be poor defense should you come under attack."

"Let the clerics come. They just have to give us a wide berth so I'm not identified."

Before Willum can give his assent, Master Querin appears at the threshold. The very presence of the Master of Inculcation causes a shudder to sweep through the room. Responsible for every image and word dispensed by the Masters of the City, Querin is second in power only to the Great Seer and feared by all. With a voice like a whip and eyes that could pierce stone, he addresses Darius just above a whisper. "Archbishop, you're required."

The Eldest motions him over. Querin leans in, but they are far too close to her for Stowe not to hear what's being said.

"A shipment has been waylaid."

Darius glowers. "How?"

"Intercepted by the Brothers."

Suddenly distracted by matters of state, Darius rises.

"Father?"

Preoccupied, Darius pauses momentarily to consider his problem child. "Very well. See to the arrangements, Willum, will you?"

The Eldest sweeps out of the room and for one brief moment Stowe is caught in the harsh glare of Querin's eye. This master single-handedly took a hapless little girl rescued from the Farlands and turned her into Our Stowe—does he think her unworthy of the title? She smiles fearlessly, and with the merest hint of a bow, he slithers out the door.

Willum turns to the doctor. "With your permission, I'll escort Our Stowe back to her quarters and make preparations for our outing. Any special instructions, Dr. Arcanthas?"

"Not necessary. I'll be coming too. In the event of a relapse."

Stowe bristles, but Willum seems unconcerned. "Good. I'll send word before we set out. The farce being performed this evening promises to be excellent."

Stowe considers her reflection. In these amber robes, she's every inch an undercleric. Though most start their training at a later age than hers, no one will suspect that Our Stowe lurks beneath this hooded garb.

Willum slides into view behind her, an approving look on his face. "The robes suit you."

Her head quakes, pain slashes across her eyes. Struggling to hold back the screeching wail, she stumbles against Willum, exhausted.

In one graceful sweep, Willum lifts Stowe in his arms, then sets her down on the bed. Eyes riveted on hers, he presses his palm against her forehead. Stowe feels him connect with the insane wailing that possesses her. The tingling in her abdomen becomes a heat so intense she believes she will explode... and then the agony ceases, all quiets and is still.

"You'll be alright for a while," consoles Willum. "I've silenced the cry within you. It sleeps, but only briefly."

"What's happening to me?" Stowe stammers.

He says the word with an oppressive gravity. "Ferrell."

Ferrell? The lizard!

Finally she understands. She thought Ferrell had died. But she never really killed the lizard, he'd just wanted her to think she had. "How?"

"He is the creator of the Wall," says Willum. "No one knows better than he how to use its power. What happened to you inside the Wall, Stowe? Can you remember anything that might help answer your question?"

Stowe hesitates, not wanting to reveal her secret. But perhaps, her secret was never what she thought it was at all. "The lights within the Wall found a way inside me. I thought it was energy making me stronger. More powerful."

"He was distracting you while he found the way in."

And once in, she became his eyes and ears. He took advantage of her dependence on Dirt, used her to spy on Darius, the machinations of the City, the Quarry. He pushed her to check all the rooms... "He tried to make me kill those recruits."

"The Eaters fear that if more advanced travelers are found, the Masters will attack fiercely and finally overtake the Dreamfield."

"It'll be with my blessing."

"You say that because you do not understand the stakes."

"What do I care about stakes? He's been trying to take me over completely, make me into a weapon against the City. It's vile. Get him out. Now!"

"I cannot, not here, not now. But it must be done. Darius has his suspicions, and if he discovers the truth, he will extract Ferrell even if it means leaving nothing of you behind."

Stowe needs no further convincing, and immediately begins calming herself, composing her mind. She does not doubt the chilling accuracy of Willum's prediction. She already knows she's becoming expendable.

"What do I do?"

"It will be difficult to achieve, but I have friends who can smuggle you out of the City."

"Who?"

"We're going to meet them now."

She rises quickly and moves purposefully toward the door, but Willum stops her.

"Blank this conversation out of your mind, Stowe. Ferrell has a mission, here, in the City. He will not accept a change in plan. He will wake, and when he does, he must not hear your thoughts. You know how to do this. Keep your mind clear. Even if you did not have Ferrell to contend with, your survival would depend on it. When you are discovered missing, the Masters will draw on every skill they possess to locate you. Though they fear you, they intend to use you until they've accomplished their goals. Only then will you be destroyed. Stowe, you know your abilities exceed theirs in scope and magnitude. Shield yourself when the need arises, and you will have no trouble evading their reach."

Stowe gazes at the man, who until recently she had dismissed as a lowly tutor. "Who are you, Willum?"

The weight of the world upon him, he sighs, a small smile gracing his weary face. "A friend."

famıly REUNION

sнe wıLL kɴow wнat нe cannot see aɴd нe wıLL
see wнat sнe cannot kɴow. тнus, тноuɢн тнe
desтıny оf тнe son and dauɢнter оf LonɢLiɢнt
вe joined, ıт sнaLL never вe sнared.
　　　　　　　　　—тнe вook оf LonɢLiɢнt

O NE HOUR, TWO MINUTES. One hour, one minute, fifty-
five seconds. Roan can't help but be tortured by time
that goes so slowly, so impossibly slowly. He'd seen clocks
like these before, antiques in an outdoor market, but then
the dials were a cipher, the featureless gray windows that
opened onto nothing, a mystery. Now the crimson light
burns through his closed eyelids, the time meted out in
painfully equal allotments of hope and rage and fear.

As he expected, after the meal, Gunther Seventy-Nine was
worn down by the constant requests to explore the library.
Normally that would be the obvious place for Roan to spend
time, but today he wanted quiet and solitude to focus his
mind. So he stayed here, because he found the lush green of
the Gunthers' hydroponic gardens a comfort. The fragrance

of the herbs keep pulling him back to memories of the gardens in Longlight, of sneaking in one afternoon with Stowe to steal a ripe tomato. Stowe, who had always been so mischievous and funny.

Now she is Our Stowe, Master-in-Training, as powerful and dangerous as any of the Turned. She could have him arrested, have them all seized. What if she attacks him? How will he react? Will he panic like he did when Saint grabbed him? No. He'll go down fighting before he allows anyone in the troupe to be captured.

His approach has to be perfect; everything depends on it. No matter how much she's changed, she is his sister and if anyone can touch her, he can. Will she accept the gift he's tucked so carefully in his pocket? And then, most importantly, will she accept him?

He opens one eye. Gunther Number Seventy-Nine waits respectfully for Roan's acknowledgment. Perhaps there's a little more to the Gunthers' invisibility than they shared, because he didn't sense her arrival. Opening his eyes fully, he greets her.

"Roan of Longlight. May I see your cricket?" she asks.

Grateful for the diversion, he opens his pocket and gives her an apologetic look. "It's really not up to me if it comes out or not. Like most of this species, it has a mind of its own."

"I know. I've been researching them."

"You have books on white crickets?"

"No, no book has been written yet. The purpose of my research is to fill that gap. But the only information available is unconfirmed. It is terribly frustrating. You see, after the Abominations, many species, including humans, experienced genetic change. I have seen many examples of these mutations in the laboratories of the Masters—Gunthers have access—but they have never succeeded in capturing a white cricket."

Gunther Number Seventy-Nine lifts her glasses and moves her face close to Roan's chest, her nose almost touching the white cricket that has emerged from his pocket.

"Smaller than I imagined. Not pure white, almost ivory. Does it sing?"

"I've never seen one that hasn't."

"And this organ." She points out a tubular structure at the end of its abdomen. "Do all white crickets have this as well?"

Roan peers at the tiny tube. "I think so."

"Were you aware they are hermaphrodites?" she asks.

"I'm not sure what you mean."

"Normally, the male cricket sings to attract females. But this cricket has an ovipositor, that organ at the end of its abdomen. It lays eggs. Your cricket seems to be both male and female. Do you think it might stand in this?" Seventy-Nine opens her palm to reveal a cube so transparent it is almost invisible. And though Roan is a bit discomfited by the idea, his cricket complies instantly.

"Excellent. This device will collect invaluable information on all aspects of the cricket's physiology."

Tiny filaments of light trace geometric patterns over the entire cube and it hums a pitch Roan identifies as middle C.

"Now, if only it would sing..." the Gunther says hopefully.

As if in answer to her request, the cricket immediately begins to weave an intricate harmony around the solo note.

"Astonishing," Gunther Number Seventy-Nine whispers, the first indication of deep feeling Roan has witnessed from a Gunther.

Though Roan can tell the cricket is not threatened by the device, he can't stem the anxiety he feels being separated from it. The snow cricket has been his constant companion since Longlight perished, guiding him through many rough passages. The idea of ever losing it is unthinkable.

"My hypothesis is that some of the mutations we're seeing are more than adaptations to the extreme environmental pressures of the last century. I believe they're part of an overall evolutionary shift that goes beyond the physical body."

"I'm not sure that I understand."

The Gunther pauses from her intent study of the data she's collecting and, lowering her glasses, directs her cool gray eyes at Roan. "You must. For you are part of this same evolutionary shift. Did you not realize it?"

Of course, he knows he's different, that he can do things others cannot, but part of an "evolutionary shift"? What does that mean? Shift to what? Before Roan can question the Gunther further, a trap door snaps open from the floor above and Lumpy's head appears, wrong side up. "Time to go." Seeing the white cricket inside the strange little cube, he asks, "What's that?"

"An interactive tonal amplifier," she explains.

"Obviously," says Lumpy.

Seventy-Nine leans in close to the cricket. "Thank you very much for your cooperation." With a wiggle of its feelers, it jumps back onto Roan's shoulder as he rises to join the others.

By the time they arrive at Conurbation Park, the celebrations are in full swing. Why they call this a park is a mystery to Roan, as it's simply a square block of white concrete, without a tree or bush in sight. The entire area is hemmed in by green glass towers that hover ominously over the celebration, but no one seems to mind. The revelers, most wearing masks, many fully costumed, are a cacophony of color rippling to the pounding rhythm of steel drums. Roan positions himself between Mabatan and Lumpy, in hopes of distancing himself from the overwhelming swells of emotion radiating from the merrymakers. He has to keep his head clear for his encounter with Stowe.

"Why aren't these people enabled?" Roan whispers to Talia.

"Hey—how can you tell?"

"There's too much feeling."

"Huh. Well, they're the rich. Citizens who contribute to the glorification of the Conurbation aren't candidates for the enabler. At least not yet. They owe their wealth to the Masters—and they know it. That's control enough."

"You sure we won't get mobbed?" Lumpy asks anxiously. "I mean, the play does make these guys look pretty stupid."

"You'd be surprised how much you can get away with when

you make people laugh," Talia says with a wink.

Roan strains his eyes trying to locate, in this mass of gesticulating bodies, the person he's come so far to see. He closes his eyes, hoping to sense her, but Mabatan cuts his search short.

"Take care you do not risk everyone's safety," she warns. "There are those in the City who can detect your abilities. You must wait for her to reveal herself."

Before Roan can respond, Kamyar settles his bulk between them. His arms enclosing them both, he whispers, "Do not look so serious, my friends. This is, after all, the party of all parties. On top of which," he grins, "we're on!"

A car stops in a quiet street a few blocks from Conurbation Park. A small hooded undercleric, a minor City official, and a doctor in his emerald greatcoat step out. Ahead of and behind them, several other cars lurch to a halt. Clerics ooze out of the vehicles to surround the undercleric. The hooded figure, however, gives the guards such a threatening look that they disperse, not as far as Stowe would like, but as much as they dare. She notes the presence of each, across a street, far ahead, behind. Maybe they'd offer some protection from an assault, but all of them put together are not worth one Willum. How could Darius be so blind? Because Willum wants him to be? Could he be that powerful? One thing is sure, these clerics are not even a match for her. Especially now that they know what she can do to them.

The business district is devoid of people and activity, but

when they turn the corner, festively dressed citizens eagerly converging on the park press against them on all sides.

"Stay close, Doctor Arcanthas, we don't want to lose you," cautions Willum.

"I'll stick to you like glue," promises the doctor. But as a dozen inebriated celebrants barge their way past, the doctor is dislodged and Willum and Stowe blend seamlessly into the crowd, leaving Arcanthas and the clerics scurrying frantically behind.

Banners festoon the park, revelers are everywhere. Jugglers, stilt-walkers, and fire-breathers wander through the square and a bizarrely masked musical group plays a rollicking jig on an outdoor stage.

Stowe jerks to a stop, suddenly nauseated. Her insides are roiling, her throat tightening. A voice, not her own, vomits out of her mouth. "What are we doing here?"

It's Ferrell, his every word low and raspy, scraping its way into existence.

"Help me," Stowe pleads, clutching desperately at her throat.

Willum seizes her elbow. "We have to keep moving or the others will catch up." He twines his long fingers through hers. "I am with you. I will not allow him to harm you. Do not fight, leave the way open, permit him to speak."

The moment Stowe relaxes, the voice barks, "I asked, what are we doing here?"

"We are here for a show, it is a mere diversion," Willum says.

"I don't believe you!"

Willum twists Stowe round and lifts her so he can look squarely into her eyes. "Ferrell, whatever else she is, she remains a child."

"She is no child. She's a freak, a monstrosity!"

Touching his forehead to Stowe's, Willum whispers, "Be at peace." This time, the mounting heat from her wound is instantly quenched by an energy that washes over her like cascades of cool water. Willum holds her tightly to stop her shivering, and in a soothing voice assures her, "All is well."

But when he sets her down, Stowe feels small, more childlike than she's ever remembered feeling. She hates these emotions of vulnerability and fear; they make her want to strike out, to explode.

"Come. There isn't much time." Willum takes her hand and guides her toward the stage. A tall man with black curly hair waves for the music to stop and addresses the crowd. "And now, in honor of the Masters of the City and the annual Festival of the Consolidation, we bring you our modest offering, entitled *A Clerical Error.*"

The showman bows to the whistling and applauding audience and is nearly bowled over by a boy with a bag over his head.

With a wink to the audience, the man pulls the boy up by his shirt. "Pardon me, lad, but why the bag?"

"You don't want to know," says the muffled voice inside the bag. The man looks at the audience. "Oh, I think we do, don't we?"

The people roar back. "We do!"

With a grin to the crowd, he yanks the bag off the boy's head, revealing a horrible mask. It's pitted with craters, the flesh red and raw.

The audience lets out a collective gasp, but a few people boo, unimpressed. "Where are the Mor-Ticks!" they jeer. The showman, backing away, gestures widely to the crowd. "Enjoy the show!"

A musician in a fire mask plays a wild tune on a recorder while the fake Mor-Tick victim hops to the rhythm, arms flapping. The music whips round Stowe's heart, seizing her attention. Her mind reaches out to the masked figure. Blocked. He's shielding himself. Impossible.

Willum nudges her closer to the side of the stage, where the showman contentedly observes the audience, apparently unaware of their approach. A young girl, holding a drum, stands near him, her eyes focused on Stowe. She has an oddly soothing gaze.

"Ah, Willum, gained a few gray hairs, I see, since last we met," says the showman, eyes still on the crowd.

Willum glances nervously in the direction of the stage.

"Relax, that cleric is one of ours. The play's stooge."

"Yes, that one, but not the others, they'll be on top of us in moments." Willum turns to Stowe. "This is Kamyar, the friend I told you about."

"This way," Kamyar murmurs as he directs them into the canvas tent behind the stage. Reaching into a trunk, he pulls out a drab ocher apprentice robe. "Put this on. Time for a change in professions. Make haste, please."

Stowe lowers her hood and Kamyar's mouth drops open. "It *is* her! I was sure I'd misread the code or that you were having us on, even though I know you to be monumentally humorless."

"It's incredibly risky, probably impossible. That's why I asked *you*."

"In this case, flattery salts the wound."

Nodding reassuringly to Stowe, Willum urgently takes Kamyar's arm. "There's something else."

"I know I'm not going to like this," grumbles Kamyar as Willum pulls him back outside the tent.

Stowe, knowing full well what the subject of their agitated whispers will be, takes the opportunity to change her clothes. She throws off the undercleric robes and replaces them with the tattered apprentice's. When she looks up to inspect herself in a small battered mirror, she sees the fire-masked recorder player instead, almost near enough to touch, staring. He's the one who blocked her outside—that's why she didn't sense him come in. As he reaches into his pocket, Stowe readies herself. It will have to be a scream, one strong enough to blow his head right off. She won't try to fight someone who can sneak up on her like that.

What has he got in his hand?

A rag doll, wrapped in a faded purple shawl.

Her doll. The doll that dropped in the snow. The bloody snow beside Roan's hand. Roan's hand. Stowe's breath is coming in gasps, her heart thundering in her ears. She takes the doll.

The player lifts the fire-mask from his face. "I missed you." His voice, so tender, just as she remembers it. This is the brother she scoured the Farlands for, the one Darius lost. "Roan."

Roan, spellbound, looks at his sister. She's grown so much. She looks exactly like their mother the last time he saw her. The same auburn hair, the same eyes wet with tears. Slowly, carefully, he reaches his hand out to her.

She stares at his hand. It's the same one she lost so long ago, the hand ripped from hers as he fell bleeding to the snow.

Roan doesn't speak, but keeps his palm open to her, reaching out with his mind, begging her: *Take it, Stowe, take it.*

She wants so badly to have her family again, to be with her brother, for life to be simple, and happy, and good again, the way she remembers it. The life of a child.

You are still a child, his eyes say to her as she smiles sadly. *You're barely ten.*

No. My childhood was lost when you left me in the clutches of the City, evaded all my attempts to find you, ignored my calls.

Roan desperately shakes his head, taking a step toward her. With all his strength, he wills her to take his hand. *Why won't you take my hand?*

Clutching the doll to her side, Stowe moves a step back from her brother. She cannot take his hand. If she did, he would know that the Stowe he believes in is dead. And the Stowe she's become needs to focus. There are five clerics and a doctor close by.

"No!" Roan shouts before the pain detonates in his head.

He gapes in horror as a pair of shadows topple, smearing the canvas red. With a slash of his hook-sword, the material splits, revealing two writhing clerics. Willum's crouched over a man in an emerald greatcoat who's convulsing, blood gushing from his ears. Roan rushes out to help several celebrants who are rocking on their knees, heads clutched in their hands, noses bleeding. A child shrieks and within seconds, there's a chorus of screams as panic spreads. People run over each other in an attempt to get away, so that Roan can't tell his sister's victims from the riot's. Seeking out his friends, he sees Kamyar charging over to where the pony's frantically rearing despite Talia's best efforts to calm it. Dobbs and Mejan are lifting children onto the stage out of harm's way. Before Roan can locate the others, sirens wail and dozens of clerics, brandishing rods, pour into the park, stunning any in their way.

A piercing howl of loneliness ghosts through Roan, and he bolts back to the tent, but Stowe is gone.

Lumpy grabs his arm.

"We have to get out of here. Now."

"Stowe..."

The man who arrived with Stowe grasps Roan's shoulder and looks steadily into his eyes. "I am Willum. I will see to her safety."

"She's my sister and I will find her." Roan tries to pull away, but Willum's grip holds him back with preternatural strength.

"Roan, understand: the entire City will be on alert. Every

Master will be searching for her. And you would be a great prize."

"What difference does that make?" Roan, blind with fury, reaches for his sword.

Willum stays his hand, his voice moving deep into Roan's consciousness. "I will make explanations to the Masters. Then I will seek her out."

"That's my responsibility."

"No. You must attend to other matters. You know this. I promise. I will bring her to you."

"Who are you—why should I trust you?"

In a heartbeat, a multitude of images flashes before Roan's eyes. The Novakin, clinging to the rift. Saint's fevered eyes in the grip of hell. His mate, Kira, smiling in welcome, gesturing for Roan to come to her. The faces of more children. The eye of a cricket.

When the bond is broken, Roan knows that he and Willum are linked. Beyond words, beyond experience. Though he has no notion how.

"Go to Kira," Willum whispers. "You have my word, Roan. I *will* find her and bring her to you."

"Why? Why would you do such a thing—take such a risk?"

"Because everything depends on it."

A score of clerics smash and stumble onto the stage.

"Journey well, Roan of Longlight!" says Willum, turning toward the clerics.

"Let's go, go, go!" shouts Kamyar, and pushing Roan through the panicked mob, they make their escape.

tHe LittLe gIRL

tHe aRCHBISHOP BeSTOWS ON HIS CITY a pHOeNIX,
RISeN fROM tHe asHeS Of tHe DeMON BaSTION CaLLeD
LONgLIgHt. a gOLDeN CHILD. HIS aDOPTeD DaUgHTeR.
CURatRIX tO US aLL. OUR STOWe. LONg May SHe SeRVe
tHe CONgRegaTION.

—pROCLamatION Of maSTeR QUeRIN

R EMORSE CHASING HER LIKE A HOUND, Stowe runs.
Enemies surround her, but what she's escaping is the
distressed face of her brother—that face so much like her
own, yet also far different. Tucking the doll securely beneath
her tunic, she hurls herself into the pandemonium, dipping
and weaving through the panicking crowd. Stowe coaxes the
tempest of her emotions into a gentle spiral as she clears her
mind, then allows the spiral to curl over her surface like fog.
The shimmering saffron aura that glistens over her every
inch is well concealed by her tattered robes. And the clerics
that glance at Stowe do so without recognition, their narrow
consciousness easily deceived by this shield.

Allowing herself to be swept along with the stampede of

bodies, she scrambles out of the park and down the street. Ahead, a truck blocks the way, its headlights blinding the oncoming citizens. Clerics stand on top of the vehicle, holding huge stun sticks, poised for battle.

"Remain where you are," a booming voice commands. "Cooperation ensures safety."

Stowe watches in disgust as the clerics bring order to the crowd. Citizens of the Conurbation are all so timid, all so willing to obey. They will allow themselves to be moved along, shepherded out one by one, their papers examined. Well, there are thousands of them and only one of her. There's enough time to calm herself and set her mind to planning an escape.

Slowly she scans the street for a way out. Steel, concrete, and glass surround her on all sides, the crowd can only go forward or back, and both directions lead to clerics. Then she spots it—a narrow lane between two of the buildings, but getting there would mean moving against the tide, and she wouldn't go far before she'd be noticed. Luck, however, is with her, for as another wave of terrified citizens rounds the corner, the ensuing tumult masks Stowe's charge. Two years of training with Willum has prepared her for much greater obstacles. She is sure of her stealth as she glides into the lane and along its walls. But it soon opens onto a sparkling commercial street, windows aglow with elegantly dressed mannequins, no shoppers in sight. Too dangerous, she'd be exposed.

Stowe swiftly cuts across the thoroughfare and follows the lane to the next street and the next until she arrives at a City she does not know. Here the people are walking corpses, as ancient and dirty as the buildings that surround them. Their hollow eyes stare right back at her, no knowledge to share, nothing to lose. Fading posters of Our Stowe are pasted to every wall, to every boarded doorway. A man, his face unshaven, mouth toothless, picking through a mass of stinking garbage, looks at her and holds out his open palm. Stowe backs away, only to bump into an ashen-faced woman.

"Are you lost, dear?" the woman gently asks.

"No," Stowe mumbles, backing away.

The woman peeks beneath the cowl with her pallid eyes, trying to make out Stowe's features. "Why do you hide your face, child?"

"The festivities."

The woman sadly smiles. "You are scarred, aren't you?"

"Yes," says Stowe. "I have scars."

"It is safe to show yourself, little one. The clerics do not bother us here. Come out of the night. I have a warm room you can share."

Taking advantage of the woman's kindness, Stowe allows her hand to be taken, making sure it remains concealed in the drape of her sleeve. She needs to get off the street and out of view. As a decrepit door swings open, the woman draws her into a dimly lit room that smells of mold and smoke and urine. In one corner, there is a small, threadbare carpet covered with dozens of broken plastic dolls. A hairless one-armed baby doll with no eyes, dolls with elaborate curls but no legs, or fusty cracked heads without bodies, all carefully arranged to surround and stare at the visitor. She feels her own rag doll and protectively presses it against her skin. Unable to avert her gaze from the eerie assembly, she draws closer to a little shrine. A few moldy grapes sit on a stained plate and two burning candles light a tiny photograph of Our Stowe.

"She looks after us all," says the woman. "Our Stowe is our guardian angel."

Stowe says nothing, for there's nothing she can say, and obediently sits when the woman offers her a little red child's chair.

"You must be hungry." The woman reaches into a box and takes out a small container. She lifts the lid, removes some tissue, and presses a chocolate chip cookie on Stowe. "I've been saving this for you."

Stowe stares speechless at the morsel in her hand.

"Eat. It's very good."

Stowe takes a small bite. Old and stale. She wipes the crumbs off her tongue.

"I'll give you one every day if you stay with me. You can be my little girl. I promise I won't sell you."

Stowe drops her cookie and stands. The woman picks it up, brushes it off. "My little girl always finished her cookies. She ate them all up. She ate me out of house and home. I'm glad you don't eat too much." Her eyes well up and she extends her arms. "I'll love you better, I promise."

Stowe pushes the madwoman away and, leaving her collapsed in the mass of mangled dolls, runs out the door. Back on the street, other wasted lives wait, and they all would like a piece of her. "Little girl," they call, "little girl."

They all want to sell her, so she can be cut to pieces and fed into the City's machine. Just hours ago, she would have wanted to cleanse this place, erase them all. It would have been so easy, one thought and they'd be gone. But that was before. Now she just wants to run.

Stowe's jolted by a familiar scent. It takes a moment to place it. Motor oil. It leads her to a chain link fence, behind which a score of official Conurbation cars and trucks in various stages of repair are parked. The sign reads VEHICLE MAINTENANCE. The fence is topped by razor wire and a heavy padlock secures the wide gate. The sirens sound like they're closing in; she's running out of time. She steals along the perimeter, steadying her breath, until she finds what she's looking for: a gap along the ground wide enough for her to squeeze through. Sensing no presence, she ducks down and crawls through.

One of the vehicles might serve as a place to spend the night, if she can find one that's suitable. The sirens wail louder. Her eyes dart from vehicle to vehicle. Then she sees it. A white truck with a giant tongue licking an ice cream cone. She tries the cargo compartment. Open.

Shutting the door behind her, she inspects her new sanctuary. The interior brings back a wave of not altogether unpleasant memories. Rows of seats in front of a long storage cabinet filled with pillows and blankets, food and snacks. Ah, yes, there's the small icebox. Could it be stocked? Stowe peers in and smiles at the sight. Ice cream. She picks one up, takes off the wrapper and bites. Strawberry.

the sewers of the city

COUSIN TO THE SON AND DAUGHTER OF LONGLIGHT,
HE SHALL STAND BETWEEN THEM AND THEIR ENEMIES
AND THEY SHALL KNOW HIM ALWAYS.
　　　　　　　　　　—THE BOOK OF LONGLIGHT

HALOED IN PALE YELLOW LIGHT, Gunther Number Six, still pushing his cart, guides the troupe through the ancient storm sewers of the City, tunnels made of huge concrete pipe wide enough for a large caravan to drive through. Abandoned long ago, these sewers are known only to the Gunthers, who, in Roan's mind, are using them to greater purpose. The first hundred paces or so into the conduit, however, were revolting: terrible fumes rose off fetid mud smeared across dark, dank walls and a few of their members retched. None too soon, they were led through a well-hidden portal, and everyone seemed happier now that they were traveling down a dry, clean-smelling passage.

"Why couldn't we fight a little before we ran?" complains Talia, still a little testy from her recent bout of nausea.

"That was not a backyard brawl, my lass," says Kamyar.

"No, it was a center of the City brawl, and I can't believe we missed it."

Mejan lets out a well-worn sigh. "Any excuse to kill a few clerics."

"Yes, and if she doesn't learn a little restraint, soon one of them is going to kill her right back," growls Kamyar.

"Easy, Shanah, easy now," coos Dobbs to the pony, who is completely unnerved by the trumpeting voices and claustrophobic surroundings. A chastening glance from Dobbs forces the troupe into a restrained silence.

With Mabatan and Lumpy at either side, Roan relaxes his defenses. Obsessing over every microsecond of his meeting with Stowe, he wallows in a morass of regret. He worries over the manic, frightened look in her eyes. The ache in her voice when she whispered his name. The way she radiated Dirt. How much has she been taking? He never should have given her the doll, it shocked her, made her remember her past in a flood, the trauma of loss drowning her. In his mind's eye, he takes out the doll again and again, recalling her reaction. The tangled mass of conflicting emotions: hate, fear, sadness. He could feel a trace of love and longing, but it was tempered by deep resentment. She hated him as much as she loved him, felt betrayed by his absence, and envious. Of what? He focuses on the memory, freezing and examining each moment, each fragment of the emotion that cascaded over him. She is jealous of what he's grown into, because she hates what she's become. She thinks she is a monster.

"They have hurt your sister's mind," says Mabatan.

Roan emerges from his deep silence. "The Turned?"

"I do not speak only of the Turned," says Mabatan.

"Then who else?"

"She is inhabited. I sensed another presence within her."

"It's a Dirt Eater," says Kamyar. "Stowe went through the Wall. She attacked the Dirt Eaters and was attacked in turn. It's Ferrell. At least that's what Willum said."

Roan finds no comfort in having his suspicions about the Dirt Eaters confirmed—they may be responsible, but he has to face the cold truth. "Her feelings were clear. Carrying an entity inside her is no doubt adding to her problems, but her unhappiness, the core of the rage that fed her attack, that was her own."

"She did no more with her mind than you might have done with a weapon," says Mabatan.

"If the clerics hadn't been there, if she hadn't had something to focus her anger on, I think she might have turned on me."

"I only got a glimpse of her," says Lumpy. "But she looked sad, not angry."

"Of the two, only anger offers a release," says Mabatan.

Roan cries out in frustration. "Alandra was right. The Turned have broken her. The Stowe I knew is gone. I could smell the Dirt in her sweat. How could they do that to her?"

Kamyar tries to reassure him. "Willum will take care of her, just like he said."

"If the clerics don't get her first."

Kamyar laughs. "They won't. They're no match for Willum.

And if he has to, he'll give those Masters a run for their money as well."

Roan struggles to accept Kamyar's assurances. Why did he feel that deep connection with Willum? If he is such a friend, why didn't he do something about Stowe sooner? Why would he let it progress so far? "Tell me more about this Willum. Is he Turned or Dirt Eater?"

Kamyar taps his finger on the mesh metal screen that covers a yellow bulb. "A little of both, I guess."

"And neither," adds Mabatan.

Lumpy's getting impatient. "Is it possible to get a straight answer from anyone?"

"There are none, my good Lump," says Kamyar. "But I can offer what little I know. I met him fifteen years ago, wandering the Farlands. We were both about your age. He'd just spent a month alone, trekking in the Devastation, on some kind of spiritual search. He was in pretty rough shape, hadn't eaten in weeks, kept muttering nonsense. I fed him but he didn't offer much in return, except to tell me his calling was in the City. He had to prepare the way, he claimed. For what? I asked. But that was all he would say. I can't explain why, really, but I decided to assist. Set him up with the Gunthers, who helped him blend in as only they can, so he could acquire a position that would allow him to work. And work he did, all the way into the Masters' circle. I never breathed a word of it to the Dirt Eaters. Over the years, he's become a good friend, if not a very forthcoming one."

Thirty days in the Devastation would have been an eternity. Roan knows that he never would have survived his time there if Lumpy hadn't happened along.

"He knew about the children. Showed me Kira. Crickets."

"Willum also told you where to go," says Mabatan. "He has given you a map."

"I don't remember a map."

"You will."

"A map? Maybe it'll help us free the children." The eagerness in Lumpy's voice betrays the anxiety he's been repressing.

Mabatan places a reassuring hand on Lumpy's arm. "They are the ones for whom Willum paves the way."

Their pace is swift and silence settles over the troupe. Their careworn expressions and fixed concentration show their concern over the riot and all its possible repercussions. Roan wonders what else was revealed to the Storytellers in the City. Humor may dominate their conversations, but their eyes look deeply into everything that crosses their path. What tales will they weave from this experience?

Under the unrelenting banks of yellow light that line the passages, Roan's thoughts shift from the Storytellers to the Novakin. He had not thought much past his hopes of finding his sister and enlisting her help. And now that he's failed, he's lost his direction and he fears he may have made the wrong decision. Having learned, time and again, not to trust strangers, leaving Stowe in the hands of one could be one of the most foolish things he's ever done. But Mabatan and Kamyar trust

Willum, and Roan has a greater responsibility—or so he's told: Guardian of the Novakin. But what kind of guardian is he when he's constantly questioning the virtue of his abilities and whether to use them? How can he help the children if he has no idea where to begin?

Shanah picks up her pace, trotting through the tunnel. Dobbs, panting, runs past the Gunther to follow her.

"The animal has a highly efficient sense of smell. The exitway is just a few paces ahead," says Gunther Number Six.

When they catch up to the pony, Shanah is softly bumping her head against a circular metal door, Dobbs gently patting her neck, trying to soothe her. "I'll be glad to get outta this place too, Shanah," he coos.

The Gunther, squeezing by the horse, reaches up to the middle of the door and slides open a small peephole. He puts his eye to it. Nods to himself, then reaches into his cart and takes out a long, thin tube. He pushes it through the hole and looks again, twisting the tube this way and that. Pulling it out, he replaces it tidily in the cart. Only then is he ready for his eager audience.

"All clear," he says. "In theory." He unbolts the door and swings it open. The pony gallops out, followed by the troupe, all gratefully breathing in the cool night air. A sliver of moon casts its pale shadow along the trench of a steep ravine.

"Follow this east. It should take you safely to the edge of the Farlands." Reaching into his cart, the Gunther presents them with a box. "This contains nutritious and appetizing energy bars for your consumption, a twenty-day supply."

Kamyar offers effusive thanks, which only seems to make Number Six uncomfortable. Scooting around Kamyar, he points a finger at Roan. "You must stay. In the morning, I will give you the thing you need."

"Thing?" Lumpy asks.

"In the morning," says the Gunther.

"My assumption," says Kamyar, "is that your journey takes you in another direction, so here is where we part ways. It was good to see you, Roan of Longlight. With any luck, our paths will cross again."

"Thank you for everything," Roan says, and takes his hand. "You were right about so much."

"That could always change, but for the moment I will accept your gratitude. Though I do have one regret." Kamyar pauses dramatically before turning to Lumpy. "You never got your opening night. And you would have been marvelous, Lump. You're a natural if I ever saw one."

"One of these days we'll get our chance," says Mejan, giving Lumpy a hug. After many thumps on the back and friendly punches, Talia and Dobbs also make their farewells, and with promises to journey safely, the Storytellers, knitting needles at the ready, set off down the ravine.

"I must leave as well," says Mabatan. "Roan, you will find your strength in the song that speaks most powerfully to your heart. Listen well, so that you may hear it."

"Where are you going?"

"Willum has asked me to help him find your sister."

Surprised, Lumpy says, "I didn't see you talk to him."

"Words are not always necessary, dear friend. Be well." Mabatan bows her head to both of them, and without a sound, disappears into the night.

"You must stay inside for the night," says Gunther Number Six. "Come."

But Lumpy doesn't move, straining his eyes for a glimpse of Mabatan. "Just making sure she gets out safe."

"She was on her own for a long time before we came along," says Roan. "She'll be alright."

"Based on our current information, there is a high probability of her safe passage. Go inside now," the Gunther presses.

But Lumpy, still peering into the darkness, doesn't respond. The Gunther twitches impatiently.

Roan nudges his friend. "You know, right now I think you ought to be more worried about Gunther Number Six."

"Yeah, I suppose," frowns Lumpy, grudgingly following the Gunther back into the tunnel.

After securing the circular metal door, Gunther Number Six is noticeably more relaxed. "Sleep. Your departure is scheduled for ten minutes prior to sunrise." After giving them a few energy bars, the Gunther slumps over his cart, and disappears down the gloomy tunnel.

"Will we see Mabatan again?" Lumpy's voice is choked with emotion.

"I feel certain we will," says Roan, and strangely enough, he does.

"Well, you're usually right about these things," sighs Lumpy, looking dispiritedly at the bars in his hand. "I suppose a meal before bed wouldn't hurt. I *am* starved." Peeling off the wrapper of one bar, he sniffs it dejectedly, then tries a tiny bite. As he chews, his face lights up. "Bugs!"

Roan looks grimly at his bar. "Practical folk, those Gunthers."

"Delicious," grins Lumpy, and gulps his down.

They silently set down their bedrolls on the cold concrete. Still melancholy over Mabatan's departure, Roan starts thinking about all the people who've walked into and then out of his life these past few years: Kira, who might not be who he thought she was; the Forgotten, who'd sheltered him when he was a fugitive from the Brothers—Orin, Haron, and Sari, all three probably Dirt Eaters although they never openly admitted it; Alandra—if he thought he could contact her without the other Dirt Eaters knowing, he would. He imagines she's still hovering over the children, trying to bring them back. They'd come to him as a surprise, but she'd sacrificed a lot to be there for them when the time came. He wonders if she has any inkling at all of where or who they really are, these Novakin.

Drifting into sleep, Roan's shoulder tingles, recalling the sensation he had when Willum touched him there yesterday. Then, in a gathering mist, a gigantic map appears. Rippling, multi-colored light on a transparent, fluid surface, it slowly extends itself to float before him. Focusing at any point on the map, he immediately knows the name and purpose of the site. He recognizes the City and its environs, the Quarry where the Dirt is mined, the approach roads, factories, guard gates, and security walls. Roan imagines himself high above the map and, as the City grows smaller, the surrounding area comes into view. He can see the Farlands, Barren Mountain, and the Devastation beyond. He finds the plateau where he spent a year with the Brothers, then on the distant horizon he sees a triangle of glowing red light. Without question, this is the place Willum wants him to go.

The sound of Gunther Number Six clearing his throat rouses Roan. "Time to leave."

Roan shares a bleary look with Lumpy.

"But we just went to sleep," Lumpy yawns.

"Sunrise in ten minutes, fifteen seconds. Pack up."

"Just another fifteen seconds," moans Lumpy, lying back down.

Despite Lumpy's protestations, they roll up their blankets while Number Six slides opens the door, bringing in a welcome draft of fresh air. The pre-dawn damp makes them shiver as they shuffle into the thinning darkness outside. Chewing on a breakfast bug bar, they watch with growing interest while Number Six negotiates the steep slope of the ravine.

"This way, this way," Number Six says, and Roan and Lumpy realize with dismay that they are supposed to follow.

"By the way, Roan," asks Lumpy, "do you have any idea where this Kira lives?"

"Yeh. I had another dream."

"You know," says Lumpy blithely, "sometimes I think you dream too much for your own good—or mine."

They scale the top of the ravine just as the pale golden dawn breaks.

"You'll want these." The Gunther hands Roan and Lumpy each a pair of goggles, then walks up to a small tree, kneels down, and starts patting his hands on the ground. Digging his fingers in the soil, he pulls up a flat piece of earth. "Willum requested we design a vehicle for his use, should he ever need to escape." He puts his hand down a hole and his arm sinks all the way in. "And now he's asked that we provide it to you." Gripping some unseen object, Gunther Number Six pulls, and listening intently, waits.

"You two should stand next to me," he suggests offhand-edly. There's a low rumbling, then the ground shakes violently and begins to rise at their feet.

Scooting behind Number Six, Roan and Lumpy watch in awe as a huge camouflaged platform lifts. Revealed beneath it are two pairs of vast wings made of the translucent material they'd seen in the Gunthers' manufacturing section the day before.

Lumpy gently runs his finger down the curve of a wing. "Do these things really do... what they look like they're supposed to do?"

"Our proudest accomplishment. A flying device of our own invention using the strong, lightweight material we developed for the Masters. As Seventy-Nine mentioned, they use it for body armor and windows, while we use it for our own purposes."

"I see there's two sets of these," says Lumpy.

"Yes."

"... Am I supposed to fly one of them?"

"Yes."

"How?" asks Lumpy, his anxiety escalating.

"They are intuitive."

"Ah," he peeps.

"Watch." With great precision, the Gunther places his palms over the juncture of two transparent wings. As he raises his hands, the wings lift and seemingly without effort the Gunther maneuvers them until they are perched over Roan's shoulders. "Extend your arms. Imagine you and the device are one."

Their touch is so gentle, Roan has to look to be sure he's wearing them. He is struck by how weightless they are, as if they were actually a part of him.

"We've embedded sensors in the material that draw the wings toward updrafts and thermals. The reports indicate it will be a hot day, so you should have all the current you need. Your will controls altitude and direction, so your thoughts must be disciplined and focused. The sensors will take care of the rest."

"One problem," says Lumpy. "I'm not exactly what you'd

call trained in the mental focus and discipline department."

The Gunther slips the other pair of wings over Lumpy's shoulders. "We have anticipated that inequity. Roan's wings have been recalibrated to control yours as well."

"Here I go, putting my life in your hands again," mutters Lumpy, with a sideways glance at Roan. He gives the wings a little flap. "So now what?" he asks Number Six.

"Just jump off the ridge. The wings will find the wind. Once they've adjusted to your size and weight, you'll feel a slight quiver. That means they await a direction. Give it and they will seek out the correct thermal current."

"Thank you," says Roan.

"The Gunthers wish you good fortune, Roan of Longlight." And with that, the Gunther steps onto the platform that held the wings and disappears into the ground.

Careful not to drag their wings, Roan and Lumpy cautiously make their way toward the cliff. Peering over the edge, Lumpy squeaks, "Seems pretty high, doesn't it?"

"Yeh," says Roan. "Good thing you trust me." And without another thought, he catapults himself into freefall. Just as he's about to lose his stomach, Roan feels the wings catch the wind. He looks up at Lumpy still staring anxiously over the side.

"Are you focused?" yells Lumpy.

"Last call!" shouts Roan as he's drawn along the flow of warm air.

Lumpy shakes his fist and Roan laughs, knowing full well the terror his friend has of heights.

Closing his eyes, Lumpy steps off the cliff. He bellows when he drops like a stone, but moments later, soaring beside Roan, he manages an offhand look. "So exactly what direction are we headed in?"

Roan calls up Willum's map. He marvels as it superimposes itself onto the landscape. Whoever this Willum is, he's got a few tricks up his sleeve that Roan wouldn't mind knowing.

"Northwest," Roan yells, focusing in that direction. The wings instantly respond, tilting slightly and going into a quick ascent.

Roan has flown in the Dreamfield, but there the wind does not scream through his senses, the cool breeze catch in his breath, nor the sun unite him with the air and the earth under its light. Nothing compares to this, the pure exhilaration and freedom of flight in the real world. He glances back at an ecstatic Lumpy, illuminated in the sunrise, its rays emblazing his diaphanous wings. Like the angels he once read about, they're flying.

stowaways

TRANSPORT VEHICLE EVALUATION. CONCLUSION:
DESPITE POOR ASSESSMENTS IN VEHICLE MANEUVERABILITY
AND ENERGY CONSUMPTION, THE efficacy of THE
JABBERWOCK fLEET REMAINS UNPARALLELED.
REPLACEMENT AT THIS JUNCTURE IS DEEMED INADVISABLE.

—ECCLESIASTICAL REPORTS

MEN... THE SOUND OF MEN'S VOICES. Stowe draws herself up slowly, silently. How long has she been sleeping? What are they saying? The words aren't clear, something about the Farlands, picking up a shipment. Something is jangling. Keys? To this truck? Slipping down to the floor, she creeps to the cabinet where the blankets are stored, crawls in, and closes the door. Huddled in the darkness, she reaches under her robe and touches the doll. The door of the cab opens, then slams shut. The truck shudders as the engine turns over. It rolls slowly forward, then pauses. The gate, they're opening the gate. It moves again, with more speed now. They're on one of the service roads; she can feel every bump.

The smell of filthy water tells her they are traveling by the inlet, through the old industrial section of the City. Willum showed her this place, the way lined with giant rusting silos, while he was instructing her on the history of the City. He explained how mountains of grain or sugar brought in from the east on "trains" were held here until they were taken on huge "freighters" across the Great Ocean. An ocean no one's traveled since the Abominations.

This road leads to the highway that will take them to the Farlands. Good. As far away from Darius and the Masters as she can get sounds like the right destination.

The truck's on a steep incline, so they must be at the bridge. She knows this place—there's a major barricade, where all who come and go are investigated. Will the truck be searched? The guards seem to be waving them through. They must know the driver. Of course, he takes this route all the time. They must have been told to keep watch for her, but it would be unthinkable to search for Our Stowe in such a vehicle. She's too pampered and soft to climb into a truck and head to the Farlands alone. Fools! What better place than an ice cream truck such as this one to hide in, with its blankets and pillows and sweets. It is made for shipping people. Little people. Children who, if they do not pass the tests, will be dismantled and redistributed for the exclusive use of the Masters.

Stowe opens the cabinet and inches back out. The truck will be empty until the first shipment is picked up. Until then, she's safe—unless the driver comes back here to eat or sleep. But if he does, the truck will stop first and she will have time to hide. And if she is discovered, there are other options. Lethal options.

Looking down at her hands, Stowe breathes deeply and watches as the amber aura of her shield fades with each exhalation. Prying open the icebox, her still-tingling fingers poke around until they find her favorite: an ice cream sandwich. Pleased with herself, she relaxes on a bench to enjoy it. For the first time since she came to the City, she is free of responsibilities and cares. Our Stowe does not exist in this cabin, Darius cannot reach her here, no one knows where she is. She has finally found freedom.

You will never be free.

"Well, well. Ferrell," she says, with the utmost care. "That is your name, is it not?"

You have no life outside the City. You won't survive for a week. If you want to live, you should go back.

"Why would you want me to do that, Ferrell?"

As long as you survive, I survive.

"Yes. To spy on Darius and the Masters and try to force me to kill all his new recruits. You fear them. Why?"

Ask Darius.

"What good would that do me, Ferrell? Darius is a liar. It's over, parasite. Your mission has failed. Go back to where you came from."

If only I could, my little house, but alas, I am part of you now.

"You are nothing but a virus. Willum says there's a way to get rid of you. I will find it and destroy you if you do not leave willingly."

I'm afraid death is the only way out.

"You are wrong. If I go back to the Dreamfield, back inside the Wall, I could open myself up again and shove you out."

How are you to do that without Dirt? Even if you were bright enough to know how, what you so blithely call the Wall is being watched by both Turned and Dirt Eater. You wouldn't stand a chance. There is only one way.

"How?"

I've lived long and loved well, but now that Lania is gone my life has lost all meaning. So it would not trouble me if you were to take your own life. You'd be rid of me then.

Stowe stifles her emotions. She will not believe him. "Willum said—"

Willum! What does he know? Nothing. I accepted this mission with no hope of return. It was worthwhile, when you consider the benefit. Think of it: inhabiting Our Stowe in the center of the City. Traveling the barricades and barriers Darius constructed on the Turned side of the Field. A wealth of information to be gleaned for the Dirt Eaters. And I wouldn't be alone for long. Lania was to join me.

"What!"

An unconventional marriage, to be sure, but at least we would have been together. Our love was strong. Strong enough to survive even you.

"I'm glad she's dead. The two of you—inhabiting me!" Stowe shudders with disgust at the thought. "You Dirt Eaters really are the vermin Darius claims."

Ah, Darius. When he catches you, he will want to conduct more of his own tests. He will discover me. He is a very inventive man. My interrogation will be a slow, difficult process. By the end of it we will both be praying for death, but he will not grant our wish. And then, Stowe, my perfect little hostess, you will have wished you'd ended it all now, when you had the chance.

"You're presuming a lot, Ferrell. I will not be caught. I'm going to escape. Willum will find me and rid me of you forever."

Oh? And then what? Where can he take you? You might hide from Darius for a while, but you can't hide from yourself. Stowe, it's true that you hate the Masters, but most especially you hate yourself. You despise what you've become: a diseased, unstable, child-monster. On top of which, your power is waning, I sense its ebb. Oh, you are so weak.

"Shut up."

I'll prove it to you.

Stowe feels her arm rising against her will. Her legs quiver, shaking spasmodically. Her hands and legs thrust forward. "I... won't..." she says, resisting the force inside her that bangs her against the sides of the truck, footsteps echoing on the bare metal floor. She strains to control her muscles—the driver will surely hear—but they refuse to obey.

Surrender.

Propelled down the aisle toward the doors, she realizes that Ferrell might force her to open them, then she'd fall, fly and spin over the hard ground, crack her bones, snap her neck.

The truck brakes and she reels back from the doors. Tumbling with the momentum, she crashes into the cabinet and lands on the floor.

As it slows to a stop, she finds her body is hers again.

Don't let him find you.

"Why would I? Idiot!"

Bruised from the fall, she opens the cabinet and buries herself in the blankets. The driver's getting out. Six heavy steps and the back door opens. He's moving through the aisle, coming closer. She hears the man's breathing as he bends over. The blanket was left out. And the wrappers.

Stupid child!

Quiet, quiet.

The man is muttering to himself. "He's done it again, sneaking naps, stealing food. I'm gonna report him this time."

His hands appear, holding the blanket. He shoves it beside Stowe's head, then slams the cabinet door but it will not shut—Stowe's body is pushing the blankets forward just enough to keep it from closing. The driver tries a few more times, checking it. He must think the noise he heard was the loose door.

"I'll have Hawkes look at that when we get back."

He retreats, and moments later the engine starts and the truck gains momentum. With a sigh of relief, Stowe carefully slips out of the cabinet and sits back in her seat. "Why do you try to frighten me when it is clear you don't want me hurt? What do you hope to gain?" She focuses all her frustration where she senses Ferrell's presence most strongly within her, grasping at anything that might push him back, give her time to think.

Don't you realize what Darius is doing? If you refuse to go back, then I have no reason to live and it is nothing to me if you end your life and mine. But soon no one will escape Darius's grip. He will be puppet master to us all. This is what I seek to stop. This is worth living to achieve.

"We want the same thing, then. Leave me alone and I'll kill Darius for you. I want to kill him. I can kill him."

You overestimate your abilities.

"It would already be done if you hadn't slithered inside me."

I have no reason to believe you would act for the benefit of others.

"And whose benefit do you serve now, Ferrell? I think you're the one going mad, cooped up inside me, grieving over your poor incinerated wife. No body, no love, not even your own mind anymore. I offer my help and still you want me destroyed. Who does that serve?"

A thousand jagged nails rip into Stowe's brain.

She'd scream but her throat is paralyzed with pain; nails tear into her legs. She tells herself that the pain's an illusion, he's just tweaking her nerves. She wills it to stop, but it builds, swelling hot inside her skull.

When she tries to numb herself, push Ferrell's invisible

fingers from her synapses, wave after wave of blinding, searing pain slices through her.

She staggers down the aisle, clinging to the seat backs. With each step, a firestorm erupts behind her eyes, her vision doubling, her limbs flailing. She is ready to surrender, to die, to smash herself against the pavement spinning past. Blindly pitching herself at the door, she flings it open.

No!

The instant the pain stops, the memories rise like a flood. *Blood in the snow. Slashing. Burning. Her mother's kiss.*

The door!

She starts to cough uncontrollably. Her eyes snap into focus. Dust. A cloud of it, all around. She can hear horses galloping on either side. It must be warriors sent to escort the truck.

Shut it!

Ferrell's scream sends her reaching for the handle. Groping, she grabs it, shuts the door, then totters back.

Hide, hide!

But her legs won't hold, the cabinet is too far, much too far. She collapses in the nearest seat, utterly spent.

You don't know what they'll do. They may not know who you are. Hide!

"What for, Ferrell?"

Move!

But Stowe will not move. She cannot.

Tears in her mother's eyes. Be brave, my pumpkin. Be brave.

She struggles to clear her mind. That's what Willum said

she should do, clear her mind. But it's so difficult.

The red skull. Blood in the snow. Her brother's hand slipping from hers. Everything on fire.

For the first time in her life, she envies all those enabled fools. They have peace, at least. More and more people choose enablers... more... how many did Fortin say? She remembers the look in those weepy eyes of his: power. From simply controlling their manufacture? No. That doesn't make sense. How could she have thought that? It's something else... some secret knowledge... something to do with Darius's new plans... perhaps even his new Construction—She's suddenly aware that the truck's movement has slowed.

"Haven't spotted any Brothers yet, but the further we go, the more I keep expecting them," the driver calls out as the truck stops.

"Rest easy. We'll be your escort from this time on," says a man's voice, cringingly familiar.

"No, *you* rest easy, Sir," says the driver. Make yourself comfortable."

The back door opens. She can hear labored breathing as the man shuts the door and draws closer. She senses his mounting excitement at the sight of her. The truck jerks forward and she hears his high, cackling laugh. Her eyes snap open.

We are lost.

Ferrell knows she is too exhausted to attack the man beneath the brilliant feathered gown, the yellow-beaked mask.

"Our Stowe! What a pleasant surprise," says Raven.

the fortress of the
red - haired woman

AND THE FRIEND BROUGHT THE VISION TO THE BROTHERS
as they slept. and at every raising of the sun,
they searched the horizon waiting for the sign.
—orin's history of the friend

ROAN IS RELISHING THIS EXPERIENCE. Soon after their
drop off the cliff, he discovered braces under the wings
to support his arms and legs, so his energy's high even after
flying all day. The temptation to experiment is ever present,
but he hasn't succumbed to it. Staying focused when the only
information he has about where he's going is a dot on a floating map proves enough of a challenge. Time is of the essence,
so it's probably more efficient to trust the sensors to opti-
mize the thermals. Still, it would be nice to try a loop or a
dive just to see what would happen.

Under a deep billowing cloud, the wings find a perfect
updraft, spiraling him and Lumpy higher and higher.

Closing his eyes, Lumpy gasps for breath. "Hey, the air's getting thinner!"

"That's what's supposed to happen."

"Yeah? So when do we start to suffocate?"

"I think the wings must have oxygen sensors. Soon as it gets hard to breathe, they glide down," says Roan.

"You mean we've already been up this high?"

"More than once," Roan grins.

"I guess I shouldn't have looked down!"

But Roan loves looking down from above, has adored it since he started climbing the Big Empty with his friends in Longlight, and being this high is better than he ever imagined. He'd stay up forever if he could.

He can't help but wonder why it's important for him to see Kira. Why did the cricket show him her face, and then Willum, too? Willum knows her. But how? From the City, or before?

Kira, Saint's mate. Roan's sure she knows he's responsible for Saint's death, even if he didn't strike the final blow. Is he being sent to submit to her judgment, as he did with the Hhroxhi? Is this another trial he must face before he can return to Saint? Remembering the skulls on Kira's mantelpiece makes it almost impossible to focus on his destination.

Roan's and Lumpy's wings lower, dipping them in a long downward arc toward a mist of overhanging cloud. As they build tremendous speed, icy wind blasts in their faces. The ground is dangerously close when the next updraft vaults them skyward again.

"How much farther, do you think?" Lumpy gasps, looking a little green. Those near brushes with the earth don't agree with him.

"Soon."

"Better be. We're losing sun, and that means no more warm air."

Roan eyes the horizon—in less than an hour, Barren Mountain will swallow the sun. Concentrating his vision, Roan can see fine particles of dust riding a strong, steady stream along the side of a ridge.

"You're thinking something. What are you thinking?" asks Lumpy nervously.

"We could make some time if we caught the wind along that ridge."

Lumpy peers down at the jagged mountain range. "Okay… but how close do we get to the rocks?"

"As close as the wind."

"Isn't that dangerous?"

Roan laughs. "A minute ago, we were flying too high."

Lumpy glares at him but it doesn't diminish Roan's excitement. No harm in a little experiment if it hastens the journey. Taking a steep descent, they gain speed and in moments they are soaring alongside the ridge. The thrill of maneuvering between wind-eroded towers of stone, avoiding sharp overhangs that could rip their wings to shreds, exceeds all of Roan's expectations. And for all his griping, Lumpy has a grin on his face. The constant dipping and swooping to evade disaster isn't nerve-wracking, it's fun. It's flying.

The sun's bottom edge is flaring over the horizon when Roan sees one mountain rising above the others, its peak obscured by clouds. Checking the map, he confirms that this is their destination, then signals to Lumpy. They simultaneously veer away from the ridge at high speed, gliding over a wooded plateau. Roan shivers, realizing that the thermals that keep them aloft have provided a lot of warmth. As the sun vanishes and the mountain air turns cold, they're getting seriously chilled.

"Wh—where's the next thermal?" Lumpy calls out, his teeth chattering.

"Not much further!" Roan yells back. "We've just got to get past these trees."

As they approach the outer edge of the forest, Roan spots a dark patch of stone radiating heat in the distance. Looking behind, Roan makes his decision. More than a third of the sun has been lost to them; there's too little time not to take things into his own hands. Positioning the wings for a dive, he forces the glide lower and lower. As they accelerate, they come dangerously close to the treetops, but they reach the edge of the forest safely. It'll be clear sailing to the thermal that will give them the warmth and loft they need.

Just past the woods—

Arrows!

Out from the trees, a half dozen Fandor appear on horseback, in close pursuit. An arrow barely misses Lumpy's wing. Urgently scanning ahead, Roan tucks their wings for maximum velocity, and they soar toward it, so close to the ground that Roan can hear whips cracking against horse flanks. The Fandor are gaining on them.

There's only a hundred feet to the black stone, but they're within sword's reach of the Fandor now, and one warrior, weapon raised high, is almost upon them. He takes a swing as they hit the thermal. Though it isn't strong, it's enough to send them spiraling up. Arrows whiz past, but their shifting positions and steady ascent make them difficult targets. The Fandor can do nothing but watch them rise.

"What goes up, comes down," says Lumpy. "That's a rule even those numbnogs know."

If they end up on the ground, it won't be arrows they're facing but swords and battle-axes. Roan wouldn't even have time to shuck the wings before they'd run him through. He should have kept in mind the possibility of roving bands of Fandor. So much for experiments.

They hear the Fandor shouting angrily at each other and look down to see them raise their weapons threateningly at five women on horseback, all well-armed, charging down the mountain in their direction. The first female warrior is swiftly upon them, and with one clean sweep she removes the head of a Fandor.

"Did you just see what I just saw?" Lumpy shouts in amazement. "Who *are* those women—are we next?"

"We'll be finding out soon enough!" Roan yells back, as another Fandor topples headless from his horse.

The battle is brief, the Fandors' brute force no match for the women's martial skills. They hardly waste a sword stroke, methodically eliminating each Fandor. The carnage complete, the victors quickly lift the dead back into their empty saddles and tie the reins around the corpses. Once secured, the horses are given a slap and gallop off carrying their lifeless Fandor masters. Roan has seen these techniques used before—by the Brothers.

Roan looks down at the victorious riders, then at the formidable peak before them. "Seems they're headed in the same direction we are."

"I guess they're the welcoming committee."

A long, downward arc takes them to the black foothills of the mountain. They swerve abruptly to avoid a geyser heated by hot volcanic rock deep below the surface. The surrounding warm air provides the strongest updraft they've had yet. They ascend higher and higher, over jagged cliffs and jutting outcrops.

Just as the sun slips under the horizon, Lumpy shouts, "Okay, so where's the village?"

Roan tries to hide his discomfort—there are no caves along the sheer rock face, this mountain is uninhabitable. Why would Kira leave her comfortable home for this desolation? Surely the Brothers wouldn't have withdrawn their protection of her village after Saint's death.

The updraft carries them so high, they enter the cloud that covers the peak. The cool mist blurs Roan's vision and he loses sight of his companion.

"Roan!" Lumpy calls out, not bothering to hide the fear in his voice.

"I'm here! Trust the wings!" Roan replies, but he shares Lumpy's concern. How long can they stay airborne, given the cloud's lower temperature?

Having little choice but to entrust the flight to the sensors, he closes his eyes, reaches out with his senses—and is startled by the smell of grass and... yes, he's sure of it... he can hear the laughter of children.

Rising over the apex of the mountain, the mist breaks, revealing that the peak isn't pointed, as Roan expected, but flat. The wings' gentle arc takes him and Lumpy past a high stone lip and down onto a lush green field. As their feet touch ground, they stare open-mouthed at blossoming shrubs and tall bamboo plants, the breeze rustling through their thin green leaves. Dozens of children play in the center of a village hewn directly into the volcanic rock. Roan and Lumpy smile and raise their hands in greeting, but the woman tending the children quietly shoos them away.

Without hesitation, Roan and Lumpy shuck their wings. As elegant as they are aloft, the wings will be no help at all if the situation becomes threatening. Three women, much like the ones who so easily massacred the Fandor, stride toward them. Roan keeps his empty hands in plain view.

The woman in the lead takes their full measure before she speaks. "Nice of you to drop in, Roan of Longlight."

Not detecting any overt hostility in her voice, he answers respectfully. "Always a pleasure, Kira."

But Kira is unyielding. "That remains to be seen."

Roan might not have been the one to kill her lover, but he was fighting Saint to the death when the blow was struck. Will she demand a price?

"Who's your friend?" she asks.

"I'm Lumpy. No Mor-Ticks, but if you'd like, I'm more than happy to go back down."

"That's alright, as long as you don't mind people staring."

"Better than being dead and tied to a horse any day."

Kira laughs. "The Fandor need to respect certain boundaries."

"What is this place?" asks Roan.

Though her look is amiable, Kira dodges the question. "You must be hungry. Come."

This whole community is built upon the caldera of the dormant volcano. That's why it feels warm, Roan realizes, and why green things grow here. The village looks to have been here for decades. The black stone is painted in places with bright designs, and toys are littered everywhere. The children they saw certainly seemed healthy and happy. They must be safe up here, far from the gaping maw of the City.

The interior of Kira's house recalls the one in the village he once visited with Saint, and is an unpleasant reminder of those turbulent times. The year Roan spent as an acolyte of the

Brothers, a year of tests and trials, has left its mark. Though he had felt the Brothers' faith was genuine, he'd had his doubts about whether Saint really believed in what he preached. Now, looking back, he thinks he may have been wrong: the Friend hadn't been real to Roan, but it's quite possible that He had been very real to Saint.

Lumpy stares at the solar-powered lights and at the huge mural that depicts a warrior bursting out of a stone.

"It's the birth of the Friend," Lumpy says, "the god of the Brothers."

"I thought about leaving it behind," says Kira, "but I had it brought here to remember him."

"The Friend?"

"No, Saint."

Lumpy sniffs eagerly. "Is that food?"

"Absolutely. But you might want to use the basins and fresh water at the end of the hall," Kira says, biting her bottom lip.

Looking closely at each other for the first time since their arrival, Roan and Lumpy burst into laughter. Flying non-stop all day may have felt carefree, but it had given each of them an appearance halfway between mad hermit and pig-boy.

Lumpy devours the vegetable stew with gusto, peppering Kira with questions about her warriors and their attack on the Fandor.

"That's not something we do very often. It's not in our

best interest to expose ourselves. But having witnesses to your arrival was unacceptable."

"Why send back their dead on their horses?"

"It's what the Brothers would do. They're more than happy to let us mimic them. Bolsters their ferocious reputation."

"Speaking of which, where are all the men, Kira?" asks Lumpy.

The rage emanating from Kira speaks volumes. Eyes fixed on some invisible point uncomfortably close to Lumpy's nose, she whispers, "There aren't any," and resumes eating her meal. But her breath, deep and measured, warns them off any further enquiries.

The many questions neither of them feel free to ask, and the radical shift in mood, make for a subdued dinner. So by the time it's over and Kira's thanked, Lumpy needs no coaxing to make a quick exit.

"If it's true I won't be stoned, with your permission, I'd love to have a look around."

"Feel free to go wherever you are welcomed, Lumpy No Mor-Ticks."

By his smile, it's obvious Lumpy's hoping to have his habitual success as a fact-finding emissary, but if Kira's people are anything like her, Roan thinks Lumpy may have finally met his match.

Roan's eyes drift to a recess in the stone wall where two skulls now lie. "Are they really your mother, and the man who killed her?"

"I'm not best known as a liar," says Kira.

Roan repeats the words she spoke to him almost two years before. "The day you execute your parents' killers, that day the pain that strangles you will lose its grip."

Kira smiles ruefully. "You took that advice to heart."

"I share in the responsibility for Saint's death, but I did not deal the killing blow."

"Oh? How did he die then?"

"He had mortally wounded my friend Lelbit, and was about to kill me. She slew him with an arrow before she died."

"He did not suffer. A good death, then."

"He suffers now."

Her face pale, Kira gasps, "He walks in death? You saw him?"

"Briefly."

"What did he say?"

The expectation in her eyes makes Roan feel ashamed. "I... had to leave."

Kira leans her head against the stone wall and sighs, clearly disappointed.

"Kira, it was terrifying, more than I could stand. It took a long time to recover, but I want to go back, I have to."

"Are you sure?"

"I was told you might be able to help me."

Kira scrutinizes Roan, then asks, "Do you still have the ring Saint gave you?"

Reaching into his pack, Roan finds the deep pocket where

he keeps the badger-shaped ring. "Saint told me it symbol-
ized resurrection."

"According to the original owner."

"And who was that?"

Kira smiles. "Your great-grandfather."

an old family friend

when fog rolls off the Lake and into fairview,
beware.
the ghosts of a thousand murdered enemies
are there
despair in their hearts, revenge in their eyes
for the smell they've endured
ever since their demise

      —Lore of the storytellers

T HE BIRD MAN TAKES OFF HIS BEAKED MASK and smiles.
"A pleasure to meet you at last, Our Stowe. I am Raven,
always your loyal servant." His thin yellow hair hangs straight
and oily down to his shoulders, and red blotches spot his face.

"You don't look well, my dear. Are you ill?"

Wait. Do not speak.

How stupid do you think I am?

"We have no real doctor with us. Perhaps some water?"
Nearly losing his balance as the truck accelerates, he braces
himself against the cabinet. After quickly locating a shallow
bowl, he reaches into his bag and pulls out a water skin. He

takes his time removing the cap, observing her as closely as he dares, then judiciously tips some water into the makeshift cup.

It's obvious he knows this truck and its contents well. Stowe sips the water slowly, never taking her eyes off the repulsive man, though he keeps a respectful distance. Ha! She may look weak but clearly he's heard the stories. Not a complete fool.

"The Masters are very unhappy. The City is under martial law, shut down tight. Word from on high is that you've been abducted. But, if I may be so bold, judging from what I see, it's more a case of flight, is it not?"

Stowe remains silent, reading his every gesture.

"Running away is something I know a lot about. Of course, I may be mistaken, overstepping my bounds. If so, I offer my most humble apologies. Whatever you wish is my command, Our Stowe. If you desire safe passage back to the City, I'm more than happy to comply." Raven fairly glows with anticipation.

As Stowe suspected would happen, the absence of a response provides the gloating freak sufficient answer.

"I see, I see. Well, in that case, I would be happy to order our escort to offer you transport to a safe haven. Darius has, of course, put up a significant reward for your return. Naturally, you will have guessed that. Shocking, that I should go against his command. Yet you are, after all, not only his Stowe but Our Stowe and since you are known to have eased the suffering of so many, you deserve to choose."

Stowe finally breaks her silence. "Why should I trust you?"

"You mean why would I take such a huge risk when returning you to the City would win me the favor of Darius?" Raven opens the flask on his belt and takes a long drink. "Our Stowe, you ask me this question because you do not know what I owe you. I spent a good year in Darius's dungeons only because I knew a saint who harbored a mutual friend of ours. This friend, your... brother, was such a sad case, so obviously not wanting to be found, how could I reveal his whereabouts? But after Roan escaped and his sojourn with the Brothers was revealed, well... I was punished. Oh, yes! I'm sure you, of all people, can imagine what I went through. It takes something special to survive that kind of torture. A faith to sustain the spirit. You were my guiding light in that darkness." Raven hangs his head as if this will convince her of the sincerity of his words.

Fool. I've been lied to by far cleverer men than you.

"So," Raven continues, looking up meekly at Stowe, "if you require my assistance, I will give it. Consider me your servant and friend."

"Where would you take me?"

"A town, large and comfortable, where I can assure your anonymity. In the meantime, may I offer you some fruit?" Rummaging in his bag, he makes a show of withdrawing two bright yellow apples and a bunch of purple grapes. "Beautiful, aren't they? I do love fresh fruit. The farmers here are incredibly generous. Go ahead. These are the best of the season."

Stowe cannot resist one sweet grape. He's right, it's heavenly. "You knew my brother well?"

He's trying to trap you. Don't rise to the bait.

You will stop assuming I am a fool and be quiet or I will find the closest knife and use it to dislodge you from my chest.

Stowe almost sighs audibly as Ferrell's presence seems to shrink to a mere dot at the base of her heart. She is not unaware of the first rule of combat: turn your enemy's weapon upon him.

"Why yes, I knew him very well indeed," says Raven. He settles back into his seat, takes another long swig of his flask, then bites into an apple, letting its juice dribble down his chin. "He was very lonely in his early days with the Brothers. Oh, he suffered horrible nightmares. I gave him what solace I could. He certainly loved apples. Do you?" Raven says, trying to entice Stowe with one.

What a coincidence that it is the same variety cultivated in Longlight. She and Roan had fought over yellow apples like this one: Roan had run off with the apples Mother'd given her. She'd chased him up Big Empty. She was furious at the thought he'd eaten them all, but it had only been pretend, a ruse to tease her.

Ignoring the proffered apple, she whispers dangerously, "I remember you, Raven."

"Well, I thought you might, Our Stowe. But as you can see, I have taken every opportunity to make amends," he says sadly. "I was given my directive by Darius, did you know? To bring all of the children to the City. He had a particular interest in you and your brother. If you'd been handed over peacefully, the tragedy could have been avoided.

"I begged Saint just to ride in and give your village a glimpse of the threat, then let me come back and try again from a stronger negotiating position. But those Brothers are animals. They massacred everyone. I was heartbroken. So I took Roan under my wing. It was the least I could do. And I'll help you now, too, for the same reason."

"Do you hear that?" Stowe asks innocently. Beyond the clatter of the truck and galloping of the Fandor guard, she can hear ten, maybe twelve men approaching on horseback. To her ears, it's like thunder. But this man has the sensory perception of a gnat. Why had they ever dreamed he could become a Master? But it's clear he's finally understood, because his face blanches considerably.

"The Brothers," he whispers hoarsely. Raven's sword is on a nearby seat, but he doesn't reach for it. Coward. "Down, down!" he cries, sliding onto the floor.

Stowe eyes him contemptuously. Does he think she will grovel down there, beside him? From what she's heard, the Brothers are moving against the City. They might be the allies she requires. She's overheard Darius's conversations: the Fandor cannot match the Brothers' skill or courage. Outnumbered as they are, the Fandor guard will be mercilessly cut down.

The truck begins to careen wildly. Wheeling precariously on a steep incline, it jolts and bounces on uneven ground. There's a sickening squeal, and for a moment Stowe feels weightless. Thrown off her seat, she tumbles until the ceiling becomes the floor and her head hits something hard. She finds herself pinned under the body of Raven, and as the truck crashes to a stop she loses consciousness.

Blood drips into her swollen eye. Forcing it open, she peers into a blue haze. Blankets—they're suffocating her. With a free arm, Stowe pushes them away. Breathing more easily, she directs her senses outside. It's quiet. The others are gone, or dead. Feeling that it's safe to move, she tries to squirm out from under the Bird Man. The sickly sweet scent that taints his breath is nauseating.

Inch by inch, she manages to pull one leg out, then another, all the time waiting for Ferrell to assert himself. But he remains tucked away in his little corner, cowering from her last threat against him—or perhaps he doesn't want her to know what he's thinking... Could she? Invade his mind as he's invaded hers? Why has the thought not occurred to her before? She's prevented from pursuing this intriguing notion, however. When one last tug finally sets her free, Raven groans and slowly lifts his head.

"Oh, Our Stowe, you're alright, thank heaven!" He exclaims, then catching himself, whispers, "Are the Brothers gone?"

"Yes. And your troops seem to be gone as well."

Raven growls. "Blasted Fandor, ill-trained, ill-mannered louts. You're injured, Our Stowe," he says, reaching out to the cut above her eye.

She quickly steps away. "It's only a scratch."

Sitting up unsteadily, he carefully squeezes his arms and legs, rotating his neck, bending this way and that to check his spine. His examination complete, he cackles with relief. "All in one piece!"

For now.

"Come, let's have a look outside and see about our prospects."

He walks to the rear, avoiding the seats that now hang above him. Reaching up, Raven twists the handle of the back door. "My Lady," he snivels, holding out his interlaced palms to boost her up. "You have only to push it open."

As if you couldn't, you stinking sycophant. I know what's on your mind: if some ugly surprise is waiting, it'll eat me first. Fortunately, her safety depends on her senses, not his, and without a second thought, she lodges her foot firmly in his hands and allows him to lift her, her head emerging for a clear look. The truck's catastrophic path is evident from the mess of earth and broken brush it left in its wake.

"What do you make of it?" asks the trembling wretch.

"Apart from a few field mice, it's clear. Are you afraid of mice?"

"Not at all, dear lady," Raven trumpets as they both scramble out into the daylight.

The truck lies like a dead animal: on its back, wheels in the air. The windshield is splattered with blood, the driver's head inclined against it.

Raven sniffs. "Dead, very dead."

But something very alive is grazing at the edge of the slope leading up to the road. Raven scurries over to it, gingerly stepping over the corpse of a fallen Fandor. The horse does not acknowledge him, just keeps chewing. "You are blessed, Our Stowe, as your brother once was. The Brothers seldom leave dead rider or horse behind."

Unobservant fool. They are at the bottom of a ravine. And it's obvious the body fell from a great height. Following the scent of its rider, the horse must have found a path down— which means there's an easy way out.

After gathering some food from the truck, Stowe climbs onto the animal and holds out the reins to Raven. "Do you need these to lead the horse?" she inquires in her most regal tone.

Unsuccessfully trying to mask a scowl, Raven straps his precious bird suit behind the saddle and accepts the menial duty.

Darius must be offering a pretty high price.

I'm sure he is. But this disgusting apple-polisher might have something altogether different in mind.

I wouldn't overestimate this one.

"I think we're very close to that route I spoke of." The fear that spurs Raven's uncertainty is painful in its intensity. Has he no self-control whatsoever?

"I believe the horse entered the ravine from over there," Stowe smiles sweetly, pointing to a narrow path that cuts through a stand of red stick trees.

"I agree." The poor Raven heaves a great sigh of relief. "Well... we should have no trouble reaching our destination by sunset."

He has some skills at least, for, true to his word, the sun is still visible when the town comes into view. And with it comes a stench as foul as any Stowe has ever had the misfortune of encountering.

Raven points to a lake in the distance as the source. "It eats whatever it touches, My Lady. They say your brother died traveling it."

Suddenly nauseated, she retches. If Roan had found a way to convince the Masters that he was dead, why had he risked coming to the City?

"My Lady..."

Waving him back, Stowe heaves and heaves until she is nothing but a hollow shell, unable to contain anything, not even feeling. Certainly not that.

"It would be wise to raise your hood, My Lady," says Raven, indicating the approaching walls of the town.

She presses her head far back into the apprentice's cowl, as Raven waves to the guard in the watchtower and the gates swing open. Leading the horse into the main square, Raven whispers, "Welcome to Fairview, Our Stowe."

Stowe's never seen anything so painfully quaint. Little houses decorated with bright ceramic tiles line streets of gleaming slate. Flowers are in bloom everywhere. Daisies, roses, snapdragons, marigolds—all an attempt to mask that stink, no doubt.

Then she notices that light twinkles through the shutters behind the window boxes. Light! Looking up, she sees the wires. Electricity! What do they possibly do here to have such riches?

Raven stops at a picturesque house. "This is my home away

from home," he announces with such irony she can't help but wonder what truth lies behind his words. After stifling an urge to give Raven a kick as he helps her dismount, Stowe strides past him and into the well-kept cottage. Books! Books in flagrant disobedience of the law. Her eyes scan the titles. Many on medicine and the healing arts. Well, that is sometimes permitted, but there is also poetry, history, even texts in long-dead languages she is certain Raven does not speak.

He sniggers at her questioning glance. "Oh, no, those aren't my books. In fact, this isn't my house. Just where I stay when I'm in town. It once belonged to the local healer. A friend of your brother's, actually. After she escaped with him, I was given it to use."

Roan was in this town, in this very house. She runs her hand along a table, over a counter... and senses something... an unexpected, delectable sensation. Yes. Yes! The unmistakable resonance of Dirt.

Ferrell, wake up!

Yes?

A Dirt Eater lived here, did she not?

Very much so. Alandra. You met her. She was the best of our young ones, though still only partially formed.

The Goat-woman. The one who didn't fight.

Stowe walks past Raven and opens the door to a small room. An apothecary. She quickly scans the many jars that load the shelves. Stowe points to a small, plain one too high for her to reach. "Would you get that down for me, please?"

Raven's fingers wrap around the precious jar, but before he can examine it, Stowe excitedly takes it from his hand. Opening the lid, her spirit sinks. It's empty, empty apart from the scattering of grains she'd detected. When this Alandra left, she must have taken her Dirt with her.

You're accustomed to an endless supply, but Dirt is not something we leave behind. You consumed in a week what all of us together nurse through a year.

"What an unexpected pleasure, Raven."

The voice is smooth, self-confident. She can tell instantly that this man is the power in this town. With surprising speed, Raven steps out of the apothecary, leaving Stowe behind.

"Governor Brack! Wonderful to see you again!"

"My dear Raven, has something happened?"

"We were attacked again by the Brothers."

"Thank goodness you've arrived unscathed."

"Unscathed and undaunted. I've spent the last few weeks meeting with the governors and they are all seething. The Brothers' attacks have had a devastating effect on commerce, and the governors, like you, resent being held responsible."

"And high time!"

"I am doing what I can. I cannot be blamed if Darius balks at letting his precious technology out of the City. He promised me the necessary resources to put down the Brothers, and it is only right that he be pressured to live up to his word. Some risks are worth taking. We cannot neutralize the opposition without more advanced weapons."

"I wholeheartedly agree. If the stories of the City's weapons caches are true, it is suicide for the Masters to procrastinate any longer. But my friend, aren't you going introduce me to your guest?"

Before Raven can utter another word, Stowe steps out to meet the silver-haired man. Governor, Raven called him. Yes. He fancies himself important in his black, high-collared suit. He smiles and holds out his hand, but his composure collapses when she tosses back her hood.

"Is it—Masters be praised—is it—?"

"I do appreciate your confidence in this matter, Governor Brack."

Brack, shaken, clears his throat. "What... what may I ask... gives us the honor... of this esteemed visit?"

"I am on a secret mission, Governor. No one is to know I am here. My meals must be brought to this door. No one, not even a maid, may see me. You must not communicate my presence to anyone. I depend upon the strictest confidentiality. Can you provide me with that?"

Brack bows his head. "Our Stowe, you have my word. Remain here, under our watchful eyes and silent lips, for as long as you deem necessary."

"Thank you," says Stowe, her sweet tone belying her distaste for the man. "Now you may leave me."

Brack smiles broadly, bows again, and stumbles out the door, shutting it delicately behind him.

Raven cackles uproariously. "You are extraordinary, Our

Stowe, remarkable!" His obnoxious laughter grates on her. Time to knock this bird from his perch.

"Are you finished?" she inquires icily, as if speaking to an errant child.

Raven pulls himself to attention.

"Can Brack be trusted?"

"Be at ease. He'd be a fool to cross us."

Us? Raven's suit should resemble a vulture's. Edging cautiously ever closer, making sure the meal's not going to bite. No wonder Kordan wanted to see him dead—birds of a feather, these two, and only room for one in the Eldest's nest.

"Now if you'll excuse me, I'll look after our arrangements." He bows. "By your leave?" And at her nod, he quickly disappears out the door.

When they return, they'll hurt you.

I don't know what they'll do. Yet. But I'll find out.

Making herself comfortable in a soft chair, Stowe closes her eyes and breathes deeply, once, twice, a dozen times. She sees the spark, then the flame, tries to follow the light, but a force clutches at her, holding her back.

Let me go.

No. There's no time. Don't you understand, they're going to try to use you.

You don't know that.

Naïve child! You waste the gifts given to you. Get up!

Stowe strains to stay seated, but her hands thrust down,

pushing her to her feet. She lurches toward a table, gripping its leg, but one hand yanks on the other, and as she jerks away, she pulls the table over, its contents smashing all around her. Like a badly handled marionette, she stiffly feels herself being drawn closer and closer to Alandra's apothecary.

What do you want from me?

I want you to cooperate!

Sweat pouring down her forehead, she pushes her arms against the doorway but her grip weakens, slips, and she's inside.

Take the shining green jar. Take it! It will calm you.

Her hand throws the jar against the wall. "Calm me! You think I don't know it's *you* who wants to control me? Or is it just to *be* me? Well, two can play at that game!" She focuses on Ferrell, pushing on the edges of his consciousness.

Tasting blood, she realizes he's forcing her hand to smash a mortar against her skull again and again.

I'll happily kill you and die rather than share my thoughts with you.

Stowe's nerves ignite, a thousand wasps stinging her. Her arms flail madly, knocking jars off the shelves. Spinning into the living room, she grabs hold of the bookcase. Everything collapses, books, bottles, candles, most of them on Stowe.

She's lying helpless, body aching everywhere, amongst shards of glass and clay, when the door opens. Governor Brack and Raven recoil, aghast at the destruction. Raven rushes to her.

"Our Stowe? What has happened?"

But she's so weak, she can barely focus on their faces. Letting her eyes close, she reserves her energy to listen to their hushed conversation as they huddle on the far side of the room.

"She's had some kind of fit."

"Do you think she's mad?" asks the Governor.

"All the better for us."

"It's too risky. We should just inform Darius."

"No. The device will work. Then she'll be ours."

Brack exhales deeply. "Insurance."

"If the rumors are true, she's more powerful than all the Masters put together. You deserve more than this small town, Governor. This is your chance. We must always grasp our opportunities, Brack."

There's a pause. "Alright, then. Do it."

Raven hovers over her, his breath vile. "We can help you, Stowe. There's so much we could do together." He lifts her hair, exposing her neck.

"You've done this before?" asks Brack.

"On occasion. Hold her down in case she squirms."

Wake, wake, wake!

I could be happy, Ferrell.

You'd be a slave and you know it.

No more pain.

Don't be stupid!

Two strong hands weigh on her wrists.

Do something!

There's the click of a blade unfolding.

What are you waiting for? Coward. You'd serve the man who brought death to your people? Disgusting malignant child!

Cold metal drawing a path over her flushed skin. Stowe moans. This is the man who killed her family; it was his word that brought Longlight's destruction. If not for Raven, I would still be a child, chasing my brother for an apple. Stowe opens her mouth as if to speak.

"Wait!" hisses Brack.

The two men lean in to hear what she's saying. They're startled when her eyes snap open, wide. But not for long.

When she screams, their faces twist in agony, then their hands grip their heads, trying to hold in the blood that spurts between their fingers. Raven totters toward the door, trying to escape, and though his hand reaches the latch, he hasn't the strength to turn it. Slipping to the floor, crimson tears flowing from his eyes, he implores Stowe to spare him. But there is no stopping until the great feathered dissembler is silent and lifeless beside his comrade, the late Governor Brack.

And Our Stowe, Icon of the City, Heir to the Archbishop, Idol of the Conurbation, Our Very Best and Beloved, closes her eyes, her doll clutched to her chest, and drifts into a dark, pestilent slumber.

the fires of hell

their decision determined the outcome of the war, but its details were known only to its participants. four of the most important rebel leaders, roan, haron, yana, and steppe, then disappeared with their armies. those who remained were decimated by the conurbation.

—the war chronicles

Under the moon's numinous light, Kira walks past the rocky scars that mark the lifeless volcano's ancient collapse. Roan studies the lines of smooth stone that were once burning lava.

"Do you know how long it's been dormant?"

"I'm told the last eruption was seventy thousand years ago. Another could come at any time, but if Darius has his way we'll be long gone before then."

In the deepening gloom, Roan can make out pillars. Carved into the igneous rock, they appear to be the facade of a temple. Kira signals him to take off his footwear and wait.

Roan grips the ring in his hand. How could something

that once belonged to his great-grandfather end up in the possession of Saint? Why was it given to him? Kira's whispers beckon him. Perhaps he'll find his answers inside.

In the vaulted open space beyond the pillars, a hundred female warriors are sitting cross-legged, swords across their laps, meditating. A wiry gray-haired woman, straight and tall, faces them, without a doubt their leader. Roan is instantly struck by their combined strength and complete focus. It was no wonder they made such short work of the Fandor.

"Our troops rotate once a month. A third are on patrol, a third with their families in the villages, and a third return here to augment their training."

Roan is unsettled by how much they remind him of the Brothers, but he tries not to show his discomfort. "An elite army," is all he says.

"They are unparalleled. Better than the best of the Brothers," Kira replies, as if reading his thoughts.

"Do Brothers Wolf and Asp help with the training?"

Kira laughs. "Other way around. Ende taught them many years ago, before Saint founded the Brotherhood. All the skills you learned from the Brothers derived from that woman." Kira's eyes shift to the older woman leading the group.

Roan studies her sedate face, high cheekbones, and wide brow. "She looks like you."

"My grandmother. The work that she's been doing has one purpose: to bring down the City. The armies of the City are many and centralized. We know they have weapons whose nature and number we can only guess at. We are few by comparison, and scattered. Knives, swords, and arrows are effective only if you can get close enough to use them. We've been waiting for the one who will gather the armies together and command them. Saint believed he might be that man but he learned otherwise. He discovered that half the battle will be fought in the Dreamfield, where very few can go—and who among the Walkers still cares enough for flesh and blood to protect the needs of ordinary people? He came to believe that you were the one who was awaited—as did we all, Roan of Longlight."

"I've seen the City. I could never send people into battle against them—they would be slaughtered."

Kira stares at Roan, grim-faced. Then she smiles. "You are as they have said. I will be proud to serve you."

"You don't understand—"

Ende, the gray-haired woman, suddenly rises.

Roan blushes, realizing that he raised his voice. "I beg your pardon," he apologizes.

"You will have to earn it," retorts Ende, her voice sharp. She signals one of the women to toss Roan a sword. With astounding speed, she bounds across the room and swings at his neck. He counters, but Ende's fast, faster than he's ever seen. Her sword slashes and jabs from every angle. The clatter of their blades echoes through the stone room, until, just as suddenly as she started, Ende stops.

The warriors, who've been watching with keen interest,

break into applause. A quick look from their teacher and they immediately quiet. Ende, stone-faced, turns to Roan.

"Well, you're who you say you are, that's for certain," she says. "But you're rusty. What have you been doing for the last year, farming?"

"Yes," say Roan, truthfully.

"Don't let Grandmother rile you, Roan. You're the best I've seen, next to her."

"Oh, he's better than me, just out of shape," sniffs Ende as she walks toward a heavy door. "Come, Roan, I've long been awaiting this conversation."

The thick stone door opens onto a room, spare but elegant in its simplicity, every item in it graced with a singular beauty, creating an atmosphere of tranquility Roan's seldom experienced. Ende sits, her back to him, and pours three cups of mint tea.

"Do join me, Roan," she offers, and gestures to the bamboo mat opposite her.

But as he rounds the low table, Roan is stopped by a picture on the wall. Our Stowe.

"I've been monitoring her progress with interest," says Ende. "I hear she's grown quite powerful."

"She's run away."

"Ah," says Ende.

"A man I met, Willum, is looking for her. He thinks he can help her."

"I'm sure he will. He's a good boy, that Willum."

"You know him?"

Kira and Ende share a smile. "He's my brother," says Kira.

Roan studies the faces of both women and sees the resemblance. "You all have the same eyes."

"And more," says Ende, handing Roan his cup of tea. He takes his place across from her and sets the ring on the table between them.

Ende finishes her tea in one gulp. "As you probably know, there were four groups in the Parting. One became Longlight, one Oasis, one became the Gunthers, and the fourth was destroyed by a plague unleashed upon them by Darius, some fifty years ago."

Roan's already put some of the pieces together. "But his virus only did half the job, didn't it? The women survived and escaped to the top of this dormant volcano, far from Darius's view. They swore never to be defeated again and became great warriors."

Kira laughs. "I told you he was quick, Grandmother!"

"What I don't understand," says Roan, "is your connection to that village, and the Brothers."

Kira shrugs. "We wanted to preserve the myth of our extinction, but we still needed mates. So our women all lead double lives, taking strong, healthy partners in the villages for breeding. In the beginning, only the girls were smuggled here to be raised and trained, our boys left in the villages with their fathers."

"But it's different now," adds Ende. "When that prune of a man started taking the children from the villages, we began smuggling out what few we could and hiding them here."

Roan stares at Kira, astounded. "So you were pretending with Saint? Just using him to... breed?"

"Despite our best efforts, many of us grow fond of our mates," Kira says, laughing ruefully. "I believe Saint desired to make a better world but was misguided. He thought he'd formed a temporary alliance with Darius. The truth was that Darius's hand gripped Saint firmly by the neck. Still, when I encouraged his involvement with our campaign to recover as many children as possible, he did not hesitate."

Roan stiffens. "But you couldn't get him to save Longlight."

Though Kira does not shrink from his gaze, her sadness is palpable. "Saint didn't tell me that Darius had given him an order to deliver you and your sister. Clerics were sent, so he knew you must both be important, but he didn't realize who you were. Legends of Longlight were considered fairy tales and as far as he could see yours was just another village scheduled for destruction, whether he did the deed or not. He believed it a necessary exchange for the lives of the children he'd yet to save.

"For his own reasons, he decided to hold one of the two requested back. And we can be thankful that he did, whatever his motivation—it is unlikely you both would be alive, otherwise.

"His eyes were opened once he'd spent time with you. He began to realize that there were many things about you and your talents that were beyond his comprehension. It was too late to save Longlight, but not too late to save you. He'd become convinced you were the destined leader we'd been waiting for, and there was no turning back. Despite the wound you inflicted on him, he kept searching and hoping. I warned him that you wouldn't be convinced, that since you'd discovered his hand in Longlight's destruction, you could never trust him. But he wouldn't let me deter him. Then, in his last encounter with Darius, something Saint saw terrified him. Though he wasn't able to speak of it, it clearly decided him—he'd win you over or die trying."

Roan's thoughts return to their last meeting, the battle— Saint had been trying to tell him something. He'd been unable to listen, and his inability had resulted in many unnecessary deaths. "I need to find out what he knows."

Ende picks up the silver ring, holding it in her palm. "I feared you would lose it."

"I often wished I'd lost it. I kept it as a reminder of the first wound I inflicted on another."

"That was wise, Roan. Do you ever wonder why it's so light?"

"I thought it was hollow."

"Not truly hollow. Inside is an energy from the Dreamfield."

"I suppose you're all Dirt Eaters," Roan says, heart sinking.

"No," Ende replies. "All our Dirt Eaters, men and women, were killed in the plague. So, though we had not intended it, in the end, we had to take the path Roan of the Parting had recommended. He'd come to hate the Dirt, so certain was he that it would lead to disaster. That was the cause of his break with Darius, and why he gave my mother the ring to keep for you."

"To keep for *me?*"

Ende shrugs. "Everyone thought he was half-mad, you know, even the people who loved him. The difference was we saw his madness as genius, while the others believed him insane—or so they claimed." She reaches out, gripping Roan's hand. Eyes fixed on his, she seizes his consciousness. A torrent of images pours into Roan's mind.

RED RAIN FALLING FROM THE SKY. TREES ON FIRE. A WOUNDED SOLDIER WRITHES ON A BLOODY WHITE SHEET. HUNDREDS AND HUNDREDS OF BROKEN WARRIORS HUDDLED OVER CAMPFIRES. A MAN, PERHAPS THIRTY-FIVE, WHO CARRIES SOME RESEMBLANCE TO ROAN'S FATHER, LOOKS OUT AT THE HALF MOON. HE TURNS, HIS GREEN EYES LUMINESCENT. HE LIFTS HIS HAND, TAKES THE BADGER-SHAPED RING OFF HIS FINGER AND HOLDS IT UP. "IT'S FOR SAFE PASSAGE," HE SAYS. "IT CARRIES ALL FORMS AND WILL NEVER FAIL YOU."

Ende lets go of Roan's mind.

"I'm not sure I understand."

"Understanding will come with action," Ende states. "Strength, though, comes from the heart and through the acceptance of what we know we must do. You stand at a crossroads, Roan of Longlight. In you, old hopes culminate and from you new hope will spring forth." Ende pauses, releasing Roan's arm. "But for you the way will be difficult, with no reward other than the accomplishment of your task. It is much to ask of one so young. Do you still wish to return to the place of death?"

"Yes."

"You may use this room."

"I was sick for a while after the last time. It could happen again. Or worse."

"If you come back sick, I will heal you. If you do not return, we will wait until your body dies, then we will bury you well," Ende says, sending a chill up Roan's spine.

The possible risks of the venture so bluntly laid out, he turns inquringly to Kira and asks, "What about Lumpy?"

"I will inform him."

"If he wishes to sit vigil, he may," Ende offers.

Putting the badger ring on his finger, Roan takes a deep breath and tries to clear his mind. But the terror of dying in the Dreamfield, his body in this world condemned to vegetate soulless, mindless, until corporeal death sweeps it away, will not leave him. All too aware of how much depends on his success, he takes breath after breath, but these thoughts keep him grounded as surely as chains.

With a few leaps, Roan's white cricket lands on his ring. It raises its wings, and rubbing them together, begins its song. Roan's apprehension is harnessed, his unruly mind soothed, and with every inhalation, light filters in from the soles of his feet. Rising slowly, the radiance finally fuses with his tailbone, blasts up his spine and he is finally freed.

ROAN STANDS AT THE EDGE OF THE RUPTURE AND LOOKS AT HIS

CLAY HAND. ON HIS FINGER IS THE SILVER RING IN THE SHAPE OF A BADGER. IT'S MOVED WITH HIM BETWEEN THE WORLDS.

THE IRON STATUES, PELTED BY WIND AND RAIN, HAVE GROWN THICK WITH RUST. THE CLOSEST ONE SLOWLY TURNS HER HEAD. SHE TRIES TO SMILE BUT CAN BARELY MOVE.

"ROAN!" MURMURS LONA, HER VOICE GROWN WEAK.

"I WANTED TO SEE HOW YOU WERE."

"WE'RE DOING GOOD, ROAN," WHISPERS BUB. "WE'RE GOOD AT THIS JOB."

"I'VE STILL GOT A LOT TO DO. YOU HAVE TO KEEP HOLDING ON."

"WE'LL HOLD ON," SAYS JAW.

"WE'RE NOT AFRAID," SAYS LONA.

"WE KNOW YOU WON'T LET US DOWN," GIP TELLS HIM.

LIGHTNING FLASHES, ILLUMINATING THE FOURTEEN CHILDREN OF IRON. THEY SEEM SO MUCH AT EASE WITH THEIR SACRIFICE— ROAN CAN ONLY GUESS AT THE COST... HOW LONG WILL THEY LAST IF HE FAILS TO FIND A WAY TO CLOSE THE RIFT??

MAYBE SAINT HAS THE INFORMATION HE NEEDS, SOMETHING THAT WILL GIVE HIM DIRECTION. NURSING THAT HOPE, HE TURNS AWAY FROM THE CHILDREN AND IN SECONDS IS AT THE WATER'S EDGE. LEAPING ONTO AN ICEBERG, HE IS HURLED OVER THE TUMULTUOUS SEA TO THE BRINK OF THE WHIRLPOOL.

WITHOUT HESITATION, ROAN DROPS INTO THE MAELSTROM. AS HE SPINS DOWNWARD, THE STENCH OF DEATH GAGS HIM. ALL TOO SOON, HE SPLASHES INTO THE LEECH-INFESTED SLIME, AND REACHING PAST HANDFUL AFTER HANDFUL OF THE PARASITES, HE

LOCATES HIS NEMESIS. SAINT'S EYES SNAP OPEN AND HIS COLD FIN-
GERS CURL AROUND ROAN'S ARMS, DRAGGING HIM BENEATH THE
UNDULATING MASS. HOPING TO HASTEN HIS SURRENDER, ROAN
BREATHES IN THE VILE SOUP. HIS LUNGS FILL WITH LEECHES AND
SCUM, BUT THEY ALSO SWELL WITH AIR. WARM AIR. HE'S SQUINT-
ING IN THE BLAZING SUN, STANDING ON THE PRECIPICE OF A BOT-
TOMLESS RAVINE. THE SAME TERRIBLE GORGE WHERE BOTH SAINT
AND LELBIT DIED.

HE HEARS A BATTLE CRY. SAINT IS CHARGING TOWARD HIM,
SWORD HELD HIGH. ROAN LOWERS HIS HEAD, AWAITING THE DEATH
BLOW. HIS CHIN RAISES INVOLUNTARILY. HE'S NOT IN HIS CUR-
RENT BODY, BUT IN THE BODY FROM THAT DAY, HIS HOOK-SWORD
MEETING SAINT'S WEAPON WITH A CRASH. HE TRIES TO STOP
FIGHTING, WANTING TO INVITE THE DEATH MABATAN TOLD HIM
HE MUST SEEK, BUT THIS ROAN IS THE ROAN SAINT WANTS HIM TO
BE AND WILL NOT QUIT. THE BATTLE RAGES, EVERY SWORD STROKE
AND BLOW REENACTED. ONLY NOW THERE ARE JUST THE TWO OF
THEM. NO LELBIT WILL COME FORWARD TO SAVE ROAN.

THEY CLASH UNSTEADILY ON THE NARROW LEDGE, NEITHER
GAINING THE ADVANTAGE. UNTIL SAINT SPOTS THE OOZING ARROW
WOUND ON ROAN'S ARM AND PUNCHES IT WITH HIS FIST. THE
ORIGINAL FLASH OF PAIN COURSES THROUGH ROAN AND HE JABS
OUT WITH HIS SWORD, CATCHING SAINT ON THE THIGH. ENRAGED,
SAINT SMASHES THE WOUND AGAIN. ROAN FALLS AND SAINT'S
BLADE IS AT HIS NECK.

"NOW DO WHAT MUST BE DONE," SAINT WHISPERS AS HIS
BLADE SLICES ROAN'S THROAT.

Blood gushes down Roan's arms and streams into the abyss. His body grows cold, and tumbling off the cliff, he plunges downward like a tailless kite. Through the haze of his death, he glimpses a crimson sheen in the eyes of the badger ring. The glow spreads over his hands, his arms. His body begins to shift and change, arms transform into legs, while his jaw elongates and bristly hair sprouts from every pore. He has taken the form of a badger.

Roan's descent slows, then he reverses, gaining speed as he bullets toward the dead prophet. Saint waits at the precipice, sword lowered, hands by his sides, and offers no resistance when Roan dives into his eye.

Through Saint's eyes, Roan sees the polished corridor, the handsome oak door, Saint's hand reaching for a brass claw. When the door swings open, a narrow-eyed, tight-skinned, oddly ageless man welcomes him to come and sit.

"Greetings, Saint. I trust your new motorcycle is up to standard?"

"Your generosity is legend, Master Darius. I am honored."

"Yes. Then why have you secretly kept from me the very boy for whom you knew I was searching?"

"If I had known, Keeper, you would have had him. We found only the girl the night of the raid. The boy I discovered later, far from the village. He claimed he'd been wandering. He said he could read and I thought he might be useful."

"What would you do with a reader?"

"Doctor Arcanthas has requested that medical books be salvaged. I thought the boy might help identify those books. We seek to serve the Masters."

"Your governance of the Farlands has been, for the most part, impeccable."

"Thank you."

"You are my prince."

Saint lowers his head. "You honor me, Seer."

There is a sly grin on Darius's face. He motions for Saint to come nearer. "I want to show you something."

A panel opens in the wall and a glass shelf glides out. Under a bell jar a huge hand reaches up into a surging coral sky. The base of its arm sits deep in a silver pool.

"One day soon this structure will be completed. But, like the motorcycle, it requires fuel. That boy, his sister, the children you are about to fetch in Fairview—it is their destiny to power my machine."

Is that all we are to the masters? Fuel? Roan would lash out at Darius if he were more than a memory.

Something flows up from the silver pool through the arm. The skin seems to be kinetic and as Saint looks closer Roan discerns a multitude of shapes, writhing, screaming, twisting in torment.

"What does it remind you of, Saint?"

"May the Friend save us all."

"Very astute. Your Friend is, of course, friend to us all. My device has been created to honor him and to benefit humankind. Help me and you help the Friend and the world. You must earn my faith again, Saint. To do that means delivering the boy and the children."

"I will find them."

"I should be very disappointed if you don't. Nothing vexes me more than waste. But it is my curse as a leader to have to, on occasion, eradicate even a prince if he veers off course."

"I will not fail."

Darius smiles, teeth flashing, and his visage moves farther and farther away.

Back on the precipice, the badger is hurled from Saint's eye. Taking his human form, Roan faces the killer of his family.

"Could you see?" pleads Saint. "Darius seeks to capture souls and imprison them in his machine. I don't understand how he will use what he steals, but he lies when he says it will honor the Friend. He means to take the Friend's place, the very place of God. He is evil, Roan. You could see it, couldn't you? Sense it? He means to end everything. Go to the Brothers, gather the armies together, and lead them against the City. Darius must be stopped. "

Roan stares at the dead prophet in disbelief. "You're asking me to declare an all-out war?"

"Darius already wages war. You've seen its victims: thousands of defenseless children, whole villages annihilated—he destroys any who stand in the Masters' way. Do you not want to shield them from further harm?"

"But you helped him. How can you now—"

"For my part in it, I am here. And I do not ask you, Roan, I beg."

"There must be another way to do that besides fighting."

The dead man's eyes cloud over. "I knew of no other way. That was my downfall. You have heard what you were meant to hear."

The cliff they stand upon begins to soften into an undulating mass that crawls up Saint's legs, his chest, his neck, until his eyes, still fixed in despair on Roan, sink back into the living bog.

Weary, Roan ascends toward the whirling light that funnels from this sea of wretchedness, leaving Saint behind. To lead armies, to send people to a certain death, how can he accept such responsibility? How can anyone?

Reaching the vortex, he hears voices. His people. The people of Longlight. Their song entices him, begging him to surrender to grief and yearning, to let tears fall, but he desires nothing more than to be working by his parents' sides again, free of the burdens that weigh upon him.

The voices rise, each a thread connecting him to a

PERSON HE LOVED. THEY ENTANGLE AND INTERWEAVE, COCOON-
ING HIM IN LAUGHTER AND LIGHT UNTIL HE IS BROUGHT BEFORE
HIS MOTHER AND FATHER. HIS MOTHER IS DRESSED IN HER WORK-
CLOTHES, A SMUDGE OF SAWDUST ON HER CHEEK. HIS FATHER IS
IN HIS FORMAL ROBE, THE ONE HE WORE EVERY YEAR AT THE
REMEMBERING.

THEY HOLD OUT THEIR ARMS AND ROAN EMBRACES THEM.
WIPING AWAY HIS TEARS, HIS MOTHER KISSES HIM. "WE'RE SO
PROUD OF YOU."

"BUT I'VE FAILED. I'VE BROKEN EVERY RULE. EATEN MEAT,
STRUCK OUT IN ANGER, KILLED."

"YOU WERE TAUGHT TO REJECT VIOLENCE AND AVOID THE
DESTRUCTION OF LIFE," SAYS HIS FATHER. "AND YOU LEARNED
THOSE LESSONS WELL. BUT THOUGH THEY ENHANCE HUMANITY'S
CHANCES OF SURVIVAL, ROAN, THEY DO NOT GUARANTEE IT.
YOU WITNESSED THEIR FAILURE THE NIGHT LONGLIGHT WAS
DESTROYED."

"EVERYONE SAYS I AM MEANT TO LEAD THEM INTO WAR."

"THERE IS NO OTHER WHO CAN," SAYS HIS MOTHER.

ROAN LOOKS AT THEM BOTH, INCREDULOUS. "BUT THAT
DOESN'T MEAN I SHOULD."

ALTHOUGH HE MEETS HIS SON'S GAZE WITH A STEADY EYE,
ROAN'S FATHER'S VOICE IS BURDENED WITH SORROW. "THE WAR
WILL HAPPEN WHETHER YOU LEAD OR NOT. ROAN, THE GIFT YOU
POSSESS WOULD BRING A VISION OF PEACE INTO THE CONFLICT.
THAT WAS THE LEGACY OF LONGLIGHT. HOW TO USE IT IS A DECI-
SION ONLY YOU CAN MAKE."

For a brief moment, Roan lowers his eyes. He has so many questions, but he knows none of them will be answered, that they cannot be answered, and perhaps he does not want them answered. His parents made their choices, now he must make his own. He looks up to find his surroundings translucent, his parents shifting into luminescence.

"Wait, please!"

"Walk free, Roan of Longlight," they whisper as their shimmering light envelops and soothes him.

Lumpy, his face fraught with worry, looms over Roan. "Are you alright?"

Roan smiles. "Yes," he says. And for the first time in years, he truly believes it.

the dormant volcano

when the moon dies in the eye of taurus,
set your vigil to the east. await with patience
its appearance upon the joined hands of gemini,
for it will presage the coming of the new age.
                                    —the book of Longlight

R OAN'S SHOULDER TINGLES, the same sensation he had
when Willum touched him, and a brown-speckled rat
appears. Roan follows it as it scurries across a verdant landscape and onto Willum's knee. Willum sits cross-legged, staring
at his empty palms. Behind him, in the distance, a tree burns.
Flames leap from its outstretched branches, cracking and spit-
ting, an angry dance of shifting color. Roan can almost hear
the screams in the frigid night air, the pounding of horse
hooves, the roaring of warriors. The tree, Roan understands, is
Stowe. He can see her face, the tears streaming from her eyes.

He rushes to her, desperate to smother the blaze, but the
fire repels him.

Beneath the whispers of crackling light, Stowe's voice is
unmistakable. "Don't worry. It is what's meant to be but

couldn't be. I have been waiting for this. The future waits for you, Roan. I will meet you there, I promise."

The crimson flames shift to a brilliant blue, then in a burst of white light they engulf Stowe, leaving only a mound of golden dust. As Willum kneels to carefully collect the gleaming powder, a wolf howls. When Roan seeks out the source of the cry, he's transported over the landscape to the crest of a hill. There, a huge bull stands, the setting sun a robe of red incandescence on the beast's glistening black coat. The wolf holds Roan's hook-sword in its teeth and drops the weapon in his hand. With great reluctance, Roan grips the hilt, the bull kneeling on its forelegs before him.

The ground beneath him shudders and the earth peels open at the bull's hooves, plunging them to where the rusting Novakin are stretched to breaking point across the fathomless abyss. Blood drips onto the iron forms like balm on a wound, the metal itself sighing with relief.

Roan sees that the blood is coming from his sword. Stumbling back, he tries to drop his weapon, but it has become part of his hand and he can do nothing to dislodge it.

Stepping past him, Willum lets the golden dust that was Stowe drift from his fingers onto the children, then turning to Roan, he smiles. "We have until the bull rises in the east. After that comes the end of all possibility."

Roan wakes with a start. The white cricket's song lulled him to sleep while he waited here, on the edge of the volcano. The gentle noon sun still glints through the mist. How much of what he saw came from Willum? How much from himself—from his hopes, his fears?

As if in prayer, he says their names out loud. "Lona. Bub. Jaw. Jam. Gip. Runk. Sake. Dani. Beck. Anais. Tamm. Korina. Geemo. Theo." They have not left his thoughts for a moment. He has until the bull rises in the east to keep his promise. Next spring, six months away. He will not let them down.

Roan's musings are broken by wild laughter. Lumpy is hunkered down with Kira and a few other women, and he's said something that's amused them. They're drawing out a map on a piece of parchment. The sight is like a great wind blowing the future inexorably toward Roan.

As if he too senses its inevitability, Lumpy catches Roan's eye. He points to the cliff edge. There, climbing up the trail, are two men. Warriors.

Breathing deep, Roan lets the crisp air fill his lungs and steady his emotions. He rises to meet Brother Wolf and Brother Asp, sword in hand and Longlight in mind.

acknowledgments

I WOULD LIKE TO THANK Pamela Robertson, Susan Madsen, and Barbara Pulling for their effort and support. This book would not have been possible without the contribution of Elizabeth Dancoes, who is responsible, in good part, for whatever grace this book achieves.

Be sure to read the first book in *The Longlight Legacy*, *The Dirt Eaters*.

about the author

DENNIS FOON has written more than twenty plays for the stage. His body of work is staged internationally and published in numerous languages. Recognition for his work as a playwright has come in the form of the British Theatre Award, two Chalmers awards, the Jesse Richardson Career Achievement Award, and the International Arts for Young Audiences Award.

In addition to his many plays, Dennis has written extensively for television and film, including the award-winning shows *Little Criminals*, *White Lies*, and *Long Life, Happiness and Prosperity*.

Dennis has written three other acclaimed novels for young adults: *Double or Nothing*, the award-winning *Skud*, and the first book in *The Longlight Legacy*, *The Dirt Eaters*.

Dennis lives with his family in Vancouver, B.C.